SWORD FIGHT

KINGDOM OF ENGINES

NATHAN VAN COOPS

Skylighter
Press

AUTHOR'S NOTE

Authors are frequently asked, "Where do you get your ideas?" The answer is usually something vague, like "I don't know, they just come to me." Or sometimes the more whimsical might reply "My muse brings them."

My typical response is that I ask a lot of "What if" questions. What if time travel were possible and lots of people could do it? Or, what if people and creatures could live in the sky and have grand adventures?

For this novel, the question was "What if the war car replaced the war horse?"

I was fascinated by the idea and imagined what would occur if medieval castles dotted the hillsides of North America and the British monarchy hadn't lost power.

The question, of course, bred more questions. "What would it take to make that world possible?" In the interest of not boring readers with mountains of backstory, I narrowed it down to the essential facts.

An alteration in two major historical events shaped the world of the characters you are about to meet.

~

AD 820: China

A Taoist monk, endeavoring to create an elixir of life, involuntarily creates black powder. Half an hour later, while lighting his pipe, he accidentally ignites the substance, burning his entire monastery to the ground. The monk perishes, and the secrets of black powder vanish with him.

AD 1217: The Second Battle of Lincoln

With the city of Lincoln overrun by the French, and Lincoln Castle under siege, a mad inventor unleashes a steam-powered armored vehicle that assists in routing the French forces and evicting Prince Louis from England.

Military leaders of the time downplay the machine's effectiveness, claiming the battle would have been won without it, but the madman's invention is brought to the attention of King Henry III, who is ten years old. Upon visiting the remains of the battle-damaged machine, the young king requests that his workmen immediately begin construction of new motor-driven vehicles.

Now:

North America is the Kingdom of New Avalon, and war cars roam the streets.

Adhering to the laws of chivalry, road knights wield only weapons used for one-on-one combat, fighting at a range meant to look an enemy in the eye. The world remains at the mercy of the sword.

The era of the war horse is gone, and in its place now reigns the war car.

It is my sincere wish that you thoroughly enjoy this new take on history.

Welcome to the Kingdom of Engines.

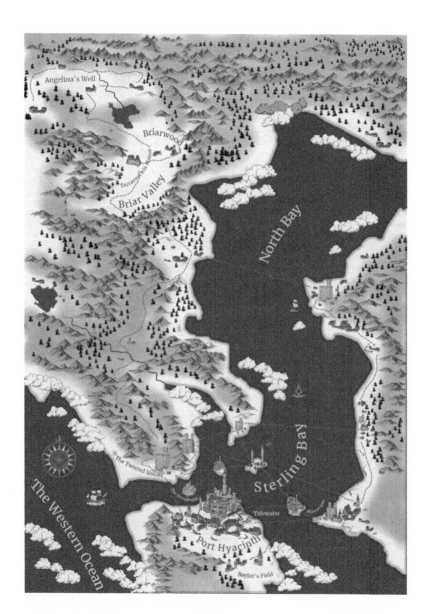

PROLOGUE

S parks erupted from the fender of the Spitfire as it slammed into the guardrail. The roar of the engines reverberated from the cliffs as two vehicles came out of the turn, narrowly missing the drop-off to the sea and rocks below.

Lady Maggie Sutton snarled into her helmet and wrestled the steering wheel, forcing her war car back to the center of the road. The vehicle beside her swerved away, cutting the corner of the next turn and pulling ahead by a car length.

"Oh no, you don't," Maggie muttered, shifting gears. Her car ate up the asphalt as she pursued her competition.

Maggie hadn't expected the Omega driver to be so aggressive in a charity-exhibition road race, but if that's how he wanted to play it, she could drive harder. She hadn't lost a match-up in months. She wasn't about to start now.

The sky-blue Spitfire Maggie was driving was lighter than the Rockwell Omega and nimbler in the turns. It was an advantage she planned to exploit. As the Omega straightened out of the next curve in the highway, she made her move.

Flooring the accelerator, she flung her car around the driver's side of the Omega and made a break for the open road beyond.

The needle on the speedometer hit 100.

As she drew alongside the other car, Maggie dared a quick glance at her competitor. To her surprise, the window grate on the Omega dropped open, and the driver pushed the face mask of his helmet up. He was grinning.

The Omega suddenly dropped back, yielding the road.

Maggie shifted her attention to the rear-view mirror. "What the —"

When she looked forward again, she slammed on the brakes.

The car rolling into the lane ahead was timed perfectly.

Maggie only had an instant to register the empty driver's seat as the junker rammed into the front of her Spitfire. Her body impacted the restraining harness, then her car was airborne.

The Spitfire flipped end over end before slamming into the concrete upside down and sideways. All breath left her lungs as glass exploded around her.

Metal screamed.

The momentum of the car sent it rolling — once, twice, and a third time — before it thudded into the guardrail.

Maggie clenched her gut at the force of the impact. The car was left teetering back and forth on the cliff's edge, its rear wheels dangling over the brink.

She groaned as she exhaled.

The windshield was gone. The protective steel grating that formed the driver's cage had held, but all the windows had blown out. The hood was crumpled enough that the Golden Stag of the Sutton House crest was now angled toward her. Maggie shifted in her seat and winced as pain shot up her back, but the movement gave her a view of the open air beneath the rear end of the car.

Her heart jolted in her chest.

It was at least a hundred feet to the rocks and waves below.

Seabirds whirled through the air beneath her, darting in and out of their cliffside nests. Their cries filled her ears with screeching. Maggie fumbled at the door frame, for the first time registering the pain in her arm.

Something was broken. Her wrist didn't move the way it should, and her fingers fluttered uselessly against the door latch. Her legs were numb, and everything about her body felt wrong. She coughed and tried to orient herself.

Her ears were ringing, blending with the shrillness of the birds outside.

Then she noticed the engine noise. The low rumble was coming from the Rockwell Omega. It glided into view from her left, easing along the shoulder of the highway.

At least he'd stopped to help.

As the car idled, the driver's door opened and the racer climbed out.

The man moved slowly, boots crunching gravel as he walked around the front of the car and crossed the shoulder to where Maggie's Spitfire was perched.

"Sterling," Maggie said, the word coming out as a croak. "Help me."

The other racer removed his helmet, shaking blond locks from beneath it. The silver helmet matched the reflective armor of his racing jacket. The ice-blue eyes found hers but betrayed no emotion.

"This is quite the state you've found yourself in, Lady Magdalena." Lord Jasper Sterling's eyes roamed over the car, settling on the stag emblazoned on the hood. "Did you know that the Regional List has House Sutton as the premier racing team of the season? They said you'd be the clear favorite in the King's Tournament. What was it they said about you this week? Something like 'Maggie Sutton is the perfect blend of competitive skill and moral courage.' Did you read that?"

Maggie coughed and attempted to get her fingers on the windshield grate latch.

Why was he just standing there quoting race reports?

The car reeked of gasoline, and something was smoking. She managed to get her helmet off—it clattered to the floor next to her—but the effort left her light-headed.

"Jasper. Help me. I don't think I can get out."

"I'm actually surprised the car stayed on the road. I thought for sure you'd go over."

"Stop talking," Maggie said. "And get me out of here."

The smell of gasoline was overwhelming now, and she was getting dizzier. She fumbled with the latches of her safety harness with her one good hand, then coughed and attempted to reach the passenger-side door. The latch moved but the door wouldn't budge.

She'd need a rescue team. Door cutters.

She fumbled for the microphone on the radio, but it slipped from her slick fingers and fell to the floor. That's when she noticed the blood dripping down her arm. She got her fingers around the microphone cord and attempted to drag it up to her lap.

"Here. I'll get that." Jasper Sterling reached through the passenger window and snatched the microphone out of her hand.

"Rescue. I'll need the medics."

Jasper's face was impassive. "Calm down. I'll call it in for you." He yanked the microphone out of its jack and bundled the cord into his fist. He tossed it over the brink, then turned and walked back to his car.

"Sterling?" Maggie called out after him, her head swimming. She tried to focus. What was he doing? She watched with confusion as Jasper climbed back into the Omega.

The radio crackled with static, and Jasper's voice came over the race channel.

"Safety team, this is Lord Jasper Sterling. There's been an accident on the coast highway. The Sutton car took a turn too fast. Went through the guardrail."

"Copy, Team Sterling, this is Safety. We'll get Rescue on its way. What is the condition of the Sutton vehicle?"

"Not good. Looks like it went onto the rocks. It was a long drop."

The words registered belatedly in Maggie's mind. "No." She

stretched for the radio, her fingers clawing at the empty microphone jack. "I'm still up here! I'm still—"

She jolted in her seat as the car rocked from an impact.

She looked up to find the Omega's brake lights pressed against her hood. The Spitfire tilted forward as the car pulled away, then the reverse lights on the Omega came on again.

"No. No no no!" Maggie shouted. The Omega's rear tires kicked up gravel as they caught, launching the vehicle backward, faster this time. She could just make out Jasper through the rear window, one arm draped casually across the seat as he raced toward her. The rear bumper of the Omega slammed into the Spitfire again, and this time, whatever was holding the car gave way. The hood of the Spitfire pitched skyward, the golden stag leaping gracefully into the air. The windshield filled with nothing but blue sky.

The Spitfire slid over the edge of the cliff to the sound of metal scraping stone, then the world went quiet.

Maggie came out of her seat.

For a brief moment, she was weightless.

The air once again filled with the screeches of startled seabirds.

Her fingers found the steering wheel, gripping uselessly. As the car turned over, she recognized the hard line where the ocean met the sky, but now it was inverted. Down was up, ocean replaced heaven and she was flying toward a firmament made of jagged rocks and frothing waves.

The last thing Maggie Sutton had time to think was—

～

"Copy. We'll send medical. Safety out."

"Roger that." Jasper Sterling smirked as he hung up the microphone.

5

The air was ripe with the scent of rubber and fuel, and a fresh cloud of smoke drifted up from the rocks below.

He took a deep breath, relishing the smell, then tossed his helmet into the passenger seat. He ran a hand through his messy, blond hair, then donned his sunglasses before shifting into gear and pulling back onto the highway.

He drove north for several minutes before turning onto the mile-long bridge that crossed the South Bay. To either side, whitecaps dotted the water in a view that was nothing short of breathtaking.

Three of the castles that guarded Sterling Bay were visible today. Their towers and battlements stood watch over the many bridges crisscrossing the waves.

When he reached the fortified outer walls of Port Hyacinth, the gates stood open for him. He navigated the remainder of the race course in a state of pleasant contentment until pulling into the heart of the arena. Several thousand spectators had turned out to witness the end of the exhibition.

He hung an arm out the open window of the Omega as he crossed the finish line, then pulled the car around to the winner's circle. He climbed out and waved to the crowd on either side of the nobles' section, turning slowly in place to allow time for the sun to sparkle from the plates of his polished driving armor. He then bowed graciously to each occupant of the elite boxes.

Finally, he pushed his hair back from his face and looked up to the central point of the stands, to the Sterling box, but his smile faded.

His family's seats were empty.

∼

A clash of steel echoed through the corridors of Sterling Castle as Jasper descended to the old dungeons.

Unlike the cramped and claustrophobic cells of old, the lowest floor of his family's ancestral home was a cavernous place of high arches and elaborate stonework. The broad flagstones were worn from several centuries of hard use, but rubber mats now lined each one, and the only torture being done in the ancient rooms was voluntary.

Masked fighters of all shapes and sizes sparred with one another using staves and swords in the dungeon-turned-gymnasium. The spot where an iron maiden had once stood now featured a dueling ring encircled by steps. Atop the platform, fighters were taking turns defending the highest position, holding off as many attackers as possible before some stronger or faster swordsman could topple them.

Jasper found his father, Lord Alister Sterling, supervising the sparring from his director's chair. His usual glass of whiskey was in one hand, and his mistress, the Baroness of Manchester, was at his side.

"No," Lord Sterling said as Jasper walked up.

Jasper frowned. "I haven't said anything yet."

"But you were about to, and I know what you're going to ask. The answer is still no."

Jasper looked down at the trophy in his hand and shifted his feet.

Lord Sterling's eyes didn't leave the fighters atop the tower. "The king is coming to our city to look for a knight to sit at the Round Table. A knight that is more than just a pretty suit of armor in a fancy car." He waved vaguely toward the room full of fighters. "One of these men will represent our house in the tournament."

"I'm your son," Jasper said. "I should be our house champion."

"You should be, yes," Lord Sterling replied. "And yet here we are."

Jasper bristled. "If you ever showed up for anything, you'd

7

know I've just won the East Bay Exhibition Cup. And I've eliminated House Sutton from the lists."

"No doubt ruining yet another of my cars," Lord Sterling replied. He straightened in his chair and shouted to a man in a black mask that had a crimson streak across one eye. "You there! You next! I want to see what you can do atop the fool's tower."

Jasper could only seethe as the masked man climbed the steps to the platform.

Lord Sterling turned to the baroness. "I've been watching this one all day. I have yet to see him lose an event."

The baroness merely sipped her drink and examined her manicure.

The contender atop the tower raised his sword and saluted his opponents, then, one after another, his competitors began their attacks. Blades flashed separately and at once, assaults coming from all angles as the warriors attempted to gain the platform and force the masked man from the circle. The swordsman moved with the grace of a tiger, fluidly defending blows and delivering devastating counterattacks. One-by-one, each challenger was sent tumbling down the steps.

When there were no more competitors left, Lord Sterling stood to applaud. "Bravo! Well done!" He turned to Jasper. "Do you also feel up to besting a dozen men atop the tower today?"

Jasper scowled.

"I didn't think so," his father replied. He gestured for the man in the crimson-streaked mask to descend. When the swordsman was standing before them, Lord Sterling sized him up. Jasper noted with irritation that the man stood several inches taller than he did. "What is your name, swordsman?"

"I fight under the name Red Reaper," the masked man said.

"A name the city must come to know," Lord Sterling replied. He pulled a wad of bills from his pocket and counted them out. "Consider this a down payment for your services. You've just earned yourself a spot on the Sterling team."

The swordsman accepted the bills, bowed, then moved away.

Jasper fumed.

Lord Sterling turned to his son. "Don't look so sour. You'll still be entering the tournament but not as a representative of this house."

Jasper furrowed his brow. "What other house would I represent?"

"It's time you learn what sacrifices must be made in the interest of our family." He reached into his pocket and removed an envelope, then handed it to Jasper. "Everyone should know their place." When Jasper had accepted the envelope, Lord Sterling held a hand out to the Baroness of Manchester, and she rose from her seat. "Come along, my dear. Our work here is finished." With one last glance at Jasper, he strode away, the baroness gliding on his arm.

Jasper tore into the envelope, his eyes scanning quickly over each line of the letter. As the contents sunk in, the corners of his mouth turned upward. He smirked at the doorway where his father had disappeared and headed the other direction.

When he reached the garage, he walked past row upon row of cars until he located the metallic-navy Phaeton speedster. Blaise Cavendish was there, leaning against the fender.

"You've certainly given me plenty of work today," Blaise said. "I've already been fielding calls from House Sutton inquiring about the incident on the track."

"It is what I pay you for." Jasper stripped out of his road armor, tossing it into the back seat of the convertible. "I assume the loose ends have been dealt with?"

"No one will trace the junker to us, and our supplier said he's happy to work for us again. He even suggested filling it with extra fuel next time for a more explosive impact."

"I don't need to know details," Jasper said.

"Did it work?" Blaise asked. "Did your father appoint you house champion?"

"No. But he's given me something else." Jasper handed the letter to Blaise.

Blaise skimmed to the heart of the text. "The widow?"

Jasper opened the the car door and slid into the driver's seat. "There is more than one path to the Round Table." He turned the key in the ignition and the speedster's engine rumbled to life.

Blaise climbed into the passenger seat and pulled a flask from his pocket. "Then here's to love." He took a swig before offering it to Jasper. Jasper took a long pull as well.

He shifted into gear and released the clutch. The speedster leapt from its place and launched down the angled drive, rocketing across the lowered drawbridge and onto the barrier road. In a matter of minutes they were on the Governor's Highway heading north.

Blaise let out a whoop as the highway raced to meet them.

Jasper watched the castle shrink in the mirror behind him and smiled. He would finally show his father what he was capable of. His future was waiting on the horizon. It was time for him to claim it.

1

DRIVE

The light at the corner of Holley and Main glowed a stale red.

Valerie Terravecchia let her gaze settle a quarter mile down the road, but her focus was on the accelerator pedal quivering beneath her right foot. The three hundred and fifty horsepower engine sent vibrations through the floorboards of her custom Rogue fastback and the rumble from under the hood kept time with her heartbeat. The rest of the world was just noise.

"Get ready to suck tailpipe, ladies!" The shout from the car beside her was punctuated with an extra revving of its engine. The taunt didn't faze Valerie, but it sat her passenger up in her seat.

Thea Johansen got to her knees on the seat cushion and shouted out the window over Valerie's shoulder. "My girl's going to dust you into last week, Remi!" Her friend then lowered her voice to whisper in her ear. "You can beat these guys, right?"

"They're driving an off-the-shelf four-banger princess wagon, and Remi Rothschild is a jack-whacker," Valerie replied.

"I assume that means yes," Thea said.

"You should buckle up," Valerie replied, not taking her eyes from the road.

The light turned green.

Valerie's foot came off the clutch in one smooth motion and the rear tires bit asphalt with a squeal. The intake on the hood scoop yawned wide, sucking liters of air into the turbo like a junkie snorting funk. Thea was bent over the seat before she could get turned around, her hair whipping her face as she struggled to get her butt back to the cushion. Valerie kept her foot on the accelerator.

The roadster tried to keep pace for the first eighth of a mile, but each poorly-timed thrust Remi made with the shifter only left him farther behind. By a quarter mile, the boys in the passenger seats were throwing up their hands and swearing. Valerie noted the scowl on Remi's face via her rear-view mirror, but never let off the gas.

"Whoo! That's right!" Thea shouted. "Better luck next time, boys!" She grinned as she waved out the back window. Valerie cut the corner of the next curve and blasted along the forested valley highway, dappled sunlight flickering across the hood as it filtered through the Redwood boughs overhead.

Thea slid across the seat and thumped against the door column. "Can we slow down now?"

"What for?" Valerie asked. "Don't you want to live a little?" She swung into the next curve and Thea slid back across the bench seat, colliding with her.

Thea laughed and scrambled for traction on the ripped leather seat, reaching for the door handle. "Where'd you say the seat belt was in this thing?"

"Check the seat crack," Valerie said, easing off the accelerator as she made the next turn. They floated over the rise in the road, lightening in their seats as they crested the hill. Valerie took her eyes off the road just long enough to help her friend find the end of the belt. Thea was feeling for it between the cushions. "Here, you just need to—"

She glanced up just in time to see the creature in the road.

Valerie wrenched hard on the steering wheel, her feet

mashing the brake and the clutch pedal simultaneously. The car's back end came loose and the passenger-side wheels left the ground for a gut-wrenching second as she swerved. The immense black shape whipped past Valerie's door as the car canted sideways.

There was no more pavement.

The fastback went airborne off the shoulder of the road, launching a dozen feet through a wall of branches before slamming back onto four wheels. The car careened through the underbrush, successively crushing sapling trees beneath its front bumper. It finally came to a stop with a lurch.

Valerie's breath caught from the jolt against her harness.

"Good God," Thea gasped. One of her palms was planted on the dashboard and the other had a death grip on the seat cushion behind Valerie's head. Her bare legs were sprawled halfway up the windshield and she had lost a sandal.

Valerie checked the rear-view mirror and caught the shadow moving off into the woods. "Holy hell. Did you see that?" she asked.

"See you drive us off the road into the woods? Yeah, I noticed," Thea said, attempting to extricate herself from the foot well.

"It was a bear. Right in the road." Valerie twisted in her seat to look behind them.

Thea got her feet back on the floor and finally made it upright. She looked out the rear window at the hill they had just come down.

"Is it still there?"

Valerie craned her neck. "I think . . . I think it's gone."

Thea located her missing sandal. "We're so lucky we're not dead."

Valerie noted the steam coming from under the crumpled hood and steeled herself for what she would find outside. She tried opening her door but it caught on something. She was forced to roll down the window and climb out, swinging her legs over the windowsill and dropping into the weeds.

Unlike Thea, who was already dressed for the pool in a slim-fitting black cover-up and bikini, Valerie was wearing jeans and boots. They gave some protection from the brambles as she made her way around the front of the car to assess the damage.

It wasn't good.

While it could be argued that the saplings they had plowed through were better than having collided with a full-grown tree, there would be no driving out. A good welder might be able to salvage the body eventually, but the hood was buckled beyond repair and the cooling system was caved in all the way to the engine block. She pushed open the hood and discovered that the motor was canted severely to one side by the sheared-off sapling that had finally arrested their momentum. At least one motor mount had snapped.

Damn.

She'd spent a lot of hours on that engine. Now her hopes of having a car for the summer racing season were toast.

"Nice driving!"

The shout came from the road. Valerie looked up to find Remi's roadster creeping along the shoulder. A couple of his friends leered from the passenger seats, pointing and laughing.

"Better luck next time, ladies!" Remi gunned the throttle and performed a burnout as he rocketed away, leaving only a lingering cloud of rubber-scented smoke.

"Wait, they're not even stopping to help?" Thea asked. "How are we supposed to get home?"

Valerie let the hood fall and wiped her palms off on her black tank top. "Forget it. We're better off without him. We can walk."

"Walk?" Thea blanched. "You just said there was a bear."

"We crossed the border of my family's land a mile back. It's not far to the manor house if we take the back roads. Someone will probably come along. If not, we can still make it by dark."

"Dark? Val, you promised me that this weekend would be

wine and hot-tubbing with cute boys, not hiking through the woods with bears."

"It's a winery, Thea. I promise we won't run out of wine. And aren't you the one always saying we're supposed to be fashionably late?"

"Fashionably late, not fashionably eaten alive."

"Wherever that bear came from, I'm sure it's long gone. Come on."

She gave Thea a hand as she slid out the window. While her friend reached back into the car for her bag, Valerie scanned the woods one last time for the bear. There was no sign of it. She was vaguely disappointed.

Valerie led the way downhill, making her way through the underbrush.

Thea grumbled at every bush and briar they had to push through, but Valerie was pleased to see that her mood improved when they reached the vineyards.

Bees were hard at work on the mustard and clover that dotted the forest's edge. Valerie and Thea emerged from the woods and plunged directly into the neatly ordered rows of vines that made up the southern acreage of the Terravecchia vineyards. It was an uphill walk, but a pleasant one. They caught a few interested looks from field hands tending the irrigation canals, but Valerie kept a straight course and didn't stop.

She fished a hair tie from her jeans pocket and pulled her dark brown hair back into a ponytail, allowing the early summer breeze to brush across the back of her neck.

They reached a planting road and followed it north, winding their way up the hill under a sunny, cloudless sky. Before long they were breathing heavily and both of them were damp with perspiration.

Valerie had just crested the hill and begun her descent on the other side when the engine noise reached her.

"Don't tell me they're coming back to laugh at us again," Thea said, searching the road.

Valerie turned to watch as well, but a smile turned the corner of her mouth as she listened. "That's not Remi's motor. That's my brother!"

As if on cue, a car came over the next hill. The sporty, cranberry-red coupe decelerated as it drew closer, gliding to a stop beside them. The Reliant 300's engine settled to a steady purr under the hood. Henry Terravecchia rested an arm on the windowsill and pushed his sunglasses to the top of his head to get a better look at them. "Hey, Val, you look like you're working up a nice sweat out here. Need a lift?"

"Yes!" Thea exclaimed before Valerie could even get her mouth open. Her friend hustled to the other side of the car and threw open the door, tossing her bag into the back seat before crawling in after it.

A playful smile parted Henry's lips. "Good to see you, sis."

Valerie shook her head, but walked around the other side of the car and climbed in.

"So, you still know your way home after all." She glanced up at the sword clipped to the ceiling rack. "New toy?"

"Yeah, sorry I haven't been around much. It was a busy tournament season this year. I assume you heard we took regionals." Henry unclipped the shiny sword and scabbard from the ceiling rack. "This was the trophy this year. They even engraved it for me."

Valerie buckled her seatbelt, then accepted the sword, reading the elegant script etched along the scabbard. *Henry Terravecchia III, Regional Longsword Champion.*

There were more deadly weapons in the world. A spear, a pike, or even a sturdy quarterstaff could thrash a swordsman in a fight. But she had to admit there was an elegant beauty to a sword that nothing else could match. She admired the way the sunlight danced off the polished hilt.

Henry shifted into gear and the Reliant continued along the

planting road, the vines out the window blurring together as the car sped up.

"I heard you had the winningest season in Bembrook University history," Thea said from the back. She leaned forward and grasped Henry's seat. "If you need a date to the King's Tournament Masquerade, my calendar is still open."

Valerie shook her head. "Thea, we've had this conversation. Henry is off-limits to your scheming. Besides, the King's Tournament is only for knights."

"They opened it up to all comers this time. Didn't you hear?" Henry said. "They're letting anyone with a car enter, even commoners. The Westland lords are in an uproar about it."

Valerie furrowed her brow. "I thought the winner of a King's Tournament got a place at the Round Table? The king wants commoners competing for a place at the high court?"

"Like I said, it's got the lords all riled up. The winner will take over the position of Knight Warden of the West. He'll technically outrank the governor."

"Could be a she," Valerie said. "We have two women at the Round Table now."

"Sure," Henry said. "In any event, it's big news. I bet it brings every warrior and war car driver on this side of the continent out to fight." He studied his sister. "Speaking of drivers, what happened to your car? Where's this hot-rod you wanted to show off?"

"I don't want to talk about it," Valerie replied, slumping in her seat.

"We almost died," Thea said. She gave Henry a dramatic account of the car's demise, exaggerating nearly all of their experience.

"Sounds like you two are lucky to be alive," Henry said, though his eyes were playful.

"Exactly," Thea replied. "And if you hadn't come along, we probably would've been murdered on the road or eaten by that bear."

Valerie rolled her eyes but kept her mouth shut.

"Been a lot of years since we've seen bears on our land," Henry mused. "I wonder what brought them back." He patted Valerie's knee. "Sorry about the car though."

Henry pulled the Reliant over and let it idle on the side of the road. "Hey Thea, how would you feel about taking the car ahead for us? I want a chance to chat with Valerie and we can make it the rest of the way on foot."

Thea looked skeptical, but when Henry got out and offered her a hand, she climbed out of the back seat. "You want to walk?"

"It's not far. We'll be there before you know it. Plus, I want to see how you look behind the wheel of this thing."

Thea grinned. "Okay." She slid into the driver's seat and Henry closed the door for her. "Which one is which again?" she asked, staring at the pedals.

"Clutch, brake, gas," Henry said, pointing them out.

Valerie joined her brother in the road and observed as Thea put the car in gear.

"You look like a pro," Henry said.

Thea flashed a smile and depressed the accelerator, lurching into motion as the clutch engaged. The coupe pulled away with the engine at high RPM as Thea struggled to find second gear. "I think I got it!" she shouted out the window, and the car sped away, the engine complaining at its mistreatment.

"You realize she'll probably have your transmission stripped by the time she makes the house, right?" Valerie asked.

"She'll get the hang of it," Henry said. He wrapped an arm around her shoulder. "Good to see you, Val. I missed this." His fingers went for her side to tickle her. "Aren't you happy to see me?"

"Stop!" Valerie tried to shrug out of his embrace, but he just squeezed her harder. She laughed despite the annoyance. "Fine, it's good to see you too."

Henry grinned and let her go.

Valerie straightened her tank top. "I swear, anytime we're alone, you're like a five-year-old."

After a quarter mile of walking, they left the paved road, opting for the footpath that led through the heart of Briarwood Village. The quaint cottages of the village housed the majority of the growers that worked their family lands. To Valerie, it always felt like home.

The air smelled of wildflowers and the blackberry bushes were already in bloom. The scents took her back to summer days long before boarding school—before Charlotte—the days when she might still catch sight of her father touring the vineyards and checking on the season's crop of grapes.

Anywhere in New Avalon, Terravecchia wines were still the most desirable labels to have adorning your table. While Valerie had heard the occasional grumbling that the current vintage didn't hold up to the old standards, she put it down to the bickering of disgruntled competitors. The name Terravecchia meant something in this hamlet, and across the valley, and would as long as she had anything to say about it.

When they reached the top of the next hill, Henry paused. His eyes drifted west. Valerie didn't need to ask. She knew what he was looking for. Her eyes likewise settled on the distant hilltop and the terracotta tile roof that was just visible beyond the trees.

"I've decided to ask her," Henry said. "I think it's time."

"Tonight? We said we would wait till I turned eighteen and ask her together," Valerie said.

"I know we talked about waiting, but that's time I could spend fixing up the old house," Henry said. "Villa Rosa should belong to us. I can't imagine Charlotte wants to hold onto it anyway. Besides, I'm a graduate now. It's time I claim my inheritance."

"Our inheritance," Valerie corrected.

"Of course. And you can live there too, if you like. Mom would've loved that. Charlotte can keep the stuffy old manor house. She can keep it all until she rots as far as I'm concerned. Just so long as she lets us have something to call our own."

"Listen to you sounding all grown up," Valerie said. "What's next? You going to go find a wife and have a bunch of kids? Turn your sword in for some vine trimmers?"

Henry shrugged. "Maybe. Who knows? It's just time to stop playing around, you know? I think Dad would have wanted us to take care of this land and not let Charlotte have her way with it."

"Why didn't Dad see what she was like? I don't know why he ever married her."

"I think she had everyone fooled back then. Even him."

They crossed through the sleepy hamlet of Briarwood, and Henry paused in front of the old theater that was once the heart of the village. A few window panes were missing and the front door was boarded up. "Remember when Dad used to take us to shows here after Mom died? He used to tell me that she was still looking down from the floodlights. That she could see us whenever she wanted."

"I don't remember that," Valerie replied.

"I guess you were too little."

"What's happened to this place?" Valerie studied the crumbling facade of the old theater building, trying to recall the last time she had seen it.

"You know how Charlotte feels about actors. She knows he only brought us here to remember Mom. I heard she stopped letting performers even stop in town the last few years."

"She's the worst."

Henry squeezed her hand. "We can fix this up along with the rest once we have what's ours. Maybe you can start that car shop you're always talking about."

"Speed shop," Valerie said.

"Right. What was it you were planning to call it?"

"Black Bear Motors. After Dad."

20

Henry dipped his chin and studied her over his sunglasses. "Might want to rethink that one now, huh?"

Valerie crossed her arms and shrugged.

"Well, whatever you call it, if we get Villa Rosa, we'll only have to see Charlotte once or twice a year. Think of the freedom."

"Sounds like a nice life."

Henry gripped her shoulder and gave it a squeeze, then his focus shifted back to the walk ahead of them. "We'd better get up to the house before she sends the dogs out after us. We're not free yet."

They made the climb to the manor house via the same route they had used so often as kids. The footpath wound through the woods to emerge onto the back side of the manor. They passed through the open gate of the outer wall, then crossed the manicured lawn to the stone steps that led to the raised patio. After climbing the worn steps, they entered the gate next to the pool house. They emerged onto the pool deck amid the sound of laughter and discovered their stepmother lounging in the hot tub with a young man Valerie vaguely recognized.

"Oh, look who finally made it," Lady Charlotte said. "When your friends showed up and said you were walking, we thought we might not see you." She indicated the nearby pool where a number of Henry's classmates had arrived and were joking around with one another. Thea was there too, tossing her hair and laughing, and doing a great job of keeping the boys' interest. So much so that none of Henry's friends even noticed their arrival.

"I hope you don't mind the intrusion," the man in the hot tub said. "But Lady Charlotte and I decided that we should get in on the fun, especially since she looks so great in a bikini."

Lady Charlotte laughed, blushing at the compliment, but obviously pleased. "Of course, you know Jasper Sterling." Charlotte said. "Jasper is the eldest son of Lord Alister Sterling."

Valerie blinked. Jasper Sterling. That's who he was. She knew she'd seen him before, on race posters and at formal events for the nobility, but never like this, half naked in her family's hot tub with an arm around her stepmother.

"Lord Sterling." Henry bowed stiffly, clearly uncomfortable with bowing to someone wearing swim trunks. Valerie wondered whether she was supposed to curtsy.

"To what do we owe the pleasure of your company, my lord?" Valerie asked.

A corner of Jasper's mouth quirked into a smile. "Well, I expect we'll be seeing a great deal more of one another soon. Your exquisite stepmother has in fact stolen my heart." He turned to gaze at Charlotte. "It's been a bit of a whirlwind, but I'd like to think that if she continues to feel the way I do, that we might all become quite close indeed."

Lady Charlotte nestled closer to him in the water until their noses touched, then she turned her attention back to Valerie and Henry. "I wanted to wait to surprise you when you got home." She lifted a dripping-wet hand from the bubbling water and displayed the glistening, jewel-encrusted ring on her finger. "We're engaged."

Valerie's mouth fell open.

Engaged.

Engaged?

How old was he? Valerie stared into Jasper's ice-blue eyes and thought he couldn't be much older than Henry. He wanted to marry Charlotte?

Jasper and Charlotte both rose from the hot tub, climbing out and coming around to join them. Valerie took an involuntary step backward as the two dripping lovers drew close. Jasper extended a hand to Henry. Lady Charlotte gripped Valerie's shoulders.

"Isn't it wonderful? We're going to be Sterlings!"

2

INHERITANCE

Valerie stared at the bathing suit laid out on her dresser and frowned.

"You have to come back out," Thea said. "You promised." Wrapped in a towel and balancing on the balls of her feet, she was practically bouncing in her enthusiasm to get back downstairs.

"There is no one in that pool I want to talk to," Valerie said.

"They're graduating seniors," Thea argued. "And every single one of them is an heir to titled lands. How often will we have them all to ourselves? Any other girl in first year would kill for this."

"We don't have to do everything the other girls do."

"*You* don't," Thea said. "You can just talk about race cars and engines all day, and the boys think you're fascinating. Some of us have to get their attention the old-fashioned way." Thea pressed her hands together. "Please?"

Valerie chewed her cheek and finally acquiesced, stripping out of her jeans. "Fine. But I'm doing this for you, not them."

Thea really did bounce up and down this time.

Valerie dressed in the bathing suit but snatched a tank top and some cut-off denim shorts from her drawer as well, pulling them over her bikini as they made their way back downstairs. Thea's return was greeted with whoops of enthusiasm from the boys in the pool. She dropped her towel and ran to rejoin them.

Valerie lingered on the pool deck, and her eyes drifted back to the hot tub where her stepmother was toweling off. Charlotte laughed at something Jasper said, then headed into the house. Jasper met Valerie's stare and winked at her.

"I can't believe she's falling for this," Henry said. Valerie turned to find her brother next to her, his brows knitted. He held an open beer in one hand, but it appeared to be untouched. "She has to know this can't be for real."

"You saw that ring on her finger," Valerie said. "I think she means it."

Henry was openly scowling toward the hot tub but finally pulled his eyes away. He stared at the beer in his hand as if realizing he held it for the first time, then handed it to Valerie. "I have to talk to her."

Valerie accepted the bottle, and Henry vanished back through the patio doors.

Thea was absorbed in conversation with two of Henry's friends at the shallow end of the pool and didn't seem to be lacking for attention. The other boys had begun a game of catch that involved creating huge waves as they dove about. Valerie turned to follow her brother inside.

"Valerie." Jasper Sterling vaulted over the edge of the hot tub and dripped his way over to her. "Don't run off."

"I'm not running anywhere," she replied.

Jasper reached her side and took her hand, lifting it to his lips and lightly brushing her fingers with a kiss. His grip tightened as he admired her signet ring. "To think, the House of the Bear and the House of a Thousand Swords will be joined at last." His thumb obscured the bear claw symbol on her ring for a moment. "Last time I saw you, I think you were wearing braces. Now. . ." His eyes roamed over her figure, lingering on her bare legs. "You've really grown up."

Valerie pulled her hand away. "I've never had braces. You must be thinking of some other girlfriend's daughter."

"Whoa, hey. There's no need to be upset," Jasper said. "If you escaped notice before, you certainly have my attention now."

Was he for real?

"Lady Charlotte must be missing you."

Jasper tossed the hair from his eyes and licked his lips. "She's getting ready for our night out. I'm taking her to the city tonight to celebrate in style." His gaze drifted to Thea laughing in the pool. "The nightlife in a village like this must be miserable. You and your friend will have to come to the city sometime too. I can show you how the grown-ups play."

"Why are you doing this?" Valerie asked. "Why Charlotte?"

"Don't tell me an exquisite, young thing like you is already a cynic about love," Jasper said. "That would be a tragedy." He reached for her hand again, but this time he took the untouched beer from her and took a sip.

Valerie narrowed her eyes. "You really want us to believe this is about love?"

Jasper brushed the hair away from his face again and offered the beer back. "Is it so hard to believe your mother would fall for me?"

"Yes," Valerie replied. "And she's not my mother." She turned her back on him and strode into the house.

She was walking a thin line.

Jasper was a Sterling, and her family owed them loyalty. He wasn't her liege lord yet, but his father was, and he would be soon enough. But when she glanced back, Jasper didn't look angry. The smirk was back on his face, and he took another sip from the beer, his eyes never leaving her.

She found Henry and Charlotte in the hallway outside her father's study.

"He's half your age," Henry said.

"He most certainly is not," Charlotte objected. "I may be a few years older than him, but who's to say what matters. A

25

decade here or there is all the same anymore. Something you'll understand when you're an adult."

"I *am* an adult," Henry said. "And you should've consulted us before agreeing to join our house to the Sterlings'."

"Consult you? Why should I have to consult you?"

"Father's estate—" Henry began.

"Your father would have wanted me to move on," Charlotte said. "He didn't expect me to spend my life pining away for him." She gathered her towel to herself, noting Valerie for the first time. "Now I must get dressed. Jasper is throwing us a party in the city tonight as soon as we arrive. *His* family wants to congratulate us."

Valerie opened her mouth to speak, but Henry cut her off.

"I want Villa Rosa."

Charlotte stopped in her tracks and turned around. "I beg your pardon?"

"Villa Rosa." Henry glanced at Valerie. "We want it. It belonged to our mother, and it's time we had a property of our own."

"Valerie isn't even eighteen," Charlotte objected. "She can't own property."

"I'll be eighteen this summer," Valerie said.

"And I'm graduating university," Henry added. "It's time for us to have what Father and Mother would have wanted for us," Henry said. "God knows you've held onto it for long enough."

"We'll discuss it later," Charlotte said. "After the wedding. Jasper wants to be married right away, and we'll have all the time in the world after that. I'm sure we can locate some little piece of land you two can have and—"

"Villa Rosa," Henry said. "And not someday. Now."

Lady Charlotte's mouth tightened. "Is this because of that tournament? You think if you own land that you'd be permitted to fight? More reason I wouldn't give you Villa Rosa even if it were possible. The last thing this family needs is you playing at being your father any more than you already do."

"What do you mean 'even if it were possible'?" Henry said. "Why can't you give us Villa Rosa?"

Charlotte scrunched up her face even more but finally broke under Henry's stare. "If you must know, I've given quite a few properties to Jasper. I don't recall exactly which ones . . ."

"You gave our mother's lands to the Sterlings?" Henry exclaimed.

"I had to give him something. He's representing our family in the tournament. And it's not as though I won't still own them," Charlotte said. "We're getting *married*. We'll all be one happy family."

"You mean the Sterlings will be happy," Valerie interjected.

"You're letting Jasper fight in the tournament as a Terravecchia champion?" Henry asked. "Are you out of your mind?"

Charlotte frowned at them. "Honestly, I thought you two could at least show a shred of decency and celebrate this occasion with me, but all you care about is getting your hands on more of what's mine. I never would have thought you would be so ungrateful, especially you." She rounded on Valerie. "Considering the fortune I'm spending for you to attend that university, you could do something useful with it. Instead, you spend all your time playing around with silly cars."

"It's not playing," Valerie argued. "I'm starting a business."

"It's a waste of time." Charlotte glared at Valerie.

"She can do what she likes," Henry argued. "It's not hurting anyone."

"Isn't it? Every dinner I attend, I have to listen to how everyone's children are doing so well, and my stepdaughter wants to roll around in motor oil with the peasants. And *you* aren't much better. A boy, play-fighting with swords. If you want to throw away your lives, so be it, but you won't be getting any more handouts from me." She tossed her hair and picked up her champagne glass, then forged her way down the hall.

Henry had been angry before, but his face was now an

unnatural shade of red. He muttered under his breath at Charlotte's retreating figure, then turned and slammed his fist into the wall. He then disappeared through the door to their father's study.

Valerie followed.

Cedar.

Ash.

The smell of old books.

The tension from the hallway ebbed as she absorbed the scents around her.

This was the one room in the house that still looked as she remembered from before. Her father's massive desk and bookshelves had been assembled in the room and were much too broad and heavy to make it back out the door. This fact had preserved the look of the study and spared it the overhaul that had occurred in the rest of the house after her father's disappearance.

Henry was standing in the center of the room, staring at the oil painting that hung over the fireplace. The family portrait featured a much younger Lady Charlotte, smiling alongside their father. Valerie's younger self stared back at her with rosy cheeks and a childish grin. Henry's portrait appeared every bit as handsome and capable as he was in real life. Age had now brought a maturity to his muscled frame, but Valerie could still see the boy in the painting when she looked at him.

"This can't be what he wanted for us," Henry said.

Valerie crossed the woolen rug to join her brother. Her eyes fell on the empty sword rack above the mantle. "Was Charlotte right? Is that why you didn't want to wait? You want to register for the King's Tournament?"

Henry shifted his feet. "Under the king's rules, if you want to represent your family name, someone has to appoint you champion. I knew Charlotte would never name me, but I thought if I could get out from under her and get land of my own, I could name myself. I could compete as a different Terravecchia household. It would be a chance to revive our family legacy."

"You want to be a knight? Wouldn't that mean leaving?" The distance across the continent suddenly became real. The Knight Warden of the West spent as much time at the king's court as he did at home, and the king's court was nearly three thousand miles away.

"I'm not saying I'd win," Henry said. "But even placing would get me noticed."

"Plenty of people have noticed you. You've won championships."

"For school," Henry said. "Wearing school colors and school emblems. I'm ready to fight for myself. For the Terravecchia name. But it'll never happen until Charlotte gives us what's ours."

"She hates tournaments. If she knows you want to fight like dad, there's no chance."

"I know."

"Mister Henry? Miss Valerie?" Valerie turned to find Eugenia, the housekeeper, standing in the doorway. "There is someone at the door who would like to speak with you. A Miss Livingston."

"Show her in," Henry replied.

A few moments later, a tall woman in a light gray suit entered the room. She had a French manicure and was carrying a briefcase. "Mister Terravecchia, Miss Terravecchia, my name is Berkley Livingston, of Gable, Livingston, and Hughes. Do you have a moment to talk?"

"What's this about?" Henry asked. "Some other trouble Charlotte's brought on us?"

"It's not my place to say," Livingston replied. "I'm merely the messenger."

The lawyer rested her briefcase on the edge of the desk while she unlocked it. She then removed two envelopes and handed one to each of them. "As you know, Gable, Livingston, and

Hughes has handled your family affairs for several generations. I was instructed to deliver these messages at the time you both became adults or in the event that Lady Charlotte should remarry. After we received word of your stepmother's upcoming wedding plans and several of her recent real-estate decisions, our firm felt that now was the appropriate time."

Valerie was about to ask who had made the agreement, but as she turned the envelope over in her hands, her breath caught. Her name was written across the envelope in neat script, and she immediately recognized the handwriting.

It was unmistakable.

3

RIDE

D ad. Valerie tore into the envelope as though her life depended on it.

She found a yellowed sheet of paper within. As she unfolded it, an iron key slid into her palm. She considered the key briefly, then searched the slip of paper. Her heart sank. It had only a single line written on it. "For my Valerie. With loving memory of our best times together."

She turned the paper over to find a map of the valley highlighting their family lands. An X on the map bore an annotation that read, "Angelina's Well."

She glanced at her brother, but he was busy tearing into his envelope. A moment later, he held up a key of his own. He flashed the paper at the lawyer. "This is it? There's nothing else? No letter to explain it?"

Valerie read the line of text on Henry's paper. It was their family motto, again written in their father's careful handwriting.

"He only requested that we present them both together. But he did include one additional instruction," Livingston said. "He requested that someone read your family motto aloud at the time these items are bequeathed. Shall I do it for you?"

Henry and Valerie exchanged glances, and Valerie shrugged.

The lawyer removed a pair of spectacles from her jacket and took the sheet of paper from Henry. She focused on the words and read, "Rimani sempre nobile di cuore."

She looked at them knowingly but, getting no response, folded the paper again and handed it back to Henry. "And that's it, I'm afraid. Gable, Livingston, and Hughes was given no further instructions." She closed her briefcase.

"What are we supposed to do with these?" Henry asked, holding up his key.

"It's not my privilege to know," Livingston said. She turned to leave, hesitated, then faced them once more. "If it's any small help, your father did say something in person at the time he made this bequest. He emphasized that he truly believed in your family's words and felt they would be enough to guide you." The lawyer gripped her briefcase handle with both hands. "It's a beautiful sentiment, really. That nobility is a product of the heart, not the blood. In light of some of your stepmother's recent choices, I thought you may find that comforting. No lack of title or property can ever take away a noble heart you carry with you."

"I'm sure that will be of great consolation when our inheritance is given to the Sterlings," Henry muttered.

Livingston sighed, then strode into the hall, her briefcase swinging gently beside her.

Valerie watched the lawyer disappear, then turned back to Henry. "What now?"

Henry studied his key. "Let's hope that whatever these unlock gives us more answers. Did your letter have anything useful?"

Valerie handed him the map. "It's the old estate. Angelina's Well."

"Out at River House, where Dad grew up," Henry said. "Where he and Mom met." He examined the map. "We could make it in an hour if we leave now."

"Sure," Valerie said. "This night is a downer anyway."

They walked back to the main hall and stepped out the front doors to the circular drive. Outside, Charlotte was already in the passenger seat of a convertible Phaeton speedster. She gave them both a cold glare. Jasper was climbing into the driver's seat. He revved the engine several times to the delight of the teenage valets.

Jasper caught Valerie's stare for a brief moment, and he gave her another wink. He saluted the valets, then shifted into gear and tore out of the driveway, tires squealing and leaving the scent of burnt rubber lingering in the air. The pair sped down the tree-lined drive until the car's taillights disappeared into the twilight.

Someone gripped Valerie's arm, and she turned to find Thea behind her. Her eyes were glassy.

"Val Val! Just the person we need." She slurred a few more words Valerie didn't catch. Every member of the group was carrying their own bottle of wine. They had obviously made a pitstop in the cellar and were determined to start summer break with nothing held back.

"I'll be along eventually," Valerie said. "Save some wine for the rest of us."

"No promises," Thea said. She eyed Henry. "What about it, captain? You, me, hot tub?"

Valerie steered Thea away and gave her a gentle shove toward the rest of the group that was slowly making its way toward the back of the house. "Be good, Thea."

Thea pouted but cheered up at the sight of the other members of Henry's dueling club making their way toward the pool house. She hurried to catch up.

"She'll be all right," Henry said, taking Valerie's hand and towing her toward the garages. "Come on. We can take Charlotte's convertible. She clearly won't be using it tonight."

They were through the manor house gates and onto the open

road minutes later, Henry behind the wheel of Charlotte's Easton convertible. Valerie attempted to direct him to the correct route. How many years had it been since she had been to River House? Nearly a decade of living at boarding schools divided her from the last time she was a real resident of her family's land, but she knew enough. Hadn't her father driven these lanes with her nearly every weekend of her childhood? His spirit lingered in every curve.

The purr of the engine kept time with the speed of Valerie's thoughts as they hurtled over hills and around bends. Her mind raced to catch up with the turmoil of the evening and sudden appearance of her father's messages.

The headlights startled a herd of deer at the side of the road and sent them bounding away into the vineyards. Henry focused on the road and took them north into the heart of the valley.

The minutes blurred by with the hills and trees. When they reached the road to River House, the tires chirped as Henry swerved onto the pavement of the drive. They tore down the long lane leading to her father's favorite summer residence. Old oaks lined the road, drooping blankets of moss that reached for them with wispy fingers. The passing car left them flailing in the wind like angry ghosts.

The house was still small in the distance when they reached the turnoff for the well. Henry launched the car down the old pump road but had to slow when they encountered the ruts left by last year's rainy season.

Frequent switchbacks punctuated a steady decline until they reached the second turnoff they were looking for. While the pump road had always maintained occasional traffic from servants or family members headed for the river, the route to Angelina's Well was so overgrown that they were soon forced to abandon the car and walk.

Henry plucked a flashlight from the car's glove box and lit the way.

"What do you think is hiding out here?" Valerie asked.

"Your guess is as good as mine."

Henry pried his way through the underbrush and they finally emerged in the clearing cut around the old stone well.

Valerie had been here a few times as a child. She recalled staring down the unfathomable well and tossing rocks into its depths, her voice echoing back up at her when she yelled.

To one side of the well was a dilapidated barn that had once housed horses. She had a vague memory of feeding a painted mare an apple from her hand. The corral in the back was now nothing but a few rotting fence posts.

The old barn had three separate bays. The largest, central bay stood open and empty. The other two doors were closed and padlocked.

Valerie and Henry exchanged glances, and both removed their keys from their pockets.

As they approached the first bay, Henry tried his key. Despite the age of the barn, the locks were well lubricated and should have turned easily enough, but Henry's key didn't work.

He stepped aside and let Valerie try. She twisted her key and the lock snapped open immediately. She held her breath as Henry swung the door open.

Inside the barn sat a vision straight from her memory.

"Good God," Henry said.

The sleek, black vehicle was a panther in crouch, power pulsing in every line of its form.

"Dad," Valerie whispered.

It had been a long time since she'd seen the car, but it was as though the years had been rolled back and she was standing on the sidewalk in front of school again. Any moment, her father would open the door and step out to greet her.

Valerie smiled at the memory.

The day her father had showed up in this machine had left students gaping and bullies afraid to antagonize her for the next decade.

Because it wasn't just a car. It was a Guardian 770. A machine of war. A legend.

She didn't notice how hard she was squeezing her brother's arm until he pried her fingers off.

"I promise it's not a ghost, Val."

"Charlotte said she sold it. She said she had it stripped for parts." Valerie kept her eyes on the car as though it might vanish. It was all there. The ravenous intake scoop of the supercharger. The Terravecchia crest on the rims. Valerie took a few tentative steps forward, stretching a hand out, still unsure if the apparition might dissolve before her eyes.

When her fingertips grazed the hood, she finally exhaled.

It was real.

She brushed her hand along the car's bold fender and up to the mirror. The window was open only a crack, but the scent of the interior was enough to bring back a flood of memories. Saturday afternoons in the passenger seat, her father's hand resting gently on hers, teaching her to shift the gears. The addictive smell of leather and gasoline.

She clenched at her throat when she saw the pocket watch. It was still there, dangling from a frayed cord on the rearview mirror.

"I can't believe it. It's really his."

"Someone's been taking good care of it," Henry said. "It's barely even dusty."

He was right. This wasn't a car that had been neglected for a decade. There were a few scars on the body—evidence of past battles—but the leather was polished, the controls still shiny.

She spotted the keychain dangling from the ignition.

Opening the door, she slid into the driver's seat. A metal tag hanging from the ignition key had a single word engraved on it. *Valerie.*

"I'll see what's in the other bay," Henry said.

"Okay," Valerie replied, though she wasn't really listening. Her hands were busy finding their places on the steering wheel.

She stepped on the clutch and twisted the ignition key.

The engine awoke with a roar.

Yes.

Shifting into gear, she eased the Guardian out of the barn. The engine trembled with anticipation, a stallion chomping at its bit, eager to run. Valerie teased the accelerator and glanced at the third bay of the barn. The door hung open, but there was no sign of Henry.

She'd come back for him.

Valerie turned the wheel and eased the Guardian down the gravel path that led through the woods to the old river road. If she took it far enough, it would loop around the house and back to the route they came in by. If her memory served her, it was a little over three miles.

She'd be back in no time.

Valerie gave the Guardian the gas and it leapt into motion. Her body trembled with its raw power, and she was immediately awash with nostalgia.

It still smelled like him. The rough leather beneath her was familiar, the shine from the glistening instrument panel too. The vibration from the 640-horsepower engine may as well have been bubbling up from her past.

She rocketed down the river road, whipping past ancient trees and only slowing in places where tree roots had found their way to the surface or been exposed by the river's annual floods.

This was home. This memory. This car.

As the Guardian surged onto the main drive, she had the sudden feeling she had gone back in time.

She let out a whoop of unconstrained joy.

But almost as soon as the sound had left her mouth, she was brought back to the present.

The windows of River House were lit.

Valerie eased off the gas. Who else was out here?

She approached cautiously, then turned around the drive, the headlights sweeping over the house. It was too late for servants to be working. Perhaps the mysterious caretaker? She rolled down the windows. She could just make out the babble of the river beyond the house as it rushed past the old bridge she had jumped from so many times as a child. But there were other noises. Voices.

A moment later, the front door opened and three people walked out. She recognized the couple but couldn't place them. The man accompanying them was shaking their hands.

"I think you'll be incredibly happy with the purchase. I know that Lord Sterling was especially pleased that you'll be neighbors." The man stopped speaking when the couple caught sight of the Guardian.

Valerie left the engine running as she got out of the car. "What's going on here? What are you people doing on our land?"

The couple exchanged glances, then looked to the third man with a questioning gaze. The man gave Valerie a quick appraisal that took in the car as well, then stepped off the porch. "This is actually now the property of the Baron and Baroness of Winthrop. They've just purchased it."

The words were a slap in the face.

"This is Terravecchia land. It's been in my family for a century."

"And now it's not," the man said without even a hint of apology. He reached into his pocket and retrieved a card. "Blaise Cavendish, personal attorney of Lord Jasper Sterling. I can assure you that this sale has gone through all the proper channels. I have the documentation right here." He indicated a silver briefcase at his side.

"This house isn't his to sell," Valerie hissed.

"I assure you, it is," Blaise replied. "The paperwork is done. Would you care to see your stepmother's signature on the deed transfer? I have it. But perhaps you should simply ask her." He took a few steps and grasped Valerie's elbow, turning her toward the car. "Valerie, is it? Why don't you run along and let the grown-ups handle their business."

Valerie jerked her arm free of his grasp. She wanted to punch him right in his condescending mouth.

Then her eyes took in the house beyond him.

They were going to lose it.

The place her mother and father had fallen in love. The docks where her mother used to sit and laugh as Valerie and Henry performed stunts from the rope swings. The shallow pools where her father had first taught her to swim. All of it would belong to someone else.

It wasn't possible.

"This isn't right," Valerie said, raising a threatening finger. "You'll have my brother to deal with."

"I have a train to catch," Blaise said, checking his watch. "But I'll be sure to tell Lord Sterling to expect his call."

Valerie climbed back into the Guardian and slammed the door. The Baron and Baroness looked on as she shifted into gear and stomped on the accelerator. The tires of the Guardian squealed and smoked. She sent a cloud of dust toward the lawyer, then raced away down the drive.

Valerie launched the car back along the river road, letting the wind tear through the open windows. Her thoughts were as wild and unruly as the hair that flailed about her head.

Everything was coming undone.

It wasn't supposed to be like this.

Jasper Sterling.

What circle of hell had he crawled up from?

When the dark figure stepped into the road, Valerie's stomach went into her throat.

She yanked hard on the wheel, stomping the brake and sending the car into a sideways skid, clawing for traction as it fishtailed. The car finally came to stop amid a cloud of dust, mere inches from contact.

The masked man in the road was brandishing a sword. His

face was that of an elemental beast. Stubbed ears framed a snarling face and a mouth with silver teeth.

He stepped closer, moving around the front of the car.

Valerie stared at the figure as he approached her window. A mask of judgment. A mask of vengeance. What long-forgotten sins were being paid for tonight?

She noted the sword in the man's hand. She'd seen it a hundred times in her dreams. *Durendal*, the blade that could cut through stone. Legend held it was the sharpest sword in existence. She had thought it lost. Past and present were once again blurring together.

The figure lifted the sword and studied the blade, then the voice came from beyond the mask. "Do you remember it being so beautiful?" He pulled the mask from his face with his free hand.

He was no longer Il Orso Nero, the fearsome bear—only Henry, her brother. And the sword was just a sword again.

"We have a problem," Valerie said. Henry lowered the weapon, and she relayed the conversation she had at the house.

"Sold," he repeated. "You're certain?"

"By some lawyer. He claimed he worked for Jasper Sterling."

"That thieving bastard," Henry muttered. "He isn't even attempting to wait till the wedding to show his true colors. I bet he'll sell Villa Rosa too."

He pulled the scabbard from his belt and sheathed the sword, then moved around to the passenger side of the car. He attached the sword to the built-in rack on the car's ceiling, then slid into the passenger seat. He pointed through the windshield. "Port Hyacinth."

"That's a long drive," Valerie replied. "The tunnel will be closed. Only the auto train gets through the border at night."

"We'll take the coast highway. We can still be in the city by morning."

Valerie searched his face. "What's your plan?"

"Justice," Henry snarled. "If Charlotte is too blind to see that Jasper is swindling her, it's on us to defend our family's honor."

"How will our honor help us?"

"You know how."

She glanced at the sword. "You expect to duel the entire House of Sterling till you get our land back?"

"If Jasper wants to steal our future, then I'll take it back in the court of steel and blood. The only court that will be on our side."

"He's the son of our liege lord. You'd be pitting our family's honor against centuries of tradition."

Henry's jaw clenched. "All I know is, father left me a sword." He focused his stare on her. "And he left you a car."

Valerie looked into his eyes for several long seconds, then reached for the five-point harness and buckled it across her chest. "This thing really moves. You'd better hold on to something."

Henry smiled.

Valerie shifted into gear and stepped on the gas.

4

ARRIVAL

They reached the city walls at sunrise. Valerie had made only one stop, needing fuel for the car and herself. The coffee cup now sat empty in the cup holder between the seats. She had also made an impulse decision to buy a pair of boots to replace the sandals she had previously had on and a jacket to cover her bare shoulders. She was still in her cut-off shorts and her bathing suit peeked from beneath the shoulder straps of her tank top, but at least her feet now looked like they were ready for the business at hand.

Henry had been asleep for the last several hours and Valerie hadn't wanted to wake him. He would need his energy.

She flashed her signet ring to the guards at the North Bay bridge gate, though the car went just as far to clarify their status as nobles. If there was any place where the dividing line between the nameless and the high families was easily defined, it was on the elevated roads of Port Hyacinth.

The highways of the "Silver City" stretched from hilltop to hilltop and island to island, linking the bay's various walled fortresses. The fortified high roads kept the sights and smells of Port Hyacinth's less-desirable underside a distant and infrequently thought of concern.

From the height of the Bay Bridge, Valerie could only make out a few details of the scattered rim villages hidden in the shadow of the city walls. Shanties clung precariously to the cliffs, and twisting roads that were little more than animal trails connected junkyards and dumps.

She returned her focus to the pristine highway awash in the dawn light. When they crossed the last bridge into the city proper, they climbed a series of winding streets toward the commerce district.

It had only been a few months since she'd last been to Port Hyacinth—on a shopping trip with friends—but now she eyed the tall buildings with darker purpose.

Henry stretched and opened his eyes. "Oh wow. We're here already?"

"You missed the dark parts of the drive."

When they reached the city center, Valerie pulled into a parking space outside Sterling Tower. It stretched skyward over thirty stories, the highest point on the hilltop. "You're sure you want to do this?"

"You think somehow a few hours have changed my mind?" Henry asked.

"I don't know. It's morning. Dad used to say the morning was for making new plans."

"I have a plan already. Make Jasper Sterling pay for his crimes." Henry snatched up the glass bottle of tea Valerie had purchased for him at the roadside store and drank. When he had wiped his mouth and tightened the lid back on the bottle, he reached for the sword.

Valerie climbed out of the car, tugging at her cutoffs. She wished she would have taken the time to change. The air was cool and her bare legs prickled with goosebumps.

Morning sun was reflecting in the glass of the tower across the street. The glittering spire was the home of the Sterlings' power, but they would need to get Jasper outside to face them. Those were the rules.

43

Henry fastened *Durendal* to his belt and shook out his arms. Then he picked up their father's mask and hung it over the hilt of the sword.

"You're positive you can beat him?" Valerie asked.

Henry gave her a derisive glare.

"I'm just making sure," Valerie said.

"I've beaten him before," Henry replied. "I beat him when I was only a sophomore in prep school and he was a college senior."

"That was a school tournament. This is the real thing."

"And I've won three district championships since then," Henry said. "I think I'll be able to handle myself."

Valerie popped the trunk of the car and walked around back to look inside. There were several miscellaneous dueling blades attached to the trunk lid. She pulled one of the unnamed swords from the rack and carried it with her.

"What do you plan to do with that?" Henry asked.

"You need a second, don't you? A second needs a sword too."

"Not unless things go badly."

Valerie accompanied her brother across the plaza toward the doors of the Sterling building. The lower two floors of the tower were sheer concrete and fortified with an iron gate. Several armed guards lingered just inside the bars. Beyond them, antique wooden doors granted access into the building.

"We've come to settle a grievance with Lord Jasper Sterling," Henry said as soon as he reached the gate. "I demand that he show himself at once and face the consequences of his dishonorable actions."

The guard at the door was nonplussed. "His lordship isn't to be disturbed unless you have an appointment."

"I have a grievance that is a matter of highest honor. Lord Sterling has wronged me and my family and must account for what he's done. If necessary, I shall fetch a magistrate, but a gentleman would not hide from his actions. Are you suggesting your lord and master is a coward?"

The guard blinked and seemed to contemplate the corner he had been backed into. "He's . . . I'll send word of your request."

"It's a challenge, not a request," Henry said. "Tell him Henry Terravecchia III demands satisfaction."

"Aye, m'lord. I'll tell him."

The guard mumbled something to his companion, who then took up the forward post at the gate. The first guard rapped on a small door built into the larger wooden gate and was admitted. He vanished inside.

Henry and Valerie were obliged to linger in the plaza outside the building.

A few early morning arrivals crisscrossed the plaza, headed for various offices in the buildings around them. Some approached the Sterling Building and were admitted by the guard after displaying their appointment cards.

Valerie and her brother drew curious glances from passersby, and several people lingered on benches, eyeing their swords and waiting to see what trouble might be brewing.

Henry drew *Durendal* and felt the balance of it in his hand, then made a few quick slashes in the air.

"You think it will come to an actual fight?" Valerie asked.

"I don't know. If he's smart, he'll admit to being a shark who preyed on our family and make amends. If not, he'll be facing my steel."

"You won't really demand satisfaction, will you?" Valerie asked. "You should fight to first blood, tournament style."

"I'll fight as the situation demands," Henry replied. "I'm not scared of him."

"Well, I am. And you getting yourself maimed or killed won't do us any good. Fight to first blood or not at all."

Henry scoffed, but after searching her face, he nodded. "As long as honor is served and he admits to defrauding our family, I don't need to see him seriously injured. I just want our future back."

Valerie pulled her jacket tighter and tried to ignore the fresh goosebumps on her skin. She didn't know if it was the wind whipping through the buildings or the thought of the fight ahead. Her body was tired from the night of driving, but she was too nervous to relax.

She fidgeted with the sword in her hand, pulling it from its scabbard and finding that the blade was still shining and clean. No rust had formed and she could see her own reflection in the steel. Her hair was a mess and her mascara had smeared. She used the sleeve of her jacket to try to wipe at the corner of her eye.

"Well, aren't you two the most eager fools I've ever seen."

Valerie spun around to find a trio of vehicles pulling up behind them. The silver limousine had tinted windows, but the rear window was down and Jasper Sterling had one arm hanging out. He smirked at Valerie. "Did you miss me so badly that you had to drive all night to see me again? That's sweet. Love the outfit."

Valerie scowled at him, but Henry was the first to speak. "You have a lot to answer for, Sterling. You'd best wipe that grin off your face."

The other two cars continued around their position, encircling them inside a ring of vehicles.

Jasper opened his door and stepped out. He was wearing an expensive navy suit but no tie. His shirt hung open at the collar. He sized up Valerie. "You should have taken me up on my offer. We had a wild night."

"Where's Charlotte?" Valerie asked.

"She went home early. Couldn't keep up."

A few of Jasper's companions stepped from the other cars, several men and one woman. All of them were still dressed in their clothes from the night before and most still looked intoxicated.

Jasper straightened his jacket sleeves, then reached inside the limo for his sword. He slid the scabbard into the extension on his belt. "Now what seems to be the trouble, dear Henry?"

Henry stepped up to Jasper and stood toe to toe with him. "You know what you've done. You're a thief. I demand that you give back the property you've stolen from us."

"A serious accusation, boy," Jasper said. "You'd best reconsider your words."

"I don't know how you got Charlotte to buy into this lie of yours, but it won't work on us."

Several of Jasper's companions closed in around them. Valerie recognized one of them as the lawyer she had encountered at River House. He met her stare with an expression of disdain.

"Your stepmother is in love with me," Jasper said. "Her generosity can hardly be considered my fault."

"You're playing her for a fool," Valerie said.

"Such an unkind thing to say about Lady Charlotte. You think she has nothing to offer? You're quite wrong. I'm sure you could learn a lot from a woman with her . . . experience."

Valerie wrinkled her nose. "You're disgusting."

"Stop evading the issue, Jasper," Henry said. "That property you sold is our inheritance. Did you think you could steal from us without facing the consequences?"

"Perhaps if you had ever taken the time to endear yourself to Lady Charlotte instead of making a spectacle of yourself all over the country, you might have been the recipient of her generosity as well."

"More words from a rat looking to escape retribution," Henry said.

"You should be thanking me," Jasper said. "I'll be a better husband to Lady Charlotte than your father ever was. She says he was sadly unimpressive once you saw behind the mask."

Henry growled. He turned and walked a few steps, then pivoted to face Jasper, brandishing his sword. "In the view of these witnesses, I name you a thief. You've dishonored the title of gentleman and I challenge you to admit your wrongdoing or face the consequences."

Jasper Sterling glanced at his companions and smiled. "Do you think any of these witnesses find your grievance sufficient for a challenge of this kind?"

"I do," Valerie said. "His challenge is seconded."

Jasper glared at her. "Another challenge of no account from a child of no account."

Henry aimed the tip of his sword toward Jasper. "Will you face me or shall all here present name you a coward?" He spoke the words loudly enough that the curious onlookers around the plaza could hear.

Jasper's upper lip curled. "Very well. You'll get your wish." He reached into his jacket pocket and removed a pen. "If we're going to do this, let's make it legal." He turned to his companions. "Blaise, fetch me a dueling contract."

"What's the matter, Sterling?" Valerie asked. "Is your word so worthless that not even your friends trust it?"

"I live in the real world," Jasper replied. "A place you should visit sometime."

"Don't worry. I'll handle this," Henry said. He gave her a handkerchief from his pocket. "Mark a starting position for me."

Blaise retrieved his silver briefcase from the car and removed a prewritten dueling contract.

"Blaise attended Huffington Law. He'll soon be employed at the most elite firm in the capitol," Jasper said.

"Well, bully for him," Valerie replied, dropping Henry's monogrammed handkerchief a half dozen paces away. She tried to ignore the stares from the other men in Jasper's crew as she walked back to her brother's side. He was leaning over the trunk of the limo reviewing the terms of the contract, a pen poised in his hand.

Valerie looked over his shoulder. The desired outcomes of the duel were listed in sequential checkboxes beneath one another. The most serious outcome was "To the death." Henry's pen hovered over "Until too injured to continue."

"Henry," Valerie whispered through her teeth.

"Fine," Henry muttered and moved his pen down to "To first-blood" and checked the box. He then signed his signature at the bottom and handed the pen to Valerie. She signed her name on the line for seconds, then passed the contract to one of Jasper's seconds. Three of the men signed as witnesses for Jasper before he signed it himself.

Henry squeezed Valerie's shoulder. "Now we get justice." He walked to the mark Valerie had dropped for him. Three of Jasper's crew likewise dropped handkerchiefs to define the space for the duel. The limousines formed a sort of wall, barring interference from onlookers.

Jasper removed his jacket and rolled up his sleeves but then proceeded to lean against the side of the limo.

"Are you waiting for a doctor?" Henry asked.

"Actually, Huxley can serve as doctor for this duel," Jasper said. "He attends Canterbury Medical."

Valerie rolled her eyes. "Must we wait for you to list the credentials of your entire playground circle then?"

Jasper smirked. "We're waiting for your brother's competition. But speak of the devil and he shall appear."

Valerie blinked in confusion and turned to find a fourth vehicle arriving across the plaza. A sleek charcoal-gray Easton Blackbird 900 pulled up behind the circle of limousines and idled. She couldn't see through the windshield, but the sight of the war car twisted her stomach.

"You plan to cower behind a hired sword in a duel of honor?" Henry asked.

"The dueling contract allows a surrogate to stand in my place if I am ill. I'm feeling a little dehydrated this morning, therefore, I have assigned my role to a champion."

"Dehydrated," Valerie said. "You mean you drank too much last night."

"Among other things." Jasper turned to the man standing in as doctor. "Hux, dehydration is a serious medical concern, isn't it?"

"Most serious," Huxley replied. "I can't recommend a duel in your current condition."

Jasper held up his hands as though that settled the matter.

The door of the Blackbird opened and a masked figure stepped into the sunlight.

The man stood several inches taller than Henry. His dueling mask was a thing from a nightmare, black eyes rimmed with silver, and a slice of crimson that cut through the black from above one brow and all the way across the right cheek. The mouth of the mask was a void that could swallow the world.

The swordsman was dressed in all black. Even the metal armor that studded various parts of his jacket had been painted black. The only other splash of color the man presented was the bright red of his sword hilt.

"I trust you've heard of the *Sword with the Red Hilt*," Jasper said. "Legend says it belonged to Lancelot and also Sir Balin. Crafted by Merlin himself. A worthy match for your *Durendal*, wouldn't you say?" Jasper eased himself off the limousine. "You had to know I wouldn't face the sword of Orlando without a legacy sword of my own. What sort of fight would that be?"

Valerie turned to her brother and found his face had gone pale.

"They knew we were coming," Valerie said. "He was planning for this. You shouldn't go through with it."

"Oh, I think he should," Jasper said. "Your brother knows the code as well as any. Three-time regional champion, wasn't he? I trust he will remember *all* the rules. Especially what happens if he backs out now."

"No one is backing out," Henry said, shaking out his sword arm. "A named sword and a mask don't make a swordsman. Only skill determines that." He squeezed Valerie's shoulder, then approached the man in the mask. "May I have your name, sir?"

The figure remained silent.

"He doesn't talk much," Jasper explained. "But he calls himself the Red Reaper. I think it suits him."

Henry set his jaw and walked back to his place. "Let's have it over with. You're merely delaying justice with your gutless tactics."

Jasper smiled. "By all means. Let justice commence."

Valerie took her position next to her brother, noting the eyes of the Reaper following her as she moved.

"I don't like this," she whispered.

"Don't worry," Henry replied. "From here I let father's sword do the talking." He donned his mask.

Valerie tightened her grip on the weapon in her hands but had never felt more powerless.

Across the circle the Red Reaper drew his blade.

The lawyer, Blaise, lifted his hand and tossed a single silver coin to the ground, signaling the duel had begun.

Henry sprang into the circle and his opponent surged forward as well. Valerie's heart went into her mouth as morning sun flashed from the blades and the two men met with a clash of ancient steel.

5

UNAVENGED

Valerie used to love watching her brother fight. There was a grace to the way he moved.

Lunge. Retreat. Parry. Riposte.

She had grown up in the shadow of his movements, eagerly following along as he would practice on the rear lawn of the manor house.

They had waged a thousand battles with one another as children, wooden swords clacking in the yard. She was fast but Henry was quicker. While they had acted out hundreds of noble victories, she had never really defeated him.

To Valerie, swordplay was a fun game, but she had lost interest as she grew. Henry turned it into art.

As the sound of blade on blade resounded across the plaza, more onlookers gathered around the circle of vehicles to see what was going on. Valerie kept her eyes locked on the two combatants.

Henry was moving with a furious energy, his sword flashing forward in bold attacks and deceptive feints. Valerie recognized many of his moves, but there were complex combinations of thrusts and master cuts she had never seen him employ.

She absorbed every scrape of their boots on the concrete, and each crash of the swords echoed in her ears.

It was evident that Henry was looking to end the fight quickly. Her brother's opponent was on the defensive, at times deflecting Henry's blows with millimeters to spare.

The ancient hand-and-a-half swords were heavier and sharper than university competition blades, but Henry wielded *Durendal* with confidence, switching from single to double-handed strokes with ease. Several times, Valerie cringed in expectation as it seemed the heavy cuts were sure to end with the Red Reaper losing a limb. But for minute after minute, steel only found steel.

The mask of her brother's opponent revealed even less than Henry's. The lenses of the black eye sockets were nearly flush with the rest of the mask, making it seem as though Henry was dueling a faceless wraith. The dark swordsman moved with precision, seeming to exert only the energy needed to avoid being impaled, though with the ferocity of Henry's attacks, that required remarkable speed.

Henry's face was mostly concealed as well, but Valerie could still see the fervor in his eyes, the way he focused and moved, guarding his position and continually pressing the attack.

The fight moved around the designated circle, the Red Reaper at times being pressed all the way to where a handkerchief had been dropped, but he never stepped out of the predetermined area for the duel. Each time Valerie felt certain that he would have to yield more ground and be backed out of the circle, he would feint and move, redirecting Henry's attacks enough to buy himself more space to maneuver.

The swelling crowd around the fight grew louder. Cheers went up during the more furious thrusts. As the fight wore on, Henry found himself increasingly on defense. Sweat was staining his shirt now, and he paused longer between attacks to gain his breath. As he backed toward Valerie, she could hear his panting.

Jasper's companions began to cheer and jeer with enthusiasm as the Red Reaper pressed the attack.

"You have this! Don't let up!" Valerie shouted.

Her encouragement seemed to help. Henry spun away from the Reaper's lunge and made a fearsome cut of his own that required the Reaper to drop and roll. Henry's blow shattered a window on the neighboring limousine, causing a shout to go up from the crowd.

The Red Reaper was back on his feet, but Henry lunged for him, slicing the air as the man dodged and weaved. The swords met with a resounding clang as the Reaper regained his footing. Valerie held her breath as the two men began a bewildering series of counterattacks and parries. The blades moved so quickly that she couldn't follow the individual movements. She could only wince and hold her fist to her mouth, her nails biting into her palm as she waited for a blow to land.

Henry let out a tremendous shout as he delivered a powerful combination of cuts that sent the Reaper staggering backward, but the retreat was only momentary. The masked man waited as Henry's momentum carried him forward and unleashed a fierce upward cut that sent Henry's blade high and wide. The Reaper brought his own sword back with a lightning-fast twist of his wrist and drove the point into Henry's shoulder just below his collarbone.

Henry screamed and staggered backward. *Durendal* fell from his grip and clattered to the flagstones at his feet. He stumbled, his left hand finding his shoulder where his shirt was already blooming red with blood.

"Henry!" Valerie shouted, lunging forward to assist him, but her brother was already regaining his balance. He muttered curses under his breath as his fingers pressed to the wound, but he straightened up to wave Valerie off.

"I'm okay."

Valerie let her hand fall to her side. He wasn't mortally wounded, but they had lost. It was over.

She tore her eyes from Henry and back to his opponent. The Red Reaper's shoulders had slumped with exhaustion. He lifted his sword and cleaned the tip before sheathing it in its scabbard. The voids that ought to be eyes found Valerie, lingering on her briefly, but then he turned back to the open door of the Blackbird where he had draped his jacket.

Jasper Sterling began to clap, a grin spreading across his face. The crowd around the circle likewise applauded.

"Now that was a fight!" Jasper strode forward, his eyes on Henry. "I have to say you had me worried." He stooped and picked up *Durendal* from where it had fallen. "I've never seen anyone work my man so hard." He turned to address the Red Reaper. "Maybe you're softer than you look, huh, buddy? You're supposed to be my ace."

The Red Reaper donned his jacket and seemed to pay Jasper no attention. He adjusted the sword hanging at his hip, then simply crossed his arms.

"So damn serious," Jasper said, turning to Valerie. "It's tough always having to carry the conversation with these types."

"This doesn't change what you did," Henry said.

"But it does change things for you, doesn't it?" Jasper replied. He balanced *Durendal* in his hand, then held it up to catch the sunlight. He drew his own sword, *Nocteflamme*, and compared the two side by side. "*Durendal*. Sharpest sword in the world. Isn't that the legend? I think I prefer my own. Still, yours will make a fine addition to the family collection."

"That wasn't part of the terms," Henry said.

"No? I think I'll take it anyway."

"Over my dead body," Henry said.

"Well, okay," Jasper replied. He stepped forward and plunged *Nocteflamme* directly into Henry's chest.

Henry's eyes widened in shock.

Valerie reached for him. "Henry!"

Henry stared at the sword penetrating his ribs, his mouth moving wordlessly. Then he fell.

Valerie caught her brother in her arms, dropping to her knees as he crashed into her.

"Henry!" She grasped frantically at his chest, applying pressure to the wound. The gaps between her fingers welled with blood.

"Val," Henry said. His hand reached for hers. She clasped his cold, already clammy fingers, then he coughed and spit a trickle of blood onto his chin.

The next moment, his head fell back into her lap, and he was gone.

The world froze in a monochromatic nightmare. The only color Valerie could see was red.

Her hands.

The stain across Henry's face.

The tip of Jasper's sword.

Her mind failed to reconcile the movement of time with the reality she was seeing. A second ago, her brother was breathing. Twenty seconds ago, he was standing, full of life, fire in his eyes.

How could a few seconds become the difference between life and the destruction of her entire world?

"Henry," she said, calmly this time as though to call him back gently from the realm of their imagination. A thousand times they had play-acted the ending to a thousand imagined battles. It was time to wake up.

"Henry!" This time she screamed it.

She looked up. There was a circle of shocked faces surrounding the ring of cars. Open mouths. Wide eyes. But no one moved. No one was helping. And Jasper Sterling was walking away.

Valerie's body was no longer limited by conscious thought. It moved of its own accord.

Her mind was elsewhere, lingering in the past—a place before the last, inexplicable minute of existence—but her body sprang into action, crawling on hands and knees to the spot where she had dropped her sword. Yanking it free of its scabbard, she rose to her feet.

There was a noise coming from her throat, but it wasn't words. It was a primal sound made of rage and pain and unadulterated hate.

He could not walk away.

She lunged after Jasper, arm lifted, sword raised. His back was to her, only a few feet separating them. She plunged the sword toward him. But he turned. His blade came up, caught hers and deflected it. Easily. Carelessly. Jasper Sterling was smiling.

Devils shouldn't smile.

Devils shouldn't live.

Valerie swung the sword again with both hands, aiming for the devil's neck. Her blade vanished in a flash of light, struck aside by the weapon in Jasper's hand. Her sword clattered to the pavement. A second later, his fist struck her in the eye, and she flailed backward into something hard and unyielding. Her head ricocheted off glass.

She wilted down the side of a limousine as though her legs had turned to liquid. The world was blurry and populated with tiny stars.

"See? Yet another forgettable member of a forgettable family." His voice came to her through a fog.

Valerie managed to focus on Jasper, then saw the sword poised to skewer her.

She had to move.

Somehow, she needed to erase the last few minutes of this nightmare. She wanted to slay the devil in front of her with her eyes, but all she could do was watch as the blade plunged toward her chest.

Red.

A second sword crossed her vision and knocked away the first. Jasper's blade penetrated the car door beside her head. Valerie focused on the red hilt of the sword that had intervened and followed the arm up to the face. The black mask with the crimson slash across the cheek. Her other enemy.

"Jasper. Stop. She's underage." The voice came from a third man. Blaise. Law School. He and Jasper's other friends were grabbing his shoulders, hauling him back.

"The City Watch are here. We have to go!"

Uniformed officers pushed through the crowd, knocking aside bystanders with long-handled pole axes. One was wielding a mace.

"Hey! Break this up. What's the meaning of this?" The armored soldier in the lead was doing the talking, waving his mace in everyone's face.

Valerie shook her head and tried to clear her mind.

"...a legal duel. He was challenged as a matter of honor. Here are the signatures." Law School brandished the contract. "The challenger's second lashed out and tried to attack him after the duel. It turns out she's underage."

"And that one?" The watch captain pointed the mace.

"I believe he's dead."

Valerie's eyes followed the movement and alighted on the figure on the ground.

Henry.

Clarity came back.

"Murderer!" The yell erupted from her lips. She pushed off the concrete and struggled to her feet. She had no weapon but she had fists. She would use anything she had to make him pay. She rushed Jasper with her teeth bared and her fingers stretching for his windpipe.

She was intercepted by two armored men who swept her back. She clawed at their arms, writhing and squirming, but strong hands wrapped around her wrists. Someone twisted her arm behind her back. She was swung violently to the side and slammed into one of the vehicles.

"Stay down!"

She wouldn't stay down. She couldn't. Not while Henry

needed her. She needed to take it back, the lost minutes between now and when he had last spoken to her. He'd said her name. This was on her to fix.

Her sword was on the ground a few yards away. So close.

She slammed her elbow into the face of the man attempting to pin her to the car. He reeled and put a hand to his nose. It came away bloody.

She broke free of her captors and sprinted for the sword. A few feet more. Her fingers wrapped around the handle, and she turned, brandishing the weapon. She searched for her enemies, finding the Red Reaper. She focused on the black recesses of the nightmare mask staring back at her. He was ten feet away, watching.

Her scream of rage came from the void where her heart had been.

Then the handle of the mace came down on her head.

Her enemy's masked face was now just a crimson blur fading into night.

The world tilted sideways on its axis, and everything went black.

6

LOCK-UP

There were sounds in Valerie's brain that she couldn't account for. Clomping feet. Rough voices. She tried to open her eyes but instantly regretted it. The ceiling was lopsided and much too bright.

Her left eye wouldn't open all the way. She reached for it, and her fingers found a puffy, sore lump where her eye should be.

Someone was breathing. Loudly. Their breath smelled of onions and cigarettes.

Valerie opened her right eye and rolled onto her side.

The onion breather was a woman on a cot with a broad, leathery face. Her eyebrows presented a unified front across her forehead, uninterrupted by the demands of the large nose beneath. Despite its impressive size, it seemed the nose had been broken several times in its life. Valerie didn't want to meet whomever had accomplished that feat.

She tried to sit up but had to pause midway to find equilibrium. She groaned as she made it the rest of the way to vertical.

Then she saw the blood. It stained her fingers—lodged

beneath her nails and in the crevices of her palms. Henry's blood.

She nearly choked on the sob that rose from her chest. The pain of realization made her gut clench. She tried to convince herself that it wasn't real, but her hands showed the truth.

Henry was dead.

Valerie felt the eyes of the onion breather on her. Each of her choking gasps were being scrutinized. It was only for that reason she tried to pull herself together. If she was home in her own bed, she would simply dissolve into her misery. Here, wherever here was, she had even been deprived of that luxury.

She pushed herself off the cot and shuffled to the wall of iron bars that defined the tiny space she was in. Choking back her tears, she wrapped her fingers around the bars and shouted, "Hey! Somebody! Somebody let me out!"

Her call echoed down a corridor lined with a dozen other cells.

"They already looked at you."

Valerie turned to find the onion woman staring at her.

"I shouldn't be here," Valerie said. "They've made a mistake. I'm not the one who's the criminal."

"Ain't never made a difference before. When you're in, you're in."

Valerie shook her head and pressed her hand over her swollen eye. "No. You don't understand. I'm a noble. Daughter of a knight. Sir Henry Terravecchia."

The woman's eyebrow raised slightly, but she shrugged. "Ain't no names that matter down here. This is the Underside."

Valerie frowned and wiped her face, then continued her yelling down the corridor. All she got in response was angry shouts to shut up from other cells.

An hour later, someone finally approached the cell. Valerie had long since given up her shouting and retreated to the cot, but she rose again at the sound of footsteps.

"You've got a visitor," the guard said before gesturing to his companion to open the door. He slapped his mace against his palm.

Valerie allowed herself to be shackled and led down the corridor to a room with a table and several chairs. When she saw the woman seated at the table, she rushed inside.

"Livingston! Thank God. You have to help me! Tell these men there's been a mistake."

Their family lawyer studied Valerie's face. "You look even worse than I imagined." She gestured to the chair opposite her.

"Henry," Valerie said. "Jasper Sterling—"

"I know."

"Did they arrest Jasper? He's the one who should be locked up. Has the Watch brought him in?"

"The city prosecutor caught me up on the situation," Livingston said. She gestured again for Valerie to take a seat. "I'm afraid the news isn't good."

Valerie eased herself onto the chair but sat on the edge of the seat. "What's happening?"

"They won't arrest Jasper Sterling. He has witnesses that affirm your brother challenged him to a duel to satisfaction, and he was within his rights to kill him."

"That's a lie!" Valerie exclaimed, exploding from her chair. "He's lying. Henry never wanted a duel to satisfaction. It was a duel, but it was to first blood, and everyone knew it!"

"The magistrate is in possession of a document that says differently. It shows your brother's signature and your co-signature and is clearly marked as a duel to satisfaction, meaning his death was within the bounds of the law."

"That's impossible," Valerie objected. "I saw the document I signed. I know what it said."

"Without any evidence to back up your version of the story, there's no way to charge Jasper Sterling with murder."

Valerie wrestled with her manacles, then pointed a finger at the door. "They're lying to you. There were dozens of people watching. They all saw Jasper stab my brother after the fight was over. You can ask anyone!"

"None of the bystanders read the contract prior to the duel. They didn't know the terms. Only the other signees on the contract can be witnesses, and everyone that Jasper had sign it backs up his version of the story. He has three witness signatures to your one, and even yours backs up his statement."

"You're not looking at the right contract then. I swear it shows what we signed. It doesn't matter what anyone says."

Berkley Livingston knitted her fingers together. "This will be difficult. You'll have a chance to face the magistrate and give your side of the story, but I'm afraid there's more bad news."

"How can anything be worse?"

"Lord Sterling has put forth that you've proven yourself a violent threat by unlawfully attacking your liege lord's family and has therefore requested custody of you. They want to declare you unfit for society."

Valerie could only stare at the lawyer. "The Sterlings want custody of me?"

"You're in an extremely unique circumstance. After your stepmother was informed of the incident, she declined responsibility for you. With no other legal adults alive in your immediate family, there is no one to vouch for your honor. Typically, in these cases, the lack of an immediate family member means the right to your guardianship falls on your liege lord. They would be the ones to vouch for you no matter your age. But, in this case, your liege lord is the family you've attacked." Livingston leaned back in her chair. "You've managed to make a bad situation much worse."

"I'll be eighteen soon. I'm almost a legal adult. No one should have to vouch for me."

"Unfortunately, that may be too late. They can have you committed to an asylum well before you turn eighteen. Once inside, your birthday won't matter. Your legal rights as an adult will no longer apply."

Valerie opened her mouth to object but could no longer contain her tears. She began to cry, her body giving in to the overwhelming sadness that was poised to crush her. Her body shook, and she sobbed into her arms on the table.

A hand rested on the back of her head.

"I know this is something you never would have imagined possible," Livingston said. "And I believe you, Valerie. I really do."

Valerie lifted her face from her arm. "Then why can't you help me?"

"I'm trying," Livingston replied. "But you've picked a fight with the most powerful family in the western colonies."

"What about outside the colonies then? The queen! Could I appeal to the queen?"

"The Court of Pendragon won't hear a case that hasn't even made it out of district court. And they're a continent away. As of now, you don't have the money for an appeal in lower court, let alone an appeal to the Pendragons. Without your stepmother taking responsibility for you, you don't have the money for anything."

Valerie's shoulders slumped; her body defeated. But her mind refused to accept the reality of the situation. Finally, she asked the question she'd been avoiding thinking about. "Where's Henry?"

Livingston pressed her lips together, then spoke. "His body is in the city morgue. Someone will need to decide where he'll be laid to rest."

"Home. It has to be there. Next to mother. Can you take him? I don't want him to be alone."

"I can at least do that much," Livingston replied. "I wish there was more I could do."

"He didn't deserve this," Valerie said, her voice softening. "He was the one who—"

"I know," Livingston replied. She rested her hand on Valerie's. After a moment, she slid her chair back from the table. "The magistrate will summon you soon. If there is any justice in the world, he'll hear you. Stay strong." Livingston rose. She rapped on the door and the guards returned.

"I won't let them win," Valerie said. "I don't care what I have to do. They won't get away with this."

Livingston turned to face her. "I pray you get your justice."

Valerie watched the lawyer go, then the guards returned and escorted her back to her cell.

It was hours before someone else showed their face. Her cellmate was released in the early afternoon, but it was evening by the time someone collected her for the magistrate. Valerie had managed a few fitful hours of rest, but her eyes were puffy from crying and she still had Henry's blood on her hands.

The courtroom was a narrow place with few amenities, just barely enough space for the plaintiffs and accused and a smattering of seats for family or friends. Valerie had neither. The magistrate was seated at a high bench and wore a wig that looked like it hadn't been properly powdered in a decade. He was frowning before Valerie was even in position.

A door at the right side of the room opened, and a person Valerie recognized entered. It was Blaise Cavendish, Jasper Sterling's lawyer.

"You!" Valerie said. "How dare you show your face here!"

"Order!" The magistrate banged his gavel. "Silence in my courtroom." He glared at Valerie and Blaise as if daring one of them to speak again. "The court will now hear the city's case against Valerie of the House of . . . Terravecchia. You are accused of assaulting a member of your liege lord's family with deadly intent and attempting to duel underage. How do you plead, young lady?"

"Innocent!"

The magistrate sighed. "The bill of grievances for this case is lengthy. You are prepared to defend yourself?"

"Jasper Sterling is the criminal, your honor. He should be the one in court. This man was a witness." She pointed to Blaise.

Blaise chimed in. "Your honor, the Sterling family insists that the contract signed by Henry Terravecchia was dutifully witnessed and provides ample proof that Lord Sterling was within his rights to terminate the duel in question by any means he saw fit. I did witness the contract myself."

"You refer to this contract?" The judge held up a document and looked it over. He turned to Valerie. "Miss, this contract is marked as a duel to satisfaction and is in fact signed by several witnesses."

"It can't be, your honor. My brother signed a duel to first blood. I swear it."

"Despite the fact that your own signature says otherwise? This *is* your signature, is it not?"

Valerie approached the bench to view the document. She had to admit that it did appear to be her signature. "I don't know how to explain it, but that isn't the contract we signed."

Blaise approached the bench as well. "Your honor, the House of Sterling insists that Valerie Terravecchia acted outside the law, letting her passions reign and endangering law-abiding citizens of the city. You will find their full statement in the documents provided. It is their position that, due to her precarious mental state, she is a danger to any and all, and they wish to see her removed from society immediately."

The magistrate reviewed the document, then addressed Valerie. "Miss Terravecchia, do you know that the House of Sterling is your legal guardian at this moment? Without another member of your family present to vouch for you, you are entirely at their mercy. According to these documents, even if I accept your plea of innocence and forgo any sentencing, they intend to have you admitted to St. Anselm's Institute for the Mentally Unstable. However, if you plead guilty to this crime, it's possible that they may be more lenient. Are you certain you wish to continue with this claim of innocence?"

"Your honor, they're lying. He's lying." She pointed to Blaise. "I know the truth. I swear it on my life."

The magistrate rubbed his chin and considered her. "I don't feel you adequately understand the circumstances. If I *don't* pass a sentence of my own involving jail time, as an underage vassal of the Sterling family, they would be within their rights to do anything they like with you. Once you leave this courtroom, you will have no further protection from the law."

"They're trying to claim my family's lands. They defrauded my stepmother, and now they've murdered my brother in cold blood. All of this is their doing! I promise you I am not a criminal or insane. Please. You have to believe me."

The judge turned to the city prosecutor. "Will Lord Jasper Sterling be in attendance today?"

"No, your honor," Blaise replied. "Lord Sterling was occupied with other matters."

"Too busy to attend a hearing that might decide the fate of an entire house and send a young woman to a lifetime at St. Anselm's? I find that hard to believe."

Blaise shrugged. "I'm sure that the business of the House of Sterling is their own. I'm merely the messenger."

"Indeed," the magistrate replied. He shuffled through the papers a bit more, reading the various statements, then he addressed Valerie again. "You said you would swear on your life that your statement is the truth. You believe that Lord Jasper Sterling, your liege lord, deliberately murdered your brother as a way to secure the ownership of your family lands. Am I getting that right?"

"Yes, sir. I swear it."

"Oaths are a solemn thing, young lady. I take them quite seriously."

"Your honor, I swear to God, to you, on the honor of my family and anything else good in the world, I'm telling the truth."

The magistrate studied her face. "Young woman, there is a preponderance of evidence against you, but despite all that, I do feel you at least believe you are telling the truth. Unfortunately, as an underage noble, I am obliged to deliver you to your guardians. The law forbids me from doing otherwise. It is very specific when it comes to the guardianship of heirs and vassals. Do you understand the predicament you are in?"

"Please, your honor, Jasper Sterling nearly killed me once already today. Don't turn me over to them. They're the ones who should be prosecuted."

The magistrate reached for his pen and began writing on a document she couldn't see.

"I feel there is only one avenue left to you, Miss Terravecchia. It's possible you are telling the truth. You have small chance of resolving anything, however, if you are a resident of St. Anselm's. I also feel it highly distasteful to turn over guardianship of a young woman to the same family that has caused her such harm. Therefore, I have only one alternative that may give you an opportunity to prove your case. Though I fear you won't like it."

"I'll take any opportunity," Valerie replied.

"Then I hope you find a way to prove that," the magistrate said. "Hand me your signet ring."

Valerie balked at the request, but when he held his hand out again, she wriggled her ring loose and handed it to him.

He finished signing the documents, stamping them each with his own seal and with Valerie's signet ring, then handed a completed document across the desk. "You are still underage. If you can return to this court as an adult with some proof of what you say, I will listen to you again. But that is the best I can do."

"Your honor, this is highly irregular," Blaise objected. "What have you—"

The magistrate held up a hand to silence him.

Valerie took the document and read it. "But, sir, this is a revocation of title."

"That's correct," the magistrate replied, making a point of

dropping her signet ring into a drawer of his desk. "As your sentence for the crime of attacking your liege lord, I hereby decree that you have dishonored your family name. I therefore rescind any and all noble titles that you hold and declare you to be a commoner from this day forward. You are therefore free to go."

Valerie's mouth dropped open. "My family name. You can't—"

"I really must object," Blaise said. "The House of Sterling wants her to be put away, not left free to roam the streets."

"That may be true," the magistrate replied. "But as of several seconds ago, this young woman is no longer the legal responsibility of the Sterling family. She is declared nameless and therefore no longer bound to the obligations of the ruling class."

The prosecutor merely stared at him, gobsmacked.

"You took . . . you took away my name?" Valerie said.

"And in so doing, gave you back your freedom," the magistrate replied. "Use it well, young lady. Otherwise, I feel you may soon run out of second chances."

"But nameless are commoners," Valerie objected. "I'm *not* a commoner."

The magistrate waved his hand. "Bailiff, please escort this young woman to the door."

A burly man with a full metal breastplate and a mace lumbered over to Valerie. He shoved a bag into her arms that she realized contained her personal belongings, then he took her by the arm, hauling her toward the exit.

"Wait. You can't do this!" Valerie objected. "This isn't how it's supposed to go. You were supposed to help me!" She attempted to hold on to the doorframe as the bailiff pushed her through the door.

"I gave you freedom, young lady," the magistrate called out. "I pray you use it well."

Then, with a final heave from the bailiff, Valerie was ejected from the courtroom. She lost her footing on the damp steps and tumbled to the muddy street outside. She looked up to find the immense height of the city wall looming above her. She was back on her feet in an instant and racing toward the flickering light of the courtroom, but the bailiff slammed the door in her face. The heavy lock rammed home with a decisive thud.

Valerie pounded on the metal door for several minutes but to no avail.

This couldn't be happening.

She continued hammering until her fist could no longer take the abuse.

Finally, she descended the steps and cautiously took in her surroundings.

She nearly fell again on the slippery walking path. The ground sloped away from the city wall at a steep angle, and the perimeter road, if it could even be called that, was pitched so severely that any misstep threatened to send her tumbling downhill.

Fog had descended on the bay for the night, shrouding the water from view, but Valerie could glimpse the rusted tin roofs of fishing shanties far below in the mist. Boat bells and the shouts of sailors drifted up from the fog.

She had been tossed into an area midway between two of the city's elevated connecting bridges. The highways loomed overhead to either side, but this middle space simply sloped away into the fog. The door she had just exited was the only one in sight along this stretch of the city wall. Someone had graffitied the stones above the door with the moniker "Satan's Arsehole."

Valerie shivered.

Bits of trash littered the footpath that ran along the perimeter of the wall. She slipped and slid her way downward until it met a serpentine road coming up from the bay. A few precarious-looking shacks lined the sides of the road, clinging in the shadow of the heavy wall stones, but they were little more than rundown wrecks. The people coming and going from the shanties weren't much better. A toothless man who smelled of urine staggered past her on his way up the hill, muttering to himself.

The setting sun was lost beyond the fog, and its light was dimming rapidly as it neared the invisible horizon. As bad as her day had been, Valerie had the sinking realization that it was about to get worse.

7

IMPOUND

I f there was ever a time to curse the powers that be, Valerie had found it. A torrent of profanity escaped her as she made her way along the darkening road outside the city wall, searching for a way back inside. To her frustration, the ramshackle assemblage of housing clinging to the slopes forced her to detour farther downhill.

She pulled her jacket from the bag she had been given and wrapped it tightly around herself, regretting her choice in clothing with every step. She did appreciate the boots she had purchased, as the ruts and potholes in the streets hid a multitude of puddles, but the cut-off shorts made her an object of scrutiny from passersby. She was humiliated and dirty, and the last thing in the world she wanted was to be looked at.

Her journey along the serpentine hillside route only led to confusion. After several involuntary return trips to the same street corner, she finally approached a prostitute and asked for directions.

The woman sized her up from beneath colorful false lashes. "What are you out here for? Don't be thinking you can work my block."

"I need to get to a city gate," Valerie said.

The prostitute rolled her eyes, then casually pointed skyward. "Like that one?" When Valerie followed her gesture, she could just make out the span of the bridge passing high overhead. It was almost lost in the fog. She hadn't realized how far down the hill she had already come.

"I've been trying to get back up there. Seems like this road never connects. Is there another way up for pedestrians?"

"Unless you got wings you ain't showing, you can take the stairs like everybody else." The woman gestured to a rusted metal staircase attached to one of the bridge's stone supports.

Valerie immediately began walking that way.

"You're welcome," the prostitute said.

Valerie kept her head down and walked as quickly as she could, ignoring the muttering from darkened stoops and windows as she passed. She could only imagine the conversations, but they couldn't match the reproach she had for herself.

A million scenarios kept running through her mind, mostly ways this day could have been avoided. If she had made any one of a thousand different choices, Henry might still be alive. If she had bothered to find out what her stepmother was doing with their estate while she was away at school—if she had convinced Henry not to come to the city . . . the litany of poor decisions went on forever. It was only matched by her innumerable thoughts of hatred toward Jasper Sterling.

With every step she took, she saw Jasper's leering smile—his coy greeting at the manor, all the while knowing he was destroying her life. Her mind replayed the seconds when she had him in front of her, the sword in her hand ready to strike him down.

If she could get to the car, get another sword. . . But it was no use. He had been a step ahead of them at every turn. He clearly knew Henry would seek retribution with a duel. Jasper had left them no other options and had the Red Reaper waiting and a crew of liars to validate his actions.

She still didn't know how he had forged the dueling contract. Everything about this city was revealing itself as deception and shadow—tricks of the light.

She focused her attention on getting back to the car.

Escaping this nightmare was her only hope.

She finally reached the bridge support and frowned at the rickety metal staircase attached to it, but having no other options, she began to climb.

She was out of breath by the time she reached the third landing. The air was so thick with moisture that it felt like breathing in a cloud. The world outside the staircase was lost in a sea of gray, and before long, even the ground was swallowed up.

When she finally reached the top of the bridge, she paused to catch her breath, then trudged the dozen yards to the lowered portcullis blocking entrance to the city.

A trio of guards sat in the murky shadows within the gateway. She could make out hands of cards being played as they talked.

Valerie leaned into one of the openings in the portcullis and shouted.

"Excuse me. Can you open this gate?"

"Get lost!" The guard speaking hadn't even turned his head.

Valerie bristled. "Hey! Listen to me. I'm Valerie Terravecchia of the House of—" She cut herself off at the sight of her bare finger.

She wasn't anyone anymore.

One of the men had looked up in curiosity at her shout, but now that it was evident she wasn't continuing, he let his head dip back to his cards.

Valerie tucked her hand out of sight and tried again. "Listen, my car is parked downtown, near Sterling Plaza. I just need to get to it, and I'll be out of your hair."

One of the guards threw down his cards in frustration, obviously the loser of that hand. He slapped the table and stood. His eyes found Valerie a moment later.

"What is this ruckus you're on about? What car?"

"It's a Guardian 770 war car. I left it parked downtown."

The guard smirked and turned to his card-player buddies. "Hey, get a load of this one. Claims she has a Guardian 770. Buzz off, little girl. The gates are closed to commoners till morning. Everybody knows that." He waved her away, then wandered back to his card table and sat down.

"Hey! I'm serious!" Valerie shouted. "I promise, I just want to get to my car. Come back!"

"Was that really your Guardian?"

Valerie spun around to discover a boy of perhaps twelve watching her. He was astride a bicycle. His clothes were dirty and ragged, but his face was sympathetic. Valerie looked him over, then went back to pounding on the portcullis.

"They took that car away."

Valerie turned to face him this time. "What? You know about my car?"

"Sure. All the kids were talking about it. Some came all the way from the smelters to see it. There hasn't been a Guardian 770 in Port Hyacinth since . . . forever. Coleslaw says he's seen one before, but Coleslaw lies about everything. He once made up that he seen a Belmont coupe convertible." The boy grinned as if expecting Valerie to laugh. "But you know they never even made a convertible Belmont. Coleslaw is full of it."

Valerie tried to piece together what he was saying. "Hang on. You or this Coleslaw person did see a Guardian though?"

"Sure. They took it to the impound, down on the South Side. I talked to the hauler. Said they'd never seen such a beautiful car."

"Where is it now?"

He turned and pointed into the fog. "Outside the south city gate. The iron district. This side of the wall."

Valerie studied the darkness in the direction he was pointing. "How far? Can I walk it?"

"I guess so. Might be a long time though."

"God, aren't there any cabs outside the walls? How does anyone get anywhere out here?"

The boy shrugged. "The worker trolleys start running at sunrise. No cars on the roads past eleven unless it's official business."

"I can't wait till sunrise. I need to get out of this damn city right now." Valerie studied the boy's bicycle. "How much do you want for your bike?" She rummaged in her bag and found her wallet.

"It ain't for sale," the boy replied.

Valerie unsnapped her wallet and assessed how much cash she had. "Tell me a number, kid. I'm a lady, and I'm telling you I need your bike."

"You can't have it."

Valerie again felt the urge to point to her hand but realized her signet ring was still missing. She frowned at her naked finger.

The boy turned his bike around and prepared to pedal away.

"Wait! Please. I need your help," Valerie pleaded. "Tell me how to get to the impound. If you help me get there, I'll . . . I'll let you ride in the car."

The boy put a foot down and studied her. "Really?"

"Really."

"I guess I can let you ride on the back."

"Of your bike?" Valerie asked.

"If you'll be my girlfriend."

"What?"

"I mean, you're kind of beat up, but you're still pretty," the boy said.

Valerie put her hands on her hips. "You've sure got a mouth."

The boy shrugged. "You want a ride or not?"

Valerie studied the long, dim road along the city wall. Even if it weren't so far to walk, she felt a little company along the way would be welcome. Even a cheeky peasant boy was better than nothing.

"Fine. I'll ride on the bike with you. How do we do that?"

The boy smiled. "You can have the seat. Just hold on to me and I'll pedal."

Valerie cursed her choice of clothing for yet another time today as she tried to figure out how to get on the bike without giving this kid a peep show.

"Turn around," she ordered. "Don't look this way for a minute."

The boy seemed disappointed but complied. Valerie managed to get her leg over the bike and got herself seated. Her first order of business after getting the car back would be to locate some leggings.

"Okay. Now we can go."

Valerie soon found herself rolling down the exit ramp with her feet in the air and a tight grip on the waist of a boy she couldn't even conceive of talking to in other circumstances. Whatever had become of her life, she was grateful that at least no one she knew was around to see it.

She had somehow sunk to a level previously undreamt of. Even so, there was a slight familiarity here, a lingering memory from childhood. She recalled riding on the back of Henry's bicycle as a child, feet splayed in a similar position, getting a lift home from school on the day someone had stolen her bicycle. It had been the tragedy of her life up to that point—the shock that anyone would take what was hers and get away with it. She recalled the indignation her young self felt at the injustice of that situation.

If she only knew.

After fifteen minutes of steady pedaling, they found the impound lot where the boy said it was. He laid his bike down in the grass near the entrance to the fenced lot, still breathing heavily from exertion.

"I can handle it from here," Valerie said, tugging at the frayed hem of her shorts again. "Wait outside."

"You said you'd give me a ride," the boy replied.

"And I will once I get the car. Just stay here."

Valerie entered the impound and made her way to an entrance station. The rotund clerk at the counter sized her up while sipping a cup of coffee.

"I'm here for my car," Valerie said.

"Imagine that," the woman replied. "You need to fill out the form." She slid a clipboard across the counter and plopped a pen atop it.

Valerie dutifully entered her information on the form and handed it back.

The clerk glanced at it, then looked up in surprise. "You're the one who owns the Guardian? Hang on a sec." She ambled to an office door at the back of the room and cracked it open. "Bern, you wanted me to let you know when the Guardian's owner showed up. She's here."

"She?" A low voice emanated from the back office, and a chair scraped across the floor. A man that was almost twice the width of the clerk clomped his way out of the office and crossed the room to the counter. He was wearing a food-stained shirt with a name tag that said Bernard.

"That's a hell of car you got there, Miss . . ." He reached for the clipboard and read the name she had written. "Terravecchia."

"I'd like it back now," Valerie replied.

Bernard shuffled a few papers. "Seems you left it unattended in a short-term parking area. Had to pull it."

"I understand that," Valerie said. "I'd just like to get it back."

"There was a fine, of course," Bernard replied, watching her carefully. "Even for ladies from noble families. Say, how old are you?"

"I don't see how that's relevant," Valerie replied. "How much is the fine? If I can just pay it, I'll be on my way."

"It was a bit of a custom job towing that car," Bernard replied. He licked his lips. "Didn't have any of the standard hookups. Took extra work."

Valerie simply waited, one hand on the wallet in her bag. It was clear he was sizing her up. If he knew the name Terravecchia, it wasn't apparent. He certainly didn't seem intimidated.

"Wasn't easy," Bernard continued.

"I'm sure nothing is for you," Valerie muttered.

Bernard narrowed his eyes. "And what do you mean by that?"

Valerie tried to brush off the comment with a thin-lipped smile. "I only meant that this business is clearly complex. I don't imagine just anyone can . . . tow cars and give them back."

"It takes precision," Bernard said. "Especially with a car like that."

"I'm sure it does," Valerie replied. "Now, about that fine. I really do have to get going."

Bernard sized her up one more time, then sniffed. "Two hundred."

Valerie balked. "What? Two hundred? To pull a car a couple of miles?"

Bernard crossed his arms. "Like I said, it was technical."

Valerie muttered under her breath and thumbed through the cash in her wallet. She looked up and shook her head. "I don't have that much."

"Then I guess you don't get your car tonight."

"I need that car!" Valerie exclaimed. "It's the only way I have to—just give it to me already, will you? Look, I've got . . . a hundred and sixty-five crowns. I swear that's all I have."

"Call your daddy then," Bernard said.

Valerie felt her face warming. "How dare you speak to me like this! Do you have any idea who—if I have to call—" Valerie stumbled over her usual defenses. There was no one to call. She wasn't even a noble anymore. She had no one left to ask for help. For all her fury, there was no curse she could invoke on this commoner to smite him back to his place.

Her righteous indignation seemed to have an effect, however. Bernard's composure wavered. "Now don't get upset . . . your ladyship. The car will still be here. If you need to make a call or come back, I promise we'll hold it for you."

Valerie choked back the profanity she wanted to unleash on him. "Very well," she growled. "Can I have your assurance that the car will be safe and unmolested?"

"Of course, your ladyship," Bernard said. Then cracked a smile. "With a small deposit."

Valerie clenched her fist and prepared to unload on him, but once again she realized that she had nothing to hold over him. He had all the power and he knew it.

"How much is the deposit?" she asked.

Bernard was openly grinning now. "A hundred . . . and fifty."

"A deposit of a hundred and fifty," Valerie said. "Paid against two hundred. Fifty more gets the car."

"Yes, ma'am."

"This is ridiculous," she muttered. "Put it in writing." She extracted some money from her wallet.

"Oh, I don't think we need to do that. A deal is a deal around here."

"In writing," Valerie insisted. She held the money up. "Please."

"I don't mind writing something up," the clerk interjected, visibly uncomfortable with the standoff.

"All right, fine," Bernard replied. "But the deposit only gets you a week."

"Usually it's thirty days," the clerk mumbled.

"What do you know about it?" Bernard said.

"Everything," the clerk retorted. "Been here ten years, haven't I?"

"I'd like the thirty days then," Valerie said, as calmly as she could manage.

Bernard glared at the clerk, then stretched his hand out for the money. "Fifteen. Give it here."

Valerie handed over the money and Bernard began to count it. The clerk sheepishly slid another form across the desk. She had already filled in the deposit amount. "The thirty days is in the boilerplate," she whispered.

Valerie nodded but skimmed over the contract anyway. "I'll be needing a copy of my own."

The clerk slid a second form across the desk, and Valerie signed both. The clerk stamped them and added her own signature before folding Valerie's copy into an envelope for her.

Bernard disappeared back into his office without further input.

Valerie tucked her wallet away and thanked the clerk. The woman gave her a nod. One small sign of solidarity against a system that was doing neither of them any favors.

Valerie then walked back out the door and pondered her options.

Two hundred crowns. Where on earth could she come up with another fifty this time of night?

The boy with the bicycle was still there, leaning against the fence.

"Where's the car?"

"I need to make a phone call," Valerie said. "Where's the nearest pay phone around here?"

"You're supposed to give me a ride in the Guardian."

"Who says I'm not? But I need to make a call first."

The boy eyed her suspiciously.

"Look, kid, am I your girlfriend or not? A boyfriend needs to help a girl out if she's going to hang around."

"What's your name?" the boy asked. "If you're my girlfriend, then I should at least know your name."

"Val."

"Val," he repeated. "I'm Eli, like the prophet."

"Can you foretell where we'll find a pay phone, prophet Eli, because that would really help me out."

Eli shrugged. "Maybe in the village?" He pointed down the coast road to a glow of lights. "One of the sailor bars probably has one."

The village wasn't much to look at from this distance, just a battered wharf full of dilapidated, clapboard buildings jammed between the two bridges that jutted out from this side of the city wall. Houses clung precariously to the steep hillside, and the road twisted into hairpin turns all the way there.

She had to hope that at least one of the establishments would have a public phone. Commoners weren't entitled to private lines, but there would be a community one somewhere in the neighborhood. Even so, she eyed the wharf with suspicion.

She'd never lingered outside the city walls of Port Hyacinth before, especially at night. A rim village was far afield of the shopping districts and theaters she'd visited with friends from school. This place was already rougher than anywhere she'd been in her life.

The infrequent streetlights did a poor job of lighting the route, and there was a closed-off and inhospitable quality to everything in view, evidenced by barred windows and heavy, iron-reinforced doors. Even the shadows seemed laden with secrets. But there was nothing else to be done.

"Fine. Let's go," Valerie said, making up her mind before she could be convinced otherwise.

"You don't want to ride?"

The acrobatics required to get back aboard the bike with her decency intact were more than she felt capable of at the moment.

"I'll walk."

Eli scooted along beside her as they went, coasting on the bicycle and stopping frequently to allow Valerie time to catch up. The ground grew progressively muddier as they worked their way to the village, and water sprayed up from the bike's back tire as the boy rode ahead, speckling his back with mud. It reaffirmed Valerie's choice to walk, though her boots were acquiring their share of filth as well.

Eli paused a dozen yards ahead, putting his foot down to wait for her.

What was this kid doing out so late? Didn't he have parents

worrying about him? Valerie almost voiced her concern but then thought better of it. If she offended him and he left, she'd be all alone out here and, selfishly, she wasn't willing to part with him yet.

The nightlife along the wharf consisted of a half dozen fried fish stalls, several brothels, and a string of taverns that spilled flickering firelight and tinny music onto cobblestone streets. Somewhere, someone was singing.

Valerie got more than a few sideways glances from passersby as she walked along the waterfront. The swelling in her eye had lessened, allowing her to see where she was going, but she knew she must look terrible. She tried to arrange her hair to cover the bruised side of her face. She wasn't sure how much it helped.

She spotted a sign on the side of a building that read "Public Phone." An arrow pointed down a side street where another tavern stood perhaps a hundred yards away. There was a gigantic octopus on the sign. She immediately started down the street while Eli rode ahead, passing from one circle of streetlight to the next before disappearing into blackness in between. Valerie watched him fade into the darkness a block away but then fail to reappear in the next pool of light.

Was he waiting for her in the shadows?

"Hey, kid!" Valerie shouted.

A scuffling sound and a squeal followed. Then came a shout. It sounded like Eli.

Valerie dashed forward to the point where she had seen the boy vanish and found the opening to a side alley. Shadows in the alley were moving and shifting. A groan came from a puddle of darkness on the ground a short way in. At least two figures were standing over it. One was holding the bike.

"Hey!" Valerie shouted. "What are you doing?" She started down the alley, and the shadows shifted, taking on definition. Eli was on the ground, holding his face. One of the figures standing over him had a wooden cudgel in his hand, and he turned to assess Valerie. "Leave him alone!" she said, rushing to assist Eli. She didn't make it far.

A shadow she failed to account for materialized from a wall to her right and seized her by the back of her hair.

"Hey! Get off me!" She elbowed her attacker hard in the gut, and he let out a grunt. It was enough for her to escape his grip momentarily, but the figures ahead of her moved to encircle her. The one with the cudgel advanced first. Valerie ducked to the side and backed away, but there was nowhere to go. A stone wall blocked her for a dozen yards.

"Well, what do we have here?" the shadow asked.

The man she had elbowed stepped closer, one hand lingering on his belly. His face was lean and pockmarked, with one eye that was partially lidded. "She's got some fight in her. I like that."

The men carried weapons openly on their belts and wore a hodgepodge of leather and metal armor—hedge knights or mercenaries of some sort. She caught a glint of steel as the man in front of her drew a blade from his belt. The knife was wide and stubby but held a jagged edge.

Utilizing the distraction, Eli scrambled away from the man who had knocked him down. He cast a glance at his bicycle and another at Valerie but then he fled, disappearing into the fog.

"Yeah, you'd better run," the man with the knife snarled.

Valerie cursed under her breath. She was happy Eli was getting away, but her good deed had simply meant swapping places as victims. These men were looking at her with hungry eyes that roamed over her exposed legs and lingered in places that showed a lack of imagination. It was clear they were used to preying on the weak in the dark, and here she was looking like an easy meal. But Valerie had one thing Eli didn't, something these men couldn't have suspected.

She had nearly twenty-four hours of bottled-up rage.

As the man closest to her reached for her bag, a smug grin spreading on his face, his features morphed into those of Jasper Sterling. The self-important smirk. The soulless mirth that came from his untouchable status as a Sterling. It was all there in her mind. These three were now the embodiment of everything she hated about her last day of life. And when she balled her fist and sent it sailing into the man's smug face, he never saw it coming.

The would-be thief's nose broke with a satisfying crunch. Valerie shouted, and she struck him again with her other hand. It was without thought or strategy, just pure and uncontrolled hate. She tore at his eyes and grabbed big handfuls of his hair, yanking hard and coming away with strands of it tangled between her fingers. The man reeled from the assault and fell to his knees, clutching his nose. Valerie attempted to kick him but missed and stumbled forward, only to be caught by the man with the cudgel. He may as well have been wrangling a rattlesnake. Valerie twisted and writhed in his one-handed grasp, punching and scratching with her teeth bared. She swung at any part of him in sight, hammering his chest and middle with blow after blow and forcing him backward. He dropped the cudgel in his attempts to shield his face.

Valerie knew she should run while she still had the element of surprise. Some part of her knew the danger she was in and that she ought to flee for the safety of the street. Someone might see her there, a constable or peace warden. Even a passerby might pity her. But she didn't want pity. She wanted justice.

The man with the knife was next. His eyes were wide as she scooped up the cudgel from the ground and brandished it at him. For a moment, she thought he would turn and run, but she had miscalculated. The man sprung forward and snatched at the cudgel, wrestling her with one hand and waving the knife with the other. The blade flashed close to her face and nicked her ear. She shrieked and relinquished her grip on the cudgel to get away from the dancing steel.

It was a mistake.

She stumbled into the man with the broken nose. He was back on his feet and angry. Blood flowed freely from one nostril. He snarled at her and advanced as she spun away and tried to flee. The righteous indignation she had felt was evaporating, replaced by an icy chill of fear.

The man she'd stolen the cudgel from closed in. This time he reached for his belt and pulled out a wicked-looking sword.

Valerie was trapped. Despite her desire to unleash her vengeance on each one of these thugs, she was outnumbered, outmatched—and as they slowly cut off the last of her escape routes, she was also out of options.

"I won't let you have me," Valerie said.

"Like I said," the thug with the sword whispered, "I like when they fight." He tossed the cudgel through the air to his companion. The man caught it with an outstretched hand, then brought it down in one swift motion, connecting with Valerie's skull.

8

THE TWISTED TENTACLE

V alerie didn't pass out.

She would have liked to. It would have been easier that way. She'd have liked to check out of this seemingly endless parade of calamity that had befallen her life. Some part of her knew that it had only been a little over a day since she was walking through Briarwood Village with Henry, planning their future, but that felt like a lifetime ago.

Her vision was blurry, and she could make out few details. Boots mostly, and cobblestones.

Her head throbbed and she shivered, holding the terror of her situation deep beneath the surface of her conscious mind. If she let it up, she would have to admit this was real and that she was probably going to die.

She focused on her senses instead.

It smelled of garbage and cat piss down here. Someone's hands were on her, pulling at her arms, dragging her somewhere, somewhere worse, no doubt. This back alley perfumed by homeless felines was far too public a place for the kind of human filth she was now in the company of. Where would they take her? A sewer? Through the gates of hell?

These demons were surely citizens of an underworld much

darker and deeper than this place. Their marauding of the surface world had netted them a prize and she would soon be dragged beneath the earth and lost forever in the black.

But it wasn't all blackness.

Light spilled onto the cobblestones, momentarily chasing the fog from her vision. A tall figure stood in a doorway, silhouetted by firelight.

Someone cursed.

"Fun's over," the silhouette said.

"Mind your business, stranger," one of her captor's hissed. "You've seen nothing that pertains to you. Go back inside."

But the stranger didn't retreat. He strode into the alley and blocked their path. His long shadow stretched up the wall and loomed like a wraith overhead.

"Leave us be, or learn to regret it," another of her captors snarled from above her. Valerie turned her head and caught the glint of the sword in the man's hand, shimmering in the light from the still-open doorway. But it wasn't the only steel making an appearance. The figure in the alleyway drew a sword as well.

More curses punctuated the air above her. One of the men released her arm and she fell to the cobblestones, barely able to catch herself before her head struck.

The stranger was outnumbered but he didn't waver. He lowered his sword into a front guard. Two of her captors took a step back, but the third man had another trick up his sleeve. He unfolded a collapsible staff, then affixed his knife to the head. This portable pike gave him range he had lacked before and apparently boosted his confidence. "Come and get stuck," he spat. He lowered the pike toward the man in the street.

The man with the sword strode forward, his eyes on Valerie. Her captor lunged and attempted to skewer him quickly. He never came close. The swordsman parried the blow, then leapt forward, piercing the pikeman's shoulder. The man howled and sprung back. Far from learning his lesson, however, the experience only seemed to enrage him. He swung his pike again, slashing the air and making wild jabs.

The swordsman sidestepped the attacks, not even bothering to block the cuts. The pikeman received another piercing for his efforts, this time in the thigh.

Valerie felt a hand on her collar. One of the other men was attempting to haul her to her feet. The swordsman intervened, his blade slicing the air above Valerie's head. The man who had grabbed her shouted and released his grip. He backed away clenching his wrist.

Valerie rolled to her side and scurried backward, pressing herself to the wall and attempting to extricate herself from the fight. The shadowy swordsman took a position with his back to her, guarding her from the three would-be kidnappers.

The man with the pike still led the attack, his companions at his flanks. They both drew blades of their own. For a brief moment they looked eager, counting on their superior numbers and position. They pressed their advantage, but the swordsman needed no additional ground to maneuver. With his feet fixed in place, his arms moved only slightly, but his wrists did the work. His sword sliced through the darkness with such rapidity that the three men were all cut and bleeding before they could even realize their blunder. Pressing in on the swordsman had only given him the opportunity he needed to reach them all at once. The dagger and cudgel fell to the ground as their owners clutched fresh wounds to their arms and shoulders. The man with the pike looked down to find several of his fingers littering the alleyway.

The fight was over.

The men shrieked and ran, cursing and shouting as they disappeared into the darkness.

In a matter of seconds, the alleyway was deserted.

Valerie took a breath and shivered.

The swordsman turned around and offered her a hand up. "Can you stand?"

Valerie stared up at him, unsure what she was capable of anymore. It was still blurry here. Even his features wouldn't seem to settle into place. What she could see was a stubbled jawline, dark, intense eyes, and a serious brow. His hair was chopped short on the sides, but the rest of his hair flowed forward in a sort of unruly wave that broke over his forehead. He wore an earring and a scowl.

"Bunch of bastards," Valerie said. She knocked his hand away. "I can help myself up."

"Have it your way," the man said.

"Will she live?" The voice belonged to a young woman peering into the alley from the doorway the man had exited.

"Unless she dies of stubbornness," the swordsman replied. He made his way back to the doorway and, without another word, vanished back inside.

The young woman scurried forward. She tottered across the cobblestones on precariously high heels and stooped to help. Only then did Valerie realize it wasn't a woman, but a man in women's clothing. He was wearing a sequined shirt that sparkled and shimmered, even in the dim light of the alleyway. He had a kind face accented with garish makeup, and bright eyes that sparkled as much as his shirt. "Let me help you," he said, not bothering to wait for a response. He tucked an arm under Valerie's shoulder and hoisted her to her feet.

"Oh honey, you don't smell so good. We need to get you cleaned up." He wrinkled his nose but tightened his grip on her and half carried her toward the glowing doorway.

A woman appeared in the doorway. She had a face lined with many years of hard work, but Valerie would have had a difficult time saying just how many. Dressed in forest-green trousers and a denim shirt, she might have been thirty-five or fifty-five. Either way she was frowning. At her side stood Eli, looking sheepish. "Just what this night needed. More trouble," the woman said. But she stood aside and let the young man carry Valerie through the doorway.

The doorway led to a tavern. At least a brief glimpse of a tavern. Valerie had time to note a bar lined with liquor bottles and a handful of patrons seated on stools. There was more noise and a cacophony of voices around the corner out of view, but she never had a chance to see what else might lie ahead. She was hauled into a storeroom full of shelves that were lined with towels, spare stools, and the other unglamorous necessities of a public house. She was deposited on a bench across from a stack of toilet paper rolls and three-gallon cartons of industrial-strength cleaner.

The lights finally allowed her a better look at her rescuers. The young man in the wig and flashy shirt was perhaps twenty, short and thin with an athletic frame. He had dimples on both cheeks that appeared when he pursed his lips. It was something he was doing now as he looked Valerie over. "I don't even know where to start with you. Do you need a drink? I know you need a hot bath. Maybe some bandages? Honey, you are bleeding all over the place."

Valerie finally noticed that she had skinned one of her knees in the street. The wound had collected some debris. Her head was throbbing from the thump she had received with the cudgel and the less recent impact from the watchman's mace. A brief inspection with her fingers revealed blood in her hair.

"Is she okay?" Eli asked. The boy was lingering in the doorway with a stricken look on his face.

"Of course she is," the woman in the denim shirt replied. "But you won't be. Get on out of here and get home. This isn't any place for a kid to be hanging around at this hour." The woman took a firm grip on Eli's collar and hauled him away.

"But she's my girlfriend!" Eli objected.

"I'll grab us some hot water from the kitchen," the woman said, ignoring Eli's protestations. She vanished through the door, returning a few moments later with a vat of warm water and no Eli.

Valerie was too tired and dazed to object as these strangers began dabbing and prodding at the wounds on her head and knees. She merely sat and took it. She hadn't fully appreciated how filthy she was until the towels came away blackened and disgusting.

"You think she has brain damage?" the man asked. He and the denim woman were inspecting the lump on her head with suspicion.

"I'll send Carlyn in to help you," the woman replied. "I've got a bar to run. Can't spend all night playing good Samaritan." She vanished again.

"Don't worry, honey. I already did my set tonight," the man said. "I won't let you pass out and die." He reached for a bottle on the shelf. "Here. Drink this. Might make you feel better. Worst case it will at least disinfect your insides a bit." He helped her tilt the bottle into her mouth. She sputtered a little but then drank. Whatever it was, Valerie felt her insides warming and her senses sharpen. She took another swig and kept her hand on the bottle. "It's okay. You hold onto that," the young man said. "You earned it."

"Who are you?" Valerie mumbled. "What is this place?"

"I'm Rico Caliente," the man replied. "And this is the Twisted Tentacle. It's a bit of a dive, I'm not gonna lie, but it's a classy dive, you know? You could be a lot worse off."

Valerie lacked the energy to decipher the meaning behind his words. She simply let him continue wiping her down. A few minutes later, Rico was joined by a young woman with dyed purple hair wearing a chef's apron. The woman, whose name was apparently Carlyn, immediately shook her head at the sight of Valerie's hair and clothing.

"No way. We have to get her upstairs to the bathroom," she insisted. "There aren't enough hand towels in the world to make this right."

Rico and the purple-haired woman helped Valerie up a set of adjacent stairs and eased her down a hallway toward a bathroom. Valerie objected to nearly everything that was

happening to her on principle, but couldn't see what good it
would do her to say so out loud.

Carlyn twisted the tap on the bathtub while Rico pulled
Valerie's jacket from her shoulders. He sized up the torn tank top
and ripped cut-offs she was wearing, then eased her onto a bench
before working on her boots.

"I can do it myself," Valerie said, but made no move to help.
It was as though her body didn't believe her. Rico got her boots
off and stood. "You handle the rest of this situation. I'll go see if I
can find her something to wear."

"Oh, lucky me," Carlyn replied. She gestured for Valerie to
turn and began pulling off her shirt. Valerie would normally have
been incensed by the nerve of a perfect stranger undressing her,
but the bath smelled incredible and the warmth of the water was
so inviting she felt she could melt into it. She finished undressing
and slipped gingerly into the water, wincing as she discovered
new cuts and scratches. The tub was deep and soon the water
covered all but her shoulders. She laid her head back on the rim
and exhaled.

"Don't go to sleep. With a bump like that on your head, you
might not wake up," Carlyn said.

"That doesn't sound so bad," Valerie replied.

Carlyn frowned and gestured for Valerie to sit up. "Come on
then. I'll help you with your hair."

When Valerie emerged from the bathroom some time later, she
was still sore and had a headache, but the scent of garbage and
cat urine had vanished, replaced by lavender and jasmine. Her
skin was clean and newly bandaged in several places. Carlyn had
sworn to burn her old clothes, but Rico had reappeared with a
selection of fresh items to dress her in. Most were wildly colored
or styled after other centuries. Valerie managed to locate a pair of
leggings that fit and a sweatshirt that was far too big. It seemed
the perfect item for her to lose herself in.

Carlyn wiped her hands on her apron and disappeared back downstairs with a vague mention of having something baking.

"She's a phenomenal cook," Rico explained. "Every successful tavern runs on food, you know. Even down here."

"You said something about a tentacle?" Valerie asked. "Where are we?"

"The Twisted Tentacle Stage and Tavern," Rico replied. "Janet owns it. She was the one who helped me pull you inside. She's the boss."

"And what are you?" Valerie asked.

"I'm the talent, honey. Singer, dancer, director. Stages don't just spit up entertainment from thin air."

"It's a theater," Valerie said.

"Well, almost," Rico replied. "Let's be honest with ourselves. It's a bar, mostly filled with drunks and precious few real lovers of drama. But they come for the food and booze and I give them art."

"Where did you train? Did you go to school for music?"

"Life is school, honey. You ought to know that. Or maybe you aren't from around here. Where'd you stagger in from?"

Valerie lacked the strength to relive her past day and the events that brought her to the city. The memory was too raw. "I'm from Briar Valley," she replied. "I just need fifty crowns to get home."

Rico nodded. "Um hmm. I'm saving up too. I'm writing a show right now that's my ticket out of this neighborhood. I'll move uptown, or maybe head down the coast. Sky's the limit." He bundled up the towels and handed them to Valerie to carry. "Can't leave a mess up here. The boss will already be mad we used her bathroom. Best not make it worse."

Valerie trudged down the stairs, then realized she was missing her bag. "Hey, did you see a bag when I came in?"

"We can check the alley," Rico replied. "Could be those bastards ran off with it."

"It has my wallet and my car keys," she said.

"You've got a car? Wow. You are high class."

They emerged next to the storage room downstairs and Rico directed her to where the laundry was deposited. He then guided her back into the bar. The place had cleared out, but there were still a handful of drinkers determined to make the night last. Valerie scanned the space and noted the long bar and the dozen booths around the perimeter. A young woman was playing a guitar while singing something mournful and lovely at the front of the small, curtained stage.

"Is that your bag?" Rico asked. "Looks like you might have gotten lucky." He pointed toward a booth in the back where a lone man was sitting with a drink in his hand and watching the guitar player. Her bag was on the bench opposite him. It was the swordsman from the alley. "Better go and get it from him," Rico said.

"What's his name?" Valerie asked.

"That's Damon," Rico replied. "He showed up a few weeks ago. He rents a room next to my building. Tonight was the most I've heard him talk. Usually he just sits back there and broods. Seems all right though."

Valerie pushed back the oversized sleeves on her sweatshirt and crossed the dimly lit bar to the booth where her alleyway savior was sitting.

"Hey," she managed.

The man looked up. His eyes were glassy, but he slowly focused on her face. "Ah. The alley cat."

She had thought him twice her age when she saw him outside. Now that they were indoors, she could see he was only in his early twenties. His world-weary expression made him look older.

"Can I have my bag back?" Valerie asked.

The swordsman lifted his glass and emptied it, then grabbed the bag and slid it to the center of the table. "Do what you like. I was just leaving." He slid out of the booth and stood.

He was tall and smelled of cedar and also vaguely of gasoline.

But perhaps that was just the alcohol. He wiped his mouth with a knuckle and moved past her.

"Wait," Valerie said.

The man turned.

"Thank you. For what you did in the alley."

"It was nothing," he replied. "I'm sure you would have been fine either way."

Valerie didn't agree, but she didn't feel up to arguing. Something about his eyes made her keep her mouth shut. It was like he wasn't even looking at her, but looking through her to some past tragedy. Her argument would have been about the here and now. A place he wasn't currently occupying.

"See you around," he muttered, and headed for the door.

Valerie scooped up her bag and rummaged through the contents. She located her car key and wallet. She opened the billfold and discovered that her money was missing.

"What the—" She searched the rest of the bag, but the fifteen crowns she should have had left was gone. She looked to the doorway where the swordsman had disappeared, then back to the table where he had been sitting. The corner of a ten-crown note was protruding from under one of the empty glasses. She lifted the glass and discovered its five-crown companion as well. She scanned the collection of empty glasses on the table and swore. "That bastard."

She considered snatching her money back from the table, but at that moment, a server arrived to gather up the glasses. She gave Valerie a sideways glance. "Everything all right?"

"No. Not remotely," Valerie replied.

The server stood there with a confused expression on her face, waiting for further explanation, but Valerie gave none. She winced as the girl gathered up the money and stuffed it into her apron.

"Now what do I do?" she muttered.

She wandered back to Rico, who was perched on a stool near

the taps. Janet, the owner, was behind the bar watching her approach.

"How are you holding up?" Janet asked. "You need us to call you a ride?"

"You have a phone?" Valerie perked up at the comment. "Can I use it?"

"Sure. We share it with the place next door. In the hall through there." Janet waved the rag she was using toward a doorway at the side of the bar.

Valerie wasted no time in locating the payphone. A drunken man was slurring into the receiver but seemed to be wrapping things up. Valerie rummaged through her bag once more, searching desperately for change. She managed to locate a single coin stuffed far down in the recesses of her wallet. "Thank God," she said and fixed the man at the phone with a look that he couldn't misinterpret. He muttered a few more things into the phone, nodded to Valerie, and handed off the receiver.

Valerie held the handle gingerly, unsure of what foul organisms might be living on it, but tapped the lever atop the phone, inserted her coin, and began to dial. The phone rang for what seemed like forever before someone finally picked up.

"Hello?"

"Thea? Is that you? It's me, Val."

"Val? Oh my God, where are you?"

Valerie felt a rush of relief wash over her at the sound of her friend's voice. "Listen, Thea, things have gotten so messed up. I need help."

"I know. I heard you got arrested. Everyone's talking about it."

That news spread fast.

She tried to focus. "Look, I'm at a . . . at a bar just outside the city, but they've impounded my car. I need some money to get it back so I can get out of here."

"It's the middle of the night."

"I know but it's an emergency. Does your family have

someone here in the city that I could get help from? I'll pay you back, I just need to get out of here and . . . Maybe I can come stay with you for a bit?"

"I heard about Henry," Thea said. "Is it true what they're saying?"

Valerie swallowed and tried not to let the mental image of her brother's bloodless body completely derail her. "It's true. Can you help me, Thea? I need to get out of here and get somewhere safe."

"I'll ask my dad, okay? Hang on."

"No, wait! Thea! Thea?"

Valerie clutched the receiver and eyed the payphone suspiciously, wondering if it might cut her off any second. It had suddenly become her only lifeline.

An eternity later, Thea came back on. "Um, Val?"

"What did he say?"

"Look, I'm not supposed to be talking to you."

"What? Look, I just need help to get out of here, then I can figure out what to do to fix things."

"Dad says you've been renounced by the Sterlings. They sent word that you're supposed to be arrested if anyone finds you."

"The Sterlings are the ones that should be arrested," Valerie argued. "Jasper Sterling lied to the courts. He murdered Henry."

"That's not what they're saying," Thea whispered. "They said Henry tried to kill Jasper and he had to defend himself. They're saying you just went crazy on him after and tried to stab him in the back."

"What? Who's saying that?"

"Everyone. It's all anyone's been talking about. He's a Sterling, Val."

"He murdered Henry!" Valerie said. "He's a liar!"

"I have to go. My dad is coming."

"No. No, no Thea. Please, I need your help. Please, just fifty crowns. Let me borrow it and I swear I'll give it back right away."

"I'm sorry. I can't."

"Thea. Wait—"

"Valerie?" A man's voice came on the line. "Where are you? What are you doing calling here?"

"Mr. Johansen, I'm sorry, I need help."

"If you want help, you'll have to turn yourself in to the Sterlings. We can't be caught up in whatever you've done. Don't call here anymore."

Then the line went dead.

9

STRANDED

Valerie stared at the phone receiver as though it held some dark and evil magic.

Her only hope had evaporated into silence and all that was left in her hand was this vile snake of a device. What had it done?

"You have to put money in it," a voice said.

She turned to find an old woman with hardly any teeth pointing at the payphone. "In the slot there. You can't call nobody unless you pay." She waited patiently for several more seconds, then cleared her throat. "So, you using it, or what?"

Valerie let the receiver fall from her hand and it swung into the wall, ricocheting off and spinning several times on its cord before thumping into the wall again.

She shuffled past the old woman in a daze. What was happening to the world? What devil had she angered that had caused her life to crumble in such a violent wave of catastrophe?

Even Thea had abandoned her?

It was hopeless.

She wandered back into the bar without conscious thought. She took a seat on a stool at the end of the bar and let her bag drop to the floor next to her. Crossing her arms on the bar top, she laid her head on them and closed her eyes. Nothing mattered. She would just stay here and die.

"I take it the call didn't go well?" Janet asked.

Her footsteps approached along the inside of the bar. A glass clunked onto the wood near Valerie's head, followed by the subtle splashing of something being poured into it.

"I'll give you just one free one," Janet said. "Because I need to finish off this bottle. And because I have a hard rule around here. No sleeping on the bar."

Valerie looked up and stared at the drink next to her. She wasn't legally allowed to have hard liquor for another few weeks, but after a day like today, what was left to lose? She'd do about anything to dull the pain of this day. She took a sip, puckered her face slightly, then went back for more. The glass was empty a few moments later.

She found Janet eying her. The woman's face was care-worn and unsmiling, but there was a hint of compassion in her eyes. "You have a place to go tonight?" she asked.

"I thought I did, but I was wrong."

"Figured that might be the case." Janet said. "We'll be closing up soon. I've got a fold-out cot in the storage room that you're welcome to use for the night. Can't very well pitch you back into the alley where we found you. Not after Rico and Carlyn invested so much time and soap into you." She put a rag and a bottle of cleaner on the bar. "Here."

Valerie stared at the spray bottle. "What's this for?"

"You can help me clean tables while I close up."

"You want me to clean? I was almost murdered tonight. And that wasn't even the worst part of my day."

"Good. Then this won't be either." Janet pushed the cleaning supplies toward her. "I told you. You get one free one, which you've had. Everything else around here is earned." She called toward the stage. "Ain't that right, Rico?"

Rico paused in the act of helping the guitarist pack up her

gear. He had removed his wig, revealing short black hair that was cut close to his head. "You know I know."

Janet smirked, then turned back to Valerie. "He's a good kid that one. Hard worker. But that's anybody who makes something of themselves around here." She collected the empty bottle of liquor and tossed it into a bin with a dozen others. Then she moved off to settle someone's tab.

Valerie's head was still aching and her body was sore, but she scooped up the rag and bottle of cleaner and groaned her way over to the nearest empty booth. She wrinkled her nose as she eyed the puddles of beer and a cup of what might have been tobacco spit that someone had left behind. Getting her hands dirty wrenching on a car was one thing, but other people's fluids?

She took another look around the bar. There was no one to relieve her of this task. She finally aimed the spray bottle at the table and doused every suspicious surface with soap.

As she was wiping, Rico wandered over and leaned against a neighboring booth. "Don't worry. She's strict but she's fair. If she likes you, maybe she'll keep you around, let you work the kitchen or something. You could make that fifty crowns you need to get out of here."

"Work the kitchen? Like a servant?" Valerie said.

"Well, not if you think you're too good for it," Rico said. "Just trying to throw you a bone." He pushed off the booth and walked away.

"No. Wait," Valerie said. "I'm sorry." But Rico simply flipped a hand in the air and moved back to the stage. Valerie sighed and went back to wiping tables.

It took another twenty minutes until Janet had cleared the last of the patrons out, and a few more till she was satisfied with the state of the bar. She finally approached Valerie and extended a hand for the now filthy cleaning rag. "Come on. The rest will keep till morning. Let's get you squared away."

She led Valerie back to the storeroom where they had first

tried to clean her up. Janet tossed the dirty rag into the laundry hamper, then plucked a green canvas camp cot from the wall and extended the legs.

"It's not the most comfortable thing in the world, but it beats the floor." She retrieved a pillow and blanket from above the laundry shelf and handed those to Valerie. "I can't promise no one has ever gotten sick in here, but we do a pretty good job of cleaning up. That being said, I'd appreciate any business you need to do be conducted in the employee washroom. You'll find it through there." She pointed to a door that was partially open, revealing the corner of a basin sink. "The back door stays locked all night for safety purposes and I've got the key, so once you're in, you're in. If you decide in the middle of the night that there's someplace else you'd rather be, you'll just have to wait till morning."

"I'll be locked in?"

"I'll be upstairs if you really need me, but I lock my hall door too and I sleep like the dead so I can't promise I'll hear you knocking. If you want out, I'm happy to let you wander off into the night right now. Your choice."

Valerie considered the heavy door that lead to the back alley, then hugged the blankets tighter. "No. I'll be fine here."

"Thought you'd make it work." Janet moved to the back door and put a hand to the lock but paused as Rico made his way down the hall. "You going out the back tonight?"

"You all good here?" Rico asked, leaning in the door to assess Valerie.

"She'll make do," Janet replied.

Rico fixed Valerie with a long stare but then simply nodded to Janet. "Night then."

"See you tomorrow," Janet replied. She locked the door behind him and made her way to the stairs.

"Janet?" Valerie said.

"Yeah?"

"Thank you."

"Don't worry about it," Janet replied. "I've been left stranded a few times over the years. Sometimes it feels like the tide has gone out and taken everything good in your life along with it. But a tide has to rise too." She flipped the light switch and climbed the stairs in the dark.

Valerie listened to the sound of Janet's footfalls fading overhead, then got herself settled on the cot with the blanket and stared up at the ceiling of the storeroom. It was only her second night away from home, but it felt like years.

Twenty-four hours ago, her brother had been sleeping in the passenger seat of the Guardian. When the sun came up again, she would no longer be sharing a day when he was alive. The thought hurt, deep in the core of her, like she was betraying him by continuing to live a new day that he couldn't. What right did she have to live that he didn't?

A million regrets flooded her mind.

She should have turned the car around before they reached the city.

They should have gone home. Found a new fight.

But she had chosen this one and lost.

She rolled over on the cot and tried to get comfortable. The room smelled of laundry detergent and bleach. She clamped her eyes shut, hoping to keep out the memories of her day, but he was still there.

His carefree smile. His confident swagger.

Gone.

Valerie didn't notice when her turbulent mind switched from awake to asleep, but she did know that all of her dreams were filled with swords.

10

THEN

"Why can't I learn *Charging Rhino*?" Valerie asked, watching her brother slash at the wooden pell her father had erected in the yard.

"Because you aren't your brother."

Henry Terravecchia II was an intimidating man, barrel chested with a voice that brooked no argument, especially from ten-year-olds.

"Fix your stance. Opening position."

Valerie stepped back and planted her rear foot, then raised the wooden practice sword.

"*Burning Sky*," her father commanded.

Valerie sighed and stepped into the form she had been working on all morning. Her arms ached as she swung the weapon overhead, making the flurry of lateral cuts. Her breath erupted from her in short bursts as she swung.

As she worked through her steps, her eyes drifted to where her brother was cutting at the wooden post with aggressive overhead cuts. His muscles were like iron. He didn't even look winded.

Her sword struck steel.

Her father had intercepted her sword with the flat of his own blade and was now looming in front of her. "You're not focusing."

"Why doesn't Henry ever have to do *Burning Sky* practice? It's so boring."

Her father studied her, then dropped to one knee in front of her to be at her level. "Your brother is a boy. He has to fight like one. You're a girl."

"I can do anything he can do," Valerie argued. "Why don't you teach us the same?"

Her father's eyes softened. "Henry's path will always be different from yours." He reached out and gripped her sword, his big hands overlapping hers and tightening around her fists. "No two warriors ever fight the same battle. Each of us has our own fight. How we train for it must also be different."

"You just like him better because he's a boy."

He released the sword and rested a hand on her shoulder. "I'll tell you a secret. I never even knew how much love my heart could hold until the day I held my baby girl and she smiled at me. That little girl was you."

"I'm not smiling now."

Her father laughed. A hearty sound that welled up from his chest. His dark beard quivered and his shoulders shook. He stood and wrapped an arm around her. "You ever stop to think that maybe Henry gets extra practice because he needs it? Maybe he's not as tough as you."

"I don't believe you," Valerie argued. "He's always been stronger than me."

"There are many ways to show strength." He held up his sword. "Take *Durendal* here. You know how it got so strong?"

"No."

"It was beaten with a hammer and heated in a raging fire, then it was quenched in water and beaten some more. If it hadn't gone through all of those things, it would never be the weapon it is today." He tightened his grip on her shoulder. "One day, you'll be the weapon. But first, you have to be tested."

Valerie stared at the legendary blade in her father's hand.

"I'll be like a sword?"

"One day. If you keep practicing."

"Does it have to be *Burning Sky*?"

"Maybe we can add in a few more forms," he said. "Get your sword ready. I'll teach you a new one."

"What's this one called?" Valerie asked.

"*Burning Sky part two*."

Valerie groaned.

Her father laughed.

NEWS

Valerie blinked at the ceiling, then slowly sat up on the cot. She would have given anything to be waking up at home, and to discover that the last forty-eight hours had been a dream, but the dimly-lit storeroom was oppressively real.

Ambient light from the grimy slit of a window in the bathroom was the only indication that morning had arrived. That and her headache.

She eased her way off the cot and over to the bathroom, taking time to wash her face in the utility sink. The bar of soap was just a sliver, and the hand towel was missing, but she made do.

Valerie rubbed the creases of her fingers. Her skin was clean, the blood gone, but in her mind they were still pressed to his chest, covering the wound.

The girl staring back at her in the mirror was barely recognizable. The swelling around her eye had gone down but had left a colorful bruise. She probed it gingerly and decided it was best left alone. Her usually straight hair was a rat's nest. She combed it with her fingers and managed to calm it down, but she was still a far cry from her usual reflection.

"The morning is for making new plans," she muttered.

What was her plan? After a solemn staring contest with herself, she decided there was nothing she could do without the proper tools, the first of which was coffee.

She slipped out of the storeroom and into the bar. The front door was propped open, allowing the morning light in. The back door was open as well, and the breeze flowing through brought the sound of seagull cries and the smell of cut fish.

Valerie shuffled to the far end of the bar where Janet was already at work tallying receipts. A few clinking noises came from the kitchen.

"The excitement starts early around here," Valerie said.

"Always," Janet replied. "You want some coffee? I have a pot going."

"You'd be my hero."

While Janet located a mug and poured her a cup, Valerie's eyes roamed over the tournament posters pinned up behind the bar.

The King's Tournament. A Showcase of Honor.

In the chaos of the last day, she had almost forgotten about the tournament. One poster featured an illustration of two rugged-looking hot rods racing past a finish line, and another had two gallant swordsmen locked in a duel. She knew there were lesser events in a king's tournament—archery, jousting, and the like—but it was the car races and the sword melee that drew the crowds.

"You want cream?" Janet set the cup of coffee on the bar.

Valerie shook her head. "So, I know it's a king's tournament, but is King Logan really coming to Port Hyacinth?"

"That's the rumor. The winner of the tournament gets to fill a spot at the Round Table. People around here are thrilled. It's the first time a king's tournament has had an open list in as long as anybody can remember. Anyone with a car and a sword has a chance."

"A war car," Valerie clarified. "How many commoners have one of those?"

"You might be surprised at the ingenuity of the builders around here. As soon as the announcement came out, you could hear the engines coming to life in places you never would have thought. There's good money on a couple drivers from the Underside causing an upset." She gestured to a lower-quality dueling poster featuring the angry-looking face of a man named Connor Kane.

Valerie tried to imagine the reaction of the high-born to a commoner winning the tournament.

"Would anyone really want a commoner seated at the Round Table?"

"Certainly better than the lot we have now," Janet said. "When was the last time the nobles at court did us any favors? We need someone who will actually speak for the people."

Valerie studied the poster's place of prominence behind the bar. Janet's politics were no doubt popular here, but there was a lot of altitude between a rim village and the high houses of the city. She doubted many of the nobles shared her enthusiasm. "You expect to get a lot of business for the tournament?"

"Are you kidding? It's already the busiest we've been in years. All the shops and restaurants along the waterfront are getting ready. Of course, the rich folk and their entourages will stay inside the city walls, but we'll get our share of itinerant knights and travelers. Tidewater's not likely to get a windfall like this for another decade."

"Is that what they call this village? I didn't know the outer-wall villages had names."

"Everyone is from somewhere."

Valerie fidgeted with the coffee cup. "So, I was wondering, with all that extra business you were talking about . . . do you maybe need some help around here?"

"I can always use help. You have someone special in mind?" Janet cocked an eyebrow.

"Well, I was thinking that maybe I could stick around for a

little and try to . . . I don't know, work? Just until I get things figured out."

Janet set her completed stack of receipts in a basket and tucked it away on a shelf beneath the register. "You ever work a bar before?"

"No."

"You ever work anywhere before?"

"I've been away at school," Valerie replied.

"You study anything that qualifies you to work here?"

"Not really. I mostly studied engineering. I want to design my own race cars one day."

Janet leaned on the bar. "The thing about hiring help is, I don't like to spend the time training someone only to have them vanish on me the first time they get paid. And there's not a lot of what I know about you that suggests employment longevity."

Valerie nodded. "I know. Last night, all I wanted was to get out of this city. My car is impounded, and if it wasn't stuck in there, I would have left town as fast as I could drive. But I think I was wrong."

"How so?" Janet asked.

"Someone I love was killed by the Sterlings. My brother. And he deserves justice. The only place I can get justice is here."

"I'm sorry for your loss," Janet said. "I've certainly known my share of people who've regretted run-ins with the Sterlings. But what makes you think you'll get justice for your brother by hanging around here?"

Valerie pointed to the tournament poster. "That. No one I know will stand up to Jasper Sterling, so I'll need to go straight to the top. I'll have to talk to the king."

Janet laughed and shook her head. "The king? Sorry, I was wrong. It sounds like you will be here for a long time if that's your plan. You think the *king* will just let you walk up and explain your story, and he'll clear everything up for you? Is that how life has worked for you so far?"

"He'll give me justice. It's what kings do."

Janet crossed her arms. "This plan is a fool's errand. How will you get an audience with the king when the Sterlings are hosting him? And what makes you think he'd believe your word over theirs?"

"I'll get proof."

"You know where to find proof?"

"Not yet."

"I'd say that's a mighty big question mark." Janet wiped her hands on a rag. "But, fine. As long as you can work your justice-seeking around normal bar hours, I'll find some work for you to do. That way, your time won't be completely wasted. But if you're going up against the Sterlings, you've got your work cut out for you. And we have enough troubles. If your crazy idea starts causing any kind of problems, you're out. Got it?"

"I understand," Valerie replied.

Janet pointed to a nook behind the bar. "You'll find a broom and dustpan back there. When you're done with that coffee, make yourself acquainted with the floors. We'll see what other uses we can find for you later."

Valerie reluctantly finished the coffee and slid the mug back across the bar.

She took another long look at the tournament posters, then set to work sweeping.

While it wasn't glamorous work, the repetitive monotony gave her mind something to do other than think about her losses of the past two days. She kept at it until she had worked all the dirt in the place over to the front door. She spotted a waste bin on the sidewalk outside and began relaying the dustpans of dirt out to it, wrinkling her nose with each load. When she was on her third trip outside, a low rumbling caught her attention, and she noticed a stream of vehicles making its way across one of the bridges overhead. Armored trucks and other rugged-looking war cars were flying the banners of House Johansen.

"Thea's family," Valerie muttered.

112

Other banners followed. She recognized crests from several northern houses in the caravan as well.

The wide suspension bridge that connected the city gates to the other side of South Bay was a lot like the bridge she and Henry had crossed to drive into the city, but her view of the high road had drastically changed. Tucked among the barrier pilings and jetties, she imagined the village she was in now wouldn't even have caught her notice from so high up.

"Hey, new girl!"

Valerie turned around to find the purple-haired cook, Carlyn, standing on the front step. "You're supposed to help me prep in the kitchen this morning. Boss's orders." Valerie dumped her dustpan load in the bin and made her way back inside.

"Any idea what that's all about?" she asked, indicating the parade of vehicles making its way across the bridge.

Carlyn squinted as she looked skyward. "We've been getting caravans into the city for weeks. Early arrivals to help with the tournament setup. Come on, we've got to get to work. New people in town means new customers."

Carlyn guided Valerie into the kitchen and pointed her toward the sink. "Get the rest of the dishes cleaned up from last night, then you can help me start lunch. We open at eleven, and I expect we'll be busy."

Valerie made her way to the sink and stared at the dirty dishes, unsure of where to start. She gingerly picked up a dishrag with two fingers, then set it back down.

"What's the matter?" Carlyn asked. "You never washed dishes before?"

"Um. Not really," Valerie said. "We had maids for that at school."

Carlyn walked to the hook on the wall and snatched up an apron, then tossed it to Valerie. "It's not brain surgery. Figure it out."

Before long, customers began arriving for lunch, and Valerie was kept busy running plates of food out to the bar, assisting

Carlyn with chopping vegetables, and of course, washing more dishes.

It wasn't long before Valerie's stomach was growling, inhaling the scent of fresh-baked bread and Carlyn's popular lunchtime concoctions. The customers were mostly sailors, but there were itinerant knights as well, mercenaries avoiding the high prices of uptown by staying in the lower-cost waterfront district. Valerie thought the clientele looked rough and dangerous, but Janet supervised the group with a watchful eye, and Carlyn's food kept everyone civil. By the time the lunch rush was over, it was mid-afternoon, and Valerie's fingers were pruney from scrubbing.

Janet came into the kitchen and surveyed her work. "I'm moving you to the front of the house tonight. I've got enough kitchen help coming in, and I want to see how you do at serving. Get something to eat, take a break, but be back before the dinner rush and ready to work, got it?"

"Okay."

Janet vanished back into the office.

Valerie scooped some cheese and egg into a warm hunk of bread, then angled it toward her mouth.

"Did you toast the bread?"

Valerie turned and found Carlyn staring at her.

"If you make an egg-and-goat-cheese sandwich in my kitchen, you have to do it right." She held out her hand.

Valerie relinquished the sandwich.

Carlyn threw the contents of the sandwich onto the grill, added some peppers, then buttered each piece of bread before pressing it. She lifted the lid on a saucepan that was simmering at the back and ladled a spoonful of creamy sauce over the eggs. When the bread was thoroughly browned, she scooped the contents of the sandwich up with a spatula and deposited them back in the bread. She handed the whole assembly to Valerie, then walked off without another word.

Valerie studied the now-dripping sandwich and took a bite.

She immediately moaned in delight.

Carlyn's disembodied voice came from around the corner. "You're welcome!"

Valerie savored another mouthful of the sandwich, trying not to drip it on her shirt, then made her way out the front door, pausing on the stoop. In daylight, the village had a different feel to it. The streets were muddy, and the shanties still leaned precariously on their stilts, but the morning fog had dissipated, and the sun was warm on her shoulders.

While the streets had mostly dried overnight, the few pedestrians she spotted were keeping to rough, board walkways that connected the various buildings. Under cover of the shingled walkway roofs, the citizens appeared oblivious to the view of the immense bridges overhead. She thought that was a shame.

Descending the steps of the tavern and stepping into the street, Valerie tilted her face skyward, marveling at the way the sun shone from the gilded emblems on the support columns. She was turning in place when something warm and wet splattered across her forehead.

She lifted her fingers to her hair, and they came away white and reeking of fish guts. "Ugh," Valerie moaned.

It was only then that she spotted the gulls roosting in the recesses of the bridge supports.

Frantically flinging the bird excrement from her fingers, she dashed out of the street and onto the covered walkway.

A toothless, old woman sitting on a bench smiled and nodded. "And now you've been christened. Welcome to Tidewater."

Valerie pulled up the end of her apron and used it to wipe at her face and hair.

"Could be worse. You might have walked under the drains." The old woman pointed toward one end of the village where pipes that jutted out of the city walls dumped runoff into the street. "But that's life on the Underside. Best get yourself a rain slicker."

Seeking to escape the scene of her embarrassment and guard what remained of her sandwich, Valerie worked her way along the covered walkway to the next road before spotting a row of automotive garages. This street sat farther up from the high-water line, and the buildings didn't bother with stilts, but they all sported large awnings and covered walks despite the shade from the city walls.

There was an old car with its hood up in front of one of the garages, and two men were standing in front of it arguing about something. One of the men was Rico. The other was a towering brute of a sailor with muscles that seemed poised to rip his shirt. A menagerie of ocean-themed tattoos decorated his arms. Valerie eased along the street and listened in to their conversation.

"It's twice what I'd pay on the Northside," the man was saying. "You trying to rip me off?"

"This is a low-mileage, competition pump," Rico replied. "Variable displacement and automatic leaning capabilities. I overhauled it myself. If you want your fuel lines to cavitate and vapor lock as soon as your engine hits peak temperatures, go right ahead and buy whatever they've got on the Northside. But you'll be watching from the shoulder while someone rocking this pump goes blowing by you. I guarantee it."

The man considered the part in his hand, then grunted and reached for his wallet.

"I'll put it in a bag for you," Rico said. A fabric sack materialized from his back pocket. He bagged the fuel pump and exchanged it for the cash the sailor offered.

The man bunched the handles of the bag into his meaty fist and aimed a free finger at Rico's chest. "If it doesn't work, you'll be seeing me a lot less friendly."

"I'll watch for you on the track, Kane," Rico replied.

The sailor grunted again and began to walk away. He had

only made it a few yards before turning around. "If you get your hands on anything else you think is primo . . ."

"You'll be my first stop," Rico said. "You know I know."

"Right," Kane replied. He noticed Valerie and eyed her suspiciously as he walked by but didn't bother to greet her.

Valerie watched him go, recognizing his ornery expression from the poster in the tavern. She ate the last of her sandwich as she continued toward Rico.

Rico finished counting his money, then looked up as she approached, glancing at her apron. "I see you took my advice."

"Yeah, thanks," Valerie said. "I'm glad I ran into you. I wanted to say sorry about last night. I was kind of . . ."

"A snot? Yeah, you were." Rico pocketed his cash, then squared up with the car's engine compartment. He reached into a toolbox on the fender and extracted a socket wrench, but when he glanced back at her, he paused. Putting his free hand out, he brushed his fingertips along her face. "Oh honey, that bruise looks like it hurts. You want me to see if I can find something to cover that up? You're turning so purple you're an eggplant."

Valerie covered the bruise with her hand and tried to rearrange her messy hair to cover it. "I'm fine."

"You don't look fine," Rico said, but he didn't push the issue. "Whenever you need it, you let me know. I'll fix you right up."

"What are you doing with this old Commander?" Valerie asked, eager to change the subject.

Rico looked up in surprise. "You know cars? Most people always assume it's a Rogue Challenger."

"No. Challenger only came with square headlights and has a narrower hood profile," Valerie replied. "I have a Rogue fastback at home. Well, used to anyway. I wrecked it. I'll probably have to part it out."

"That's all this one is good for too," Rico said. "But at least with the tournament coming to town, everything is in demand. Seems like just about everyone is trying to build a war car right now."

"Do any of these run?" Valerie asked, noting the array of junkers scattered around the back lot.

"Nah. None of these. But living this close to the junkyards has its perks. One of these days I'll have my own rally ride fixed up, then I'll roll out of here and never look back."

"Whose is that?" Valerie said, pointing to a primer-gray Rockwell Vulcan parked outside the warehouse next door. It seemed to have all of its parts.

"Oh, that's your boy, Damon's, ride." Rico gestured toward the loft apartments above the warehouse.

At that moment, the ground-floor door to the warehouse opened.

"Speak of the devil," Rico said.

The dark-haired swordsman stepped outside, locked the door to the warehouse, then made his way over to the Vulcan. He was dressed in jeans, a white T-shirt, and heavy boots and was carrying a longsword by its scabbard. His eyes were hidden by dark sunglasses. He looked up and caught sight of Valerie just as he was reaching the door to his car. He gave Rico a nod.

"Hey," Valerie said.

The swordsman unlocked the car door and deposited his sword inside.

"Hope you enjoyed those beers last night," Valerie added, unable to help herself.

Damon leaned on the doorframe momentarily, then walked over to where she was standing. "Surprised you're still here this morning. Figured you would have caught the first train home."

"I have debts to settle," Valerie said.

"Uh huh." Damon nodded. He ignored her glare and eyed Rico's handiwork. "That a five liter?"

"Nah, three point eight," Rico replied. "Cracked case. Love to get my hands on a five-oh, though."

Valerie studied Damon's muscled chest and arms. Several long scars lined his forearms. It was clear the sword wasn't just for show. "You're a hired sword? You fight people for money?"

Damon glanced at her, but his expression was unreadable behind his dark sunglasses. "You don't need to worry about what I do."

The idea that had been slowly coalescing in her mind finally took form.

"What if I want to hire you?"

Damon shook his head. "You can't afford me."

"You haven't even heard the job."

"I can guess," he replied. "You want me to enact revenge on all the people who have wronged you? Solve your problems with cold steel and spilled blood? Because that's what everyone wants. You'll have to get in line."

"Actually, that's not what I'm after," Valerie said. "I need . . . I need someone to fight in the King's Tournament."

Damon lowered his chin and peered at her over the rim of his sunglasses. "The King's Tournament. What do you know about sponsoring a tournament team?"

"Plenty," Valerie replied. "My dad was a tournament champion. Il Orso Nero. The Black Bear. And my brother fought too."

"I think we know who Il Orso Nero was," Damon said.

"Hang on. I didn't know this," Rico said. "Your dad was Il Orso Nero? I still have a poster of him in the garage. He was one of my all-time favorite melee drivers."

"Having a famous father won't get you into the King's Tournament," Damon said. "And a tournament isn't just about the fighter. You'd need a war car."

"I have a war car," Valerie said.

Damon raised an eyebrow and glanced around the lot. "In your . . . imagination?"

"No." Valerie scowled. "Here. In the city."

"Like a legit battle ride?" Rico asked.

"It's a Guardian 770," Valerie said. "It was my dad's."

"Oh sweet Mary," Rico said, his hands finding his face and involuntarily smearing grease on his forehead. "For real?"

Damon studied her. "You're serious. You want to sponsor a tournament team? Who would be your driver?"

"I'd drive," Valerie said. "I know how to handle it."

"You'd need a mechanic," Damon said.

Valerie pointed to Rico. "I'm looking at one right now."

Rico rubbed his hands together. "Work on Il Orso Nero's Guardian? Oh, hell yeah. I'd be in for that."

"You know you'd have to put the car up as collateral," Damon said. "Unless you've got a serious stack of cash laying around or something else worth the price of admission."

"I know," Valerie replied. The thought hadn't actually occurred to her, but she couldn't back down now.

"What makes you think you'd stand a chance against the other teams in this thing?" Damon asked.

"Because I don't need to win," Valerie said. "I just need to get in front of the king. Even a finalist team gets to do that, right?"

Rico nodded. "Sure. Finalists all get to go to the masquerade. Why are you trying to talk to him?"

"Jasper Sterling killed my brother. Unless I find a way to get revenge myself, I need the king to give me justice."

"Oh, damn," Rico muttered.

Damon pushed his sunglasses to the top of his head and crossed his arms, surveying her. Valerie locked eyes with him, refusing to blink. There was something about the way he was staring at her, as though he was reading her face. Whatever it was he was looking for, she didn't flinch.

"So you're not after the prize? The spot at the Round Table?"

"I have no interest in becoming a knight," Valerie replied. "I just need to get in front of the king and tell him what happened to my brother."

"What makes you think he'd side with you?"

"Because King Logan is a just king," Valerie replied. "And I need justice."

Damon stared at her for another long second, then finally broke eye contact. "Okay. I'll tell you what. If you're serious, you show me the car, and we'll talk about putting together a team. What time are you off work?"

"Eleven."

"Fine. I'll see you here at 11:05. Bring the car." He lowered his sunglasses back over his eyes, then walked to the Vulcan.

Once Damon had driven away, Valerie finally turned to Rico. He was staring at her with an open mouth.

"What?"

"You seriously have Il Orso Nero's Guardian? You're not making this up, right?"

"I'm not making it up. Only problem is, it's in the impound right now."

Rico's expression darkened. "Wait. What impound?"

"One right outside the city walls. It got towed there last night."

"Oh no. That's not good. Did it belong to a guy named Bernard Ipswich?"

"Yeah. I think so. Why?"

Rico shook his head. "Sorry to tell you this, honey. But that car is gone."

GUARDIAN

"What do you mean, 'gone'?" Valerie sputtered. "He said I only had to pay him fifty more crowns, then I could have it back!" The ground was shifting under her again just when she thought she had found her feet.

"He knew you didn't have the money? How long ago did you leave it there?" Rico asked.

"Last night," Valerie replied.

"All I know is that Bernard Ipswich moves more stolen cars than anyone in the city. If it's not chopped and parted out already, it will be soon."

"That bastard," Valerie spat. She looked around to orient herself. "I need to get down there."

"It's a long walk to the impound," Rico said.

A worker trolley dinged its bell as it made its way around the corner.

"Hey, wait." Rico dug into his jeans pocket. "I have a couple of punches left on my city pass. If we hitch a ride, I can save you some time. I'll have to go with you, though. It's got my name on it." He flashed the pass. The name Ricardo Cabrera was printed on it, and Rico's teenage face grinned back from the photo.

"I still don't have fifty crowns," Valerie said.

Rico reached into his pocket and brandished his recently acquired cash. "I can spot you the money. Consider it a loan."

"You'd do that?"

"Flag down that trolley," Rico said. "Let's go get your car."

Valerie tried to judge the height of the sun in the sky as they stepped off the trolley at the corner of the impound lot. "What time is it?"

"Time for you to stop asking me for the hundredth time," Rico said. "Your car is gone. You'll be late getting back to work, and Janet will murder you. You just have to live with it."

"I'm not sure what you're doing counts as helping," Valerie replied. She cursed inwardly and pushed her way through the gate. The woman behind the desk was the same lady she had dealt with the night before. Her eyes widened as Valerie walked through the door. "Oh, wow. You're back."

"I have the money," Valerie said. "Where's my car?"

The woman blanched. "Um, you might want to hurry. He didn't think you would be back so soon."

"He said I had two weeks," Valerie replied.

The woman shrugged.

Valerie rushed past the desk and through the back door of the office.

Rows of old wrecks made a maze of the back lot, but her path ahead was clear. Her car was sitting in the open at the far side of the lot, but a wrecker was hooking up to the back of the vehicle, preparing to pull it onto a trailer. Bernard was directing the driver of the wrecker. "Get it good and tight, then haul away." He looked down and started counting a wad of cash in his hand.

"Hey!" Valerie shouted. "Hey, that's mine!" She broke into a run.

Bernard turned at the shout and his eyes widened.

"Put that down!" Valerie shouted.

The driver of the wrecker looked to Bernard for help.

"Pull it up!" Bernard shouted.

The wrecker driver activated the winch and started hauling the Guardian up the inclined ramp of the truck bed.

"Stop!" Valerie shouted, rushing up to the car and gripping the door handle.

Bernard tucked the wad of money behind his back and held a hand up to her. "Calm down, there's no cause for alarm."

"Give me back my car!" Valerie demanded.

"I can't do that. It's been purchased by a private collector."

"You can't sell my car!" Valerie objected. "It's mine!"

"Actually, an addendum to your impound contract states that failure to pay the necessary fees in advance makes the car liable for resale. You never asked to have that section of the contract waived, therefore—"

Valerie's fist struck him right in the mouth. Bernard reeled backward, losing his grip on the cash in his hand. Bills fluttered to the ground and immediately began to blow away in the wind.

Valerie stood shaking with fury. She looked down at her closed fist. She hadn't intended to hit him, but it had just come out of her.

It felt good.

She moved to the controls at the side of the wrecker and slammed the release lever.

"Hey!" The driver kicked open the door to the cab and started climbing out.

He was too late. The Guardian was rolling, gaining speed as it thudded back to the ground and onto all four tires. Valerie raced after it. As the car slowed to a stop, she scrambled under the bumper and released the tow cable from the frame.

Bernard and the wrecker driver stormed after her, and Valerie retreated to the passenger side of the car, keeping it between them.

"You little brat. You assaulted me," Bernard said. "I'll have you whipped for that."

The wrecker driver moved around the front of the car. He was taller than Bernard with a neck thicker than Valerie's leg. She took one look at him and realized there would be no winning a physical confrontation with him. She yanked open the passenger door and leapt inside, locking the door behind her.

Bernard shouted and lunged for the driver's side door, but Valerie hit the lock just before he could yank the handle. She fished the keys from her pocket and held them up with a smile.

Bernard's face reddened. He shouted something to the wrecker driver, but it was drowned out by the snarl of the Guardian's engine as Valerie slid into the driver's seat and turned the ignition.

Clutch. Shifter. Accelerator.

The Guardian leapt into reverse. Bernard's lost bills flew into the air in a colorful tornado as the car passed over them.

The wrecker driver was shouting. Bernard chased his airborne bits of cash.

Valerie spun the car around, shifted into gear, and raced for the gate, spotting Rico lingering on the pavement halfway to the office. She skidded to a stop beside him and flung open the passenger door. "Get in!"

"Oh my God, are you stealing it?" Rico asked as he scrambled inside.

"They're the thieves," Valerie said. "Let's go."

As soon as Rico had his feet inside, she stomped on the accelerator again. The door slammed shut and Rico searched for the seat belt.

"Hold on to something!" Valerie said. She pulled the handle on the ceiling of the car, and the protective metal grate slid forward to cover the windshield. Then she shifted into third and put both hands on the wheel, aiming straight for the gate.

"Oh God. Oh God," Rico sputtered.

Bernard was waving wildly in the rear-view mirror. Then she noticed the clerk from the office standing next to the gate.

"They have tire spikes," Rico said, pointing to a row of holes in the pavement. "She's going to stop us."

Valerie pressed harder on the accelerator and shifted into fourth.

The clerk's hand was at the gate controls. Valerie locked eyes with her.

"Come on. Come on," she whispered.

Rico finally found the safety harness, snapped it together, and braced himself.

They'd passed the point of no return. There was no stopping an impact now.

The clerk threw the lever.

But instead of spikes erupting from the pavement, the lever sprung the lock on the gate. The center of the gate fanned outward, opening just in time for the Guardian to go blasting through. Sparks flew from the car's armored fenders as it knocked the gate open the rest of the way.

"Yes!" Valerie shouted. She cut the wheel hard and braked once she was through, fishtailing across the dirt road before spinning to a stop, facing the office. She gave the horn a few joyous blasts.

The clerk at the gate was grinning and gave her a wave.

Valerie whooped, then she shifted back into gear and gave the car the gas. A rooster tail of dirt and gravel erupted from beneath the rear tires as they found traction, and she aimed the car up the street, racing away before Bernard and the wrecker driver could even think to follow.

"Yes, yes, yes!" Valerie shouted, pounding the steering wheel.

Rico still looked petrified, but his death grip on the door started to relax. "Oh God. If you could feel how puckered my butt cheeks are right now . . . I think they were hanging on to this seat for dear life."

"I knew we'd make it," Valerie said.

"You just took years off my life."

"Yes!" she shouted again, unable to keep the grin off her face.

Valerie raced along the coast road to Tidewater and made the turn up Cannery Lane toward the tavern. "What time is it?"

"No idea," Rico replied. "But I can tell you, you won't be early."

Valerie kept her foot on the gas and only hit the brakes when they were directly in front of the tavern. The car skidded to a stop in a cloud of dust and came to rest right in front of the Twisted Tentacle's sign.

"You're parking it here?" Rico asked. "Bad enough you're late. No need to advertise it."

"I already lost this car once. I'm leaving it right where I can see it." She retracted the windshield armor, then climbed out.

Janet wasn't anywhere in sight when she walked through the front door of the tavern. That was a relief, but Ruby, the bartender, was eyeing her suspiciously.

"You should've been here half an hour ago."

"I had a thing," Valerie replied. "I'm here now. Where's Janet?"

"Out. Count yourself lucky."

"Thank God," Valerie replied. She quickly crossed to the back of the bar and donned a fresh serving apron. There were several customers in the tavern to wait on, but at the moment, every one of them was gathered at the front windows or wandering out the front door.

"Is that a real Guardian?"

"Wow, what a classic."

"Is that a Bear Claw emblem on the grill?"

"No way that's the real thing."

Valerie did her best to focus on her job but couldn't help but be distracted by their conversations.

"Whose car is it?"

"Think it's seen actual battle?"

A half hour later, Janet walked through the front door. She made straight for the bar.

"Ruby, why on earth is there a war car parked in front of my tavern?"

Ruby finished setting a cocktail on the tray Valerie was waiting to serve and smirked. "I don't know. You'll have to ask the new girl."

Janet turned and stared at Valerie. "This is your doing?"

"Sorry. I didn't have anywhere else to park it." She tried to look repentant.

Janet wandered over to the window and pulled back the curtain to get a better view. A crowd had gathered around the car. The din of their conversation carried from outside. Janet surveyed the street. "Ruby, how many of these people have come in and bought drinks?"

"I don't know," Ruby replied. "Maybe a dozen. It's attracting a lot of attention."

Janet pursed her lips and nodded. "Okay, then." She turned to Valerie. "You can leave it there." She admired the growing crowd again. "Maybe next time wash it first. If we're sponsoring a car show, we might as well do it right."

Valerie smiled. "Yes, ma'am."

The rest of her shift was a blur. Word spread quickly that there was a Guardian 770 parked on Cannery Lane. Business was non-stop, and she was kept hopping all night with new customers. When the steeple clock on Lexington struck eleven, Valerie caught it over the noise of customers. She balled up her apron and stuffed if behind the bar.

"Where are you going?" Janet asked. "We're still busy. I was planning to keep the doors open another hour if this keeps up."

"I'm sorry," Valerie replied. "I have to go. And I have to take the car."

Janet threw up her hands in exasperation. "Now?"

"There's somewhere I have to be."

"You'd better have a damned good reason," Janet replied. "We haven't had a weeknight like this in ages."

"I'll start early tomorrow. I promise."

She fished her keys from her pocket and made her way back outside. The crowd around the car had dispersed, but there were still a few people lingering around it.

"Must be part of the exhibitions," one man said. "Can't imagine which fighter though. Maybe House Agnor? I heard Gunnar Ragnarsson was competing this year. It could be his steed."

"Excuse me, gentlemen," Valerie said as she elbowed her way past. She unlocked the door and slid into the driver's seat. She tried not to laugh as their mouths fell open, but she relished the stares as she drove away.

When she pulled around to Lexington Avenue, she found the warehouse door up and the lights on.

Damon was standing in the doorway with a sheathed sword in his hand.

She idled in front of the garage, but he stepped aside and waved her onward. She drove into the warehouse and cut the engine.

"You weren't lying," he said as she climbed out of the car.

Valerie smirked. "My father used to say, 'You should never lie about beautiful cars or beautiful women. Because words can never do either justice.'"

"A wise man," Damon replied, examining the fresh scratches on the fender armor. "And apparently he also taught you how to drive it."

"He taught me enough. Are you ready to talk about our deal?"

Damon's eyes roamed over the interior appreciatively. "Full-authority traction controls. Seven-piece armament dashboard. This thing had the works." He walked around the front of the car and paused at the grill to rub a bit of dirt off the bear claw emblem. "I saw your father fight once. When I was just a lancer assisting a knight named Sir Gwalin in a tournament at Meers. Your father defeated him in twenty seconds. It was the most perfect exhibition of sword form I'd ever seen. One of the reasons I dreamed of becoming a swordsman."

Valerie ran a hand down the line of the fender. "He did that for a lot of people."

"You must have learned from him. The forms."

"Sure. Only every day. For hours." She ran a hand through her hair. "Henry and I both did. We always tried to follow along, but he was better at it than me. Henry was a natural."

"What was your father like as a teacher?"

Valerie exhaled and leaned against the car. "I don't know, relentless? He liked to pit me against my brother all the time. I was Henry's first victim."

"You must have dueled a lot."

"Pretty much every day till Dad disappeared."

"How often did you win?" Damon asked.

"Not once," Valerie said. She kicked a bit of dirt off one of her boots. "My father didn't train me the same way he did Henry. Henry got to concentrate on dueling. My dad always had me doing stupid things. Standing on one leg for an hour, balancing on beams. Practicing cuts a thousand times in a row. He said we all have our own way of training."

Damon was no longer looking at the car but at her. She hadn't noticed the color of his eyes before. They were a steel gray that seemed to pierce straight through her. She felt naked.

"So, what about our deal?" She moved around the far side of the Guardian. "You said we needed a war car. I brought you one."

"Why do you want to do this?" Damon asked.

"I told you," Valerie replied. "I need to get in front of the king. He's the only one who can help me restore my name and get justice for my brother."

"And you're willing to give up your father's car to do it?"

"My father would have wanted justice."

Damon walked toward her. As he got closer, he began rolling up the sleeves on his shirt, exposing his forearms. He held one up to her. "Do you see this scar? You want to take a guess why I got it?"

She studied the line of white in his otherwise olive skin. "You lost a fight?"

"I did. Why do you think that happened?"

"The other guy was better?"

Damon shook his head. "No. He wasn't better. But I got careless. You know why?"

Valerie shrugged.

"Because I didn't *care*," Damon said. He pointed to the other forearm and other scars. "Didn't care. Didn't care." He pushed his sleeve up past his bicep. "Really didn't care on this one."

"What are you trying to say? That you aren't a very good fighter?"

"No. I'm an excellent fighter," Damon replied. "In fact, I've never lost a fight I truly cared about. Problem is, I get hired by a lot of cowardly people. People who don't want to fight their own battles. And people who frankly don't deserve to win."

Valerie narrowed her eyes. "Is this the part where I'm supposed to make you care about my fight? You need me to tell you how noble it is and all the reasons why Jasper Sterling is a bastard? Because that could take all night."

Damon rolled his sleeves back down. He walked over to the cabinet where he had set the sword and picked it back up by its scabbard. "What I'm saying is that you came here looking for a fighter. Someone who will win this battle of yours and give you justice. I think you've found what you're looking for."

Valerie exhaled. "So you'll do it."

"Is that what you heard?" Damon said. "You want the fighter who will do anything to win." He lifted the sword, then threw it to her. She caught it two-handed. "I've got news for you. Nobody in the world cares about this fight as much as you. You want justice? Then the only qualified person for the job is you."

13

FIGHTER

"Are you crazy? I'm not a tournament fighter," Valerie said. Damon crossed the warehouse to a set of cabinets and began fiddling with a combination lock. "You just got through telling me that you dueled nearly every day of your childhood."

"If you were listening, you would have caught the part where I mentioned I lost every duel I ever fought."

"That's the part that's most encouraging," Damon said. "Failure is a far better teacher than success." He got the cabinet unlocked and swung the doors open, revealing a rack of weapons. "The fact that you spent your entire childhood losing to someone bigger and faster and stronger than you is possibly your greatest asset."

"You're telling me that being smaller and weaker is helpful?" Valerie scoffed.

"No. But it's an opportunity to think outside the box," Damon replied. He fished a broadsword out of the cabinet, thought better of it, then put it back. "You know the story of the siege of Lincoln?"

"Everyone does. It was the birth of the war car."

"What you may *not* know is that its inventor, Holbrook, had been failing at creating his imagined war machine for a decade.

Everyone thought he was insane and, from all accounts, he likely was. It was only when the French laid siege to the city and everyone was starving to death that his people fully committed to building his vision. When the drawbridge came down and that crazy machine rolled out, it changed history. They routed the French forces that day and on every battlefield for the rest of the war. Horses went to pasture, and the age of the war car was born. So that's what they put in the history books. Holbrook, the genius."

"So I'm supposed to get out in the arena and invent an entirely new method of warfare that revolutionizes history? Sure. Why didn't I think of that."

Damon donned a pair of padded gloves and took a couple of longswords from the cabinet, then pointed her toward a practice area he had set up. "Come over here. I want to see something."

Valerie eyed the various sparring rigs and training equipment. "I'm telling you, I'm not the fighter."

"Humor me," Damon said. He led her to a starting position on the mat. "Show me a sword form you're good at."

Valerie tightened her grip on the sword and thought about the hours of forms she had done as a child. She positioned her feet, then stepped into *Rising River*. She brought the blade up with flourish as she moved forward, once, twice, then ending with the blade crossed above her head.

"Good. Show me another."

Valerie stepped back and centered herself. She focused on her sword and stepped into *Burning Sky*. The series of lateral cuts again ended with her sword held over her head.

Damon lifted his own sword and brought it down gently to hers, resting it on her blade as she held the position.

"And now what can you see from this position?"

She was staring at his muscled chest. "You work out a lot?"

Damon canted his head. "You see a target."

"Right. That too." She exited the form, retreating to get out of range.

"Your clearing cuts could use work, but you move efficiently. That's good. Your enemies will underestimate you based on your size," Damon said. "And they're right to. You don't have the physical strength to compete with some of the monsters that will be in that arena. But you have other skills. Speed will be one of them."

"I've only ever done these forms slowly."

"Because making a correct move slowly is better than making the wrong move quickly. It's no use getting faster till you're doing it right. It's clear you have the muscle memory. It's just a matter of waking it up."

Valerie sighed. "You're barking up the wrong tree. I'm telling you. My brother was the fighter."

"Would he have fought for you?"

"Any day."

Damon cocked an eyebrow. "So what are you willing to do for him?"

Valerie scowled, but his expression was unmerciful.

She swung. Damon blocked the cut but was forced to take half a step back.

"Okay," he said. "Now we're getting somewhere." He lowered his sword and put it back into the cabinet. "If you were to ask me what I see here, it's someone who already has the raw skills needed to win."

"I've never won a fight."

"But you've lost a lot of them well. I say that's better. Take the night to think it over. If you still want to put a tournament run together, I'll be here. If you're serious, I'll train you every day until the tournament starts. But I won't fight your battle for you. That's the way of cowards. And if there's one thing I can say about you, you aren't a coward."

"You barely know me," Valerie replied.

"I've seen what I need to see," Damon replied. "Take that as another point in your favor."

Valerie handed him her sword. "What about the car?"

"I'll keep it here. If you win, that'll be my payment for training you."

"You want the car? If I lose, I won't have a way to pay you."

Damon closed the cabinet. "Then I'd better do a good job."

Valerie narrowed her eyes. "What makes you so confident?"

"Listen, if you lose, I'm no worse off. But I know a thing or two about fighting for what you believe in. Give it some thought. If you decide it's not for you, you can always climb into your car tomorrow and drive home. Maybe you'll find some other way to get justice. It's your choice."

Valerie walked back to the Guardian and pulled the keys from the ignition. "Tomorrow."

Damon crossed his arms. "I'll be here."

Valerie stared at the ceiling of the tavern supply closet for a long time. Despite her exhaustion, sleep was elusive. Her mind kept returning to the scene of Henry's murder.

Henry clutching his wounded shoulder but waving off her help.

The leering smile on Jasper's face just before he ran his sword through Henry's chest.

She hadn't acted.

She should've stopped him.

Henry stared up from her lap, his life leaking into her hands. How many seconds had ticked by since his death, and she still had done nothing to avenge him.

When she finally drifted off to sleep, Valerie dreamed the entire city was slick with blood. Her hands were covered in it. But this time it was hers.

In the morning, Valerie was awake before anyone else in the tavern had stirred. She rolled off the cot and walked to the hallway window that looked into the street. Fog blanketed the wharf. The fishermen were already gone, searching for their morning catch. The docks stood deserted and gray.

At the edge of the village, the stone walls of the city stretched up into the fog, an impenetrable barrier between her and her goals.

Her optimism of the day before had vanished with the sun.

Even the tavern seemed desolate. Overturned chairs sat atop tables. The curtains covering the tiny stage hung limp and static. Not so much as a clock moved inside. In the early morning light, this place looked like what it was—just a pitiful, run-down bar. A pitstop for lives going nowhere.

She pushed her palms into her eyes to wipe away the sleep. What had she been thinking? Sponsor a tournament team? Fight in the arena? It was delusional.

She took a step back from the window, and her foot landed in something sticky on the floor. She hoped it was merely residue from someone's spilled drink the night before, but it felt as though this place was grabbing hold of her. A fly caught in a glue trap.

She had the sudden urge to run. She wanted out.

The morning is for new plans.

She moved into the hallway that bisected the tavern and the neighboring restaurant and made it to the pay phone that hung on the wall.

She dropped her coins in and hesitated only a moment before dialing the number.

The phone rang three times, then someone picked up.

"Terravecchia Manor, how may I assist you?" The voice was familiar. Comforting.

"Eugenia? It's Valerie."

"Miss Valerie? Oh my goodness, we've been so worried. Are you okay?"

Valerie felt the rush of homesickness hit her like a wave. Eugenia had always answered when she needed her. "I'm all right. Is Charlotte there?"

"Her ladyship isn't here. She's down in the city with Lord Sterling."

"I figured as much."

"But she gave me a number to give you if you called. She said to contact her right away. Let me fetch the number. . . Okay. Here it is."

Valerie recited the number back to her as she read it.

"And Miss Valerie, I want you to know we are all just torn up about Mister Henry. We never could have imagined such a thing. Is it true, what they're saying?"

"He's gone," Valerie said.

"But . . . is it true you two attacked his lordship?"

"No. Jasper murdered Henry, Eugenia. While he was unarmed. I tried to . . . It doesn't matter what I did. Henry is gone."

The long silence on the other end of the phone was followed by swelling sobs. "I knew they weren't telling it straight. I knew it. I saw Henry come up since he could barely walk. He's always been a good boy." The sobbing on the other end of the phone grew worse.

"I'll make it right, Eugenia," Valerie said. "I promise." When the crying on the other end of the line didn't abate, she gently hung up the phone.

She stared at the receiver in its cradle for several long seconds, then picked it up again. She dialed the number Eugenia had given her.

A stranger's voice picked up. "Sterling Tower, how may I direct your call?"

"This is Valerie Terravecchia, calling for Lady Charlotte Terravecchia."

There were whispers between persons on the other end, then the voice came back on. "I'll connect you right away, miss."

The phone didn't even have time to ring before someone picked up.

"Valerie? Valerie, is that you?"

"It's me, Lady Charlotte."

"Oh my God, we've been looking everywhere for you. Where

are you? I've been calling the manor constantly. No one has heard a word."

"Why are you still at Sterling Tower?" Valerie asked. "Jasper killed Henry."

"I heard about what happened," Charlotte said. "It's all just so awful. If you had told me you were coming to the city, we could have resolved all of it easily. For Henry to attack Jasper in the street like that. We're all so shocked."

"He didn't attack him," Valerie argued. "It was a duel to first blood. Jasper murdered him after it was already over."

Charlotte sucked in a breath. "But Valerie, there were witnesses. They all confirmed it. I know it must have all been a shock as it happened, but Jasper never wanted to hurt your brother. He told me so. We just want you to come home so this can all be explained. Where are you?"

"There's no *explaining* what he did. You need to get out of there. I'm telling you, Jasper Sterling is a killer."

"Now please, Valerie, don't say that. This will be okay. I know you're probably scared. Just tell me where you are. I'll come to you and we can talk. I want to see you. They told me what that insane magistrate did to you—how he revoked your title. We're working on getting that fixed right away. Just let me see you, we'll talk about everything and sort it all out."

"Charlotte, Jasper's not who you think he is. If you ever cared for me, for my father, for Henry, you have to believe me."

"You know I cared for—"

"Then listen to the truth!"

Charlotte didn't reply for several moments, then finally whispered into the phone. "I want to believe you, Valerie. Just tell me where to find you."

Valerie chewed her lip as she stared out the window.

If Charlotte could see what Jasper was, she could go home. They could seek justice from there. Once she got her title back, she could at least make an appeal to the king. A letter. Charlotte could sign it too.

She'd be a noble again. Once she made her case known, she could enlist more nobles to help. Maybe Thea's family would come to their side. She wouldn't need to fight the Sterlings alone.

"Just tell me where you are," Charlotte insisted. "I'll come to you."

Valerie twisted the phone cord in her hands. "Just you, okay?"

"Just me. I promise."

"I'm outside the walls. In a waterside village called Tidewater." She glanced around the dingy bar. "I'm at the . . ." A doubt nagged her. She glanced out the window to an inn across the street with a broad porch dotted with rocking chairs. "At the Swan and Pelican. It's an Inn."

"Just stay right there. Don't go anywhere. I'll be there as fast as I can."

"Okay." Valerie slowly hung up the phone.

Charlotte wasn't the ally she wanted, but she was technically family. If she believed her.

She went back to the storeroom where she had left her few possessions. She splashed herself with water from the utility sink, toweled off with a clean dish rag, and snatched up the keys to the Guardian. She studied them. Damon would be waiting for her answer, but he must have known she couldn't go through with his crazy plan, didn't he? Her? Fight in the tournament?

She just needed to be out of this place. Looking around the room, part of her couldn't believe she had ever sunk this low. Sleeping on a cot in a tavern? She eyed her bruises in the mirror. This wasn't what she deserved.

She gathered up the handful of money she had made the day before and considered what to do with it. She could leave it for Janet. Payment for her hospitality?

But she could always send a courier from home to repay Janet for the odds and ends she had used. She would send a gift. Something nice. She stuffed the money into her pocket.

She was twisting the lock on the front door of the tavern when the voice spoke.

"Leaving without saying goodbye?" Janet was standing on the lowest step of the staircase that led up to her apartment.

"I was . . . I was going to send a courier," Valerie replied. "To let you know where I went."

"Fancy," Janet said. "I take it you found a way out."

"I'm going home," Valerie said. "I'll have more options there. I guess you were right. I'm not the best bet for employment longevity."

"It's a pity. I think the patrons liked you. You okay? You have someone looking out for you?"

"I'm meeting my stepmother across the street."

Janet nodded. "All right then."

"I promise I'll send something to pay you back for your hospitality," Valerie said. "Once I get home I can —"

Janet waved a hand to dismiss it. "Don't worry about it." She crossed the tavern and lifted the gate on the bar. When she reached the cash register, she pulled out her key and unlocked it. "You'll want your pay."

"I'm okay," Valerie said. "I got some tips from tables last night." She glanced out the door to the inn across the street. "I should get going."

"Nonsense," Janet replied. "A day's work gets a day's pay. I know my clientele are stingy bastards when it comes to tipping." She counted out several bills onto the bar top. When she was satisfied, she evened the edges and held them out. "What's fair is fair."

Valerie frowned but shuffled her way across the tavern. "You don't have to pay me. After all, you've put me up for two nights. I should repay you."

"Then let me be generous," Janet said. "A thank you from you is plenty."

Valerie took the bills. "Thank you."

"Good luck, kid."

Valerie nodded and moved back to the door. Janet began tidying up and prepping for her day, her focus already on the next task.

Valerie wanted to say something more, but the words wouldn't come. She slipped out the door and closed it behind her.

It was a hundred paces to the porch of the Swan and Pelican. She made it exactly three feet.

A trio of armored war cars roared down the street in formation. Another pair were only blocks behind. The first group skidded to a stop in front of the inn, and a half dozen armored soldiers poured out. They took up positions around the cars, scanning the inn's exits.

Valerie backed into the shadow of the Twisted Tentacle's doorway as the next pair of cars raced in. They pulled up to the Swan and Pelican and dispersed a contingent of soldiers bearing the green and silver emblems of the City Watch.

"Spread out. Find her," the captain ordered.

The soldiers advanced on the inn with weapons drawn.

Valerie fumbled for the door handle of the Twisted Tentacle and scrambled back inside. Just before she got the door shut, she caught the captain looking her way.

Damn.

"That was quick," Janet said. She moved to the window and took in the scene outside.

To Valerie's horror, the captain of the watch was still studying the tavern. He signaled to one of the soldiers and sent him their way.

"Get in the back," Janet said. "Lock the door."

Valerie rushed into the storeroom. The lock on the door looked flimsy and useless, but she slid it closed.

The pounding on the front door made her heart leap into her mouth.

"Hang on! Don't knock my damn door down," Janet shouted.

Valerie pressed her ear to the crack to listen.

A soldier's heavy boots thudded across the main room. "We're looking for a girl."

"Aren't we all," Janet replied.

"It's no laughing matter. Lord Sterling was attacked by a fugitive runaway, formerly of the house of Terravecchia. She isn't in her right mind, and we've been charged with bringing her in for her safety."

"Five war cars for one girl?" Janet said. "Seems excessive."

"Just take a look at the picture," the voice said.

"Sounds like an interesting case," Janet replied. "Is there a reward?"

"You'll have to make arrangements with his lordship. You seen this face?"

Valerie's nails dug into the wood of the door as she waited for Janet's response.

"No one as fancy as that ever comes into this place."

The soldier grunted. "I'll have a look around."

"Suit yourself."

The footsteps grew fainter, then increased in volume again as the man made his way around the tavern. The boots began to thud down the hallway toward the storeroom.

"What's back here?"

"Just supplies."

"Show me," the man said.

"I'll find the keys."

Valerie searched the space, desperate for a place to hide, but there was nothing. A few shelves, a bathroom so small you could barely get the door closed. Even if she crawled under the cot, too much of her would be exposed. The cot was still out. Was that a giveaway? She rapidly collapsed it and pushed it against the wall.

"This lock always gives me trouble," Janet said.

It was clear that she was attempting to buy Valerie time, but for what? There was nowhere to hide.

Finally, the lock turned and the door eased open. Valerie leapt behind it, pressing herself to the wall. Janet stepped all the way through and stood near the door handle, her back to Valerie. Valerie slouched as low as possible in case the soldier somehow peered over Janet's shoulder and spotted her cowering behind the door.

But the soldier didn't make Janet move.

"Need any toilet paper?" Janet offered, gesturing to the shelves.

The soldier simply grunted again and ducked back through the doorway. "If you see anything suspicious, call the Watch. This girl is considered dangerous to herself and to others. Her family is eager to get her back."

"I'm sure they are," Janet replied. "Mind if I have one of those pictures? I can hang it up in the bar." She shut the storage room door and locked it again.

Valerie slumped to the floor.

A few minutes later, the door opened again. Valerie scrambled back to her feet, but it was just Janet this time.

She held up the photo. "You ever see this girl? Apparently, she's quite the troublemaker."

Valerie recognized the image as a headshot from a middle-school formal. It wasn't even a good photo. Her younger self was grinning at the camera from behind far too much makeup with a bow on her head that she had instantly regretted.

Janet handed the photo over. "The good news is, I just had a server quit on me this morning. There's a job opening if you're looking. Doors open at eleven."

Valerie stuffed the photo into her pocket, determined to destroy the evidence of its existence. "Thanks. I'll be here. I just have one more person I need to talk to first."

An hour later, she walked onto Lexington Avenue with the hood of her sweatshirt up to hide her face. She rapped on the door of the warehouse until it finally swung open.

Damon stood in the doorway in a damp tank top and workout shorts. He was holding a weighted practice sword. His muscles gleamed with sweat, and he was out of breath.

Valerie noted the workout equipment behind him, then let her eyes come back to his.

"When can I start?"

Damon's mouth quirked into a smile, then he took a step back and gestured her inside.

14

PENTHOUSE

"I'll ask you the question again, but this time there are only three acceptable answers," Jasper said. "She's either dead, admitted to St. Anselm's, or you have her tied up in the trunk of your car waiting to be brought in. Which of the three is it?"

The captain of the City Watch shifted his feet on the foyer rug and adjusted his grip on the helmet he held in his hands. "I'm afraid we were unable to find her, my lord. Locating fugitives can be difficult outside the walls. The seaside villagers tend to not cooperate."

Jasper turned to Blaise, who was lounging on the couch in the penthouse's living room. "How much of a problem can this girl present for us?"

"A minimal inconvenience," Blaise replied. "We've made certain any noble families she might reach out to will notify us at once. She's cut off financially, and thanks to that incompetent magistrate, she doesn't even have her name to fall back on. If she's hiding out on the waterfront working street corners for food, it does you no harm. Let her become a fishwife and be done with her."

"Perhaps if we offered a reward," the Watch captain said.

"Those folks down there do get desperate. Someone might turn her in."

"Spend more of my money to get someone else to do your job?" Jasper scoffed. "If you want to shirk your responsibility, then *you* pay the reward. Get out of here before I find someone else even more useless to fill your post."

The captain bowed sheepishly and backed out the door, closing it behind him.

"It wasn't a bad idea," Blaise said once the man was gone. "A reward could be effective."

"If you'd sold the Terravecchia properties for the prices I suggested, perhaps we would have had the funds to spare. As it is, we're already running out of money." Jasper walked to the bar and began fixing himself a drink.

"You said you wanted cash fast," Blaise said, extracting a lighter from his pocket and reigniting his cigar. "That doesn't equate to top dollar. And your expenses have been coming in faster than I can make deals. I hope you don't intend to buy off all your competitors. You'll be bankrupt by the start of the tournament."

Jasper added an extra shot of gin to his drink, then walked to the windows that overlooked the bay. "Most of the competitors will be of little consequence. I only need to worry about the ones who will survive the auto melee."

"If the king discovers you've bought your way through the tournament, he'll be offering you a position in his dungeons instead of the Round Table. You'll have a lot of people to keep quiet."

"Everyone who makes this deal will have as much to lose as I do. And we've already established the solution for the ones unwilling to bargain." Jasper took a sip of his drink.

Blaise blew out a cloud of smoke. "Yes, Lady Magdalena was a bit of a square when it came to the rules." He pushed himself off the couch. As he did so, the front door opened, and Lady

Charlotte entered the penthouse wearing one of the dozen dresses she had acquired since arriving in the city.

Jasper took a deep breath and affixed a smile to his face. "My darling. You're back early."

"I was worried. Were you able to find her? Did you find Valerie?" Charlotte dropped her bag on the bureau near the door and rushed into the living room. Jasper met her halfway and grasped her hands.

"They're still looking. It seems she wasn't where she said she was. I'm afraid it's just another lie she's told you."

"I should have gone myself," Charlotte said. "I knew I should have."

"My love, it's too dangerous for you outside the walls. Our engagement is the talk of the city, and you are much too high profile. It would be as if the queen or one of the princesses were to be seen at the docks. There would be too many dangerous people hoping to harm you or hold you for ransom. These bottom-dwellers can't be trusted."

"I know, I know." Charlotte wrung her hands. "But Valerie is just a girl. I know she's been in trouble, but she's not even eighteen. How will she survive down there?"

"We'll keep searching," Jasper said, moving closer and embracing her. "If she wants to be helped, she knows how. All she has to do is find the nearest city watchman, and they'll bring her straight to us."

"This whole business is just so awful," Charlotte replied. "I did my best to raise them, you know. They had the finest schooling . . ."

"There are some things out of the control of even the best parents," Blaise interjected. He flicked the ash from his cigar into an ashtray on the end table. "Lady Charlotte, you are doing what's best for Valerie now. I'm sure she'll come to her senses soon."

"Why don't you focus on the wedding plans," Jasper said.

"That will help keep your mind off it. There's nothing to bring a family together like a wedding."

Charlotte fidgeted with the ring on her finger. "Yes, I suppose so."

"And join me in a drink," Jasper added. "We have much to celebrate. I have it on good authority that the guest list has tripled since last you checked it." He guided her to the bar and began fixing her a cocktail.

"Is the Royal Family coming?" Charlotte asked.

"Rumors abound," Jasper said. "You know they won't be able to commit just yet, but when the king spends time with you at his tournament, he'll no doubt want to extend his visit till the wedding."

"Extend? I thought you wanted to be married prior to the tournament?"

"That seems ill-advised now," Jasper said.

"On account of how many families will be busy with preparations," Blaise added.

"And after the tournament is over, we will have even more to celebrate." Jasper handed her a drink. "Especially when I win."

"I don't know why anyone even needs to compete in these silly tournaments," Charlotte said. "The king should simply choose the best man for the job. What good is it having everyone bashing each other with cars and swords when the country is at peace? We ought to just skip all that."

"The king loves tradition," Blaise said.

"And you must enjoy the pageantry of the games," Jasper said. "Not to mention the masquerade ball."

"Well, everyone loves a ball," Charlotte said.

"Can't very well have a tournament ball without a tournament." Blaise puffed on his cigar as if it settled the matter.

"Do you have a gown for the ball yet?" Jasper laid a hand on her shoulder. "Perhaps that should be in your plans today?"

"Yes, I suppose I should start looking." Charlotte took a sip from the cocktail. "It's just so much to handle all at once."

"We'll get through it together." Jasper raised his glass. "To our new life."

Charlotte clinked her glass against his and took another drink. "This is delicious. You do know how to make a good gimlet." Her shoulders relaxed. "This is helpful. I suppose I really should be working on our plans. Valerie will be okay, won't she?"

"She will be. All she has to do is call."

Charlotte nodded. "We're still on for dinner tonight, aren't we? You promised to take me to that VIP club you like."

"Anything you desire, my dearest," Jasper said.

Charlotte smiled and kissed him, then carried her drink toward the bedroom. "I'd best think about what to wear for that too. So many social engagements in this city. I don't know how I'm supposed to keep up." She vanished around the corner, and a few moments later, the music from the stereo turned on.

"You want me to keep your usual girls off the list at the clubs tonight?" Blaise asked.

"No need. A few more drinks and I doubt she'll be conscious past nine," Jasper said. He picked up his glass. "Perks of dating the geriatric."

Blaise glanced toward the bedroom hallway. "You do realize that if things don't go your way at the tournament, you may actually end up married."

Jasper finished off his drink. "Good thing your job is to make sure it does go my way."

Blaise rose from his chair, and the two men walked onto the balcony together. A container ship was steaming into the port. Blaise puffed his cigar and nodded toward the ship. "And it's a good thing I always deliver."

15

TRAIN

The deserted shoreline didn't look like much, just a thin stretch of coarse sand, tide pools, and a few large rocks covered with sunbathing sea lions. The giant, fleshy animals also occupied an old fishing pier that jutted into the surf about thirty yards.

Damon was standing near a tide pool with a canvas sack over his shoulder. He tossed it to the sand. "Good morning."

Over the last few days, Valerie had spent every non-working hour drilling on footwork and pell exercises, but this was something new.

"What are we doing down here?" she asked.

"It's time to start your specialized training." Damon opened the sack and let Valerie have a look.

She peered into the bag and discovered that it held a suit of dueling armor. She pulled out a breastplate and gauntlets as well as a gorget and helmet. The armor wasn't steel but some manner of lesser alloy. There were multiple welded repairs to the breastplate. It was rusted in places, and the attachment straps were brittle and cracked, but it looked as though it would fit her.

"Where did you get this?" Valerie asked.

"Did a bit of bartering at the smiths' market. I think the

armorer would have been happy to unload it for free any other time of the year. But the tournament on the horizon must have sent him scouring the attic for whatever bits of old junk he could sell. Made it sound as though it was his prized possession now."

"I hope you didn't trade anything too dear."

"I'll survive," Damon said. "Put it on. Let's see how you move in it."

Valerie put on the equipment and did her best to get the straps secure. Damon helped in places that were difficult to cinch. When she was done, she donned the helm. "Now what?"

Damon flipped the visor of her helmet down. "Now you run."

"What?"

He pointed down the narrow beach to a ruined lighthouse that sat atop the cliff. "Up to the lighthouse and back. I'll be timing you." He judged the distance. "I think you should be back here inside of . . . five minutes." He checked his watch.

Valerie gauged the distance over the uneven sand and rocks. "There's no way I can make it all the way up there and back by—"

"Clock's already started," Damon said.

Valerie cursed and turned, adjusting the balance of her helmet and breaking into a run.

The first few steps weren't terrible. Then she had to breathe.

The visor partially obscured her vision as well as her breathing, especially when she lowered her head to see her feet. She started along the water's edge where the sand was hard-packed, but when the first wave caught her ankles, she shifted directions and moved to the dry sand.

That was a mistake.

She stumbled through the loose sand and fell, crashing to the ground face first. Grit and shell permeated the visor, and she found herself spitting out tiny granules. She couldn't rid herself of them while still wearing the helmet, but she didn't have time to take it off. She climbed back to her feet and kept running.

After what felt like forever, she reached the lighthouse and turned to locate Damon. He was out on the fishing pier staring at the water.

She scrambled back down the rocks to the firm sand, well aware that she was never making it back on time. She ran anyway, keeping a steady pace that at least allowed her to stay upright the entire way back.

When she reached the base of the pier, she looked down the length of it to where Damon was standing and wondered if she was supposed to run all the way out to the end.

The pier was still dotted with sea lions, but somehow, Damon had managed to get past them. A heavy bull barked at her the moment she set foot on the wooden planks.

"How did you get out there?" she shouted.

Damon turned to watch her progress. "Just ignore them. Show them who's boss."

Valerie took a few cautious steps.

A female sea lion slid off the pier and into the water, but the big bull was standing his ground.

"I don't think this is a great idea," Valerie said. "Shouldn't we just let them have it?"

When Damon didn't reply, she cursed under her breath. If this was some kind of test, she was failing.

"Come on, Val. Get it together," she muttered. She took a few more deliberate steps, angling toward the narrow route around the big bull, not looking him in the eye.

The sea lion continued to bark and bluster, but as the females abandoned the pier one after another, the bull finally eased himself toward the water too. With one last, angry bark, he launched himself from the pier and splashed into the surf.

"Thank God," Valerie muttered. She worked her way to the far end of the pier and finally joined Damon.

He consulted his watch. "Ten minutes."

"I didn't know you were counting the sea lion part. I thought it was just the running."

"The knight I learned from used to call this terrain training," Damon replied. "Getting used to operating in all manner of environments in your armor. It's important to problem solve."

"Terrain training," Valerie repeated. "Okay. What's next?"

"Glad you asked." Damon shifted to the side and revealed a heavy-looking rock sitting on the railing. He scooped the rock up with both hands and held it out to Valerie. "I need you to carry this back to shore."

"Um. Okay," Valerie replied, cradling her arms and accepting it. It weighed around twenty pounds. Awkward but manageable. She took a step toward the beach.

"Uh-uh," Damon said. "You need to go this way."

He shoved her with both hands, sending her crashing through the flimsy wooden railing.

Valerie screamed.

Gray, overcast sky filled her vision—then she hit the water.

Saltwater.

Cold.

Up her nose.

Down her throat.

She immediately dropped the stone, coughed once, flailed wildly for a fleeting second above the surface, then sank.

A wave rolled her over, sending her end over end.

Bubbles raced from the crevices in her armor, rippling past her in the semi-darkness.

Valerie fought to swim but her feet touched sand.

Her mind raced. Panic made her freeze. What was she supposed to do?

The current wrenched at her, threatening to turn her over again. She flattened out on the seafloor and dug her fingers in, fighting for equilibrium.

She was at least eight feet below the surface. She got her legs under her and leapt, trying to swim. An air bubble escaped her mouth in her panic, erupting through the eye holes of her visor in its rush to the surface. She stretched and kicked, but her feet bumped sand again. The light remained impossibly far above her.

The current toppled her, and she bumped across shell and coral.

It was so dark. Which way was shore?

The helmet restricted her vision, and she fought to get it off.

Her armor was too tightly cinched. She struggled to escape it, but she could barely see, let alone find the latches.

Her lungs ached.

Where was Damon?

Was he trying to murder her?

She wanted to shout. To scream for help. Only bubbles escaped her mouth. Saltwater trickled down her throat.

Every movement she made was depriving her of oxygen.

Her stomach clenched as she concentrated on holding her breath.

She caught the vague outline of the pier pilings through the water and crawled toward them. It was agonizingly slow.

One yard. Two.

Her lungs were on fire.

The current fought her every movement.

Her head throbbing, she stretched for the algae-covered piling. Barnacles and oysters clung to the wood. She wrapped her gloved fingers around the pole and pulled. Her foot found a patch of oyster to step on. Then another. She climbed for the surface.

Almost to the light.

The oysters gave way. Her hands slipped.

A wave crashed through the pier and slammed her into the adjacent piling. All the remaining air in her lungs vanished in the impact.

No.

She was so close.

Her eyes were wide, but all around her there was nothing but turmoil. Fish darting, frantic bubbles, and blackness. It was closing in on her.

Her chest spasmed.

So this was what dying felt like. Sudden. Painful.

She couldn't hold her breath a moment longer. She gulped desperately at nothing, her lips pressed tight. Then she let out a last, gurgling scream.

The blackness closed in.

Her head broke the surface amid a torrent of seawater. She gasped and sputtered as she caught great mouthfuls of air and spray alike. She was being hauled forward, a hand on the straps of her breastplate. She was heaved upward and sent sprawling to the shell-crusted shore. Another wave crashed over her and sent a chill through her. She retched shells and seawater into the inside of her faceplate, not caring that she was splashing herself with her own spit. Her body shivered and she rolled over.

A shadow passed overhead, and she looked up to find Damon staring down at her.

"Where's my rock?"

Her anger swelled, and she fought with her visor, jerking it back and forth and finally wrenching the entire helmet from her head.

"Are you insane? You almost killed me!" She coughed more seawater as she scrambled to her feet, pushing away the hand he offered to help her up. She pressed both palms against his chest and shoved. "You're not a coach, you're a psychopath!"

"That's about what I expected you to say," Damon replied. He brushed a bit of sand from his lips.

"That's what anyone would say! You're mental."

"You're welcome," he said.

"I'm welcome?" Valerie sputtered. "For you trying to murder me?"

"For saving you."

"Screw you. You don't get credit for saving someone when you're the reason they almost died."

"Don't I? Who should get credit then? Certainly not you. You sank like a rock and stayed sunk."

"I'm wearing armor! You can't swim in armor! Or didn't they teach you that in psycho school?"

"You can walk."

"What?"

"You can walk," Damon repeated. "In armor. You can climb. You can do a lot of things."

"I was under . . . water," Valerie said, enunciating both words so that they would penetrate his thick head.

"Do it again," Damon said.

"What? No! You're crazy!"

Damon crossed his arms. Valerie stood defiant and stared him down.

Finally, Damon walked away. She exhaled, satisfied that he had bent before her fury. But he was moving to a second bag she hadn't noticed before. He pulled the sack from between two stones and began donning his own suit of rusty armor.

The steel plates were easily twice as thick as the armor she had on. He slowly cinched the pieces to his arms, legs and torso, then donned a heavy, full-faced helmet. Without a word, he turned and walked out to the end of the pier. He never so much as paused when he reached the end. He walked straight off the edge and plummeted into the waves.

"Oh my God," Valerie stammered as Damon disappeared.

She scrambled through the sand and clomped onto the pier, searching the waves. When she reached the end, she darted from side to side but saw no sign of him.

She held her breath.

A bubble erupted from the surface along one side of the pier about a third of the way back to shore. She raced to the railing and peered over the edge. She caught the glint of metal below the surface making slow but steady progress toward the shore.

He was just walking. In another dozen steps, his steel helmet broke the surface. Damon continued with his slow and deliberate pace, striding up and out of the waves, water pouring from the recesses of his armor. He was carrying the rock.

When he reached the sand, he dumped the rock and kept walking.

Valerie raced to catch up.

Damon picked up the empty sack he had used to haul his armor. He pulled his helmet from his head and used the sack to dab at his face. Sand and shell now dotted his hair, but otherwise, he appeared to be barely out of breath.

"You're certifiably insane," Valerie said, watching him strip out of his armor. His soaking-wet shirt clung to his chest.

"I feel great. It's actually quite refreshing."

Valerie wanted to hate him, but she couldn't help but crack a smile. She immediately focused on returning the scowl to her face, but it was too late. Damon had seen.

He pushed his wet hair back from his forehead. "Still think you can't do it?"

Valerie eyed the length of pier again. A few sea lions had wriggled their way back ashore nearby, awaiting her decision. They were clearly ready to reclaim their prized sunning spot.

"It's always easier the second time," Damon said.

"You are the worst sword-fighting teacher I've ever heard of," Valerie said.

Damon pulled off his shirt and began wringing it out with his hands. The scars on his forearms glistened as his muscles clenched—a tapestry of experience that said more than any amount of words. Valerie lost focus. The sight of his bare chest somehow short-circuited her anger. She felt suddenly aware of her own body and how she must look with her hair matted with shell and seaweed.

This was entirely unfair.

Damon merely smiled at her. His piercing eyes were expectant and waiting.

Valerie swore under her breath, then scooped up his dropped rock and headed for the pier.

16

HELTER SKELTER

W hen Valerie arrived at the Twisted Tentacle for the dinner shift, she found a woman sitting at the bar staring at her. She had kind eyes and a playful smile. Her curly black hair was neatly tied back behind her head. As soon as Valerie made it to her station, the woman slid off her stool and approached her. "Hey. I'm Ann. I've heard a lot about you."

Valerie shook the offered hand. "Oh! You're Janet's wife."

"Actually she's *my* wife," Ann corrected.

"Oh, um . . ."

"Just messing with you," Ann laughed. Her smile was infectious. "It's good to finally meet."

"Surprised I haven't seen you around before," Valerie said.

"Been away. Working up in Brighton Bay. I've had an apprenticeship up there."

"Oh yeah? Apprenticing for what?"

"Just a smith," Ann replied, taking a sip of her beer.

"Don't you dare be humble tonight," Janet said, emerging from the kitchen with several bottles of liquor in her hands. "Tonight we celebrate." Janet looked at Valerie. "My beautiful wife has just completed work on her first, soon-to-be-named sword."

Valerie registered the words. "A swordsmith? But that's a noble art. If you've completed a master task, then that means—"

"We just got the word that they're coming here to judge it prior to the opening of the tournament," Janet replied. "Thanks to Ann, you may be looking at the newest Craft Guild family."

"That's incredible," Valerie said.

Ascending from the ranks of the nameless to any other tier of society was always difficult, but becoming a master craftsman took years of training.

"How long have you been working on it?"

"I've been an apprentice twelve years," Ann replied. "Working on this sword for five."

"It's a thing of beauty," Janet added.

"Want to see it?" Ann asked.

"It's here?"

Ann grinned. "Upstairs. Come on, I'll show you."

Valerie looked to Janet and Janet nodded. "Go on. I'll mind your tables for a few minutes. Just seeing her like this is worth it."

Ann picked up her beer and led the way. She unlocked the stairwell door next to the storage room and climbed the steps to Janet's apartment. It was the first time Valerie had seen the top floor of the tavern since the night she had been dragged in from the alley, and it wasn't what she remembered. Somehow, she had imagined Janet disappearing upstairs to a place that more or less matched the tavern—a place of wood and iron, all its rough edges worn down from heavy traffic and overuse—but now that she saw it again, the apartment was different.

The rooms were filled with cozy blankets and warm, autumn colors. It was certainly lived-in but had the look of a place you could settle in with a book and a cup of tea and not be disturbed for hours. In that way, it was nearly the opposite of the tavern.

Ann led her down a short hallway to a bedroom that featured a four-post bed, an overstuffed armchair, and a thick rug. On the bed was a long case. That alone was gorgeous. The rich wood was inlaid with intricate metalwork, and the lock was highly polished. Ann plucked a key from her pocket and inserted it into the lock, twisting it until it clicked.

She opened the box.

The sword was a feast for the eyes. It had a pleasing, tapered shape with hints of deep, iridescent colors in the blade. The hilt was magnificent. A twisted-steel guard set off the handle, which itself had a symmetrically grooved length—a hand-and-a-half of an almost purple wood—before being capped with an elaborate silver pommel.

Ann pulled a pair of gloves from her pocket and donned them, then reached inside the box and extracted the sword. The blade caught the light in its fuller groove, reflecting on the walls as she turned it. She held the sword up so that the edge was toward Valerie. "Look."

It took Valerie a moment to notice what she was signifying, but then she saw the magic of it. The edge of the blade was so sharp that she couldn't see it. Even light found nothing to hold on to. As Valerie stared at the sword in wonder, her eyes could only pick up the wider inner diameter of the blade while the sharpened edge refused to reveal itself.

"That's incredible," Valerie said. "I've never seen anything like it."

"Let's hope the Guild judges feel the same way," Ann replied, gently placing the sword back in its case.

"I had no idea you and Janet were so close to becoming a Guild family," Valerie replied.

"We've been saving and hoping for this chance," Ann said. "With the extra tavern money coming in from tournament visitors added to what we've had in reserve, we'll finally be able to make the move up. It's a dream come true."

"Where will you go? Are you moving away?"

"Hard to say. Still feels like a fantasy, you know? Once I have the certificate in hand and we're a named family, then I guess we'll decide. I'd love to open my own forge somewhere.

I'll make my own line of noble swords if I can find the right spot."

"Sounds amazing," Valerie said.

"I've heard about your quest too," Ann said. "An audience with the Pendragons? Restore your title?"

"It's my only chance to set things right."

"Then you'll do it," Ann said. "You've got the drive. I can see it in you. It's that spark that keeps you going when nothing else will."

Valerie looked down at the sword in the case. "Let's hope my quest doesn't take twelve years."

Ann closed the box with a gentle click. "When you have a good dream, the time to build it doesn't seem so bad."

Valerie knew her own quest could never be construed as good, but she was happy that at least Janet and Ann had a way out.

She followed Ann back downstairs to the bar.

Once Janet saw that the staff had things in order, she and Ann disappeared into the night, no doubt to celebrate somewhere that came with less responsibility.

When her shift ended, Valerie headed out the door of the tavern, expecting to make the walk to Damon's garage, but she was surprised to find him lingering outside, leaning against a beat-up Lark sedan she had seen collecting bird droppings behind the warehouse.

She eyed the car, which was comprised of multi-colored panels pulled from different vehicles, all dappled with primer. "Heading to the car show uptown? Trying to win least improved?"

Damon smiled and opened the door. "Get in. We're going for a ride."

"Will this hold together until we get where we're headed?"

"We'll see," Damon replied.

Valerie walked around and climbed into the passenger side.

The seat was missing much of its upholstery, and the springs were protruding from several points. She did a double take as she reached for the shoulder harness.

"You know your car is missing the back-passenger door?"

Damon started the ignition without explanation. He drove them up the winding streets to the city gate but turned right at the bridge, crossing the bay and heading into the open country. One headlight was loose and variously lit the undersides of tree boughs and passing houses as they drove. A herd of cows they passed looked up and blinked sleepily as the wonky headlight illuminated them.

Valerie didn't know the countryside well enough to recognize where they were headed, but it seemed they weren't the only ones going. After Damon turned onto what ought to have been a lonely dirt road, Valerie was surprised to see a line of taillights. There were rugged-looking trucks, cars, and several motorcycles.

Damon reached across her and opened the glove box. He pulled a lump of purple fabric out and tossed it onto her lap. "Put that on."

Valerie lifted the lump and found it was a ski mask. Damon pulled a similar green mask from his pocket and donned it.

"Are we robbing a bank?" Valerie asked.

Damon rolled down his window as they crept forward. Up ahead, a man in an elaborate, metal mask with welded horns was slowly admitting cars through a gate. When Damon pulled up, the man leaned over and looked inside. His mask had reflective lenses that made it impossible to see his eyes. "Competing or betting?"

"Little of both," Damon said. He canted his head toward Valerie. "She's driving. I'm betting."

The man consulted a clipboard. "You can have round two, spot five. 12:30 start time."

"Got it," Damon said and pulled through the gate.

"What did you just sign me up for?" Valerie asked.

"Practice."

Damon followed the dirt road and line of vehicles until the area opened up into a well-lit clearing. Fuel-powered generators were running electric lights on portable poles. They illuminated a relatively level area that stretched for roughly a mile. Valerie recognized it as a shallow, dried lakebed.

It was also a homemade derby arena.

Vehicles of all shapes and sizes were spaced around the lakebed. Figures moved in and out of the zones of light cast by the pole lamps. All of them were masked.

The lot next to the lake was filled with cars. There were a few models she recognized—Stingrays and Scorpions, Ridge Runners, and a Vulcan or two. But many of the custom builds were like nothing she had ever seen—strange amalgamations of engines and steel that sometimes barely resembled cars. There were mono-cockpit speedsters melded with all-terrain frames. Lifted sand rails bore armor plating and grappling turrets. One beast of a vehicle was made from at least four roadster bodies cut and welded onto a truck chassis.

"Who are these people?" Valerie asked.

"Your competition. Got wind of a melee going down and wanted to have a look. It'll be a good sparring session. We'll get a feel for what you need to work on before the real tournament."

Valerie let her eyes roam over the odd collection of vehicles. "Some of these people are basically driving battering rams. And you've got me competing in a car that doesn't even have all its doors. This seems like a stupid idea."

"You have to learn to deal with these problems sometime. May as well be here where it doesn't count for much."

"Unless I get smashed to bits and die," Valerie said.

"Yeah, well, there's that." Damon reached into the back seat and pulled a pair of hand-held radios from a duffel bag. He pocketed one and put the other in the cup holder. "I'll be talking to you the whole time. I'll keep you advised of what's creeping up on you. It's time to learn some strategy."

They pulled into a spot with a flag labeled 5. Another vehicle was already lined up at the front of the bay, waiting for the starting signal.

Damon opened the door and exited the car. "Come on. We'll find a spot to watch this round. There's a fighter that we need to look for. They say he's the best contender the commoners have put up in a decade."

Valerie climbed out of the sedan and followed him, walking up the berm to a spot between starting positions where they would have a good view of the action. She'd seen melees before, but that had been when she was young. Her father had competed in tournaments all over New Avalon, and she had occasionally been allowed to follow along. But the ones she had witnessed were grand affairs with waving ceremonial flags and bleachers filled with spectators. At the time, she had been more interested in the snacks than the actual sport. She'd never encountered the sort of raw energy she was feeling now.

Engines revved all around the lake. Sparks flew from someone's vehicle as they attempted a last-minute welding repair. Someone was blasting boisterous guitar music from a speaker, and the air was ripe with the scent of gasoline. Even the sky was chaotic, punctuated by the chirps and squeaks of bats as they darted in to snatch disoriented moths from the arena lights.

Valerie's heart was racing even before the starting bell rang. But then it did ring, and a dozen vehicles roared out of their positions.

The crowd let out a collective shout.

Melee games varied, but this arena was set up for Helter Skelter. Valerie knew the basic rules.

Flagpoles were set up all around the arena space. Each was clearly marked with a point value. Knocking down the pole would earn a driver the designated amount of points. These usually fell to the participants who drove the fastest vehicles.

In this round, a contingent of caged, four-wheeled motorcycles sprang into the lead, their riders taking out several poles in short order.

But speed wasn't the only asset. If a vehicle could be disabled by another vehicle, the survivor would claim all the points held by the victim. Thus, a second wave of slower but heavier-duty vehicles made their way across the arena. Many had chosen cars, but several larger vehicles were at work as well, trucks and ramming vehicles capable of crushing or demolishing competitors. These drivers typically held the advantage the longer the match lasted. As the lighter and faster vehicles accumulated points, a lucky attacker could swoop in and disable them, claiming the reward.

The third and most dangerous method of acquiring points was to earn the pedestrian prizes. This required exiting your vehicle entirely and retrieving one of the items only reachable on foot. Exiting a vehicle left it vulnerable. While it was generally considered poor form to disable a vehicle while unoccupied, the rules did allow it, along with piracy. If a contender's vehicle was disabled and they had not retreated to the lists for safety, they could attempt to steal an unattended vehicle and continue the competition. Sometimes drivers would deliberately abandon their vehicles in an attempt to commandeer a competitor's. If successful, they were entitled to keep it, or would sometimes sell it back to the original owner for a premium after the event.

Some contenders were more famous for their abilities as car pirates than as drivers. Skilled racers could continuously upgrade vehicles that way and amass enviable collections.

"There's Kane," Damon said, pointing out a heavy-duty truck with oversized tires and orange flames up the fenders. It was parked a few stalls down from theirs. "Looks like he'll be in your round."

"I've met him," Valerie said. "He bought a fuel pump off Rico the other day." The muscled sailor climbed into the cab, and the truck started with a roar.

Valerie returned her attention to the arena, watching with interest as the vehicles maneuvered for position. What one would imagine as a straight race for points wasn't nearly as simple when the arena was dotted with barriers and obstacles.

"Keep an eye on that red Eagle," Damon said, pointing to a car with red doors that was navigating the barriers closest to them. "I'd bet anything that the driver is Mervyn Doyle. The silver Lantern Fire is likely to be one of the Patel sisters. I can't tell from here, but I'd wager that's Nikki. There are more than a few undercover nobles gauging the competition here."

The silver car slammed another lighter vehicle into a piling. The victim's car started to smoke, and the driver was forced to bail out. Several points went up on a board mounted to a makeshift wooden tower at one end of the arena. Referees watched from on top with binoculars, shouting to the scorekeepers.

The numbers began to accumulate rapidly once all the vehicles reached the center of the arena. Crunching ensued as many cars went head to head, attempting to outlast one another in brutal collisions.

"When you're out there, keep your foot on the gas, and don't let anyone pin you into a corner. The name of this game is stay moving. Nothing good ever happens to a car sitting still."

The first round ended far sooner than Valerie would have liked. As she walked back to the car, she eyed the board. The leader had knocked down five points poles and disabled three other vehicles. One contender had managed to disable five other vehicles but had been knocked out themselves before being able to claim victory.

Damon popped the trunk of the sedan and pulled out a white, open-faced helmet. He handed it to Valerie. "Remember to keep your mask on. We don't want anyone knowing who they're up against. Don't get injured. As far as we know, nobody wants to kill you out here, but I've known a few people who like to increase their odds in the tournament by taking out some of the competition in practice. Keep your head on a swivel."

Valerie donned the helmet and strapped herself into the car.

"You sure this is a good idea? What if I get taken out in the first five minutes?"

"Then you'll learn from your mistakes," Damon said. He checked his watch. "Look alive. I think they have the arena reset already."

Valerie took a deep breath and tried to dispel the growing tension in her chest. Damon clicked on his radio and depressed the mic button. His slightly scratchy voice emanated from the walkie-talkie in the cup holder. "Good luck, Alley Cat."

Valerie muttered curses under her breath, trying to figure out how she had gotten herself into this.

"Okay, no problem," she said to herself, turning the ignition key. "If these people can do it, I can too." She shifted into first and waited with the clutch in, revving the engine a few times to get the feel of the accelerator. She eyed the nearest points pole with a flag waving from the top, then made a mental map of the rest of the arena and the other visible flags.

She tightened her grip on the steering wheel.

Moments later, the starting bell rang. Around the lakebed, vehicles launched into action. Valerie released the clutch and flew into the arena.

Once in motion, the lakebed seemed a lot less level than it had appeared from the perimeter. The ground undulated with little rises, and the obstacles, which had appeared small from a distance, now loomed large in her view. It would be hard to track the competition.

She'd counted twenty-five starting positions, though she wasn't positive they were all filled.

However many cars were competing, they were kicking up enough dust for twice that number. The perimeter of the lake disappeared in a cloud of brown.

She bore down on the pole with the first points flag and centered the car on the target. It would be embarrassing to miss it in the wide open. It was a straight shot now, less than fifty yards.

Forty.

Twenty.

The radio crackled in the cup holder. What had he said?

Contact.

The pole went down with a satisfying clang, and Valerie grinned beneath her mask.

She was on the board.

She checked her rear-view mirror, saw the downed pole disappearing into the dust cloud she had raised behind her. She reached for the radio, picking it up and keying the mic.

"What did you say?"

She slammed sideways into the door, her helmet ricocheting off the window mesh.

The car was airborne.

Up. Over.

It landed on its roof with a crunch, and Valerie jolted against the shoulder straps. The roll continued, and she was tossed around the roll cage, this time with dirt and grit flying in the windows.

The momentum of the car carried it over once more, and the sedan thudded back onto its tires.

Valerie clenched the wheel and tried to orient her mind to what had just happened. Out her right window, red taillights from the massive truck disappeared into the dust. Connor Kane.

"He's coming back around!" Damon shouted from somewhere on the floor amid a blast of static.

Valerie spit sand from her mouth and reached for the ignition. The sedan fired back up.

"Which way?" She shouted the words, but she had no way to key the radio.

The dust and darkness around her revealed only distant and disorienting flashes of headlights.

"Fifty yards!" Damon shouted.

The bastard didn't have his lights on.

Valerie shifted into reverse and stomped on the gas. The car launched backward just as the armored truck careened past the front bumper. Valerie slammed on the brakes and brought the car skidding to a stop again.

"Hey! You okay?" Damon shouted into the radio.

She shifted into gear again and revved the engine.

"Oh, hell yeah. It's on."

17

DEMOLISHED

When Valerie rolled back through bay 5, the sedan's wonky headlight had gone completely missing. The roof of the car was concave, and there was a layer of dirt a quarter of an inch thick on the back seat. There were handprints back there too, from the incident where a masked man had leapt into the car and attempted to take her hostage.

Valerie's deft execution of a hard left turn had seen him exit again nearly as quickly, but it was a lesson nonetheless. In the real tournament, she wanted to be driving a vehicle with all of its doors.

The scoreboard showed she had knocked down four point flags and disabled one other vehicle, but she hadn't claimed any pedestrian prizes or taken any hostages. She did manage to avoid breaking down or getting captured herself, so her points total was enough to rank her in the top ten, but she wasn't bringing home any prizes.

Damon assessed the steaming hood of the sedan. "With a little coolant, it might even get us home. Not bad, Alley Cat."

Valerie attempted to open the driver's door but couldn't budge it. The passenger door was also stuck. With Damon looking on, she finally had to resign herself to climbing out the back through the missing rear door.

"See? Not so stupid now, is it?" Damon said.

"Whatever. I still want a real door."

"How do you feel? That rollover looked rough."

"I imagine it's what a pinball feels like."

"You did well. Pretty sure that Belmont Cruiser you knocked out at the end was Holden Rothschild. He'll be fuming." Damon reached into his pocket and extracted a wad of bills. He counted a few out and handed them to Valerie.

"What's this for?"

"Made a few prudent bets while you were busy driving. Might be enough to get you a few armaments for the Guardian."

"What kinds of weapons will the other cars have? I saw a wrecker out there with a rack that looked like it might carry a ballista."

"Could be. But anybody carrying an artillery weapon will only get one good shot at a time. No way to effectively reload and fire that without stopping. Still, you will see the occasional net launcher, and you have to watch out for tire cutters. I got a good look at the driving skills out here, and you can hold your own with any of them. From here on out, we should focus on your sword training."

Valerie tossed her helmet into the trunk. "What's next?"

"Sleep. Come on. Let's get back before anybody gets too nosy or follows us home. You've made enough of an impression for one night."

Valerie was wiping down tables the next day after the lunch rush when she caught sight of a face she hadn't seen since the night she first arrived. The boy seemed to be searching for someone.

"Hey! Eli!"

Eli located her voice and straightened up.

"I thought that was you," Valerie said, making her way to the door. "What are you doing lurking around the Twisted Tentacle?"

"Nothing," Eli replied. He stuffed his hands into his pockets. A couple of his fingers protruded through holes. "Just wanted to make sure you were okay."

Valerie crossed her arms. "You trying to make up for bailing on me and leaving me to get beat up in an alley?"

Eli scuffed one shoe against the other. "Yeah."

Valerie cocked her head and studied his forlorn posture. "You been back before today?"

"Couple of times."

She sighed. "Look, it's okay. It's not your fault."

Eli looked up, his eyes darting to her face, then back to the ground. "I still . . . still shoulda stayed."

She put a hand on his shoulder. "They would have hurt you. You went for help. If it hadn't been for that, who knows what might have happened."

Eli looked up again, this time he held her gaze. "I'm still sorry. It's not how you should be with your girlfriend."

"Yeah, well, we all make mistakes."

Eli looked encouraged. "Do you . . . Do you want to maybe go out again sometime?"

"Out? What are you talking about?"

"You know, like maybe ride on my bike again, like the last time?"

"That wasn't a date," Valerie replied. "And you do realize you're twelve, right?"

"So?"

"I'm turning eighteen in a few days."

"That's not so old," Eli replied.

"I think you're better off finding someone your own age."

Eli frowned. "What if I got you a really good birthday present? Like jewels."

"I think I'm all set," Valerie said.

A Sovereign Mark II came cruising down the street, and Valerie backed into the shadow of the tavern's doorway.

"What is it?" Eli asked.

"Nothing. Just trying to avoid attention. Someone I know drives a car like that." She watched the car go by, but the driver wasn't anyone she recognized.

"There's a couple of those Mark IIs uptown," Eli replied. "A black one and a green one, and one like that except it has a hole in the door like someone stabbed it."

Valerie focused on the boy. "You've seen that car? Was it a hole in the driver's door where a sword went through it?"

"It looks like it. Why?"

"The guy who rides around in that car is Jasper Sterling's lawyer. He's the bastard who has the documents that got me stuck down here."

Eli nodded. "I've seen that car a bunch of times."

"You ever see the guy that rides in it?"

"Sometimes," Eli said. "He has this metal box he never lets go of."

"That's him." Valerie bit her lip. "Listen, if you see that car again and the guy who drives it, can you come tell me? I'd really like to get my hands on that briefcase."

"Would that make you want to be my girlfriend again?"

Valerie shook her head. "Friends. That's what we are. But I'll give you that ride in the Guardian you wanted, or I'll buy you an ice cream or something."

"Like a date."

Valerie laughed. "Like friends."

"All right," Eli said. "I'll find the car. Then I'll change your mind about the *friends* part." He winked at her, then climbed on his bike and pedaled away.

That night after work, she made the walk to Damon's loft as usual, noting the increase in traffic on the roads. The revving of engines could be heard on nearly every block these days.

Garages all along Lexington had crews working on junkyard motors and custom cars.

Valerie had kept the Guardian under wraps for the last few weeks, and the buzz about its existence had faded as new arrivals came to town. With the exposure of new home-built war cars around Tidewater, she hoped the Guardian had been largely forgotten. When she walked into Damon's warehouse, she found Damon and Rico working on the car. It was on jacks, and the rear wheels were missing.

"What's going on in here?" Valerie asked.

Rico was in the driver's seat messing with the dash controls. "Been installing a few weapons and defense systems for you. We're trying to up your game for the tournament."

"Excellent," Valerie replied.

"This thing was state of the art ten years ago," Damon said. "But we need to make some updates if you want to hang with some of the cars coming into the city for this tournament."

"You want to talk to her about track geography?" Rico asked.

"Good idea," Damon said. "Show her the course."

Rico climbed out of the Guardian and moved to the rolling tool chest. The top workbench had been cleared and was now covered in butcher paper. But it was obvious that Rico wasn't planning to use it for wrapping sandwiches. The butcher paper had been scribbled on with dark charcoal pencil, and the drawing was a rough representation of Sterling Bay.

"They announced the route this morning," Rico said. "It's an open start south of the bay at Baylor's Field, out to Mount Oro Castle, around the Twisted Sisters, then all the way back to Sterling Arena here in Port Hyacinth via Long Bridge. It's a little over sixty miles start to finish. It's a timed run. You're not racing the other cars as much as you're racing the clock. And you've only got forty-five minutes."

Valerie studied the route. "That shouldn't be bad in a car like the Guardian. What is that, eighty miles per hour average?"

"Only you won't be going eighty the whole time," Damon said. He nodded to Rico. "Tell her the hazards."

"There's plenty," Rico said. "Getting out of the melee start will be the biggest one. You've got at least a hundred cars trying to muscle their way out of Baylor's Field. There's only one route that will get you to Mount Oro, and it'll be chaos. Expect a lot of smash and bash going on there, especially from the bigger, slower cars. They know they won't be able to catch you on the straightaways, so they'll be looking to lame their competition early. Grappling hooks, tire slashing, ballistae, it's all fair game in the opening."

He pointed to the next element. "When you make the bridge to Mount Oro, the trouble's not over. It's a moat circuit. Mount Oro's old defense moat has been drained, and you're racing through it, doing a perimeter run around the outer wall, then out the north side."

"I have to race through a moat?" Valerie asked.

"Exactly," Rico said. "And from what the spotters have said, it didn't drain well. Lots of mud puddles and sludge down there. Great place for a pileup."

"Holy hell," Valerie muttered. She glanced at the tires on the Guardian. "Mud?"

"That's why we're making modifications," Damon said.

"Okay," Rico continued. "Assuming you clear the Mount Oro moat, you're on to the Twisted Sisters. Here's where you'll have a decision to make. Either route will get you around the twin peaks of the city, but they'll have multiple roads open through the city proper. All have their disadvantages. The high roads are wider, presumably less likely to clog up due to a wreck, but it's a longer way around. The low roads are more direct, but they've got tight turns, little to no room to maneuver, and drop-offs that can have you swimming in the bay with the first mistake."

Valerie ran her hands through her hair and exhaled. "Tell me there's good news on this course somewhere."

"Sure," Rico said. "Good news is that if you survive the

Twisted Sisters, you get the Long Bridge. That's a straight run. Ten miles of full throttle drag race. It'll put you through the gates of the arena, we hope before they drop the portcullis. If you're still outside after that comes down, race is over."

Valerie stared at the route scratched out on paper. It was certainly a lot different from smoking Remi Rothschild off the line back in Briar Valley. She turned to study the war car.

She knew she ought to be worried, but somehow the clean, confident curves of the Guardian calmed her. They could handle it. Together.

"I guess we've got some work to do," she said.

Damon tossed her a tire iron. "Welcome to the pit crew."

18

DANCE MOVES

"I'm going to shoot you with this crossbow."

"Like hell you are," Valerie said.

Damon was standing thirty yards away in the pasture, holding the weapon. "Don't worry. The arrowheads aren't real. They're soft rubber."

"I don't care if they're made of marshmallows and pretzels. You'll put my eye out."

"Not if you do your job right." He hoisted the crossbow. "You need to learn to move in that armor. You're too slow. This will fix that."

Valerie muttered a few more curses under her breath but lowered the visor of her helmet and lifted her sword. This pasture they had driven to was dotted with holes and ruts, and there was no sure footing among the tufts of grass and weeds. "Are you giving me a countdown from three or —"

Damon fired.

The bolt sailed right past Valerie's blade and struck her in the chest.

"Damn it! Ow." She staggered backward, rubbing a hand over her left breast. She was armored in a mail shirt and had a boiled-leather breastplate over top, but the impact of the crossbow bolt was still painful.

"Feel free to dodge the next one. It's a lot easier than blocking it. Try to get closer."

"Closer?" Valerie had already taken several steps in the opposite direction.

"I'm your target," Damon replied. "I want you to get to me without being hit." He had already reloaded the crossbow and hoisted it to his shoulder.

"This is a sword-fighting competition. No one will be shooting at me."

"That's your excuse for being slow? Maybe I should have named you Alley Turtle." He sighted down the length of the crossbow.

"I really hate you, you know that?"

The bowstring twanged and the bolt flew at her. This time she moved to the side as she swiped at it, but the bolt still struck her, glancing off the steel pauldron on her shoulder. She raised her sword and charged, attempting to cover the ground between herself and Damon before he could get another bolt loaded. But as she closed in on him, she realized she was too late. He leveled the crossbow at her head.

She put up her hands. "This isn't fair," Valerie said.

"Let's do it again."

She returned to her starting position and raised her sword. This time, she darted sideways before Damon had a chance to fire. She zigzagged as she ran, forcing Damon to track her. He fired, and the bolt zinged off her right thigh. The force was enough to throw her off balance and send her sprawling. Her hand landed centimeters from a cow patty. She rolled over and rubbed at her leg. "Those things really hurt."

"You should stop letting them hit you," Damon replied, calmly reloading the crossbow.

"Is this one of those times where you get to show me how it's done, because I'd love to get my hands on that crossbow for a minute."

"Then come get it." Damon smiled.

Valerie climbed to her feet, picked up her sword, and limped back to her starting position. She set herself in a rear guard and attempted to form a new strategy.

When Damon raised the crossbow, she darted right. This time, instead of zigzagging, she feigned a stop but immediately continued on in the direction she had begun. Damon's bolt whizzed harmlessly behind her.

She sprinted at an angle to Damon's position that kept him clearly in view, and as he finished loading the crossbow, she cut back toward him.

He pivoted to face her, but as soon as he leveled the weapon to fire, she leapt into a slide, her legs in front of her, sword raised in a blocking position. Damon adjusted his aim, lowering to track her incoming attack, but she forced her heel into the ground and let her momentum bring her back to her feet. Her sword arm extended at the same time, bringing the blade up in a sweeping arc that caught the front of the crossbow and sent it skyward. The bolt flew off into the distance, and she brought her sword around to Damon's neck. She stopped the cut with half an inch to spare.

She was panting but her sword arm stayed steady.

Damon smiled. "Okay. Now we're getting somewhere."

Valerie withdrew her sword and nodded, lowering the weapon while she caught her breath.

Damon suddenly dropped and spun, his foot flashing around in a leg sweep. Valerie's legs went out from under her, and she landed with a thud in the grass.

She stared up breathlessly at Damon above her.

"So, you can dodge an arrow, but you can't dodge my foot?"

"You're such a bastard," Valerie said, groaning as she rose to her elbows.

"Don't worry," he said. "You can start the next round from

here." He winked at her, reloaded the crossbow, and strode
away.

~

Valerie examined her fresh bruises and studied her lean face in
the mirror. There was no disguising that she was exhausted. She
attempted to tidy her hair before walking out of the bathroom
but decided it was a lost cause. She just needed sleep.

Damon was closing up the cabinets of practice equipment.

"I'm heading out," Valerie said. "Janet has me working the
morning shift."

Damon nodded. "Before you go, I got you something." He
moved to the table and picked up a brown, paper-wrapped
parcel. It was tied together with bailing twine. "Sorry it's not
better wrapped. Happy early birthday."

"A birthday present?" She took the package from him.

"I know I've been pretty hard on you in training lately, but
you've shown some real improvement. I figured it's time you had
something to show for it."

Valerie's fingers pried at the package. The twine and paper
came away quickly in her hands and revealed a beautiful wooden
box with runes engraved on it.

"Go ahead. Open it," Damon said. His eyes glinted with
enthusiasm.

Valerie lifted the lid and gasped. "Oh my goodness. It's
gorgeous." Inside the box was an ornate, blue-green masquerade
mask. It had silver accents that glinted in the light and when she
turned it over, she noted the inside was marked with the sigil of a
wolf. "Where did you find this?"

"It was my mother's."

"What? You can't give me this," Valerie said, attempting to
hand it back. "It's too dear to you."

"It's collected enough dust," Damon said. "That mask has

been in my family a long time, but it deserves to be worn by someone I respect. Besides, if you make it through the race, you'll need one for the king's masquerade."

She let the words sink in. Someone he respects.

She admired the exquisite workmanship of the mask, then ran her finger over the emblem on the interior. "Your family sigil is a wolf?"

"House of Roark," Damon replied. "I used to hate it. Wolves terrified me as a child. But my mother used to say, 'Don't be a baby. They're just slightly more dangerous dogs.' She wasn't much for coddling us."

"How do you feel about bears?" Valerie asked, holding the mask up to her face and peering at him through it.

"To tell you the truth, they're starting to grow on me."

Valerie's face flushed. There was something about the way he was looking at her that made her want to stay hidden behind the mask. Like otherwise he'd be able to see into her mind, and she wasn't sure she wanted him to see what she was feeling. "I'd . . . I'd better get back." She quickly returned the mask to the box and set it on the table. "Thank you for the kindness, but it's too generous. I can't take it."

"It's a birthday gift."

"How about a birthday loan?" Valerie offered. "I still have to make it through the race before I'll even get an invite to the masquerade."

"I'll keep it safe for you till then."

Valerie nodded and averted her eyes. She quickly donned her sweatshirt and moved to the door. When she looked back, he was already busy tidying up the training space. It was his same routine as always, but was it? She couldn't help but feel that something about the gift had changed things. The walk back to the Twisted Tentacle was over before she knew it, but as she readied herself for sleep in the tavern's back room, her mind was still on Damon and the beautiful mask. Getting a chance to wear it was one more reason she'd hold nothing back.

"All warmed up?" Damon asked.

Valerie walked into the warehouse, after what seemed like the hundredth run this week, and sighed, then stripped down to her tank top and picked up a sword. She was mentally tired and sweaty, but despite a morning swim, a long day at the tavern, and her post work run, she was pleased to find that she still had energy.

Over the course of the last few weeks, she had worked up to running for almost a minute and a half underwater without taking a breath and could now do it carrying a stone that weighed thirty-five pounds. Her runs on land had not only gotten longer but also faster, and she could do several miles in under twenty minutes.

Leaving the mask and padded jacket off, she stepped onto the mat and worked through her sword forms.

It was a matter of routine now. She didn't even have to think about it.

Weeping Angel came first, then *Soaring Eagle*. She transitioned smoothly into *Fire of the Dragon*. Damon flipped on the radio, tuning the dial to a station playing something fast-paced and Spanish. He then picked up a sword and joined in with the forms, his body moving fluidly beside hers. They worked their way across the floor, each form flowing into the next. After weeks of practice, it was no longer the struggle it had once been.

The sight of Damon's flawless execution had infuriated her in the past, highlighting her own deficiencies, but tonight they moved like extensions of the same body. *Inside strike, parry, lunge, outside strike, step back, clearing cut.* Nodding along with Valerie's movements, Damon slipped into an opponent's position and mirrored her, his intense eyes finding hers as their blades connected.

As the music moved through her, they timed their strikes to the beat.

His body moved with hers, and the forms became a dance, at once deadly and beautiful. Valerie's heartbeat quickened with her breathing. The blows came faster as the tempo of the music and their footwork sped up. Form matched form, and she felt her lips parting into a smile as her body moved from memory. Each stroke of the sword sent vibrations through her arms.

Yes. This was how it was supposed to feel.

Before she knew it, they were dueling in earnest.

The forms flowed with attacks and counterattacks. Lunge. Riposte. *Sighing Dove, Roaring River.* Damon responded with *Whistling Grass* as she anticipated, and she felt the heat rising in her as the adrenaline pumped through her veins. She thwarted his attack almost before he started it, moving like water, her sword an extension of her body.

Ripping Tide.

Sweeping Hurricane.

Her blade advanced faster and faster until Damon suddenly disengaged, wheeling off the mat, a hand held to his shoulder.

When he pulled his palm away, she saw the tear in his T-shirt and the blood on his fingers.

"Oh my God. I'm sorry," she stammered. "I didn't expect to—"

"It's all right. Stupid of me. I should've been wearing a jacket." He set the sword against the wall and flexed his arm.

"Are you okay?" Valerie said. There was something shocking about the sight of blood coming from Damon as though she had forgotten it was possible.

"It's just a scratch." He kept pressure on the wound. "It'll mend. And I'll be more careful next time." He looked up at Valerie and smiled. "Someone found their rhythm."

Valerie grinned. "I have a good teacher."

Damon moved to the bathroom and pulled a medical kit from

the cabinet. He lifted his hand from the wound to pry the kit open, but Valerie stepped in.

"I can do that." She took the box of bandages from him and pointed to the bench just outside the bathroom. "You'll need to get that shirt off."

He attempted to pull the shirt over his head while still keeping pressure on his shoulder with one hand.

"Let me help." Valerie reached for his waist and tugged upward, peeling the sweat-dampened T-shirt up his chest and helping him get it over his head. He sank to the bench in front of her and leaned his head against the wall, letting his eyes close. She stood clutching his shirt and tried not to lose focus.

Valerie had been training hard for the tournament, but the effects had not been negligible on Damon either. His muscular body was even leaner and tougher than before. Only the fresh cut on his arm gave any hint of vulnerability.

Bandages.

Focus.

Valerie peeled Damon's hand away from the wound and placed a cotton pad there instead. He hissed through his teeth when she applied the disinfectant but didn't flinch. Fortunately, the wound wasn't deep. Valerie applied a pair of adhesive sutures and layered two bandages overtop just to be sure it would stay clean.

"You've done this before," Damon said, looking on with what she took as approval.

"I did a season as the men's dueling team medic when Henry first got to prep school. Thought it would be a good opportunity to meet older guys."

"Did it work?"

"Not really. I was always Henry Terravecchia's little sister. No one wanted to annoy the best swordsman on the team by hitting on me. It wasn't safe."

"He was good," Damon said.

"He was a natural. You would've liked him."

"I'm sure he's proud of you." Damon lifted a hand and brushed her waist with his fingertips.

It was such a small gesture. He had barely grazed the fabric of her tank top, but Valerie's breath caught. Sitting down, his head was at the level of her chest. His eyes lingered on her hips. She had the sudden urge to put her fingers in his hair and lean into him—pull his body to hers. They were so close she could feel the heat radiating from his skin.

Where had that thought come from?

His fingers trailed down her hip, just the softest caress through the fabric, but it was somehow electric.

Something was different. Ever since the night he had given her the mask, she had been waiting and watching for something to confirm it. Now she was sure.

He looked up and met her gaze. Those intense, dark eyes. Had he always looked so hungry? In this moment, he resembled the wolf of his family house, beautiful and dangerous. What force held him back?

Did she want it to?

With the bandage finished, she didn't know what to do with her hands. She clenched her fingers into fists at her sides, just to keep them to herself. If she didn't . . .

"I think you're ready," Damon said.

"Yes," Valerie whispered.

"For the tournament," Damon added.

"The tournament. Yes." Valerie pulled her eyes from his face and spun around, facing the garage. She exhaled. How long had it been since she had taken a breath?

Damon stood. She could feel him looming behind her. There was an electricity still lingering in the molecules of air pressed between their bodies, a magnetism drawing her backward.

But she wouldn't turn around. If she did, she wouldn't be able to resist the pull.

She waited, anticipating the touch of his hand on her skin.

But it didn't come.

Damon moved away.

He walked to the training area and picked up Valerie's tournament sword. He examined the tip of the blade as if wondering how such an inconsequential thing could have harmed him, then he moved to the cabinet.

Valerie tried to compose herself. What on earth was she doing?

Damon pulled on a soft, gray T-shirt and fixed her with a long stare. Was he seeing her in a new light too? Did he feel the electricity?

He broke eye contact, walking to the training area and donning an armored jacket. "We'd best get back to practicing. It's getting late."

Valerie moved into position as well, donning her own jacket and picking up a training mask. She focused on staying casual. "As long as you think you can handle it," she said. "Don't want to hurt you again."

Damon's lips cracked the briefest of smiles before his mask covered his face.

They took their positions, and Valerie put on her mask. Her breath was hot and rapid inside it, but she tried to calm herself. This was training. That's all.

They saluted.

Armored and masked, there would be no holding back this time.

Warrior's Way. She moved into action. Damon countered with *Raven's Cry.* They swept back and forth across the mat, striking and countering with vigorous enthusiasm. She transitioned into *Moon Under Water,* hoping to press Damon out of the fighting zone and force him to yield, but something was different. He countered with a form she hadn't seen before.

He suddenly switched his sword from left to right, and in one forceful motion, his blade spun around hers, lifting it. He caught her wrist with his other hand and spun into her, wrapping her arm around his neck and pulling her toward him. Her mask went flying as if it had never been on, clattering off the mat to the concrete. His mask followed. She found herself pressed up against his chest, her arm still wrapped behind his neck and her front leg caught between his. Trapped against him, she couldn't tell if the pulsing in her chest was his heartbeat or her own.

His face was a fraction of an inch from hers.

What little breath she had came in with a gasp and caught in her throat.

"I added a new form," Damon panted. "It doesn't have a name yet."

"It's my favorite so far," Valerie whispered back.

Then his lips were on hers.

Valerie's sword fell from her hand, and her fingers found their way to his hair.

So much for practice.

19

AFTERGLOW

"**A** re you even listening?" Rico asked.

"What?" Valerie snapped back to attention, finding Rico staring at her. They were on the corner of Fifteenth Street and Westbrook, handing out flyers for his show.

"It's like your head has been up in a cloud today. You want to come back down to earth with the rest of us?" Rico snatched a handful of the flyers from her. He had clearly been far more successful at getting rid of his.

"I'm here," Valerie said, adjusting the brim of the big, floppy hat she was using in an attempt to disguise her face and hair. There had been no more visits from the City Watch of late, but she still chose to keep a low profile. "I was just thinking."

"Uh-huh," Rico said. "Thinking about who'll be sitting in the seat you reserved next to yours for my show tonight?"

"You know about that?"

"Of course I know," Rico scoffed. "Just like I know who it's for too. You don't think everyone saw your giddy little schoolgirl face when he walked into the tavern this morning? Or that you spent twice as long bringing him a drink or meal than anyone else? Please. I know a lovesick puppy when I see one."

"What? I am *not* a lovesick puppy."

"Uh-huh. Cool as ice, you are."

"Damn. Was it that obvious?"

"Why do you care?" Rico said. "He's a good-looking dude. I mean, if I was you . . ."

"What? What would you do if you were me?"

"I wouldn't just be making puppy dog eyes at him, that's all I'm saying."

"It's nothing," Valerie lied. "I just had a big breakthrough in training. I beat him in a duel last night."

"Uh-huh," Rico said. "And I'm supposed to believe that's it? I don't get you competitive types. For weeks you don't give him a second glance, then you get to poke him with your sword, and suddenly he's got your panties all in a state?"

She smacked him with a handful of flyers.

"Listen, I don't know how to explain it either. I guess, before he was just teaching me, and I was always on the losing end of everything. He was untouchable."

"And now you want to do all the touching."

"Shut up."

Valerie thrust a flyer into the hand of a passing merchant. "Big show tonight at the Twisted Tentacle. Doors open at sundown. Best act in town."

The man nodded and glanced at the flyer briefly before shoving it into a jacket pocket.

"Besides," Valerie said. "I don't *just* make puppy dog eyes at him."

"Oh, really?" Rico's eyebrows stretched for his hairline. "Do tell. Maybe he's doing a little poking with his sword too?"

Valerie glared at him. "No. It's not like that. Not yet anyway."

"Slow playing it, huh? Good. I can be into that as long as it's worth the wait." He pressed a flyer into the hand of a woman pushing a pram. "Get out tonight, darling. Hire a sitter. It's worth it."

"He might be waiting till my birthday to get any more serious. I told him I turn eighteen tomorrow."

"That's sweet," Rico said. "Or maybe he doesn't want to hook up with a girl who has a death wish and plans to commit public suicide."

"I'm not committing suicide," Valerie said. "I'm good at this."

"I'm just glad you get to come to my show prior to your tragic ending."

Valerie sighed. "You're probably right. I shouldn't be getting involved with anyone. I should be focusing on getting justice for Henry."

Rico dropped his hands to his sides and turned to focus on her. "Listen to me, chica. Your brother loved you, right?"

"Of course."

"Then don't beat yourself up about it. He might be dead, but that doesn't mean he doesn't still want you to be happy. God knows there's little enough love floating around in Tidewater. Take what you can get." He handed her the rest of the flyers. "I've got to go prep. I'll see you at the show tonight."

Valerie attempted to disperse the remainder of the flyers on her way back to the tavern but ultimately stuffed the last couple into her sweatshirt pocket. The cliffside villages were buzzing with activity on her way home. There were fresh coats of paint on once-dingy shop fronts. Colorful banners and flags hung from lines strung across the roads. Food vendors had arrived towing carts. Musicians sang on street corners. And everywhere she looked, there were playbills and flyers for shows and entertainment. Everyone was eager to attract visitors and capitalize on the influx of money coming in from the countryside.

Janet and Ann were prepping the tavern for the arrival of the Guild judges. Ann's sword would be on display in a place of prominence, and they were hoping Rico's act would draw a crowd. The Twisted Tentacle would be bustling.

Janet had decided that displaying the tavern in the best

possible light—busy and profitable—would increase Ann's chances of being accepted by the Guild.

All the servers had been given strict instructions: Guild judges were to be treated like royalty.

Janet had paid top dollar for the freshest seafood catches that morning, and Carlyn was already working her magic in the kitchen.

"How are we doing?" Valerie asked as she walked in the back door of the tavern.

"So far so good," Carlyn replied. "But stay out of here. I've told this crew no distractions. Not even you."

Valerie slipped out to the bar and edged her way around the crew of workers setting up chairs and lights.

Janet was supervising from beside the bar, counting chairs with a hovering finger. She turned to Valerie as she walked in. "There you are. Anyone left in this town we haven't invited?"

"Doubt it," Valerie replied. "How's setup going?"

"We've sold about a third of the seats for Rico's show so far. If we can fill the rest before showtime, we'll be in good shape." She noted something on her clipboard. "The Guild judges are supposed to be here at eight. We'll have a private area roped off for them over there. Let's hope they're in a good mood."

"Ann's sword is a masterpiece," Valerie said. "It's a shoe-in."

"Let's hope the masters agree," Janet said. "We'll find out tonight. I'll need you here before sundown. All hands on deck tonight."

"You've got it," Valerie replied. "I'll be here."

It was clear that her presence at the tavern now, while well-intentioned, was just getting in people's way, so she made the walk to Lexington Avenue instead, eager to find Damon.

The roaring of engines echoed from the city walls. She looked up to note the slick luxury cars and intimidating machines of war cruising the bridges. The city was pulsing with anticipation. The weeks of preparation and planning had created an enthusiasm that was now streaming from every open door and window. Shop owners and merchants, locals and tourists alike were conversing in excited tones. If the city had a heartbeat, it was pounding.

When Valerie reached Damon's warehouse loft, the garage door was still closed. She rapped on the pedestrian door at the side of the building. After several rounds of knocking, the door finally opened.

Damon was wearing a tank top and athletic shorts and appeared to have just woken up, a state Valerie currently envied.

She paused briefly to study him. He was more than just tired. He looked exhausted.

"Did you go out last night?" she asked, trying to sound uncaring.

Damon moved to the water cooler and poured two cups. He brought one over to her. "Work."

"Who was the client?"

Damon downed the water, then crunched the paper cup in his palm. "You know I'm not allowed to talk about my clients." The cup arced into the trash can.

When he turned around, they found themselves face to face. She grasped him by the front of his shirt, rose up on her toes, and kissed him.

Damon's broad hands found the small of her back and pulled her closer. Everything about him was warm and firm. She balled the fabric of his shirt in her fists.

But then his lips left hers, and he pushed her away.

"Wait."

Valerie froze, studying his face. He looked every bit as hungry as she felt, but there was something else in his eyes.

"We shouldn't do this."

"What are you talking about?" Valerie said. "Look, if it's an age thing, I don't care. A few years is not that—"

"That isn't it," he replied. He ran a hand through his hair and backed away. "Last night was . . ."

"Don't you dare say a mistake."

"No. Not a mistake. But . . . ill advised. I lost control of myself, but I shouldn't have. This tournament is only days away. You need to focus, and I'm . . . I'm not a guy you want to be involved with."

She tried to read his face. "Isn't that something I should decide?"

"The king will be here soon. We have a lot to do before that happens. You don't need any more distractions."

Valerie tried to focus on his words, but he had to feel what she was feeling. The electricity in the air between them was palpable. Something about the way he smelled. His intensity of focus. The desire was written across his face.

For all of his equivocating, he hadn't once taken his eyes from her.

"I'll focus," Valerie said. "And I won't get distracted. You're right. But there's just one thing I have to say first." She took a step toward him until their bodies were an inch apart. Their breath mingled.

"One thing," he echoed.

Her hands went to his neck as she leapt into the air. She wrapped her legs around his waist, then grasped his face with both hands as she pressed her lips to his, this time harder.

For a moment, his face was stone, a statue, frozen in resistance, but then his lips melted beneath hers. He clenched her thighs in his grip.

In all the world there was nothing but this—his muscled arms wrapped around her, the feel of her fingers in his hair. The solidness of him.

Their lips finally separated, and she leaned her forehead against his, their noses still touching. "Just so you know, this is all I really wanted for my birthday."

He smiled and let his lips brush against hers again. "You have a real way with words."

She grinned.

But at that moment, someone knocked on the door of the garage.

Valerie looked up and considered it, then looked down at Damon. "Mailman?"

The knocking persisted. It wasn't a loud knock. It was a small but fervent one that increased in intensity as they stared at the door.

"I have no idea," Damon replied. He loosened his hold on Valerie and let her slide to the ground. He took her hand and moved to the door, opening it only a crack. He paused at the sight of whomever it was, and Valerie tried to read his body language.

"What do you want?" he demanded.

"I'm here to talk to Valerie," the voice said. A young boy. A voice she recognized.

"It's okay," Valerie said, moving around Damon. He opened the door to reveal the boy standing on the doorstep.

Eli.

"Hey," he said.

"Who's this?" Damon asked.

Eli eyed him suspiciously. "I'm her boyfriend. Who are you?"

Damon turned to Valerie with an eyebrow raised. "Boyfriend?"

Valerie flattened her lips. "I'll explain later."

The phone rang on the rear wall of the warehouse. Damon smirked, then moved aside, crossing behind her and heading toward the phone.

"How did you find me?" Valerie asked, addressing the boy on the stoop.

"I saw you come in," Eli said.

"You followed me?"

"No. Well, sort of," he said. Eli leaned sideways to get a look into the garage. "What are you doing hanging out with that guy?"

"He's my . . . coach," Valerie replied. She stepped outside and closed the door. "What's going on? What are you doing here?"

"You said I should tell you if I saw that car you were looking for. The Sovereign Mark II with the hole in it?"

"You found it?"

"Yeah. It's in a parking garage up on Cumberland Street. A bunch of sweet cars went inside this morning. There's something big going down in that garage today."

"How long ago was this?"

"Maybe twenty minutes? I thought you would want to know."

"Cumberland Street . . . which building?"

"The one called Regency."

Valerie contemplated the distance to uptown. "Are you going back up that way? Can you keep an eye on the garage until I make it?"

"Yeah, I guess so."

"Okay. Make sure it doesn't leave. I'll be there as soon as I can."

Valerie watched Eli pedal away, then closed the door.

Damon appeared to be wrapping up his phone call. "Fine. I'll be there." Then he hung up.

"Who was that?"

"A work thing. I need to go out for a bit, but I'll try to get back as soon as I can. For training," he added.

"How long do you think you'll be gone?" Valerie asked. "Ann's sword is getting judged tonight at the Twisted Tentacle. It's a big deal."

"I have my ticket. I'll try to make an appearance."

"Okay. I've got to run anyway." Valerie made her way toward the door. Damon caught her by the hip and spun her to him. She once again found herself pressed against his chest.

He gazed down at her. "When I get back, we focus, okay?"

Valerie traced her fingers across his chest. "I'm focused."

He released his grip on her, bit his lip in visible frustration, then snatched up his leather jacket and disappeared out the back door.

Valerie smiled.

A few moments later, the engine turned over on the Vulcan. The low rumble faded away as he left the lot.

She stood there with her fingers to her lips for several long seconds, then shook her head to snap herself out of her daydream.

She had a decision to make.

She weighed her options.

If she wanted to stay out of Jasper Sterling's grasp, his personal lawyer was probably the last person she should be around, but he had the briefcase. It would be no good getting in front of the king at the tournament if she had no evidence to back up her side of the story. If she could get her hands on phony contracts or some proof that Jasper had lied, at least she'd have something to prove her case. And she may not get another chance at it.

Crossing to the practice cabinet, she considered the swords, but then thought better of it. She'd have a hard time explaining herself if she was stopped uptown with one of those. She moved to one of Damon's toolboxes, opening drawers until she discovered a hammer. That could work.

The Guardian was far too conspicuous a vehicle for what she had in mind, but her only other option wasn't much better.

She got the rear garage door open and located the battered wreck of a car she had used in the practice melee. The rear passenger door was still missing, along with the headlight and various other pieces she had knocked off or mangled, but with the city as busy as it was, she hoped it wouldn't warrant too many stares. The ski masks she and Damon had worn were still in the glovebox.

She climbed into the car through the missing rear door, located the keys above the sun visor, and exhaled. It was just a little bit of armed robbery.

Her heart shouldn't beat so quickly.

She settled into the driver's seat.

One trip uptown. Somehow get the briefcase from Blaise. Back before anyone knew it.

Easy.

She turned the ignition, shifted into gear, and stepped on the gas.

20

STOLEN

The uptown district of Port Hyacinth was teeming with activity. Valerie had gotten lucky and trailed a caravan of parts dealers though the city gates. The guards had waved her through without stopping.

Now she was nearly at her destination.

The streets were filled with pedestrians and cars alike, and Valerie was forced to park the battered Lark sedan on a side street a block south of Cumberland and proceed on foot.

It was for the best anyway. The wreck was far too conspicuous a vehicle to breeze right up to her target in. She was bound to attract attention.

She checked her sweatshirt pocket, tossing Rico's leftover show flyers into the passenger seat and stashing the ski mask in the pocket instead. Positioning the hammer in the waistband of her jeans, she then pulled the edge of the sweatshirt overtop to hide it. No use drawing suspicion just yet.

She walked the last couple of blocks to the Golden Hill neighborhood and located the Regency Arms. The high-rise condo building was outfitted in mirrored glass and had several armored guards stationed out front.

The parking garage was gated.

How on earth had Eli gotten in?

She kept an eye out for the boy, all while attempting to keep a low profile. She pulled her hood low over her brow to try to shield her face.

As she was standing on the corner eyeing the condo building from across the street, a buzzing noise made her turn. Eli was whizzing up on his bicycle, his leg cocked and sneaker jammed against the frame and back tire, using his foot as a brake. The bike came to a skidding stop directly in front of her, and Eli tossed his hair out of his eyes.

"Hey, I almost didn't see you. You look different with that hood on."

"Kind of the idea," Valerie replied. "Is the car still here?"

"Yeah." Eli nodded. "Come on. I'll show you." He leaned his bike against the stop sign, then darted across the street on foot, gesturing for Valerie to follow.

She tailed him around the back of the condo building, cutting down an alley filled with dumpsters that was still somehow cleaner than Tidewater. Eli directed her to hide behind one of the dumpsters while he peeked out and checked the area. "Okay. I think we're clear. There's a couple of guards, but they only come around every once in a while. There's a hole in the fence."

The fence he was referring to was actually a shoulder-high, concrete wall with some chain link attached to the top as a sort of window that admitted daylight into the parking garage. "Hole" was a generous term as the area he was referring to was simply a corner of the chain link that had broken free of its mounting brackets along one column. Eli was able to pry at it and create an opening just wide enough to wriggle through. Once inside, he called for Valerie to follow.

Valerie retrieved the mask from her pocket and put it on, then squeezed through the chain link.

It was a drop of several feet into the ground floor of the parking garage. She landed softly and followed Eli farther in. There weren't a lot of cars on the ground floor, but the ones she saw were expensive. Most were sports cars. She spotted two King Edward Edition Monarch VIIs, several imported French Louis, and a gold-flecked Marvel 1600. Some bore iridescent paint jobs. Whoever drove them clearly had money to spare.

Eli waved her on, and they ascended a flight of stairs to the next floor. Here she found more than just luxury sedans and limousines. These were war cars. An entire row of the racing machines was lined up, paint sparkling even in the dim light. Diamondbacks, Hell Runners, even a Shogun. Any one of these vehicles would have been a rarity to see on its own. Together they were staggering.

She focused on her goal and kept her eye out for Blaise's Sovereign Mark II. Eli led her straight to it. It still had the hole in the rear door where Jasper's sword had punctured it.

"How did you find it?" Valerie whispered.

"My friends and I sneak into garages sometimes to look around. These are all pretty cool, but my favorite car is a Belmont Super M8. There's one in the MacDougal Street garage. My friend, Scabs, knows the guy who washes it. He let us sit in it once." His voice grew louder as he got more animated.

"Shhh. Somebody will hear you," Valerie said. She tried the door handle on the limo. As expected, it was locked. She cupped a hand like a visor and pressed her face to the window, trying to get a look through the tint. "You think the briefcase is in there?"

"I thought I saw something that looked like a briefcase," Eli said. He came close and peered through the window as well, trying to get a good angle. The dark interior made it difficult to make anything out.

"Uh-oh," Eli said. "Someone's coming."

Valerie spun around and ducked. There were indeed voices in the garage, coming from around the corner. Several women and at least three men were making their way through the garage. One of the women laughed at something her companions said. Valerie peered over the hood of the car next to her and watched as the rest of the group came into view.

Her heart sank as she recognized Blaise, the one person she most wanted to avoid. But then, a moment later, her apprehension turned to fury when Jasper Sterling and the Red Reaper came around the corner. Jasper was smiling. Laughing even. The Reaper was carrying the *Sword with the Red Hilt* again, and her mind immediately flashed back to the duel with Henry. She tightened her grip on the hammer and seethed. Jasper was only a matter of a dozen yards away. If she only had a sword . . .

The group paused in a cluster, evidently about to part ways. One of the women looked vaguely familiar to Valerie, and it took a moment for her to recognize that it was from one of the posters behind the bar at the Twisted Tentacle. Niko Okazaki. She had a set of car keys in her hand and was angling toward the rugged-looking blue-and-white Shogun.

"Okay. So you all understand the arrangement," Blaise was saying. "You'll be compensated for your performances. Half now. And proportionally to your rank at the end of the tournament. From here on out, you'll work as a team to keep anyone not in this group out of the finals."

"Just pay them already," Jasper said. "They all understand their part."

Blaise laid his silver briefcase on the hood of a neighboring car. All eyes turned toward him as he opened it and removed a document. "Your signatures are all required, then you get your money."

"And I trust you won't forget your part," one of the fighters said. "When you have your seat at the Round Table, we'll be counting on you to come through for us."

"It will be as though each of your own voices is speaking to the king's ear," Jasper said. "Only this way, you're also rich."

The fighters gathered around Blaise and signed the document. One by one, they received envelopes. One or two peeked inside, but Niko Okazaki merely tossed her package through the open gull-wing door of her car, then slid in after to put the keys in the ignition. Tensions eased, and the rest of the group milled around to watch.

The throaty snarl of the Shogun's engine filled the air. It was followed by exclamations of admiration from the other fighters.

Blaise closed up the briefcase and moved toward the car Valerie was hiding behind. She eyed the briefcase. First the falsified dueling contract, now a fixed tournament. There was no way to know what other documents he might have inside. If she could expose this to the king, he'd have to listen.

She was so close to what she wanted. The proof of Jasper's duplicitousness was practically within reach. If she didn't take this chance, she might never encounter it again. She turned to instruct Eli, but he was already gone. She glimpsed a flash of movement near the stairs as he slipped from behind one car to another.

A nagging voice told her she ought to follow. She should hide. But Blaise was getting closer. He reached the far side of the car and fumbled for his keys.

"Screw it," Valerie muttered. She vaulted onto the hood of the car and immediately leapt up to the roof.

Blaise looked up to see her looming over him. "What the —"

Valerie kicked him in the head. Blaise flailed backward and hit the concrete.

She jumped to the ground after him and snatched up the briefcase. Despite being dazed, Blaise flung a hand out to stop her, his fingers wrapping around her ankle. She stomped his arm with her other foot, causing him to shriek and lose his grip.

She ran.

"Stop him!" Jasper shouted.

Valerie sprinted for the stairs at the corner of the garage. She briefly spotted Eli, cowering behind a luxury sedan along the far wall, but he wisely ducked out of view to stay hidden.

She allowed herself one look back and was shocked to find her pursuers already closing in on her. Two women were in pursuit, one a fighter she didn't recognize, and the other was Niko Okazaki, a wicked look of determination on her face.

Valerie dashed down the stairs, crashing into walls as she flew down them, not wanting to relinquish her grip on the briefcase. She completed a full circuit of the stairs, then emerged on the ground floor. She looked around to orient herself, trying to identify the corner where she first came in.

A figure vaulted from the level above and landed in a crouch ahead of her. Niko had a sheathed sword in her hand, but as she stood, she drew the blade from its scabbard.

"Hello, thief," she said.

Valerie's eyes widened at the sight of the masterworked steel in her hand. It was Yawarakai-Te, crafted by Niko's legendary ancestor, Masamune Okazaki.

If it were any other circumstance, Valerie would have gaped in awe at the sight of the sword, but as the second fighter's hands reached for her throat, she was forced to duck her outstretched arms and sprint away across the garage.

It was a dozen yards before she came to the sickening realization that she was headed the wrong way. More of her pursuers had made it down the stairs now, including Blaise. He shouted encouragement to the ones chasing her, but it was clear he himself was unable to keep up.

Valerie turned a corner of the garage but nearly ran straight into a pair of men-at-arms, both armored in mail and shiny helms and carrying maces. "Hey! You there! Stop!" one shouted.

The exit was just beyond the guards, but the gates were still down, and these men now blocked the path to the pedestrian exit. They rushed her, and she fled the only direction left available to her, back through a pair of double doors and into another stairwell. Lacking any other options, she climbed upward, leaping the steps two at a time. She burst back into the second level and looked around.

She was on the far side of the garage from the stairwell she had come up initially. Jasper Sterling was at the opposite stairwell, peering over the railing. He looked up at the sound of Valerie's entrance, then quickly turned and shouted down the stairwell. "He's back!"

The shout was partly obscured by the low rumbling of an engine. Valerie studied the line of cars to her left and noted that Niko Okazaki's car was still idling and the driver's door was hanging open. She had evidently raced off in pursuit of Valerie so quickly that she hadn't bothered to shut the war car off.

That was lucky.

The pounding of feet in the stairwell behind her caused the single cloud of doubt to evaporate from her mind. She rushed to the idling war car, slid across the hood, then tossed the briefcase inside before flinging herself into the driver's seat.

A shriek came from the stairwell as Niko bolted toward her.

Valerie slammed the driver's door and locked it. She shifted into gear just as Niko launched herself onto the hood of the car. Her eyes were wide, and her mouth stretched into a snarl. Valerie popped the clutch and accelerated.

She was immediately thrown back in her seat from the torque of the rear wheels. She slammed on the brakes to avoid crashing into a support column ahead of her. The maneuver sent Niko flying from the hood, and the fighter rolled several times on landing, her black hair whirling around her face as she tumbled into the column. Valerie paused only long enough to see Niko look up before her foot was on the accelerator again. She cranked the wheel hard and launched away at an angle, sideswiping the taillights of one of the luxury sedans on her way out.

It took a moment to straighten out of the turn as the sheer power of the Shogun's rear end threatened to send her into a spin, but Valerie got control of the car in time to avoid crushing Blaise's limo. Thinking better of it at the last second, she sideswiped the bumper anyway, shearing it off and slamming the limo into the concrete barrier.

Jasper's eyes widened as she next aimed the car toward him.

He raced for the corner of the garage and disappeared into the stairwell.

Valerie cursed and straightened out again and was about to round the curve toward the exit ramp when she spotted a boy's head bobbing up from behind a Windsor 350. She braked hard, skidding to a stop before reaching across the seat to pop open the passenger door.

"Hey! Get in!" she shouted.

Eli took a quick look at the men and women now in pursuit, then dove into the car. Valerie was already moving by the time he got the door shut.

"Buckle up," she shouted. She slipped into her own five-point harness before steering the Shogun down the exit ramp. She took the curve at the bottom without braking, flying around the corner and onto the level surface of the ground floor. She finally slowed, coming out of the turn as she searched for the exit.

Jasper Sterling emerged from the stairwell. He was shouting something but not at them.

Eli got his harness locked in and gripped the door handle. Valerie spotted the gates at the far end of the garage, but as she aimed that direction, a pair of headlights flicked on in the far-left corner of the garage. She only caught quick glimpses of the car as she sped past the rows of columns, but it was enough to recognize the other vehicle as a charcoal-gray Easton Blackbird 900. When she looked again, she saw the driver's black mask and the crimson streak down one side. The Red Reaper.

"Oh no!" Eli shouted as the Blackbird blasted out of its parking space. It was tracking a course to intercept or possibly T-bone the Shogun. Valerie shifted gears and stomped the accelerator.

Several men-at-arms were standing guard at the exit gate, but they took one look at the vehicles speeding toward them and scattered.

Valerie aimed straight for the center of the right-hand gate, trying to judge the velocity of the intercepting Blackbird. It was going to be close.

The gates were a mix of thin, horizontal, metal rails and chain link. She tightened her grip on the steering wheel as she accelerated straight for it. The Blackbird was closing in her peripheral vision.

Thirty yards.

Fifteen.

Five.

The Blackbird's rear tires smoked as it braked, and the Shogun hit a speed bump, went airborne, and slammed through the exit gate, metal, chain, and sparks exploding from the front end of the car as they flew through.

Valerie's eyes were closed on impact, but the instant the car hit the ground, they were back open, and she fought the wheel to regain control, all while attempting to see through a windshield obscured by twisted debris.

They erupted into the street amid a screech of steel on concrete. Valerie braked hard, and the remains of the exit gate flew off the front of the car and gave her back her vision. They slammed into a parked car, crushing the entire driver's side. Valerie and Eli both jolted against their harnesses.

A quick glance in the rear-view mirror showed the carnage of the gate behind them. To her dismay, the headlights of the Reaper's Blackbird were sweeping toward the hole. Valerie shifted into reverse and backed up just far enough to extricate herself from the smashed car ahead of her.

The Blackbird growled as the Red Reaper drove it through the ruin of the exit gate.

Valerie met the Reaper's gaze through the windshield. The voids that took the place of eyes in the mask seemed intent on swallowing her.

"Bastard," Valerie hissed, shifting into gear again and accelerating away from the wreckage she had created.

She checked her rear-view mirror and found the Blackbird

accelerating out of the turn to follow. They were out of the garage, but this wasn't over.

"I need you to get that case open," Valerie said, indicating the briefcase now on the floor near Eli's feet. "Any way you can." She handed him the hammer.

Eli stretched for the briefcase but had to wriggle part way out of his safety harness to reach it. Valerie kept her eyes on the road and dodged carts, pedestrians, and a few other vehicles as she sped through uptown. She made the turn on Druid Avenue and headed east.

"That was my bike," Eli said, turning in his seat as the corner flew by.

"We'll have to come back for it."

The Blackbird raced onto the street behind her and was on her bumper in a flash. As soon as she cleared the last of the pedestrians, Valerie gunned the throttle, and the Shogun's twin turbochargers spooled up, launching her forward and plastering Eli back in his seat.

The road opened up ahead of her, and she used the space to gain some distance on the Red Reaper. He hadn't tried to ram into her again, perhaps because of the pedestrians around, but it was clear she wouldn't lose him easily.

In a matter of seconds, her problem tripled. Two armored Monarch Furies bearing the paint scheme of the City Watch pulled into the road ahead, blocking her route. The Furies bristled with weapons, including turret-mounted ballistae.

Valerie swore under her breath and turned the wheel hard, careening through an open plaza, dodging street performers and musicians and wide-eyed visitors. The only exit from the plaza was a narrow alley barely big enough for the Shogun. The broader Furies wouldn't clear the walls on either side. If she could get through . . .

One of the Furies bore down on her, flames shooting from its short-stack exhaust system. It was almost on her when it was suddenly knocked aside by the Blackbird. The Reaper forced the other car out of the way as he pursued her.

As she plummeted into the alley, the armored Easton was back on her bumper.

With a similar body width, there was no getting around the fact that wherever she could go, he could follow.

The alley twisted and turned, and the roar of the two engines echoed off the sides of the houses. People leapt from the cobblestone street into doorways to avoid the vehicles.

Valerie emerged into a second plaza south of the first and launched the Shogun down a series of broad steps toward an elaborate fountain.

Eli had a white-knuckle grip on the door handle as they bounced their way down the steps, and more tourists leapt out of their way.

"Briefcase!" Valerie shouted. "Get it open."

Eli tore his eyes from the chaotic scene ahead long enough to focus on the silver briefcase. Once the Shogun was back on level ground, he made an attempt at the combination latches but with little effect.

"It's still locked."

Another Fury flew into sight to Valerie's left. She pushed the hood of her sweatshirt away from her face, keeping her mask on but trying to maintain a better view of her pursuers. An armored troop carrier raced along the side street to her right as she flew past an intersection.

"Oh great. Just what we need," Valerie muttered.

The pursuit was causing her to flee downhill. They were forcing her that way, and she soon realized why. She was headed for the harbor. They were closing a trap.

Valerie swerved left and attempted to cut east across the water district, but the Furies formed up on that side to block her path. A car slammed into her with a squeal of metal on metal, knocking her sideview mirror forward. The gendarme in the passenger seat of the car was so close she could count the teeth in his snarl. She was forced south again, swerving around a produce cart and causing the farmer to dive beneath it to get out of the way.

The troop carriers were multiplying behind her.

She was running out of time.

The glistening harbor was now in full view. Ships lined the docks, and noblemen and merchants crowded every corner. This high-end waterfront district was crowded with passengers alighting from ferries. All around the plaza, the Furies were pouring out of side streets. Lights and sirens flashed, and their ballista turrets all swiveled toward her.

Valerie turned one way and then another, but they had her hemmed in, a noose that drew tighter with every move she made. She cursed and brought the Shogun to a skidding stop near the entrance to the ferry dock. She was out of room.

"I got it!" Eli said, springing the lid of the briefcase with the claw end of the hammer. A broad grin spread across his face, but it vanished when he looked out the windows. They were surrounded by vehicles with artillery weapons pointed straight at them.

The Red Reaper's Easton Blackbird fronted the ring of Furies.

Soldiers of the City Watch poured from the troop carriers and moved into positions with crossbows.

"Tell me there is a dueling contract in there," Valerie said, reaching for the stack of papers in the briefcase and rifling through them. "Something that proves Jasper Sterling is forging duels." She tossed forms and envelopes aside, searching for the stack of dueling contracts she'd seen Blaise pull from. "There has to be something in here."

But her search came up empty.

"Damn it!" Valerie shouted.

Eli shrunk against the seat. His eyes darted to the soldiers outside.

Valerie shuffled through the last few papers and located the form that Blaise had made the other fighters sign in the garage. She didn't have time to read the details, but the signatures were all there. She stuffed all the papers back in the briefcase.

"You there! You in the car! Shut off your engine immediately!"

Valerie looked up and eyed the vehicles and soldiers encircling them. No one was taking any chances of being run down by the Shogun, but there was nowhere to go.

Valerie glanced into the rear-view mirror at the fishing vessels crowding the harbor. Another ferry was working its way toward the dock.

"Eli. Tell me you know how to swim."

"Swim?" Eli twisted in his seat and looked behind them. "Oh no. You're not thinking about—"

"Can you or can't you?" Valerie asked.

"Yeah, but—"

Valerie didn't wait for the rest. She stomped on the accelerator and popped the clutch, the rear tires gaining traction after a squeal of rubber on stone. She spun the car around and aimed it for the long pier of the ferry dock. A shout went up from the captain of the gendarmes.

"Fire!"

A hail of crossbow bolts ricocheted off the back of the car. A normal vehicle would have suffered from the barrage, but the Shogun's armored body and reinforced windows repelled the attack with ease. The ballistae were a different matter. Valerie didn't want to find out what they would do.

Eli gave a shout as the Shogun shot across the last remaining yards of concrete and onto the wood planks of the pier. His fingers tightened on the door handle again, and Valerie didn't blame him. Her own hands may as well have been welded to the steering wheel as she kept the Shogun aimed down the length of the pier. The wooden structure wasn't designed to support a vehicle of this weight, but she could only hope the timbers would hold together long enough for her to make the channel. She glanced in the mirror.

None of the Furies had dared to follow, and even the Red Reaper was simply staring. He had climbed out of the Blackbird and was watching her escape, those black eyes still fixated on the Shogun's taillights.

"Open the door," Valerie shouted over the rumbling of their tires. "We'll either hit the water or we can jump first."

"Jump?" Eli's eyes were as wide as they could go, but he unlatched the gull-wing door and pushed it skyward.

Fishermen and longshoremen dove off the pier left and right as the Shogun gained speed. There would be a lot of people in the water. She hoped enough.

The end of the pier was approaching fast. There was only a low, wooden railing at the far end, then a long drop to the crowded blue channel.

"Time to decide!" Valerie shouted. "All the way in or jump?" She shifted her gaze from the pier to the boy next to her.

"Aaahhh, aaahhh, jump!" he shouted.

She shrugged out of her five-point harness at the same time he unbuckled his. Valerie pushed her door open as high as it could go and let go of the steering wheel just as Eli got his footing against the door frame.

She grabbed the briefcase.

The railing of the pier exploded across the hood of the car.

The next moment, the world got quiet as the Shogun's wheels left the pier. Valerie looked down to find twenty-five feet of open air and the glistening waves of the harbor beneath her. She kicked hard from the doorframe and leapt.

The rippled water rushed up to meet her.

DISCOVERED

"Give me a name," Jasper said. He stood amid the wreckage of the parking garage's exit gate and glared at the security captain.

"We don't know who the trespasser was," the captain said. "But I've got my men scouring the area for anyone who knows something."

"Let me be clear when I say that your career depends on it," Jasper said. "If you don't find me answers, you'll be taste-testing chum in the dock district for the rest of your useless existence."

The man bowed as he backed away, and Jasper turned his glare on Blaise. "And you may as well have just announced our plans to the entire city."

Blaise was still rubbing his forehead. "That little bastard kicked me in the face."

"You let them," Jasper said.

"Listen, you're the one who wanted the contract in writing," Blaise hissed. "To hold over the other fighters' heads. I advised against it!"

"We need to fix this," Jasper said.

In the aftermath of the incident, the other fighters had been so amped up to chase the thief that they hadn't had time to point the blame at him. But it was only a matter of time before they wanted to know what had become of their signatures.

They wouldn't out him to the king. They had as much to lose as he did if it came out that they were planning to cheat the tournament, but they needed to solve this problem quickly.

"Whoever it was will make contact," Blaise said. "Hold the briefcase for ransom. Or they're just after quick cash and will dump it once they see there's no money in it."

"Don't be dense," Jasper said. "If they wanted money, they would have taken a car when no one was around or gone after the briefcase *before* we dispersed the payments. This is something personal."

Footsteps pounded pavement, and the security captain and one of his underlings ran back up to them breathlessly.

"You'd better have something good," Jasper said.

"My men located a suspicious vehicle," the captain panted. "No registration. Junker. Must be from outside the walls. Found these inside." He handed over a pair of colorful flyers.

Jasper unfolded the crumpled papers and read the announcement. "This is just some second-rate drag show."

"Yes, sir. A clue, sir. Appears to be a tavern down in Tidewater."

"Tidewater?" Jasper clenched his jaw. "That little welp." He crushed the flyers.

"What is it?" Blaise asked. "That mean something to you?"

"Charlotte's prodigal daughter telephoned from that pit-stain district. I'd hoped she would have turned up dead by now."

"If she's survived this long on her own, she could be trouble."

"She's a loose end," Jasper said. "We need it cut." He turned to the security captain. "Bring the car. We're all going for a ride."

It had been a long time since Jasper Sterling had set foot in one of the city's rim districts. When he opened the door to the stink of dead fish and rotting seaweed, he remembered why. He held a handkerchief to his nose and got out of the car.

Despite being an offensive eyesore, the avenue he found himself on was surprisingly busy. Fishmongers shouted from corner stands, and noisy music blared from shop windows. The area was teeming with energy and an ever-present babble of excitement. It was clear that the King's Tournament was eliciting the requisite enthusiasm even among those who stood no real chance of benefiting from it.

His bodyguards closed his door for him, then led the way down the muddy street, pushing commoners aside to make room.

Jasper paused when he saw the sign for the Swan and Pelican Inn. He turned and noted the proximity of the tavern they had come to find. He was surprised to find several people he recognized mingling on the covered porch of the inn, talking among themselves. Guild members.

Breaking away from Blaise and his security team, Jasper strode up to the tallest of the figures on the porch and immediately extended a hand. "Richard Canton. What a pleasure it is to see you."

"Lord Sterling," the man replied. His hand was bedecked with gold and silver signet rings. "What an unexpected surprise. Don't tell me you've finally accepted the Guild's invitation to participate in a field judging."

Jasper smiled and tucked away his handkerchief. "I have indeed. The House of Sterling does so value the work of the Guild leadership. I thought it was past time I made good on your generous invitation. I'm afraid I know little of the candidate today, however. Who are we judging?"

"It's a rather unorthodox story." Jasper recognized the speaker as Rupert Pimsley, a beady-eyed man who always smelled of horses. "Our new candidate is a woman who has apprenticed in the west end for over a decade," Pimsley continued. "She's the wife of a tavern owner, and they'll be presenting just across the street there in a matter of hours." He pointed to the Twisted Tentacle.

"Just taking the time to get in the mood over here first?" Jasper nodded to the cocktail glasses in the men's hands.

"When in Rome," Canton replied. "It is tournament week after all."

"I certainly can't fault you." Jasper glanced across the street. "There haven't been many female sword masters in the Guild of late, have there? And a showing hosted in a rim village tavern, no less?"

"As we said, it's an unorthodox entry," Canton replied. "But the work is quite exquisite. In cases like this, the judging is almost a formality. The sword has the makings of a true masterwork."

"I look forward to seeing it," Jasper said. "Shall we go over there now? Surely they wouldn't want to keep us waiting."

"We are quite early," Pimsley said. "The official judging isn't scheduled until this evening, and the rest of the judges have yet to arrive."

"Sounds like you've all made up your minds already. Perhaps I'll just have a sneak peek myself then and report back," Jasper said. He turned to Blaise and the two bodyguards they had brought along. "Why don't you gentlemen wait here," Jasper said. "I'll have a look at what they have planned."

"It's typically the tradition of the Guild to judge a work in a group," Pimsley said. "But of course you should do as you wish, m'lord."

Jasper smiled at the Guild judges. "I'll keep my thoughts to myself until the official judging." He strode off the porch and crossed the street to the tavern. He immediately rapped on the door. When his initial knock gained no response, he kept up a barrage on the door until it was finally opened by a woman with short, choppy, blonde hair and a careworn face.

"You can stop that racket already; we don't reopen till—" the woman said in an irritated voice but cut herself off at the sight of him.

"Pardon the intrusion," Jasper said. "Lord Jasper Sterling."

"It's . . . an honor," the woman replied, though Jasper had the impression it wasn't the first thought that had actually crossed her mind. She adjusted her apron and fixed a smile on her face. "I'm Janet Merriweather. I'm the owner."

"I was told there would be a Guild membership judging here this evening," Jasper said. "I was invited by the Smith's Guild to participate. Do you mind if I come in?" He didn't wait for a reply but stepped past the woman.

He took in the sights and sounds of the tavern in an instant: worn booths, bad acoustics, a floor in desperate need of refinishing. It was clean, if you could call anything in this dump of a village clean, but he knew enough to recognize a dive when he saw one. The staff had clearly worked hard to tidy the place up, but there was only so much lipstick you could put on a pig.

The tavern owner dried her hands on a rag and gestured to a table adjacent to the stage. "Please come in. Can I offer you a drink?"

"I don't suppose you carry Mortal Blade."

The tavern owner shook her head. "Our top shelf whiskey is Bushmills. I can get you some of that."

"That would be adequate," Jasper said. He peered down the hall and surveyed the staff in sight. None resembled Charlotte's missing daughter. "You must be quite proud of your . . . wife is it?" He took in the threadbare curtains of the stage.

"Extremely," Janet replied. "She's an inspiration to me daily." Jasper smiled.

"Janet, there's something going on with the microphone cables back—" A young man came bursting into the hall from a back room, his face covered in makeup, but he stopped short at the sight of Jasper and gaped.

"Good afternoon," Jasper said.

The man looked past him to the tavern owner, eyes wide.

"Rico, this is Lord Jasper Sterling. He's participating in the judging of Ann's sword tonight."

Jasper thought she spoke the words with a slight edge of warning in her voice.

"I see," Rico replied. "It's such an honor to meet you," he said, bowing politely. "I'm afraid you've caught me without my hair on."

"I do always enjoy seeing what goes on behind closed doors," Jasper replied. "The truth of things, if you will."

Rico kept the smile on his face and bowed again as he backed away. "I'll just be . . . back here." He pointed to the door he had come from and waved off Janet. "I'll fix the microphone myself. I'm sure it's nothing."

"Unique character," Jasper said. He turned and accepted the glass of whiskey from Janet. "Are all of your staff so eccentric?"

"We're all very close here," Janet said. "Eccentricities and all. Like a family."

He glanced around the bar area. "Who else is part of your little family?"

"Well, my wife Ann is upstairs." Janet wiped her hands off again. "She's the star of the show, so make yourself comfortable. I'll go get her." She crossed from behind the bar to a staircase and disappeared.

Jasper pressed his lips into a line and wandered over to the kitchen door. He pushed it open to get a look inside. The area was bustling with activity, an army of misfits under the supervision of an aproned woman with purple hair. She looked up and glowered at his intrusion, but her mouth fell open at the sight of his tailored suit and the signet ring on his finger. Jasper studied each of the occupants of the kitchen, registering their faces, then removed himself back to the bar.

"Lord Sterling, I'd like for you to meet my wife," Janet said, coming down the hall. "This is Ann."

The woman who stepped from behind the tavern owner had caramel skin and a brilliant smile. Her black hair was pulled behind her head. She was modestly dressed in a white blouse and slacks. She extended her hand. "It's an honor to meet you, Lord Sterling."

He accepted her hand and shook it. "The honor is mine, I'm sure." He noted the ornate wooden case that she held cradled in her other arm. "I take it this is your masterwork. The sword of the hour."

Ann smiled. "It is. I'm looking forward to having it judged tonight."

"Well, there's no time like the present," Jasper said. "Let's have a look, shall we?"

"Now?" Ann said. "Of course. I'll find a table to—"

"Nonsense," Jasper said, reaching out and grabbing hold of the end of the box. Ann hesitantly released her grip on it. Jasper set the case on the bar top and unceremoniously flipped open the lid. But even in the poor light of the bar, the sight of the sword took him aback. "Wow. Now that . . . is a sword," he said.

He reached into the case and grasped the twisting, purplish wood of the handle, lifting the sword from its case and balancing it in his palm. Ann seemed ready to step forward at any moment as though he was dangling an infant by its toes.

"Exquisite," Jasper said. "And as a son of the House of a Thousand Swords, I should know, wouldn't you say?" He glanced at Janet. She forced a smile to her lips.

Ann was still looking on anxiously, her expression caught somewhere between hope and nausea.

"A bit of a lie though, our moniker," Jasper continued. "I doubt we have anywhere close to a thousand named swords. A few hundred, certainly. Like one I came across recently. A legacy sword. Its name is *Durendal*—rumored to be the sharpest sword in the world." He studied the edge of Ann's sword. "But I must say this one appears to be a contender for that title." He pressed a finger to the edge.

"I wouldn't—" Ann began.

But it was too late. The blade bit into his skin.

"Jeezus," he said. "That is sharp." It took a moment for the cut to bleed, but then a single droplet of blood appeared on his fingertip. He popped the finger into his mouth and sucked on it, the taste of blood registering on his tongue.

"I'll get you a towel," Janet said.

"No need," Jasper said, pulling his finger from his mouth while continuing to examine the sword. "You know someone tried to kill me with it? *Durendal*. It's hanging in Castle Sterling now of course, and my challenger is dead." He tossed Ann's sword casually from one hand to the other and back again. "But one of the would-be assassins is still loose somewhere, do you believe it?" He fixed his eyes on Janet. "A girl, no less. Completely out of her mind. Goes by the name Valerie, formerly of the house of Terravecchia."

"We're certainly sorry for your troubles," Janet said.

Her eyes were hard despite the words that came from her mouth.

"Troubles. Yes. I suppose that is one way to phrase it," Jasper replied. He dipped the blade of the sword until the tip was pointed at Ann and peered down its length at her. "It does seem like you have a fine future in store for yourself. Both of you." He casually angled the sword so that it pointed at Janet. "If you can avoid . . . troubles."

The women remained silent. Their eyes no longer followed the tip of the sword. They were both staring back at him with faces that may as well have been made of stone.

"Best of luck to you tonight," Jasper said, swinging the sword around with a flourish and presenting the grip to Ann. "It truly is a masterpiece."

Ann wrapped her fingers around the pommel, but Jasper didn't release his hold on it. "It would make a fine addition to any collection. If you ever plan to part with it, do let me know." He let go of the sword, and Ann took an involuntary step back.

Jasper bowed politely to Janet, then turned and pushed his way out the front door.

He strode directly across the street, heedless of the cart and pedestrian traffic that was forced to make way for him. Blaise and the two bodyguards rushed off the porch of the Swan and Pelican to meet him.

"Start the car," Jasper said.

The two guards leapt to comply.

"We're leaving?" Blaise asked.

Jasper reached into his pocket and removed his handkerchief, using it to cover his nose. "We'll be back."

22

WET

Valerie sucked a last breath just before the light vanished, and resisted the urge to gasp from shock.

Cold.

The deep water was more frigid than she expected, and she was turned upside down as soon as she was under.

The surge of waves from the Shogun's impact turned her end over end.

Valerie chased her own escaping air bubbles as she tried to orient which way was up. The briefcase in her grip tugged toward the surface, but she resisted the pull, staying under long enough to shed her mask and strip out of her sweatshirt. As the hoodie floated gently below the surface, she forced the briefcase beneath her and stayed submerged, kicking hard and angling away from the pier. Her boots were heavy and made swimming twice as hard, but she refused to lose them.

When she had held her breath for as long as possible, she finally surfaced to orient herself. She clenched the briefcase to her abdomen and spun around, scanning the water for any sign of Eli.

She spotted a head. He was treading water thirty yards closer to the pier.

As he bobbed over a passing wave, Eli spotted her and began splashing in her direction. The current was rapidly sweeping them both away from the pier. Valerie ducked under the waves and swam hard for Eli. When she came up again, she was less than ten yards from the boy. He was again treading water and had evidently been waiting for her to surface.

People were gathering at the end of the pier. Some were pointing to the area where the Shogun had disappeared. Valerie pointed to a cluster of sailboats anchored to the east. "We'll head that way! Stay underwater as long as you can."

Eli nodded. A glint of steel shone from the pier approach, and she noted a contingent of helmeted soldiers trooping along the boards, their lances out as they detained citizens. She ducked underwater again and swam.

The current was strong, and she could feel it pulling her along. The water was too murky to make out the seafloor, but she could still sense her speed from the changing cloud shadows on the water. When she came up for air again, she was several hundred yards from the pier, far enough that even if someone did see her, they would have a hard time making out details.

There were more heads in the water near the base of the pier as people who had leapt to safety attempted to cling to the pilings or take the direct route to shore. She hoped that the attention of the City Watch would be occupied long enough for her to escape detection. There were boats in the water, but none appeared to belong to the Watch.

A fisherman in a flat-bottomed skiff spotted her bobbing in the waves and gave a shout.

"You there! Do you need a hand?"

"Yeah!" came the reply from behind her.

Eli had surfaced a dozen yards from Valerie and immediately began swimming toward the vessel.

"No, Eli," Valerie hissed. "He might want to take us in."

But Eli paid her no attention, swimming hand over hand to the boat and clinging with relief to a line the fisherman threw overboard. Eli reached the edge of the boat and immediately climbed aboard, only turning to encourage Valerie once his feet were firmly planted on the deck.

Valerie took another look at the pier receding in the distance, then resigned herself to the rescue and swam to the skiff.

The old fisherman extended a hand over the rail and clasped her wrist with calloused fingers. He hauled her up in one swift motion, lifting Valerie far enough that she could toss the briefcase aboard and cling to the gunnel. She slid over the rail and collapsed in an undignified heap before righting herself and climbing back to her feet.

The fisherman studied her boots, then his eyes roamed up her trousers to linger unabashedly at the tank top that clung scandalously tight against her chest. Valerie scooped up the silver briefcase and hugged it, then looked at Eli who, to his credit, was not gawking at her soaking wet figure but was simply working to regain his breath. His mouth hung open as he inhaled gulps of salty air.

"Bit of a hubbub over there on the pier, eh? That splash was something to behold," the old timer said. "You two are lucky it didn't smash you under."

Eli looked like he was about to speak, but Valerie interrupted. "We leapt clear just as that car was coming by. Must have been some kind of . . . crazy person."

"Crazy to be sure," the old man said. "Did you get a good look at a face?"

"Uh, yeah." Valerie glanced uncertainly at Eli.

"Big guy," Eli said. "Looked angry."

"Very angry," Valerie said. "That man. Very big. Bearded, right?" She looked back to Eli. "You see a beard on him?"

"And he only had one eye," Eli added.

"Is that so?" the fisherman replied. "No doubt some manner of fearsome warrior then. The car looked to be a war machine if my eyes told the truth."

"Could be," Valerie replied. "Just so glad we got out of the way." She glanced around, eyeing the other boats in the area. She spotted a Sea Patrol cruiser headed in from the channel. "Hey, do you think you could get us ashore? We have friends who will be worried."

"Of course I can," the old man replied. "You want I should take you back over to the pier and put you up there?"

"No!" Valerie and Eli blurted out simultaneously.

"I mean, heading against the current isn't necessary," Valerie added. "Putting us ashore at the next dock east would be fine. Are we anywhere near Tidewater?"

"Tidewater? Why, that's the far side of the peninsula. I can take you as far as Welsh Point if that'll suit you."

"Is that closer to Tidewater?" Valerie asked.

"It is if you go over land."

She nodded. "Okay. Welsh Point then."

"Stow that for me, lad," the man said, handing the coiled line to Eli, "and let's be off."

Valerie lent a hand as well, and the little boat came around and headed downwind again. The fisherman, who finally introduced himself as Gaspar, took a firm grip on the tiller and steered them along the edge of the harbor and around the bend.

Valerie was relieved to see the pier and its new collection of patrol boats vanish from view.

They still caught some attention. Mostly, it was just friendly waves from boat captains or the crew of other fishing vessels, but Valerie caught more than a few glances from folks who recognized that she was soaking wet and clearly cold in the chilly, late afternoon breeze.

She did her best to keep her teeth from chattering, but there was no disguising the goose pimples that rose along her forearms. "Fetch yourselves some towels," Gaspar said, indicating a hold near the front of the boat. "Can't say how clean they be, but it'll keep you out of the wind."

Valerie was grateful to find the towels. They were dingy and smelled vaguely of fish, as did everything aboard, but at this point, she knew she couldn't be choosy. She handed a towel to Eli, then bundled herself up as best she could, stomping her feet occasionally in her soaking wet boots and doing her best not to think about the mess her afternoon had become.

As the little skiff was pulling up to the dock, she glanced at the sun on the horizon and queried the old man, "Do you know what time it is?"

"A bit past five o'clock, I reckon." Gaspar lifted the well-chewed end of a stubby cigar to his lips and chomped it between his teeth. "Don't have no clock aboard, but the sun'll be down in a few hours." He raised an arm and squinted over his outstretched fist, gauging the distance of the sun from the horizon. "Aye, I'd say just past five."

Valerie cursed under her breath as she waited for the boat to pull ashore.

She had no idea how to get back to the car unseen or make it to work on time.

As soon as Gaspar tied off the skiff, Valerie leapt onto the dock.

"Thanks for your help," she muttered quickly. "I hate to seem ungrateful, but I have to get uptown in a hurry. I've got to get back to work."

"Uptown, you say?" Gaspar replied. "It be a long, winding way up that way." He nodded toward the heart of the city. "We be outside the walls now. You'll have to climb back a mile or more west before finding your way through. Up the old quarry road. Get passage through the Ore Gate."

"Damn," Valerie muttered, switching the briefcase from one hand to the other. "Isn't there any other way? A way you don't have to get through the wall security?"

"Not unless you get yourself a ride in one of them fancy cars whizzing by the high road," Gaspar said. He scratched at his whiskers. "Well, I suppose there is one way. But not for a young lady like yourself," he said. "If it was just the boy here, I might suggest it, but it wouldn't be the type of route a lady would take."

Valerie considered the position of the sun above the horizon. "Try me."

Gaspar raised an eyebrow. "Well, if you're the observant sort, say maybe an old timer like me, you know that all the rainwater runoff from uptown flows down through those drains there." He pointed along the seawall to a rusty, corrugated pipe jutting through the rocks that was only partially submerged in seawater. "Used to be nothing big ever made it down the wall drains. They had the passages beneath the wall defenses barred off to prevent attacks and invasions from the old days. Used to be nothing much bigger than a rat ever found its way out through those grates.

"But that was before. Been seeing some big things floating out of the drains of late. Car tires. Tree branches. Sort of things that never would have made it out in the old days." He flicked his nose and leaned closer. "Way I see it, city maintenance ain't taking care of the drains anymore, and all those grates have rusted away. Means that pipe there is a straight shot more or less all the way to Bringham Park. That's where the drain system starts."

Valerie eyed the drainpipe suspiciously. "You're suggesting I crawl through a sewer?"

"Not recommending it, mind you. Just saying it might be possible," Gaspar replied. "The type of route I might use if I ever found myself in a situation where I needed to get uptown in a hurry and maybe do it without attracting the attention of the City Watch." He winked conspiratorially. Gaspar pulled a box of matches from his pocket and struck one to light his stub of a cigar. "Watch out for more of them flying cars though," he added. "Wouldn't want you to get yourselves into any trouble."

Valerie blushed. Their lie hadn't worked in the slightest.

At least it seemed the old man had no intention of reporting them. If he had wanted to turn her in, he could have pulled up to any one of the guarded docks dotting the harbor.

At that moment, a patrol boat motored its way around the jetty to the west. They appeared to be searching the shore. She noted a pair of patrol cars working their way down the hill as well, their lights flashing. She cursed under her breath.

Gaspar tossed Valerie the box of matches. "Looks like you might be needing those." He untied his mooring lines and pushed away from the dock again. "So long!" He gave a quick wave, then turned the skiff around, motoring away with the put-put-put of his undersized outboard motor. The smoke from his cigar blended with the boat's exhaust, and the old man drifted away downstream.

Valerie only waited till he was out of earshot, then tuned to Eli. "Well, I guess that's that. We'll have to climb a damned drainpipe."

Eli studied the pipe, then looked up the dock to where the gravel path met the quarry road. "I think I'll just take the long way back to Tidewater."

"We can't go that way," Valerie said. "They're sure to be looking for us at the gates. You heard what that boatman said."

"I know," Eli said, stomping his soggy sneakers and making little puddles on the dock. "But, I guess . . ." He glanced at her, then looked away. "I guess what I'm trying to say . . ." He finally dragged his eyes back to hers. "I think I want to see other people."

Valerie stumbled over the arguments she had been about to make, taken aback by his statement. Despite the circumstances, she couldn't stop the smirk of amusement from forming on her lips. "You're . . . breaking up with me?"

Eli looked away. "I mean, it's not that I don't still think you're pretty. You are. And I like that you can drive and everything, but . . . I think . . . I think you might be a bad influence."

Valerie laughed.

Eli watched, confused. "You think it's funny?"

"No. I get it," Valerie replied. "You're right. You deserve someone who will be better suited for you." She laid a hand on his shoulder. "You've been great. Best boyfriend a girl could ask for."

Eli straightened up at that. "Really?"

"Yeah. Stay out of trouble, okay? Be careful getting back. I'm sorry I got you into this."

"It's all right," Eli said. "It was kind of fun."

The port patrol boat was making its way toward the docks. The soldiers aboard were now scanning the docks with binoculars.

"See you around, kid." She leaned over and kissed Eli on the cheek. "Gotta run." She took a tighter grip on the briefcase and dropped off the base of the dock, then worked her way along the seawall to the runoff pipe.

"Watch out for rats," Eli said. "I've heard they get as big as cats in the drains."

"Great," Valerie said. "Just what I needed to hear." She reached the end of the pipe and peered inside. Subtle sloshing echoed from the darkness as the water lapped back and forth. She pulled a match from the box and hesitated. She looked to the dock for one last bit of reassurance, but when she scanned the dilapidated structure, Eli had vanished.

A blast of the patrol boat's horn solidified her resolve. She struck the match against the side of the rusted pipe, lifted the dimly flickering flame ahead of her, then plunged into the darkness.

23

DANK

V alerie wasn't scared of the dark.

She was scared of what she was touching in the dark.

She'd been inside the runoff drain for what felt like forever. The first few matches came and went in a hurry, but as she continued on, she had to ration them. It could be a long walk, and who knew what other need she would have before reaching the end.

One advantage of her slightly below-average height was that she barely had to stoop to avoid the top of the pipe. She could imagine that hunching over for any length of time in this cramped space would be difficult to maintain.

The walking wasn't easy either way. The ridges of the metal pipe made for uneven footing, and the curve made her feel continually off balance. She was careful to keep her feet because there were thick layers of algae and slime coating the bottom of the pipe, and she was uninterested in falling face first into the stuff.

There was little to do inside the pitch-black pipe other than to walk and to think. Think about how, a matter of weeks ago, she wouldn't have dreamed of entering this dank hole in the ground as a means of getting anywhere. No manner of prodding would have convinced the Valerie Terravecchia of those heady days that anything could have been worth it.

That Valerie wouldn't have understood.

She couldn't have comprehended the abysmal injustice of this place. She certainly couldn't have fathomed this one-person war she was now waging against the House of Sterling. Even having lived it, Valerie had a hard time comprehending how bad things had become. She barely recognized herself.

She had taken every chance offered to her so far but had lost at every turn. The theft of her inheritance, Henry's death, her condemnation as one of the nameless. All of it was bizarre. As bizarre as the person she had now become. She was a car thief. A fugitive from the law that was seeking justice by, of all things, entry into a tournament in which she was almost certainly outmatched. A person who, at this very moment, was crawling like a rat through the bowels of the city that had ruined her. Could she possibly get any lower?

The briefcase she was holding hadn't felt heavy before. It was a lead weight now. The adrenaline of the car chase had worn off. Combined with the growing self-pity she was now feeling for her circumstances, the list of her recent defeats was almost enough to make her cry. But she was tired of crying.

She would rather be angry.

Every squishy step through this drainpipe was fuel for her hatred of Jasper Sterling.

His arrogant smirk as he boasted of his engagement to Charlotte.

His merciless sneer as he stabbed Henry.

More than anything, she wanted to wipe that smug look off his face.

Valerie's foot struck stone and she nearly fell.

She caught herself on the side of the pipe but not before stumbling, inadvertently dipping her knee into God-knows-what fluid at the bottom of the pipe.

She was already soaked, so there was little change to her

overall state of dampness, but she could still feel the slime permeating the leg of her trousers. It made her want to wipe it away or possibly crawl out of her clothes, but neither were options.

She fumbled for the matches and got one lit. As the flame sputtered to life, it illuminated an iron grate with bars a half inch thick in some places. The top of the grate was still intact. The thick bars protruded down through the exterior of the pipe and had, at one time, pierced all the way through the bottom. But the days of it holding back invaders were gone.

Years of corrosion had eaten away at the iron, causing it to crumble from the bottom up. What once must have been a small opening was now, as Gaspar had suggested, a large enough hole for tree branches and tires and other flotsam to slide through.

That wasn't to say the grate had failed to stop anything.

To the contrary, a great many things, primarily trash, had accumulated against the bars and had been packed so densely that it was impossible to see much beyond. The only way forward was through the trickling stream at the bottom of the pipe. What space there was had been carved out by the flow of water along the bottom. The water's persistence had cleared a sort of tunnel though the accumulated debris.

She hadn't counted on this.

The hole was big enough for a person to get through, but only providing they were small and willing to get down on their belly to slide under the heaps of refuse pressed against the other side of the grate.

Valerie cursed again. She stooped to peer through this tinier and more constricted version of hell.

Tiny eyes reflected the flame of her match back at her. Just before the match went out, Valerie counted no less than five pairs of them, waiting.

Then darkness returned with the scent of smoke.

Every part of her mind rebelled at the idea of crawling through that hole, but she had no choice. Outside the sun was sinking, and if she went back to find another way, she would most certainly be caught. Once the City Watch had her, she might end up at St. Anselm's before the night was over. It was still hours until she legally turned eighteen. She had little doubt Jasper would make use of that time if she was caught.

No. Going back was out of the question now.

Mentally unleashing a symphony of curses, she set the briefcase down, twisted her hair into a knot atop her head, then sank to her hands and knees. She clamped her mouth shut and her eyes tight, careful to avoid any chance of injecting the muck directly into her body. Then she crawled forward, pushing the briefcase ahead of her, inch by disgusting inch.

Mud and slime squished up between her fingers, and the smell assaulted her nostrils. It had been dank enough walking through the stuff, but having it this close to her face was enough to make her gag.

To make matters worse, the tunnel constricted, and she had to sink all the way to her belly. She kept her face out of the muck but just barely. The slimy water went down her shirt and into her boots and soaked through every bit of her clothing. She crawled with one hand and one elbow, her other hand desperately clenching the box of matches and keeping it above the water.

She tried to avoid thinking about how many animals were currently using this pipe as a toilet.

An agonizing few yards later, she was able to get to her hands and knees, then finally to her feet. She had cleared the blockage.

She picked up the briefcase and listened to the steady plop of mud and sludge sliding off it. Now fueled by a blend of anger and disgust, she stomped the rest of the way through the pipe, attempting to dislodge the ooze and slime from her body. She had little luck.

She traversed the remaining length of pipe in a sort of trance, refusing to think of anything other than escape. Before long, she spotted light. The drainpipe opened up into a larger drainage system and passed beneath several streets. She was able to peer up through the runoff drains and listen to the noise of passing pedestrians.

She trudged on, grateful that at least no one knew she was down here.

As Gaspar had predicted, this portion of the drain system terminated in Bringham Park. The flow of water was cleaner here, and the tunnel was littered with stones that had washed in from a stream. Valerie staggered out of the last portion of the pipe and found herself beneath a pedestrian footbridge. People were walking above it, chatting gaily about the tournament and the impending events. She could make out a few refrains of a festive song being sung somewhere nearby.

The sun was still up.

Valerie took a moment to splash herself with the stream water, attempting to remove the worst of the foulness from her body, but it was a hopeless cause. The smell of the drainpipe still lingered in her nostrils. She felt as though the majority of the filth was now on the inside of her clothes, and that made matters even worse.

She was still several blocks from where she had parked the car, and she had the drive to Tidewater to manage. There were so many people between here and there that someone was bound to see her. What if someone she knew saw her like this?

But there was no other option.

When she crawled out of the stream and up to the footbridge, she indeed got no shortage of stares from passersby. But she didn't have time to listen to their tittering comments. She broke into a run, the briefcase thudding against her thigh and her boots squishing with each step. Little jets of water spurted out the tops of her laces for several paces.

She cut north through the park, avoiding the main footpaths, then met the street at the far side. Here there was no avoiding the stares and comments of other pedestrians.

They weren't kind.

Rim rat.

Street filth.

Gutter trash.

Peasant.

She ducked through alleyways to avoid the comments as much as the City Watchmen but kept a steady pace. She noted with some satisfaction that the endurance training Damon had been putting her through was paying off.

Finally, she reached the street where she had left Damon's junker.

The car wasn't there.

She turned a circle where she stood, double-checking the street signs. There was no sign of it.

Then she spotted a smattering of rust on the ground near the front of the parking space. The rust was partially adhered together with undercarriage sealant. It looked as though it had been scraped loose recently.

Someone took it.

A pair of City Watchmen turned the corner of the building and began walking her way. She ducked behind a parked car and waited for them to pass, then ran the way they had come, working her way downhill. "That stupid impound," Valerie muttered. "When will they stop towing my damn cars."

The sun had disappeared into the horizon, and she was miles from Tidewater on foot. She began to run.

She did her best to avoid the main roads, sprinting through parks and gardens at every opportunity. With the crowds for the tournament, there was no avoiding being seen. Fortunately, the exit gate at the city walls was getting much less attention from the guards than the entrance gate, and she was able to slip out amid a caravan of farmers returning home from the markets.

She reached the bridge but cut right instead, racing downhill along the worn and uneven road to Tidewater. Seagulls cawed from recesses in the bridge above her as she followed the glow of the village ever downward. By the time she reached the wharf and made the turn toward Rico's apartment, she was exhausted and out of breath.

The lights of the Twisted Tentacle were glowing brightly, and the place looked to be packed.

She would need a change of clothes and a shower before showing her face. There was no way around that, but she would have to somehow sneak in to get cleaned up. She knew her chances of continued employment were slim now either way, but she certainly couldn't let Janet see her show up drenched in sewer water.

Valerie made her way around the back of the building, walking up the same alley that she had been assaulted in the first night she showed up. She was almost to the back door when she noted a man lingering in the shadows a few doors down.

She froze.

He wasn't one of the homeless that sometimes picked through the trash. This man was wearing a suit. He met her gaze briefly, then looked away, gliding out of the doorway and moving off toward the far end of the block. Just before he turned the corner, he looked back and lifted a radio to his mouth.

Was he there for her? If he was with the City Watch, why hadn't he tried to apprehend her?

She searched the alley, looking for any other surprises, but it was deserted. She continued on and pushed her way into the rear of the tavern. She nearly collided with Rico. He was in a shimmery dress, wearing a wig that reeked of hair spray.

"Oh my God, no. You are not coming in here looking like that." He held up a hand. "What happened to you?"

"I'm so late," Valerie said. "I was supposed to be here to help."

"That ship has sailed," Rico said.

"Did Ann's sword pass the judging?"

"It's going down right now. And you need to get your butt out of here, pronto. Your crazy life has brought us enough trouble for one day."

"Why, what happened?"

"Jasper Sterling happened is what happened. He was here. In the bar. Now go hide before someone sees you. You can go to my place if you want." He pulled a key from his shirt and handed it to her. "Get cleaned up, and don't show your face until this is over. God, I remember you smelled bad the first time you came in from that alley, but this is so much worse."

"Okay, but hold up. Jasper Sterling was here? Why?"

"I have no idea, but you've got to go. We can talk about this later. I need to get back in there." He shoved her through the door and shut it on her.

Valerie stood on the steps in the alleyway clutching the key.

Jasper Sterling was in the Twisted Tentacle? She hastily scanned the alley again. There was no sign of the lurking man or anyone else for that matter, but she suddenly felt as though the very walls might be watching her.

She exited the alley, but when she reached the sidewalk, she had to cross north to get to Lexington. The illuminated front of the Twisted Tentacle was visible from where she crossed. Somewhere inside, Ann and Janet's fates were being decided.

She had just reached the far sidewalk and was about to head uphill when she heard the scream.

She turned in time to see a car barreling down the street. It was racing downhill with no one at the wheel. A metal drum was strapped to the roof.

"What the hell—"

Valerie watched in horror as the car continued at full speed across the road, then hit the sidewalk outside the tavern. It went airborne and sailed straight through the front of the building.

She stared in shock at the gaping hole in the tavern where the car had vanished.

The night erupted with screams.

Valerie dropped the briefcase in the street and sprinted toward the building. She was nearly there when the inside of the tavern lit up with a fiery, orange glow. The next moment, the remaining windows at the front of the tavern exploded, showering glass and flaming wood and sending Valerie flailing backward.

She hit the ground hard.

When she rolled over and lifted her head, the whole world was on fire.

24

CHARRED

F laming debris drifted slowly from the sky; receipts, paper napkins, all turning to ash even as they fell.

Valerie's ears rang.

The flash from the explosion still lingered in her vision, temporarily seared into her eyes.

Then she saw the shoe.

It hadn't been there a minute ago. It was sitting upright in the center of the street, a solitary sentry standing guard against the night.

Valerie staggered to her feet.

That's when she finally registered the screams. They had been there all along, a backdrop to the ringing, but it now matched the scene in front of her.

A chill went up her spine.

The Twisted Tentacle was engulfed in smoke. People stumbled from the massive hole in the front of the building, coughing and covered in soot.

A man tripped over a curb in the lot, fell, and didn't get back up. More casualties spilled from windows and openings blown in the walls.

No. It couldn't be real.

Janet. Rico. Ann.

Flames licked up the facade of the building. Several of the windows in the upstairs apartment had blown out and were billowing smoke. Others were illuminated with flame.

Valerie rushed toward the opening where the front door had been. The figure that came staggering out next was someone she recognized, but just barely.

"Rico! Are you okay?"

Rico's dress was blackened, and he appeared to be in a daze. His wig was on fire. Valerie snatched it off his head and threw it aside, then ran her hand over his head to check for embers. She grabbed him by the shoulders and led him out of the wreckage, past the prone man near the curb.

The street was chaos. Citizens from around the village were showing up, some gaping, some springing into action. Shouts filled the air, some calling for water, others searching for friends or family members.

"Rico, where are Janet and Ann? Are they inside?"

"I saw Janet," Rico mumbled. "I saw—" His mouth opened, but he clamped his eyes shut as though blocking out the vision. He groaned, the groan turning into a wail. He staggered, and Valerie helped him to a sitting position.

"Don't go anywhere," Valerie said. "I'm coming right back." She gently released Rico's arm and it fell into his lap. He slid onto his side on the ground, wracked with sobs.

"I'm coming back," Valerie repeated, then raced toward the hole in the tavern. She hesitated when she hit the wall of heat. The inside of the Twisted Tentacle glowed with angry, ravenous flames. They licked from the walls and ceiling in growing pockets of red and orange. She squinted and forced herself onward, focusing on the bodies littering the floor. Valerie recognized several of her regular customers, some with blank stares, others writhing in agony. Hands reached for her, and she clasped them, dragging one, then another out the hole in the front of the building.

On her third trip inside, she pulled her still-damp shirt up, attempting to shield her face from the heat of the flames on the ceiling.

The hulk of the car had landed at the center of the seating area for the stage. The blackened steel was twisted and smoking.

The rear passenger door was missing. It was the same Lark sedan she had driven uptown.

She was part of this.

Valerie staggered around the car and nearly tripped on a man pinned beneath the front bumper. His hand lifted toward her. It was covered in signet rings. The nobleman grasped at her leg. "Help. Me." His fine clothes were burned and blackened, and when he turned toward her, one side of his face was nearly melted.

His hand was red and blistered. It pawed at her leg. Valerie clasped his palm, unable to think. He was pinned, crushed, and there was no way to help him. As she held his hand, the man's arm went limp, his eyes fluttered, and his head fell back, thudding against the floor. When she looked down at her hand, bits of his skin were sticking to hers. She let go reflexively and wiped her hand on her leg. The smells from the fire were overwhelming, and she tried not to retch.

This couldn't be happening.

But there was no escaping the carnage around the room. More disfigured people were crawling across the floor or staggering toward the entrance. A few citizens from outside moved in to help.

Regaining her focus, she rose. "Janet!" She turned in place, searching the smoky room. "Ann!"

"Valerie." The voice was almost a whisper. "Valerie."

Valerie turned toward the voice and located the source. A number of tables had been overturned and now lay in a heap to her left. The voice was coming from beneath them. Valerie scrambled over to the pile and located Ann partially buried under the furniture. A heavy table lay atop her leg. Several stools covered the rest of her. Valerie quickly tossed aside the stools but struggled to budge the table.

"Don't worry. I'll get you out of here."

Ann tried to pull herself free from the table, but she was pinned fast.

Valerie turned and shouted toward the now dim opening. "Help! Someone come help me!"

The shout was partly drowned out by a groan from the timbers overhead. Part of the ceiling gave way and tumbled into the bar. Valerie flinched and tried to shield Ann from the swirling embers.

"Valerie, Janet is here somewhere," Ann said, her voice straining.

"We'll find her. I promise." She shouted toward the opening again. "Somebody help!"

"Val?" A figure appeared in the smoke.

A flood of relief filled her.

"Oh God, Damon! Over here!"

Damon climbed over the wreckage and moved toward her voice, but he froze momentarily at the sight of the car. His eyes roamed over the blackened frame.

"Help me get her out!" Valerie shouted.

Damon rushed to help as she struggled with the table. With his assistance, they were able to shove it aside.

Another piece of the ceiling crashed down a few feet from them, this time roaring with flames.

"We've got to go!" Damon shouted. He pulled Ann up and threw one of her arms over his shoulder. Valerie lifted Ann's other arm, and they hauled her out to the street.

Rico was back on his feet and rushed to help.

"Take her," Valerie said. "Help her." She passed Ann's arm to Rico and turned toward the tavern.

Damon caught her wrist. "No. It's too dangerous. That roof is coming down any second."

"Janet's still in there," Valerie said. She broke her wrist free from Damon's grip and sprinted back into the tavern. Sparks were flying around the inside of the bar, and the heat from the flames was intensifying.

Valerie's eyes watered from the smoke as she searched the area near the bar. Several prone figures lay on the floor, but none of them were Janet. As the beams creaked and moaned overhead, she squatted lower to avoid the heat and shouted, "Janet!"

Several bottles crashed from the shelves behind the bar, one of them erupting into flames as it struck the burning cash register.

Valerie scrambled around the far side of the bar and discovered two women unconscious on the ground. One was Janet and the other was Ruby, the bartender. Ruby was staring blankly into the shelves, a jagged piece of steel protruding from her neck.

Valerie struggled to roll Janet over. She couldn't tell if she was breathing.

"Val!" Damon's shout came from the front of the bar. "Get out of there!"

Valerie lifted Janet, wrapping her arms under the tavern owner's armpits and across her chest, then began to drag her. "I found her!"

She made it around the end of the bar and worked her way toward the opening. A cascade of flaming timbers suddenly rained from the ceiling, and the inrush of air made the flames around her brighten. Valerie screamed.

"It's coming down!" It was Rico's voice shouting this time. The two men were at the edge of the tavern where the door had once been, but there was no longer a way through.

"I'm going out the back!" Valerie shouted. She coughed violently as she turned the way she had come, but when she reached the hallway that led to the alley, it was engulfed in flames. She could see the exit. The door was open, but the walls and ceiling roiled with fire.

She could sprint it and possibly avoid being burned, but not hauling Janet's limp form. She hoisted Janet higher, wrapping her arms under the tavern owner's armpits. Janet's head lolled against her chest. Was she even alive?

The beam above her began to give way, groaning as it buckled. Valerie clasped her own wrist tightly as she hoisted Janet as high as she could, then she closed her eyes and ran.

Flames licked at her back and her hair. She screamed as an ember landed on her bare neck. Smoke rose from her clothing, and the lingering moisture from her crawl through the storm drain steamed out of her. Every part of her felt like it was on fire. She opened her eyes just enough to gauge the spot of darkness that signaled the only escape through the walls of orange.

Embers flew around her, and flames licked at her from every angle. Even the air seemed to be on fire.

Valerie screamed.

Then she was out.

Her foot missed the doorstep and she stumbled, crashing to the cobblestones of the alley. Janet fell on top of her, crushing what little breath she had from her lungs. Valerie opened her mouth but there was no air. She choked on her own tongue and coughed.

Finally, the breath came.

Valerie gasped and gulped at the air, ignoring the pain that was registering from a hundred points on her body.

This same infernal alley, altogether too familiar, now reeked of burnt hair and flesh.

Footsteps pounded the cobblestones. Then there were hands on her. Patting out flames. A wet shirt, a towel. Damon and Rico, also strangers. They lifted Janet off of her and hauled her away from the burning building. Two strangers stepped in and hoisted Valerie into the air as well. She was thrown over one man's shoulder and carried from the alley into the street.

There was no fire brigade, just citizens. Some relaying

buckets of seawater up from the docks, others lifting the injured into carts. Valerie was laid on the ground among other casualties.

"I'm okay," she argued, brushing away the hands that sought to aid her. "I'm okay. Where's Janet?"

She didn't have to look far. A small group was gathered around the figure of the tavern owner. Rico, Damon, and Ann.

"Is she alive?" Valerie asked, speaking to their backs.

Damon got down on his knees and breathed into Janet's mouth.

A produce truck blared its horn as it rattled to a stop nearby. The driver stepped down from the cab. "Seriously injured! Bring them here! We're taking them up the hill. Gotta get the worst hurt up to the hospital straight away."

"Over here!" someone shouted.

"Help me!" responded another.

Rico stood and grabbed the arm of the driver. "Please. Take her." He pointed to Janet.

"Get her in the back," the man said. "Quickly."

Damon and Rico and one other man lifted Janet as gently as they could and carried her to the back of the truck.

"I'm going with her," Ann said, limping her way toward the truck.

"No room for extras," the driver said.

"I'm going," Ann replied, hauling herself up the tailgate of the truck, using her arms and one good leg. Rico did his best to assist her.

Valerie got to her feet, but there was nothing else to be done.

The driver of the truck restarted the engine and moved farther along the road, gathering up other victims. The bucket brigade had given up attempting to dampen the flames consuming the Twisted Tentacle. They concentrated all of their efforts on the buildings around it.

Valerie felt someone's fingertips on her shoulders and turned to find Damon beside her. "We need to get you taken care of," he said.

"I'm okay," Valerie replied, but even she realized it wasn't true. Her skin was hot and red, and there were holes burned through her clothes. Other parts of her clothing were stuck to her.

"You're still in shock. Come on. I'll help you."

Valerie turned to take another look at the Twisted Tentacle. Most of the upstairs apartment had collapsed into the interior of the tavern. Through the carnage she could still make out the twisted steel frame of the car.

"This was my fault," she whispered.

Somehow, some way, she had brought this on them.

Damon scooped her into his arms and carried her away from the scene.

"No. I've got to try to help," Valerie said. She squirmed, but the pain made her stop. She hissed through her teeth, the burns on her neck and arms finally registering.

When she laid back in Damon's arms, she noticed the light emanating from the bridges.

Headlights.

Cars were stopped on the highway, and the distant faces of nobles crowded the guardrails. They were staring—watching the turmoil—but no one was coming to help.

Valerie closed her eyes and tried to unsee the nightmare, this next level of hell she had fallen into. But the more she tried to unsee it, the more the visions persisted. The car streaking across the road and launching into the tavern. The fireball. Ruby's face as she stared lifelessly from behind the bar.

When she opened her eyes again, Damon was shoving his way through the door of his warehouse loft. He kicked the door closed and carried her past the training gear to the bathroom where she had tended to his wounded shoulder.

"We need to cool you down," Damon said. He set her on her feet, then started the shower.

"None of this would have happened if it wasn't for me," Valerie said. "It's all my fault."

"You weren't the one who drove that car into the building."

"No, but . . ."

"It isn't your fault."

"But if I had just stayed here. I went after him. Jasper."

"It doesn't matter what you did," Damon said. "Tonight isn't on you."

"He's rigging the tournament," Valerie said. "Bribing other fighters. There's no chance of anyone else winning. He has everyone in his pocket."

Damon ignored her outburst, put a hand into the shower, and felt the water temperature, then gestured for her to step inside. "Time enough for that later."

She peeled off her boots, one at a time, then staggered forward into the shower while still dressed.

"We'll need to be gentle getting you out of those clothes," Damon said.

Cool water.

Valerie leaned against the wall with her forehead and let the water course over her.

She stayed like that until she felt Damon's fingers in her hair. She lifted her head from the wall and noted that he had climbed into the shower with her. He had stripped to his shorts and was now working the soot and sludge from her body.

Oh God.

How had she let herself get to this state?

The part of her that objected to him seeing her like this was quickly overruled by the part of her that acknowledged how much she needed it. He gently worked the grime out of her hair. She turned toward him and rested her forehead against his bare chest.

Damon slowly pulled her shirt up her body and over her head, carefully examining her skin. There were angry, red patches on her forearms and shoulders, and the skin on the back of her neck burned, even under the flow of the cool water.

She climbed out of her pants next. Her legs had fared better, protected by a thick layer of material, but there were still burn marks in places she hadn't even recalled feeling at the time.

The bottom of the shower now held clumps of her singed hair. The strands raced each other through little eddies of water around her feet.

Standing in that shower, soaked and in her underwear, it felt as though all of her ambitions were washing down the drain as well. How could she have expected justice? Whatever small irritation she could cause the Jasper Sterlings of the world, they were capable of delivering a vengeance a hundred times worse. She was nothing in their world. All of her work thus far had only brought misery and pain to everyone who had tried to help her.

"It would have been better if you'd left me in that alley," she said, muttering the words into Damon's chest.

He shut off the shower and gently wrapped her in a towel.

She closed her eyes and tried to disappear.

Valerie wasn't exactly sure what occurred after that. It was as though it all was happening to someone else. When next she opened her eyes, she was in Damon's arms being carried upstairs. Her disgusting clothes were gone, replaced by a clean, oversized T-shirt that was no doubt his. Her burns were dried and bandaged and her hair partially wrapped in a towel, though she had still managed to dampen Damon's shoulder as she rested her head on it. Little beads of water ran from his collarbone down his bare chest.

When her head hit the pillow on Damon's bed, it seemed to swallow her. She wished it would.

She stirred enough to find Damon's hand and grasp it in hers.

"Get some rest," he said.

"Don't go. Come to bed," Valerie managed. "Stay."

Damon began to pull away, but Valerie kept her grip on his hand. She concentrated her efforts and pulled.

He slid onto the bed next to her.

When he had settled into a position beside her, Valerie curled into the crook of his arm. If she tugged the covers up high enough, there would be nothing left of her to see. She pulled them over her head, disappearing from the world into the only place she could. But even the solidness of Damon's body beside her wasn't enough to shield her from the memories. Flames still danced across the inside of her eyelids, revealing a moving picture show of faces. Janet, Henry, her mother and father. In her mind, the flames continued to spread, consuming all of Tidewater. They swallowed up Rico and Damon, transforming all the waterside villages into a lake of fire that lapped against the city walls. Jasper Sterling looked down from a parapet and laughed.

She opened her eyes only long enough to dispel the visions, grounding herself in the present moment, the feel of the rough sheets beneath her and the earthy smell of Damon beside her. She listened to the rhythm of his breathing for as long as she could and then cried herself to sleep.

OTTER AND OYSTER

Valerie woke to the sound of trumpets.

She rolled over in Damon's bed and winced, rediscovering her injuries from the night before. She blinked a few times and tried to orient herself to her circumstances.

Memories came in flashes of orange flame. She could still hear the roar of the fire, and her mouth tasted like charcoal. It took a moment for her to realize it was her own breath that still held the lingering scent of smoke.

Damon wasn't in the room, but morning sunlight was filtering through curtained windows at one end of the loft.

The persistent blaring of the trumpets drove her from bed.

She staggered stiffly to the window and opened it, scattering flakes of white that went dancing from the windowsill. The roofs of the warehouses next door were all coated with ash. Another trumpet blast made her look up. High overhead, vehicles lined the Crown Bridge. The trumpeters were heralds, positioned at the sides of the road and blasting away as a caravan of vehicles rolled past. The cars were flying the banners of the House of Pendragon and the flag of Avalon.

"The king," Valerie muttered.

He had finally arrived.

The news would have thrilled her a week prior. A week ago she had a plan. She had allies. Now everyone she had come to rely on was paying the price for helping her.

A sea breeze picked up more ash from the windowsill and swirled it into the room. She closed the window.

Was Janet alive?

Whatever her condition, there were many citizens of Tidewater who hadn't woken up this morning at all. Many more were scarred or injured—all because of her.

Valerie stepped into the bathroom and had a look at her wounds in the mirror. The girl staring back at her was about what she expected.

Her run through the fire had left her hair completely burned in several places and singed in others. Her face had avoided the worst of it, but she had been scorched at her temple and several more places on her neck. The most painful of her burns—those on the back of her neck and several on her arms—were still bandaged. She gingerly checked the dressings on her arms, replacing one that she could manage on her own.

She surveyed Damon's bedroom and located a pair of shorts she could roll the waist down on and wear comfortably. She was already swimming in his T-shirt. She descended to the warehouse level and discovered her boots sitting at the base of the stairs. She stepped into them, not bothering to lace them up before searching the ground floor. But there was no sign of Damon.

Where had he disappeared to?

She clomped past the Guardian and crossed the training area to the side door, cracking it open to peer outside. Several people along the street had stepped out to watch the passing caravan overhead. It took her a second glance to realize that one of them was Rico. He was standing with his arms crossed, his face blank and unreadable, gazing up at the Crown Bridge.

As if sensing she was watching him, he glanced her way. He

stared at her for a moment, then lifted his chin in acknowledgment.

"Hey," Valerie managed, calling across the broad, vacant driveway between them. "You okay?"

"Doing as badly as expected," Rico replied. "Look at them up there. Last night proved it. Tidewater could literally be on fire, and they wouldn't even piss on us to put out the flames." He glared at the bridges, gestured toward the royal caravan with a solitary finger, then turned and made his way over to her.

"Any news about Janet?" Valerie asked, not convinced that she wanted to hear the answer.

"I tried going up to the hospital this morning. The bastards won't let anyone in who isn't family. Haven't seen Ann. No one knows anything." He kicked at someone's discarded cigarette pack that was littered on the ground. "They're setting up a board with names for missing persons down at Pier Five for people trying to find each other."

Valerie hugged herself to ward off the morning chill, wincing as she discovered more tender areas on her skin. "What about Carlyn and the kitchen staff?"

"Carlyn is safe," Rico said. "She's already helping out with a survivor's breakfast they're putting together over on Gull Street. Told me to bring you by if I found you."

"I'm not sure I could handle that," Valerie replied.

Rico shrugged. "I told her no one would have any appetite. Not after last night." He looked Valerie over. "How are you feeling?"

"I'm fine."

Rico looked skeptical but didn't argue. "Is that all you have to wear?"

Valerie glanced down at what she had on. "I'm still doing a lot of borrowing lately."

"Come on. I think I have a few things that might fit you. Maybe not well but better than that."

"I'm sure there are more important things to worry about," Valerie said.

"Just let me help," Rico said. "Let me do something."

Valerie nodded.

She followed Rico up to his apartment. Once inside, an overweight Calico cat met them at the door and immediately began rubbing its whiskers on Valerie's shins.

"That's Gertrude," Rico explained. "She's an ornery old lady most of the time, but I guess she likes you."

The cat was possibly the only resident of Tidewater unaware of the previous night's tragedy. It purred contentedly as it rubbed against her leg. Valerie scratched the cat atop its head and followed Rico into his bedroom.

Had she not known differently, she would have assumed Rico's room belonged to two different people. One was the auto mechanic she was with now. Grease-stained shirts. Coveralls. Torn jeans. The other was an elegant woman who wore flowery scarves and fancy dresses. A sewing machine had a place of honor along one wall.

When it came to choosing the person to borrow from, she was inclined toward the mechanic.

Rico found her a pair of rugged trousers that were only slightly too big for her. Cinched with a belt and with the legs tucked into her boots, she at least felt prepared to face the day. She was grateful for Rico's tendency to wear tight clothing. She fit comfortably into a soft, gray, wool sweater, only having to roll up the sleeves slightly.

"We've got to do something with your hair," Rico said. "That is a fright."

But at that moment, a horn blasted in the street. They moved to the windows and observed as a black, armored limousine with golden emblems on the doors rolled slowly down the street. A man was standing up in the car, half of his body protruding through a herald hatch, shouting as they moved. "Gather! Gather to hear the proclamation from His Royal Highness King

Logan!" A cape that featured the crest of the House of Pendragon fluttered in the wind behind him.

As the vehicle rolled on, villagers stepped from their homes and began to follow.

Valerie and Rico exchanged glances. She borrowed one of Rico's bandanas to tie up her hair, and they descended to the street, following the crowd toward the wharf.

She kept her eyes out for trouble, initially wary for sightings of the City Watch, but then it occurred to her that today was her birthday. Since she was now eighteen, they wouldn't be able to haul her off to St. Anselm's without trouble. For better or for worse, today she was legally an adult citizen of Avalon. The realization made her stand taller in her boots.

The royal limousine stopped outside the Otter and Oyster Inn on Market Street directly across from the marina. Three men in royal livery climbed out of the limousine, and one began to read from a document in his hands.

"Hear ye! Hear ye!" the herald shouted. "Let it be known that His Majesty King Logan Pendragon, the first of his name, has hereby declared his tournament open. Any man or any woman wishing to compete for the honor and privilege of a place in his honored circle of knights at Glastonbury Castle may present their qualifications at the designated tournament grounds at Candle Green and commit to the challenge of armed combat. Competitors shall demonstrate their courage and weapons skills. In addition, the winners of each round shall receive an invitation to the regional governor's ball in the king's honor to be held this Friday evening. Long live King Logan!"

A muffled echo came from the gathered crowd. "Long live the king." The response was less than enthusiastic and had come from only a few citizens. The herald inserted the document into a frame, then one of his companions hammered a nail into the front wall of the inn to hang it. The innkeeper didn't look especially pleased about it.

"What'll King Logan do about our troubles?" The voice

boomed from behind Valerie, and she turned to find the imposing, bald-headed figure of Connor Kane striding through the crowd.

The heralds looked up from their work and froze. The shortest one let his hand slide to his sword hilt.

"State your business." The herald who had issued the proclamation faced Kane.

"My business is seeing the lords of this city held accountable for what happened here last night. The City Watch will bang on doors and haul off good folk for no reason when it suits them, but some maniac nearly burned down this village, and we saw nary a soul come to help."

"There is a system in place to address your concerns," the herald replied. "If you take your complaints to the local governor, I'm certain he'll take care of it."

"He'll do nothing, you mean," an old woman shouted. "Same as ever."

A boisterous clamor of agreement erupted from the crowd.

The heralds eyed the crowd nervously. "We're just messengers of the Crown," the short one said. "It's not our job to take complaints."

"Ain't no one's job, it seems," an old man in the crowd shouted.

"You tell the king we'll be in his tournament all right," Kane said. "And when we win, there will be some changes around here."

"I wish you good fortune then," the herald said. "May God smile on your sword." The three men in livery pushed their way through the crowd, giving Kane a wide berth. They climbed hastily into the limousine and drove off in the direction of the next seaside village.

A few people stepped onto the porch to reread the notice. A couple of others thanked Kane for speaking up. Most just stood around muttering.

Kane turned and caught Valerie staring at him.

"You!" he shouted. He strode toward her.

Valerie took an involuntary step backward.

"People have been talking. They say you were outside the Twisted Tentacle last night."

"I was," Valerie replied.

"Did you see the car? Someone jump out at the last minute? Who was driving it? What did you see?" Kane reached a meaty hand out and gripped her by the shirt.

"Hey! Let her go." Rico attempted to step between them.

Kane shoved him away. "Come to think of it, we've had nothing but trouble since you showed up." Kane fixed Valerie with a glare. "You were seen driving a Lark sedan yesterday. One like ended up exploding. Could be that you were the one that bailed out of that car before it went in."

"No. I wasn't," Valerie objected.

"Some of my best mates were in that tavern last night. You gonna tell me who was driving it?" Kane shoved Valerie so hard that she lost her balance. She grunted as she hit the ground.

"Kane! Stop." Rico was there again, attempting to hold the big man back, but this time Kane caught him by the wrist and flung him to the ground.

The sailor loomed over them. He pointed a thick finger at Valerie. "Now you start talking. You tell me who the bastard was that sent that car. You tell me who killed 'em."

"I didn't see anyone —" Valerie said. "I swear I don't —"

"The car was mine." The crowd turned, Connor Kane included, to stare at the speaker. As Kane moved aside, Valerie had a clear view of Damon. He was wearing his leather jacket and motorcycle boots. He pulled his sunglasses from his face. "It was my car. A junker I left uptown."

"And where were you while your car was flaming its way into the Twisted Tentacle?" Kane said.

"Out."

Kane sneered. "Another out-of-towner who has been nothing but trouble."

"A lot of us lost friends last night," Damon said.

"You're a hired sword," Kane spat. "No honor. No loyalty to anyone but yourself." He faced off with Damon, the muscles in his back rippling with tension. "What would you know about how *we* feel?" Kane gestured to the crowd of villagers gathered around them. "We're from here." He thumped a fist against his chest. "This is our home. You don't speak for us."

Valerie scrambled to her feet. "Damon, don't fight him —"

But Damon wasn't moving into a fighting stance. He spread his arms, leaving himself open. "Your quarrel isn't with me, Kane. And it certainly isn't with them." He gestured toward Valerie and Rico. "If you want to make a statement about what happened here last night, there's only one way to make it. Use your car. Use your sword. And head to Candle Green. Make them notice."

"He can't," Valerie said.

All eyes turned toward her.

"It's rigged," Valerie explained. "Jasper Sterling is paying off the other racers. They're working together to put him at the Round Table. It won't be a fair fight for anyone else."

The crowd murmured.

"So they plan to cheat," Kane said. "What else is new?"

"Do you have the proof of this?" Damon asked.

"I did. But I lost it last night."

"It doesn't matter," Kane said. "The only thing that'll get their attention is when I'm standing in their arena with their cheating hearts on my sword."

"You two would be better off working as a team," Damon said. "Watch each other's backs."

Kane grunted. "The last thing I need is someone slowing me down." He gazed over the crowd as if suddenly recalling he had other places he needed to be. He gave Valerie one last glare. "Stay out of my way on the track. I won't go easy on you just because you're a girl." He moved off through the crowd.

Valerie was left staring at Damon. He met her gaze and set his jaw.

"That went well," she said.

He turned to Rico. "What's the word on Janet? Any news?"

Rico shook his head and repeated his experience at the hospital that morning.

"I have a few clients that have connections at the hospital. I'll see if I can learn anything." Damon turned to Valerie. "Did you do your forms yet this morning?"

Valerie frowned. "Not yet."

"We should get on it," Damon said. "I've been uptown and seen the competition you're up against. You'll need to be limber."

The three of them made their way back to Lexington.

Valerie thanked Rico again for the clothes, then followed Damon into the warehouse. It seemed he was all business this morning. He headed straight for the training gear and began gathering items to put in the trunk of the Guardian.

"Thank you," Valerie said, "for lying for me out there."

"It was my car."

"But I'm the one who left it uptown. It's my fault that they—"

"No," Damon said. He turned and glared at her, his face stone. "You didn't send that car into the tavern."

"But if I hadn't gone—"

"We're not talking about that. What's done is done."

Their eyes stayed fixed on one another for several long seconds, then Damon went back to organizing the gear for the Guardian. He worked silently, and whatever he was thinking, it was clear she was locked out.

She shifted her feet. "Did they post the order of events?"

"You'll have to touch the shields outside the registration tents at Candle Green. Archery and jousts are no good to you, so we'll enter you for war driving like we planned. Finishing there will qualify you for the swords competition melee the next day."

"All I care about is making it through to the governor's ball to see the king."

Damon checked the batteries in the hand-held radio and pocketed an extra set. "Making plans for your revenge is all well and good, but you have to place in the competition first. One thing at a time."

"One thing at a time," she echoed.

She plucked a sword from the racks and moved to the practice area, stretching and freeing up her joints. The burns on her skin left her feeling tender, and there were tinges of pain on movements she hadn't anticipated. She worked through her usual routine under Damon's watchful supervision. His comments were few, and she was once again left wondering about the state of his mind.

When they had finished the forms, Damon helped her change the dressings on her burns, but there was none of the tenderness in his touch that she had felt last night. It was as though the pall of the tavern fire had eliminated all warmth between them.

"Where were you this morning?" Valerie asked.

"I went uptown when the caravan came through the gates. I was hoping to catch an old friend from back east traveling with the king's party."

"Old friend?" Valerie asked.

"Unfortunately, I couldn't get through. It'll have to wait."

"What's her name?" Valerie said.

Damon narrowed his eyes.

"Your friend from back east."

Damon tightened the last of the bandages on her arm with what she thought was more force than necessary. "I'd rather not talk about my friends. We have other business to worry about."

Valerie rubbed her arm and noted that he hadn't disputed it being a woman.

"I put fresh batteries in your extra radio. Your gear is set for the melee. Get to Candle Green and get registered."

"You're not coming?"

"I have business to take care of. You won't see me in the morning either. You'll start on your own."

"But you're my coach. I need you."

Damon handed her the radio. "And I'll be there. Channel 28."

Valerie accepted the radio and reluctantly added it to her belongings in the Guardian. She closed the trunk and turned around to find Damon only inches from her.

She jolted. "What? I thought you had to leave."

"You'll be okay," he said. "You've trained just as hard as anyone out there. When you get in front of the king, he'll listen. He'll give you justice."

Valerie searched his face. "You're talking like I won't see you afterward."

"I just want you to know that you've got this."

"Is it someone you have to fight? What has you scared?"

Damon brushed a strand of her hair away from her face. "Don't worry about me. I'm not worth it."

"Talk to me."

"I told you. I'm not the guy you want to be mixed up with. Once this is over, you'll be free and clear."

"It's too late. This . . ." She gestured back and forth between them. " . . . is mixed up."

For a moment, it looked like he was going to speak, but his jaw set and he turned away. "I have to go."

Valerie caught him by the sleeve of his jacket. "Wait."

He stopped.

She reached for his face and turned him toward her, then rose up on her tip toes and kissed him. His lips parted beneath hers, and his hand cupped her face. He pressed his forehead to hers, his eyes closed.

She dropped back to her heels. "I'll see you after."

Damon nodded but he looked pained. He turned and strode out of the warehouse, not looking back.

She tried to puzzle through his behavior, but it was clear there was a wall he wasn't willing to bring down. She suddenly felt very alone.

Valerie listened as the Vulcan left the lot, then locked up the Guardian before walking next door to Rico's. She banged on the door until he answered.

"What? I'm here already," he said as he opened the door. "You missed me or something?"

"Get ready," Valerie said. "We're going to Candle Green. We've got a tournament to win."

CANDLE GREEN

J asper Sterling stood inside the newly erected exhibition tent and admired the machine before him. It was almost too beautiful. The paint shone an iridescent emerald, and the chrome gleamed from the fender trim. He had the unusual urge to keep the vehicle to himself and not let anyone else see it.

But that wouldn't do.

There would be thousands walking the expo tonight, admiring the cars. If it had only been the mob of Port Hyacinth citizenry touring the show, he might be tempted to keep the car a secret, but his father would be out there too.

This car would be a statement. Proof that there was no one who could compete.

Jasper walked to the door of the war car and reached for the recessed handle. The polished metal didn't have a single fingerprint on it.

It had cost a fortune to ship the car here in time for the tournament, but there would be nothing like it on the track. A marvel of Japanese engineering, beautiful and deadly.

He slid into the driver's seat and imagined the crowd in the morning. They would be feverish with excitement. His fingers brushed over the armament dashboard. No less than twenty offensive options presented themselves to his touch. He would slaughter the competition. If you could even call it that.

The speedometer markings topped out at 180.

He checked the rear-view mirror. That's where his enemies would disappear. He was still imagining the track in front of him when the flap on the tent opened, and the guard that had been posted just outside poked his head in.

"Sir? You have a visitor who wishes to speak to you."

"I told you, I'm not to be disturbed."

"It's . . ." The guard looked so uncomfortable that Jasper thought he might pass out. "It's just . . . you should come out."

Jasper climbed from the car and marched over to the guard. Disobeying him once was one thing, but to insert his useless opinion again and presume to give him orders? Jasper relished what he would to do to this cretin.

But just as he reached the tent flap, the guard was pulled out of the way and two armed men stepped inside. They were dressed in modest black suits, but their coats hung heavy with internal armor.

Jasper was just about to object to the intrusion when the men stood aside and a third man appeared between them.

Jasper froze. The new intruder was dressed casually in slacks and a blue, button-down shirt with the sleeves rolled to the elbows. There were no insignias anywhere, not even on the silly, floppy hat he was wearing. He only had a signet ring on his right hand. Had it not been for the sheer audacity of the man's entrance, Jasper would have assumed he was just some visiting merchant or nobleman. But he recognized the face. He looked different in person, shorter than he expected, and he was sporting a mustache, but there was no question that he was staring at King Logan Pendragon.

"Your Majesty." Jasper sank to a knee.

"Jasper Sterling. This is a surprise. I saw the Terravecchia crest on the tent outside. I had thought perhaps I might see young Henry here this year."

"No, Your Majesty," Jasper said, rising to his feet. "I'll be the champion racing under the banner of House Terravecchia tomorrow."

"That's right. I received word of your betrothal to Lady Charlotte. My congratulations. You must be thrilled." The king's voice remained unnervingly neutral as he spoke.

"Thank you, sire. You do me great honor." Jasper attempted to decipher the king's expression, but the man's face was a puzzle he couldn't unlock. "Pardon my confusion. This is quite a surprise. And it took me a moment to recognize you with that mustache."

"The queen hates it," the king replied, stroking his lip. "It'll have to be gone tomorrow for all the official photos, but it was a long journey to get here, and what's the use of being king if I can't have a little fun once in a while."

"It's most distinguished, Your Majesty."

"Is that a Samurai?" King Logan gestured to the war car.

Jasper finally exhaled.

"Yes. It just arrived. The Samurai X. It's the only one on this continent."

King Logan strode across the tent and peered inside. He studied the armament dashboard and controls, then straightened up and walked around the front of the car. He paused at the hood where the Sterling crest was embossed in the metal.

"Racing for House Terravecchia but no bear claw?"

"There will be house decals on the car tomorrow," Jasper explained. "For the fans."

The king nodded. "It's an impressive vehicle. I trust you'll put on quite a show."

"When the news came that you were opening a seat at the Round Table, I knew it was an honor I should spare no expense to compete for."

"Your father has spoken of your ambition," King Logan said. "He listed it as one of your primary characteristics."

"He discussed my prospects with you?"

"Not at length, but as host of the tournament, I knew he would be sponsoring a team."

"A member of our family having a place at the High Court would be an honor he would boast of for a lifetime."

"I have no doubt of that," the king replied. "Honor is what I have come in search of here. And, of course, courage, integrity, and the willingness to sacrifice for the good of the kingdom. The role of a knight at the Round Table does not come without a cost."

"I'm sure the contender who emerges as your tournament winner will be a knight for the ages."

"Let us hope so," the king replied. "We live in dangerous times, and I'm afraid the code of chivalry holds less sway than it once did."

The king moved to the exit, and Jasper followed him into the fading daylight. The king's guards moved into the foreground, scanning the bustling crowd but making no move to part it. The king was obliged to yield to a vendor pushing a cart of sweets along the walking path.

"Do your men not herald your movements?" Jasper asked. "These folk should be bowing."

"I'm not here today as anyone's king," King Logan replied. "I'm but another war car enthusiast among the crowd. There will be time enough for pomp and circumstance tomorrow." He turned and observed the Terravecchia crest on the tent banners. "It will be a pleasure to see the bear claw sigil on the track again. I assume you know Il Orso Nero was an old friend of mine. He fought in the Border War with my eldest brother. He was the one who brought my family word of my brother's death on the battlefield."

Jasper struggled to form a response. "No. I wasn't aware of that, Your Majesty."

"I trust you will do the family name proud tomorrow."

"It will be my honor to try," Jasper said.

The king nodded, then moved off, disappearing among the crowd.

Jasper stood staring at the hustle and bustle around him without seeing anything for nearly a minute until a hand shook his shoulder and he started.

"Jeezus!" He turned to find Blaise Cavendish at his side.

"Whoa! What's with the thousand-yard stare?" Blaise said.

"You ought to know better than to startle me like that," Jasper replied. "What's wrong with you?"

"You wanted me to let you know if there was any sign of the Terravecchia girl. Our spotters saw someone matching her description touch the shields at the registration tent a few minutes ago."

Jasper wheeled on him. "Under what name?"

"No family name was listed. Just a call sign. Alley Cat. I told the men to follow her and plan to detain her."

"No!" Jasper shouted it at him.

Blaise recoiled in confusion. "No? You've been looking for this girl for weeks. Why don't you—"

"I said no. Things are more complicated now." Jasper ran his hands through his hair and grasped at his scalp. "Why didn't you tell me that King Logan was a family friend of Il Orso Nero?"

"He is? How would I have known that?"

"Because it's what I pay you for!" Jasper hissed. He turned and fumed at the crowd around them. "Call off the men. We need to get as much distance from this girl as possible. Whatever happens to her from here on out can't be traced to me. Who else knows she's entered the race?"

"I assume no one of consequence," Blaise replied.

"The king still doesn't know about the brother. But he will."

"Your story is clean. Everyone is on your side. Other than the girl, no one has disputed what you did was justified. She's the only loose end."

"It'll have to be on the track," Jasper said. "Accidents happen all the time in races. If some no name contender buys it tomorrow in a pile-up, there's no way it gets tied to me."

"I'll make sure our team understands."

"And I need some bear claw decals for the Samurai tomorrow."

Blaise furrowed his brow. "You said you'd rather someone defecated all over the — "

"Just get me the decals!" Jasper shouted.

Blaise shut his mouth and nodded, then backed away.

Jasper clenched his jaw and stormed back inside the tent.

"I'd take any of these cars," Rico said. "Just pick me one."

Valerie walked beside him as they strode past the dozens of war cars on display. Nobles from nearly every western district were in attendance, each house sponsoring a different race team. The cars were lit by overhead lights, but many of them glowed on their own, featuring electric colors from every spectrum of the rainbow.

"I'd give you that one," Valerie said, pointing out a stunning, violet Renegade that had a strobe light flashing through the haze from a smoke machine.

"Done," Rico said. "Wrap it up."

Valerie laughed. Her tension had eased after touching the shields at the registration tent. No one had paid much attention to her there. They simply noted her information and gave her the registration package. She now had a number decal for the side of the Guardian and a map to her starting position swinging in the bag at her side. The fact that hundreds of other people had joined the competition was unnerving, but that was a problem for tomorrow's Valerie.

"So, it's not a car, but I did actually get you something," Rico said. He reached into the messenger satchel he had slung over his shoulder and pulled out an elongated paper bag. "Sorry I didn't have anything to wrap it in."

Valerie accepted the package and found the neck of a wine bottle protruding from the end. She removed the bottle and read the label. The Terravecchia crest was front and center. "It's the Toscana '65. That was a great year!"

"Figured you might like a taste of home on your birthday."

"You remembered," Valerie said. She attempted to hold back the wave of emotion that rose unbidden from her chest, but it came anyway. With all that had gone on in the last few days, she'd felt like anything might touch off the raw emotion she had been bottling beneath the surface. Certainly this. She put a hand to her mouth and did her best not to cry.

"Of course I remembered," Rico said. "Not every day you get to turn eighteen. Let's go find a place to drink it."

Valerie nodded, still not quite in control of herself enough to speak.

They rounded the corner of a tractor trailer, and she ran directly into someone, splashing his beer on her.

"Oh, pardon me," the man exclaimed. "How clumsy of me."

He was slender and dressed like a beach tourist in a lightweight button-down and a floppy, fabric hat. A mustache still decked with beer foam betrayed an otherwise attractive face.

"Watch where you're going there, man. You almost ran her over," Rico said.

"You have my apologies." The man bowed and circumvented them before moving farther down the path.

Valerie straightened herself and wiped some of the beer off her shirt.

"Probably drunk," Rico said.

A hulking man in a black suit passed by next, giving them an icy glare before following along the same path.

Valerie's eyes lingered on the man in the hat for a brief moment, wondering why the encounter felt odd, then Rico tugged on her arm. "Come on, I know a place we can go."

They stole a pair of cups from a soda vendor while he wasn't looking, then Rico led Valerie to an apartment building on Mason and Green. They didn't enter the main foyer but rather skirted around the back. Rico retrieved a key from a hiding place under a loose alleyway brick, then returned to the steel access door to let them in. A long climb up several sets of stairs later, they emerged onto the roof and a view of the bay that Valerie couldn't help but gawk at.

The bay bridges were all lit, and the twilight air seemed somehow more alive up here. The sounds of the city below were still present but muffled and safely distant.

"How did you know about this place?" Valerie asked, following Rico to the front of the building and peering over the edge.

"My uncle used to have a flat here when I was younger, before they raised the rents in uptown and drove out all the common folk. Landlord changed the locks on the front of the building, but she was too cheap to do the back. I found out my key still worked, and I've been coming up here ever since."

"It's beautiful."

They took seats on the gravel and tarpaper rooftop, and Rico pulled the cork from the wine bottle with the corkscrew on his multi-tool. He poured them each a cup of wine and held his aloft. "Here's to eighteen. The first day of officially knowing better but doing it anyway."

Valerie tapped her paper cup against his. "I might be too late for knowing better." She paused the cup on the way to her mouth. The aroma of the wine made her stop. She knew this vintage well. How many times had it been opened on the table with her family gathered around? How many glasses raised to health and happiness?

She took a slow sip. It was the same deep flavor. It tasted like summertime and a hundred walks through the clover and lavender in her family's fields. It all seemed a long time ago.

"You feeling nervous about tomorrow?" Rico asked.

"Yeah."

"Pretty sure everyone will be scared. It's a packed field. Plus, Connor Kane basically hates you."

"I'm not even thinking about that," Valerie replied. "I'm not scared about dying in a crash or getting hurt. I'm more worried about what happens if I don't make it through the finish line. This is my only shot at getting to the king. If I let my brother down, he'll never have justice. It'll just be over."

Rico took another sip of his wine and focused on the distant horizon. "I didn't know your brother, but he sounds like a good guy. If you die tomorrow, then at least you get to go hang out with him. It's me you ought to worry about. With you dead, I'll have nobody left whose life is more miserable than mine to feel sorry for."

Valerie punched him in the arm.

"Ow!" Rico laughed. "At least I'll be able to say I got to hang out with the daughter of Il Orso Nero the night before she died. That's worth something."

"You're no help at all in these situations," Valerie said. "Aren't you supposed to lie to me and make me feel better?"

"No. Because I don't think you should want to feel better," Rico said, his voice growing serious. "I want you to bottle all that up and use it to drive your war car right over Jasper Sterling's smug face."

Valerie chewed her lip. "Yeah, you're right. That will make me feel better."

"You and me both." Rico poured more wine into her cup. "I was thinking we might still have time to weld some spikes to your lug nuts tonight. Good for slashing Sterling tires."

"All four wheels?"

"You tell me. It's your birthday."

Valerie tipped her cup back again.

They drank until the stars were out and the bottle was empty, then returned to the garage and got to work.

REMEMBER

"It's about focus. You have to think like a car."

Her father was beside her in the passenger seat of the '68 Del Toro, his hand resting on the seat behind her head. Out the windshield, a constellation of 55-gallon drums was arranged around the lot. A path through them was laid out with white, spray-painted arrows on asphalt.

"But cars don't have brains," Valerie said.

"With you in the driver's seat, they do."

He had moved her seat all the way forward and stuffed a pillow behind her back, but even with the extra padding, her feet barely reached the pedals.

"Racers get themselves into trouble because, when they get in the driver's seat, they still think like they do the rest of the time. They get emotional. They think like a person. What does a car need to think about?"

"How much gas it has?"

"That's the pit crew's job. Unless we're talking about the distribution of weight. Why is that important?"

"So the wheels get good traction."

"So *you* get good traction. Remember, you're nothing but a car's brain right now. This is your body." He slapped his hand on the doorframe. "You don't have feet anymore. You have tires. You don't have a heart. You've got a motor." He picked her hand up and placed it on the shifter. "You feel that? That's your heartbeat now."

Valerie wrapped her fingers around the leather grip and let the vibration set her arm quivering. The engine pulsed under the slightest pressure from her foot.

"Eyes on the road. Don't worry about the gauges. Your ears will tell you when to shift. Let's get rolling. Show me how you launch off the line."

Valerie pressed the clutch to the floor and shifted into first. She touched the throttle and brought the engine RPM up to 2500. She exhaled and focused on the sensations of the car, then she slipped the clutch pedal out, applying the throttle the moment the pressure plate engaged. The engine's torque transferred cleanly, and the four tires stayed adhered to the ground without breaking loose. They bit the asphalt and hurled the car forward, pushing Valerie into her seat. She had to stretch her toes to keep the accelerator down. The engine screamed, and she pumped the clutch, the shifter moving simultaneously and taking them into second gear.

She dared a glance at the speedometer, and the Del Toro blazed through 60 mph before the tachometer redlined again. The shift into third brought a whoop of joy from the passenger seat.

"Yeah! That's my girl! Get on it!"

A smile spread across her face, and she careened into the first turn, downshifting as she went. They erupted out of the curve and blasted down the next straightaway. The speedometer crept past 80 as she got into fourth gear.

"Give me a heel-toe downshift through this next turn, then we'll hit the hairpins." He pointed to a series of barrels at the end of the lot.

She decelerated and took the turn, coming out in third gear

with the engine roaring. She downshifted again going into the first hairpin.

"Looking good. Don't oversteer coming out."

Her father's voice slowly faded into the background. It blended with the whistling wind through the windows and the steady growl of the engine. As she glanced over at him, she caught him smiling at her, the gleam in his eyes unmistakable.

But then the wind and engine noise faded, replaced by the blaring of alarm bells.

The clanging grew oppressive, and Valerie opened her eyes.

She was back in Damon's loft, the alarm clock hammering away on the nightstand. She rolled over and pressed the stop button.

In the darkness and silence, she could still feel him beside her. Just around the corner of her mind. The proud smile was still there. But then the dream faded, and the memory lost the battle with reality.

She sat up.

Stars shone out the window. She rubbed her eyes and pushed away the covers.

The bed was empty. Wherever Damon was, he hadn't come home last night.

She walked to the door and flicked on the lights.

On the floor of the garage below, the Guardian was waiting. Fueled up. Armed. They had raised the rear end to accommodate the all-terrain tires. The tires had come used but still had plenty of tread. The lug nuts now bristled with steel spikes. Even in its resting state, the car looked dangerous, its broad air intake formed into a permanent snarl. Valerie took a deep breath.

She washed and dressed quickly, only taking the time to down her water bottle and fill it again. She checked that her tournament sword was stowed on the ceiling rack of the Guardian and gently touched the watch dangling from the rear-view mirror. "Today is the day I get justice," she whispered.

Valerie worked quietly to get the Guardian out of the garage in an attempt to make a discreet exit.

She needn't have bothered. Once the bay door was open, the sound of engines could be heard throughout Tidewater. An intermittent stream of headlights was winding its way up the turns toward the Crown Bridge, then meeting the flow from the city. The caravan of vehicles coming out of the walls lit up the predawn sky and made the bridge glow.

A door slammed, and Valerie turned to find Rico descending the stairs from his apartment.

"So much for getting you out ahead of the crowd," he said.

"Everyone seems to have the same idea."

Rico opened the passenger-side door of the Guardian and climbed in while Valerie went inside the garage to lock the bay door. She cinched the chain and was working her way to the side exit when she spotted the glint of silver beneath one of the rolling toolboxes. She squinted at it in the dim light, then walked over and knelt down, fishing beneath the toolbox until she felt a handle. She dragged out a silver briefcase.

Valerie stared at the case for several long seconds before trying the latches. The briefcase was unlocked. She flipped it open to find it empty except for a few lumps of sand still wedged in the crevices and corners. There was no question that it was the same briefcase she stole from Blaise, but what on earth was it doing here?

She closed the lid gently and slid the briefcase back under the toolbox where she found it. She was still trying to come up with a reasonable answer as she locked and closed the side door of the garage and made her way to the car. As soon as she got in, she started the engine and reached for the radio. She tuned in channel twenty-eight and keyed the mic button wired into the steering wheel. "Danger Dog. This is Alley Cat. Are you there?"

"Woo hoo!" a voice replied. "This is Brickyard, Alley Cat, you got some company on the line."

She glanced at Rico's skeptical expression, then keyed the mic again. "Brickyard, are you a racer?"

"Yes, ma'am. Meanest son of a sailor this side of hell. What are you driving?"

"Guardian 770," Valerie replied.

"Woo dog, that's a hot rod," Brickyard replied. "But you see a bright-as-the-sun orange streak coming up on you on the track today, you pay no mind. That's just me and my Rockwell Hurricane. Don't look too close, you might go blind."

"I'll try to remember that," Valerie replied, unable to keep a smile from her face.

"Good luck out there, Alley Cat," he added. "See you at the finish line. Brickyard out."

"Going to be a lively day on the Citizen's Band," Rico said.

Valerie waited a few more moments to see if Damon was also on the channel but then turned down the volume. It seemed she would have to wait to get her answers. She consulted a map of the circuit, then put the car in gear, climbing up the hairpin turns of Tidewater's upper slopes. On the way up, they passed a battered produce truck that someone had attempted to convert to a war car. A few men were working furiously under the hood, and their swearing was audible even over the rumble of the Guardian's engine. The motor of the truck hadn't been strong enough to even get it out of the village.

"That's why I wanted out early," Rico said. "I bet we pass a dozen of these junkyard rust buckets clogging the road by the time we reach Baylor's Field. They're liable to stop traffic and make us miss the start."

When they reached the main highway, they joined the flow of vehicles on the Crown Bridge. The Guardian drew a fair amount of attention. Most of the city race cars were being towed via trailer out to the starting line. But Valerie and Rico weren't the only ones making the drive in a war car. They passed a pair of Outlander Rebels that had been modified with giant buzz saws on the hoods. The men driving them looked just as intimidating with red war paint on their faces and spiked collars around their necks.

"Don't worry about them," Rico said. "Everyone thinks a buzz saw is a great idea until it binds up in somebody's frame and gets stuck there."

"As long as it doesn't come through my window," Valerie said.

"You brought your road armor, right?" Rico asked.

"In the trunk. I figure I'll put it on when I get there."

They passed several drivers who had thought differently and were already wearing their gear. Road armor, by design, was meant to provide freedom for your shifting arm and your legs while protecting your upper body and head from attack through the driver's side window. Worn outside the car, it made for a lopsided look with only one arm fully protected. Sometimes drivers went so far as to protect only one half of their heads.

Rico pointed out one such driver whose helmet was formed in the shape of a bison skull, one side bearing a horn to complete the look. He looked like a monster from a storybook. Valerie had to admit it was intimidating.

"You remembered to bring the extra fuel, right?" Rico asked.

"Enough for a top off," Valerie replied. "You still think we should go with a full tank when we get there?"

"Hard to say," Rico replied. "I guess we'll need to see the track condition when we get to the start. Might need to stay light to get out in front of the pack."

When they neared the exit for Baylor's Field, the traffic slowed to a crawl. As they exited the offramp, contenders were directed away from the growing stream of spectators.

A man with a glowing wand noted the decal number on the door of the Guardian and waved them on through a barricade. "Twenty-three is on the right. Keep moving!"

Valerie pulled through a gate and down a long stretch of road leading to the starting line.

The name Baylor's Field was a misnomer. It might have

once been a green space, but over the decades, the area had sprung up clusters of low-rent high rises. Weather and a lack of upkeep had battered the buildings, leaving many as vacant shells. Today they were experiencing a revival as scores of spectators climbed the crumbling towers for a better view of the race start.

The buildings surrounded a wide lot that had once been a vibrant plaza. The area had been cleared of its old fountain and any residual obstacles with the exception of a newly erected wooden tower with an Avalon flag flying from the top. Several race officials were already in the tower and commanded a view of the start.

Valerie brought the Guardian down the line. Most of the cars were already in position; the few that weren't were being rolled off trailers. She tried not to focus on the weapons in view, but it was difficult not to notice the ballistae and spike launchers.

She backed into the space marked twenty-three between two vehicles from other cities. They both bore emblems from houses she didn't recognize. The men surrounding the cars fixed her with stony glares as she parked.

"This won't be a bad position for you," Rico said. "At least you aren't too far out on a wing."

The starting line wasn't straight. The officials had formed it into a shallow V, owing to the fact that there was only one route out of the plaza, and it would require that the racers all meet at a point at the north end with the matter-of-fact name 'The Bottleneck.'

Valerie was positioned on the right side of the V near the center. It would be a mad dash from her position through the Bottleneck and out to the highway beyond. She expected chaos prior to that, and it was anyone's guess who would make it through. The drivers in the cars beside her didn't exactly look like they planned to play nice.

Valerie shut the Guardian off and got out, then climbed onto the roof of the car for a better view.

She studied the route out of the Bottleneck, then scanned the start and the growing line of her competitors.

Her eyes caught on a brand new, emerald-green Samurai X parked at the center of the V. She was shocked to see the Bear Claw emblem of her own house emblazoned on the hood.

"What the hell?"

Then she saw the driver. Jasper Sterling had his road armor on, but his helmet was off, and his bleached blond hair was tied behind his head. The Terravecchia crest was on his chest plate as well. It was all Valerie could do to choke back a shout. How dare he wear her colors! Her fingers clenched into fists. That's when she noticed the charcoal-gray Easton Blackbird parked next to the Samurai. House Sterling's champion, The Red Reaper. The windows were too dark to see him, but she could almost feel his presence. Both of her enemies in one place.

Valerie jumped off the top of the car and reached inside for her sword.

"What are you doing?" Rico said.

"That bastard is stealing my life," Valerie said. "So I'll take his."

Rico grabbed at her wrist to stop her from pulling the sword from the rack. "Whoa, whoa! Not here! You'll deal with him on the track."

Valerie pulled the sword from the rack anyway and spun around to find her enemy. Rico's words warred with her urge to storm down the line and end Jasper this instant. Rico was right, but she didn't want him to be.

The radio crackled. "Alley Cat, this is Danger Dog. Come in."

Damon.

Valerie turned around and set the sword against the car, then reached for the volume knob. She pressed the mic. "This is Alley Cat."

"Hey."

"Hey," Valerie replied. Despite her heightened state, she

couldn't help the little flutter she felt in her chest at the sound of his voice.

"I've got a good position to watch your start. We should be all right."

"Where are you?"

"I nabbed a seat on the spectator train. I can coach you from here."

Valerie looked up to the elevated railway that passed through the west side of the plaza. The train was pulling into position for the start.

"Which train car are you in?" She scanned the various windows on the train. A few were open, and ladies and lords were waving flags and handkerchiefs with their favorite racer's colors.

"I don't think you'll be able to see me, but the train will be parallel to the track for a good sixty percent of the race. I should be able to keep you well informed. Rico's ticket is set for the mechanic car as well."

"He got it," Rico said, rubbing his hands together.

With the seat on the train, he'd be in position ahead of Valerie for most of the main track features. With limited pit assets, there wasn't a lot they'd be able to do in terms of maintenance, but if necessary, he could wait for her along the track for roadside repairs. Anything was better than nothing.

"Better get your armor on," Damon said from the radio. "You don't have long till the start."

"There are some things I need to talk to you about," Valerie said. "In person."

"First things first. You've got a race to win. Keep this channel on. I'll check back shortly. Danger Dog out."

Valerie's eyes roamed along the spectator train. Was the king aboard somewhere?

She moved to the back of the Guardian and opened the trunk. Her armor was sparse, the cast-offs from Damon's training gear that fit plus a few odds and ends they had managed to scrounge or fabricate, but it was at least enough to give her some modest protection from outside assaults. Her racing helmet would protect her face, and the neck guard and pauldron would cover most of her exposed shoulder. She was hoping to avoid anything coming through the window grate, but in a race like this, anything could happen.

Rico did last minute checks on the Guardian's tire pressures and offloaded his tool kit from the trunk. They did a run-through of the car's armament assets and tested the fire-warning light panel. Everything was in order.

"You ready for this?" Rico asked.

Valerie finished cinching up her helmet. "As ready as I can be." In truth, her heart was pounding, and she was doing her best to keep a tremor from her hands.

Rico helped strap her into the racing harness and handed her the water bottle. Valerie took a quick drink. All around them, engines revved. She turned the ignition and was relieved to feel the Guardian come to life around her. The vibration of the engine was like a salve on her nerves.

"Those four lanes through the Bottleneck will jam fast," Rico said. "Whatever you do, don't get caught behind a blockage. Some of these big boys will come right over you." He gestured to the trucks with monster tires that were as tall as a house.

"You have any positive things to say?" Valerie asked. "I could use a few of those right now."

Rico leaned in the window and smiled. "Don't worry. This war car is the best mix of tough and fast. If it was good enough for Il Orso Nero, you know it has to be good." He slapped a hand on her shoulder. "You've got this."

Valerie nodded. "I'll see you on the other side."

Rico gave her a reassuring wave before scooping up his tool kit and the spare gas can. He then joined the flow of other mechanics boarding the rear of the spectator train.

As the plaza cleared out, Valerie had an unobstructed view of her competition. Over a hundred vehicles were spread out across the starting line, every one of them aimed for the mouth of the Bottleneck. The smell of exhaust mixed with burnt rubber from tire burnouts. The air was alive with tension. The energy of it pulsed through her.

"It's about focus."

Her father's words cut through the anxiety, the memory forcing its way to her mind.

The radio crackled, and Damon came over the channel. "The official has the flag. Get ready. Fast launch and go hard for the Bottleneck. I'll call out trouble if I see it coming."

Valerie tapped the mic button and allowed herself a smile. "I'm the trouble."

"Damn straight."

She gripped the steering wheel and focused on the race official with the starting flag. "Think like a car," she muttered.

The official raised the flag. All around her, engines roared.

The flag dropped.

Valerie launched.

28

RACE

Pedal down.

A hundred cars launched off the line in a blur of chrome and flame.

Fuel burned and rubber smoked.

Valerie shifted into second, and the tachometer needle soared across the gauge. A dozen cars vanished behind her, but dozens more were eating up the ground to either side.

An emerald blur erupted from the center of the V. The charcoal streak of the Easton Blackbird was on its tail. The wall of vehicles on either side constricted, narrowing the open space every second. Tailpipes glowed orange with flame as drivers pushed their engines to the limit, fighting to stay ahead of the wave of compressing steel. The plaza's jaws were closing, and the racers were the teeth.

Valerie kept her eyes on the mouth of the Bottleneck. Her feet pumped the clutch and gas again, hurling the car into third. Her peripheral vision was now filled with the blurry shapes of the cars that were outrunning her to the opening. She was ahead of the bulk of the pack, but there were machines here built solely for speed, and they were showing it all.

An unarmored Super Seven slingshotted to the lead on its

thin racing tires, a yellow bolt of lightning straining for the freedom of the open lanes at the far side of the Bottleneck. A black-and-red Shogun swung into position behind it, engine straining to keep the car in the draft.

Then the first ballista bolt flashed from somewhere behind Valerie. The missile screamed past her window and found its mark in the back of the Super Seven. The car canted sideways at the impact. The driver fought to keep the wheels straight, but with nothing to protect it from the blow, the missile pierced directly through the thin metal protecting the rear-mounted engine. Belts and hunks of the motor exploded from the car as the motor tore apart, and the next second, the Shogun slammed into the Super Seven's bumper.

The lightweight car went airborne.

The road was chaos as a hundred vehicles shifted trajectory to avoid the blockage.

Metal screamed from somewhere to Valerie's right, and something slammed into her from the left.

Collisions rocked the wave of vehicles, some spinning out and wiping through competitors to either side. Valerie wrestled the wheel straight and kept her focus on the road—not the wide open beyond the Bottleneck but the asphalt immediately ahead—gauging the shifting vehicles around her. She was no longer an arrow but a hare, weaving and dodging as debris rained from the sky and pummeled the road.

"Pileup to the west!" Damon shouted over the radio. "Stay right!"

She swerved right and found herself behind a Ridge Runner with tail spikes the same height as her head. If it stopped suddenly, she'd lose her face. She swerved left again just as the Ridge Runner collided with something immobile and tore apart.

The road was now an obstacle course with diminishing exits. A flurry of vehicles shot toward the Bottleneck from the left, but the route through the center was full of collisions going badly.

A volley of spikes rained into the roadway ahead, launched

from some vehicle in the rear, and a half dozen cars met in a violent crash as they tried to avoid them. Connor Kane's flame-painted truck rolled into the fray, blasting his way through with a ram.

The opening Kane made was inviting, but a silver Lanternfire beat her to it before laying down a patch of tire spikes as it went.

"Bottleneck is closing!" Damon shouted. "Get out now!"

Valerie downshifted and swerved right again, finding herself alongside a jacked-up orange Rockwell Hurricane that had a plow affixed to the front of its frame. The driver looked left and met her eye.

Valerie keyed the mic. "That you, Brickyard?"

"Sure as shootin', Alley Cat!"

Valerie dodged a loose wheel in the road. "You see a way through that mess ahead?"

"I plan to make one!" He grabbed a lever overhead and yanked on it. "Oorah!" The plow on the front of the Hurricane lowered and sparked off the pavement. Valerie was headed straight for an overturned Vulcan. She braked and swerved into the lane behind Brickyard.

"Coming through!" The Hurricane plowed through the remains of the Vulcan, and metal flew in every direction.

Tucked behind the Hurricane, Valerie couldn't see much of the road ahead, but they were closing on the Bottleneck fast, and it looked to be completely clogged. An arrow shot through the grating of her open passenger window and imbedded itself in the dash. She checked her side mirror and found a heavily armored truck with a ten-pack arrow launcher aimed her direction. It looked to be targeting the Hurricane's tires.

She weaved right to block the shot, and several more arrows bounced harmlessly off her rear armor.

"You've got company, Brickyard!"

"Thanks for the defense!" he called back.

She weaved right to get a view of the track, but the Bottleneck was solidly jammed with wrecks.

"Detour!" Brickyard shouted.

Valerie turned hard to follow the Hurricane as it went off-road and plowed through the lower level of one of the buildings bordering the track.

"This is crazy!" Valerie shouted into the mic.

"Crazy like a fox!" Brickyard replied. He plowed his way through the empty building's old walls, ancient lighting and drywall raining down behind them, then they erupted onto a road running parallel to the track. He swerved left again and blasted through the low barrier wall, bringing both of their vehicles back onto the track in a spray of concrete.

They were past the Bottleneck.

Valerie checked her rear-view mirror and noted that a stream of racers had followed them through their alternate route. The truck with the arrow launcher had been lost in the fray, but a dozen other vehicles that looked just as mean had replaced it. She recognized the house emblems of Nikki Patel and Mervyn Doyle, as well as a car she had seen with Jasper in the garage. They all had her in their sights.

"Time to open it up, Brickyard!" Valerie shouted, pulling alongside him.

Brickyard whooped again and raised his plow, then stepped on the gas. "It's on!"

Valerie smiled and upshifted, keeping pace with her track mate for a few seconds. Then the Guardian's engine snarled as she accelerated and pulled ahead.

The road was clear.

However many cars had survived the Bottleneck were now screaming along the highway toward Mount Oro.

She concentrated on the chatter coming from the radio.

" . . . this is Danger Dog. Come in, Alley Cat."

"Alley Cat here," Valerie said. "I'm back."

"Tell me you made it through that pile-up."

"I'm through. Where are you?"

"The train is five miles ahead of the Bottleneck now. It'll

285

rejoin the track at Mount Oro. From the spotters' reports, you've got about twenty cars ahead of you. Time to make up some ground."

"I'm on it. Where's Jasper?"

"He's going by the callsign 'Viper.' He's two cars back from the lead and gaining. You'll need to really pour it on to catch him."

"And the Red Reaper?"

"Not sure. Keep your eyes peeled."

"Let's hope that bastard got stuck in the pile-up," Valerie muttered. "If not, I'll put him into one. Alley Cat out."

She shifted into fifth gear and floored the accelerator. The Guardian's turbo kicked into full boost and hurled the car down the highway.

~

The towers of Mount Oro Castle kept a brooding vigil over the twisting highway that climbed its mountain cliffs. For a hundred years, the castle's intimidating height and perilous maze of a moat system had kept all intruders at bay. Today the castle walls were lined with spectators. Binoculars were trained on the spillway at one end of the moat that had been linked to the road via a newly constructed stone bridge.

Jasper Sterling crossed the bridge and headed into the moat to the sound of cheering. He could hear it even over the noise of the Samurai X's high-pitched engine. So far, it had been almost too easy. Of the racers within a mile of his position, he knew at least five of them were paid off and would stay respectfully behind him, keeping his other competition at bay. The driver of the silver Stingray directly ahead of him hadn't gotten that message.

As the Samurai splashed through the muddy moat, he eyed

the armament dashboard at his fingertips. He had always wanted to see what a flaming harpoon could do to a rear-mounted fuel tank. That would give these people something to cheer about. He'd need to punch through the Stingray's armor first. His fingers found the lance lever and activated it, twin metal spikes extending from the Samurai's front bumper. He pulled into the draft of his competitor's vehicle, accelerating hard and aiming the steel spearheads for the Stingray's trunk.

"Time to face the music," Jasper muttered.

Then, to his surprise, the Stingray's trunk flew open, and three jets of fuel sprayed from the nozzles aimed directly at his windshield. Jasper gasped in horror and braked hard. It wasn't fast enough. A ball of fire ejected itself from the roof of the Stingray and exploded across the hood of Jasper's Samurai. His entire view went up in flames.

"No!" Jasper squawked and slapped at the fire controls. The car sideswiped the wall and spun out.

Jets of pressurized extinguishing agent sprayed from orifices all over the car, blanketing the vehicle with foam as he spun. When the car had stopped and the flames were out, he angrily flipped the switch for the wipers, flinging away the foamy obstruction to his view. He had lost valuable seconds and suffered an embarrassing defeat at the hands of this upstart. It wouldn't stand.

He gunned his engine, then shifted back into gear, tires slipping and sliding on the wet stones. The automatic traction control kicked in, and the Samurai leapt forward, eating up the ground. There were cars in his rear-view mirror now—a trio of vehicles entering the moat.

The radio squawked. "Viper, this is Ghost Dagger. I'm on your six. Be aware, you've got some kind of mega truck coming in hot."

Jasper checked the mirror again. There was indeed a truck closing fast. The flames decorating the paint were now splattered with mud from the oversized tires. He'd heard of this truck.

Some sailor from the out-villages that no one would shut up about. Kahn? Kane? Whoever he was, he wasn't part of the plan.

"Keep him off me!" Jasper shouted into the mic as he plunged the Samurai into a dark tunnel.

"We're trying but he's no joke."

Jasper cursed into his helmet and focused on keeping the Samurai off the walls going through the moat's twists and turns. Multi-colored murals of graffiti on the tunnel walls seemed to move with the passing of his headlights. It was almost enough to make him nauseated. He tried to keep the car at speed while listening for the competition behind him. The echo in the tunnel changed to a deep rumble as more vehicles entered.

The Samurai slipped and skidded around the turns. If he was having this much trouble, his competitors must be as well. He had the best car on the track. There was no way they could beat him.

He searched the armament dash.

Tire cutters, chainsaw, harpoon launcher. No. No. No.

Black Ice.

That could work.

He flipped the switch for the chemical pot, then hit the trigger on his steering wheel.

A fan of black fluid sprayed from beneath his rear bumper. Mixed overtop the already muddy stones, it would make a surface that was as frictionless as the ice it was named for.

"Let's see you drive on that," Jasper muttered as he watched his rearview mirror.

The big truck that had been gaining on him slid around the curve and slammed into the wall hard. The gigantic wheels spun, losing traction fast. Jasper smiled and accelerated around the next curve, putting more distance between them.

A boom echoed through the tunnel.

Jasper couldn't see what had happened, but a moment later, a woman's voice came on the radio. "Viper, this is Song of

Silence. Ghost Dagger just hit the wall hard. Someone slicked the track. I don't think he's walking away from that."

"What about the truck?"

"Still coming."

Jasper cursed.

The muddy tunnel gave way to an inclined ramp, and he shot into the sunshine again.

~

Valerie entered the Mount Oro moat system unsure of what to expect. With walls that stretched for miles around the mountaintop, this wasn't an average castle, and the route was far from ordinary.

The sloped walls made for a narrow racing lane, and while the concrete moat had served as a defense system for past attacks, it was also tied into the city's drainage system and handled the runoff from the rest of the city.

The moment her wheels touched the bottom of the inlet ramp, she was glad for the all-terrain tires.

Plumes of water fountained from her rear wheels as she tore through puddles several inches deep.

Damon's voice emanated from the radio. "Be alert. Sounds like there's a potential pile-up in the moat."

Valerie downshifted and took the next curve cautiously. She'd made up a lot of ground on the open highway, the Guardian's speedometer at times topping 150, but now wasn't the time to throw away that progress in an ill-timed corner.

She passed more inlets to the moat—steep drainage spillways from higher ground. High above, spectators looked down from battlements cheering and waving the house flags of their favorite competitors.

Seconds later, they vanished from view as she drove into a tunnel.

It didn't take long till she found the trouble, coming upon a section of tunnel illuminated by the red glow of taillights. A half dozen of her competitors were trying to get by a wreck of a war car that had piled into the wall. The driver was no longer in the vehicle, but it was upside down and blocking a third of the passage.

If it was only a matter of going around the wreck, the cars would be on their way in seconds, but one particularly stubborn driver had turned around and was deliberately blocking the road, preventing passage. The war car had engaged twin buzz saws and was also spraying jets of fire from nozzles over each headlight.

"Filthy cheaters," Valerie muttered. It didn't take much imagination to figure out that it was likely one of Jasper's paid cronies. The only positive to the situation was that the closest car being blocked was the charcoal-gray Easton Blackbird belonging to the Red Reaper. He was a sitting duck.

Valerie flipped the safety on her armament panel and deployed her spike ram. She'd hammer him into oblivion right where he sat. She revved her engine and began to let off the clutch, but her rear-view mirror suddenly flashed as twin headlight beams illuminated her rear end. Something big was coming in fast. She shifted into reverse and launched the Guardian up the incline to her right, clearing a path for the incoming truck so she wouldn't be smashed into the pile of cars ahead. To her frustration, the Reaper saw the danger too and likewise backed the Blackbird up the slanted sidewall of the tunnel on the far side. He got clear just in time for the heavily armored truck to come barreling through. The cars ahead of them took the full brunt of the impact as the truck's jacked-up frame rolled over them on fat monster tires. The truck went over the pile and into the obstructing war car without so much as a pause. The war car's buzz saws caught in the truck's tires, exploding them on impact. The chassis of the truck sheared the top off the war car in a blaze of sparks and flames. One of the car's flamethrowers was ripped bodily from the fender and exploded in a raging fireball.

Valerie ducked as flames roared across the ceiling of the tunnel. Parts and debris rained onto her hood. When she looked up again, her eyes met the black reflective visor of the Red Reaper angled toward her from the embankment on the far side of the tunnel.

She took one look at the chaotic pile of cars in the tunnel and knew there was not a moment to spare. There was no way she was getting through now, and a detour would cost valuable time. Every second counted.

She shifted into gear and blasted off the embankment, heading back the way she had come. The tires of the Blackbird smoked as well, and he launched into the tunnel right on her bumper. She wished she could deploy a defense, but there wasn't time.

Headlights glowed in her windshield as oncoming racers flew down the tunnel, oblivious to the danger ahead. Valerie swerved and dodged as the war cars careened around her. Time after time, she evaded catastrophe with mere inches to spare.

In a quarter mile, she had her chance for an exit and launched the Guardian up one of the spillway ramps, downshifting and giving the car the gas as she climbed. She downshifted again and forced the war car to accelerate. The engine screamed under the strain.

Ahead, the metal bars of the spillway's defense grate were approaching fast.

The radio crackled.

"How's it looking down there? Do you have an exit?" Damon sounded concerned.

Valerie keyed the mic. "I'm about to make one."

She pushed the accelerator all the way to the floor. "Be rusted. Be rusted," she muttered as she bore down on the metal bars. She held her breath and prayed Gaspar's predictions about the runoff drains held true in Mount Oro too.

The Guardian slammed into the iron grate. The bars weren't rusted, but the attaching hardware was. The rectangular grate sheared away from its mounting points, tearing holes in the concrete as the force of the impact sent the grate somersaulting into the air.

Valerie jolted in her harness and held on, landing the Guardian on the now level surface of Mount Oro's surface streets.

Pedestrians and race fans screamed, some in shock and others in delight as the Guardian erupted into the square and tore along the cobblestone streets.

She wasn't alone.

The Red Reaper had followed, the Blackbird making the climb and emerging fifty yards back.

She checked the position of the sun. West. She needed to get west. She made a hard right at the next street, dodging panicked race fans and trying to keep her speed up. Every second she wasted off the main track was time she was losing ground to Jasper Sterling.

She keyed the mic. "Danger Dog, you have your map handy? I'm on Chapel and Figueroa. I need an alternate onramp!"

"West Garden Street. A quarter mile."

Damon sounded stressed.

"Got it!" Valerie replied. She covered the distance in twelve seconds and took the curve at 50 mph. She spared a quick glance in the mirror as she fishtailed out of the turn, gauging the distance from her pursuer.

The route ahead was clear, word having spread fast that war cars were on the street. Pennants streamed from the battlements, and she was surprised to see several fans waving the Bear Claw emblem of House Terravecchia. Her heart thrilled at the sight until she recalled that Jasper Sterling was driving the official Terravecchia car.

She gritted her teeth and gave the Guardian more fuel.

The detour down West Garden did indeed intercept the

original route, but as she approached the racetrack, it became clear that it wouldn't be a smooth transfer. The road went over the moat via a wooden drawbridge crammed with spectators. There was no way she could make it across.

Valerie veered left at the last instant, taking a service road that ran along the inside of the wall. It was a narrow space, little more than an alley caught between the wall and the neighboring businesses. She startled cats and obliterated trash cans as she rocketed through, looking for the next opening in the wall.

Off in the distance, she spotted another broad drainage ditch grate at the far side of a three-way intersection. She eyed the front end of the Guardian, gauging the damage she'd already done. Her hood was tweaked, and the spike ram was canted to one side. She didn't like the idea of testing her luck on more solid steel bars. With the hardware mounted on this side of the concrete, it might not give way again. She glanced in the mirror and noted that the Blackbird was gaining on her.

While they were barreling along the narrow alleyway, he would be lacking the visibility she had. It might just be enough of a break. Valerie let off the gas, allowing The Reaper to close the gap.

He was right on her tail now.

As the cars sped toward the intersection, she gauged the distance to the drainage ditch, keeping the Guardian squarely in the Reaper's line of sight the entire time. He was practically nudging her bumper.

When the moment came, she accelerated to give herself a sliver of space. It was just enough so she could cut the wheel hard, yanking on the parking brake and spinning the Guardian into an aggressive 180 degree turn that landed her in the intersection facing the opposite direction.

The Blackbird blasted by, unable to slow, and launched across the street, going airborne off the other side of the intersection and slamming straight through the drainage grate in a shower of sparks and twisted metal. The car vanished underground.

"Well, what do you know? It did give," Valerie murmured. She gunned the engine and brought the Guardian around again, following the Reaper down the hole he had involuntarily made in the drain. She found the Blackbird at a standstill at the bottom of the runoff channel, now back on the track but with its hood steaming.

"Thanks for the help!" Valerie shouted through the window. She sideswiped the rear of the Blackbird with her wheel spikes as she passed. She couldn't help but grin at the sight of the crippled car diminishing in the rear-view mirror.

She focused on the road ahead and keyed the microphone.

"Danger Dog, this is Alley Cat. I'm back on the track. Going after Sterling."

The radio returned only static for a few seconds, then Damon finally replied. "Radio reports have him nearing the Twisted Sisters. You'll need to take the low route. It's less safe but the only way to catch him."

Adrenaline was pumping through her veins as she keyed the mic to reply. "Safety is overrated. I'm running him down. Alley Cat out."

Inside the battered Blackbird, the Red Reaper groaned and restarted his engine. His thumb then slid to his microphone.

"Good luck, Alley Cat. Danger Dog out."

29

FINISHER

J asper Sterling had made good time around the Twisted Sisters. He'd taken the high route, a longer path that had cost him some time, but it lacked the hairpin turns and sheer drop-offs the low route would've required him to navigate.

Let the cars in pursuit take chances. Everything was currently in his favor, and he planned to keep it that way. He shot onto Long Bridge doing 120 mph. At this pace, he'd be through the portcullis at Sterling Arena with ten minutes to spare. The only nagging irritation was the speck in his rear-view mirror that had failed to go away.

The truck with the painted flames was refusing to lose. It was all the radio announcers kept talking about. The commoner. The underdog. They were calling him a people's champion.

Jasper sneered at the mirror. *He* was the champion. Not some nameless deckhand with more brawn than brains. He certainly didn't want this upstart making it through to the sword competition. There was no telling how the crowds would react if he actually got a weapon in his hand.

No. He would have to end this now.

Jasper adjusted the controls on his armament dashboard, and the hydraulically actuated scorpion tail lifted from the Samurai's rear end. The weapon was armed with the latest in offensive tournament weapons. The ballista was loaded with broadhead, carbide-tipped darts. The tail also held a flamethrower and an air-powered thud gun that launched three-inch steel balls. If one wouldn't bring his pursuer to a stop, the rest would.

Jasper released a patch of tire spikes, then slowed to a stop, backing the Samurai around on the track and taking aim at the incoming truck.

"Just you and me now, Rim Rat," Jasper whispered.

The truck dodged the patch of tire spikes, just as he suspected. It brought the vehicle directly into the line of his weapons.

Jasper triggered them one after another.

The steel balls were the size of fists. They slammed through the window grating of the truck and ripped the mirrors off the doors. The ballista bolts found a truer target in the intake grill, the broadheaded tips ripping through the engine compartment at high velocity.

The flamethrower was just a finishing touch. The truck was still moving fast as it careened by, but the damage had been done. The truck limped on for another eighth of a mile, but it was the last spasm of a wounded beast.

Jasper actuated the ram on the front of the Samurai. This would be the fun part.

He turned and aimed for his victim, accelerating to second gear, then third. He put on a final burst of speed as he covered the last few yards. The ram worked with devastating effect, crushing the left rear wheel of the oversized truck up into the chassis and lifting the entire vehicle up and over onto its side. Jasper didn't let off the gas until the vehicle had rolled once more onto its roof. He backed away to view his handiwork.

The driver of the truck was struggling to orient himself upside down. Jasper watched him wrestle with his harness and relished the wide-eyed look of horror on the big man's face.

This was what Jasper lived for. He eyed the frothy, blue

water of the bay that lay to either side of the bridge. The wind had picked up and now sent whitecaps skipping across the surface. He knew he should simply drive on. The upstart was no longer a threat. The flame-bedecked truck wouldn't be driven again. But it was as though the bay called to him. Angry gods beneath the waves demanded a sacrifice. Who was he to disappoint?

He shifted into gear again and targeted the cab of the truck. The concrete barrier at the side of the bridge was already fractured from the truck's impact. One more good hit should push the entire vehicle through.

He revved the engine and watched the needle of the tachometer dance across the gauge. Time to launch.

The Samurai's rear tires smoked as they spun, then bit asphalt as they gained traction. Jasper rushed toward the truck at full speed, soaking up the terror on the big man's face as he flew toward him.

Then came the impact.

But not the one Jasper expected—his Samurai plowing through the inverted truck. Instead, a cataclysmic battering ram of a vehicle tore through the rear end of his car, shearing off the scorpion tail and sending him spinning in a mad whirlwind of metal and sparks. The Samurai stayed upright, but just barely. By the time he stopped thrashing around his seat like a rag doll, his car was facing a different direction. Its rear end had struck the truck, but he was now staring out the fractured windshield at an all-black monster of a car in the center of the road. It was a Guardian 770 with a girl at the wheel.

~

She'd driven like a bat out of hell. Turn after turn, twisting mile after treacherous mile. She took the low road, cut every curve. She'd poured on the gas. She'd finally caught him.

Valerie stared out the windshield at the emerald-green Samurai X and the man behind the wheel that had ruined her life.

Jasper's helmet revealed nothing of his face. That was a pity because she wanted to see his expression when she ended him.

She revved the motor and popped the clutch. The Guardian launched forward and rammed the Samurai head on, smashing it back into Kane's truck. Jasper's head rocked back and forth in the driver's seat, and he screamed in fury.

Let him scream. He had this coming.

Valerie threw the Guardian into reverse and backed away, then shifted back into first for another run. The Samurai was smashed up but was still holding together. It appeared to still be running.

Not for long.

She pressed the accelerator and the rear wheels spun, smoking as they sought traction on the oil-spattered bridge. She hurtled forward again, but the Samurai moved as well. Jasper turned hard and launched his war car at an angle, escaping her fury by millimeters.

The Guardian slammed into the truck behind it instead, pushing it partly through the fractured barrier wall.

"No!" Valerie shouted as Jasper fled. She shifted into reverse again and backed out to pursue him. That's when she saw Connor Kane. The big man appeared to be unconscious, dangling from his race harness as the truck teetered on the side of the bridge. The force of her attack had pushed his truck right to the brink of falling. Even the rumbling vibration of her engine seemed likely to send it over the edge.

She turned to the view of Jasper's Samurai fleeing ahead on the track. She could catch him again if she went now.

At the approach end of the bridge, more cars were on their way. A wave of angry steel.

Her eyes fell on the unconscious form of Kane once more, and she swore.

She pulled the Guardian around to block the approach side of the truck, leaving the engine running, then climbed out. She raced to the driver's side window of the inverted cab and got to her hands and knees.

"Kane! Can you hear me? You've got to get out!"

The big man groaned, but his eyes merely flickered beneath his eyelids. Valerie worked furiously at the latches of his harness as the rumble of approaching cars grew louder. The belts were too tight. She snatched a knife from Kane's roof mounted weapon rack and used it to saw at his harness. Finally he fell.

The truck shifted position, the front end tipping upward as the rear slid toward the water.

"Come on!" Valerie shouted, as much to herself as to Kane. She grasped both of his wrists and pulled, attempting to haul him out the damaged window. Her muscles strained as she pressed her feet into the asphalt, fighting against the inertia of his limp body.

Loose bits of concrete were beginning to dance around her feet. The first competitor car went roaring past, a Rockwell Omega. Valerie checked the narrow gap between the Guardian and the wall and watched as more racers bore down on her. The one in the lead was a sky-blue Katana bearing the Okazaki House emblem. It was close enough for her to recognize Niko Okazaki behind the wheel, the same racer whose Shogun she had stolen and dumped into the bay. From the angle of the Katana's approach, it seemed like Niko knew.

The Katana cut to the side and careened toward the back of the Guardian. It appeared as though she would ram directly into Valerie and pin her to the wall.

Valerie grunted and gave one last tremendous pull on Kane's wrists. The truck shifted, falling away from them and plummeting toward the bay. Kane's limp body came out the window as the cab slid away, and Valerie collapsed backward, successfully landing the big man on the asphalt.

Looking beneath the Guardian's undercarriage, Valerie only had a view of tires approaching, but Niko's Katana was almost on her. She rolled over and prepared to dive off the bridge, but suddenly, another car slammed into the Katana from behind, forcing Niko wide so that the car only grazed the rear corner of the Guardian. The Katana flew past and slammed into the wall a dozen yards beyond Valerie, still being pushed by the car behind it. Valerie was shocked to recognize the Blackbird of the Red Reaper. He steered back into the driving lanes and continued on, leaving Nico's Katana smoking along the wall.

Kane was coming to. He was groggy but breathing. Valerie pulled him over to the wall and tucked him into a cutout meant for drainage. There was no way she could get him into the Guardian, and she was out of time. She sprinted around the car and jumped back into the driver's seat, slamming the door just before another war car attempted to shear it off. She gunned the throttle and tore away from the wall, racing to catch up to her competitors.

The last stretch of bridge was an all-out drag race. She checked her father's watch hanging from the rear-view mirror. There were only minutes to go till the portcullis dropped on the gate of Sterling Arena. She shifted into high gear and dodged and weaved around the debris in the road. War cars ahead of her were jettisoning armaments in a last bid for speed, and she did the same, ejecting the heavy ram and rear plate armor. The Guardian's engine roared as she gave it all the fuel and air it could handle.

Her heart was pounding, but her hands were steady on the wheel. Her mind was clear.

"Think like a car," she muttered to herself. Her eyes found the ticking second hand on her father's watch and raced it toward its apex.

The gate of the arena was in view. Thousands of spectators

lined the road in bleachers, pennants waving. She kept her focus on the gate, noting that the portcullis was already lowering. She ejected the last of her spare weight and pressed her foot all the way to the floor, mashing the accelerator with all her might.

It would be close. There was no stopping now. If she was wrong about her choice, she'd end up a pile of twisted steel and burning flame, pancaked against the portcullis.

"Come on. Come on. You can make it," she whispered. Her jaw clenched as she made the final push for the closing gate.

The crowd was on its feet, shouting and cheering as she streaked across the end of the bridge. The metal spikes of the portcullis sparked off the top of the Guardian and tore long scratches down the roof, but the car kept going.

She was through.

Valerie shouted in elation and slapped the steering wheel as the Guardian erupted through the other side of the gatehouse into the heart of Sterling Arena. Trumpets blared, and the portcullis thudded into its place, announcing the end of the race.

She'd made it. She was the last of the contenders to continue, but she was moving on.

The spectator train had offloaded all of its passengers into the arena.

Slowing the car, she scanned the crowd and found Rico cheering wildly from the sideline. She angled the Guardian toward the finisher's circle, watching for Damon among the crowd, but she saw no sign of him.

The noise in the arena was deafening.

In all, only a dozen cars had completed the course. As she climbed out of the Guardian, the royal band was playing *Hail to Avalon*, and Valerie's eyes roamed up the bleachers to the seats of honor. The royal box was crowded and chaotic, and she wasn't able to make out any details of what was going on inside.

She was immediately met by a race official in a jacket and tails who handed her a piece of parchment trimmed in gold.

"Congratulations, finalist. Here is your invitation to the King's celebratory ball. He looks forward to meeting you this evening at the masquerade in his honor."

Valerie accepted the invitation breathlessly. The adrenaline from the race and this massive scene was still so intense that she couldn't find any words to reply.

"You'll find all the details you need on the invitation," the official continued. He gave her a smile. "That was some incredible driving."

"Thank . . . thank you," Valerie finally managed.

The official bowed and moved off.

A young man vaulted the line of spectators and ran toward her, startling the guards.

"It's okay! He's my mechanic!" Valerie shouted as Rico raced up. The guards nodded and went back to monitoring the crowd.

Rico grasped her by the shoulders. "You did it! That was incredible! Some of those bang-ups looked so awful I thought for sure you'd be crushed. Are you okay?"

"Not dead yet," Valerie said. She held up the masquerade invitation with a grin. "And tonight I see the King!"

30

TRANSFORMED

"Tonight is the night," Valerie whispered to herself, barely able to contain her excitement.

Her plan was working.

Her success at the race had entitled her to a celebration. The crowd had thrilled at her inclusion in the finisher's circle. She saw more people waving Terravecchia flags, and this time it was clear that they were waving them for her and not for Jasper. One young girl shouted *"L' Orsa Nera!"* from the sidelines. When Valerie had taken her bows and descended from her place at the end of the finisher's pedestal, she waved to the race fans and stopped to sign several pennants.

She froze when she saw Jasper Sterling approach. His driving armor was less shiny now, and his forehead was streaked with motor oil. The smile on his face was as fake as his blond hair, but he maintained it as he waved to the crowd. He walked up to Valerie and gave her a nod.

"Seems you're full of surprises these days," he said. He glanced at the Guardian that Rico was prepping for its drive back to Tidewater. "Your mother will be shocked you managed to hide a war car from her. I understand she had a great interest in where that had vanished to."

"Upset that there's one more piece of my family legacy you can't have?"

Jasper waved to the crowd and spoke through his forced smile. "We'll see how long you keep it." He snatched a bear claw banner from a child and signed his name across it, larger and bolder than Valerie had done.

"You don't intimidate me," Valerie said. "Your time to gloat is up. Justice is coming for you."

"I love the idealism of youth," Jasper said. "It's so refreshing to hear your charming and unrealistic views of reality." He placed a hand on her shoulder, still smiling as though to congratulate her. "Bit of advice. You should run back to whatever hole you've been living in and stay there. It'd be a shame if more of your friends had to get hurt." He waved at Rico.

Rico froze in place, staring back at them but unable to hear over the noise of the crowd.

"Stay out of this tournament," Jasper continued. "If you show up for the fight tomorrow, I promise you won't like what happens."

He patted her shoulder amiably, then waved again to the crowd as he moved off.

Valerie gave the children in front of her a reassuring smile, signed a few more banners, then walked back to the Guardian.

"What the hell did he want?" Rico asked.

"Let's just get out of here," Valerie replied. She climbed into the Guardian and slammed the door.

Their drive back to Tidewater was dotted with spectators who cheered and waved as they passed. The village itself was quiet, the mood far less festive. They passed several garages in the warehouse district that were now empty, the cars and drivers having failed to return from the race.

Valerie parked the Guardian in one of the rear bays of

Damon's garage and assessed the condition of it, noting the dents and gouges in the body.

"Pretty banged up but nothing we can't fix," Rico said.

"It'll be rough getting parts. We'll need a bit more than primer and paint."

"I'd start with hair and makeup."

Valerie turned and realized that Rico had been assessing her and not the car.

She looked down at the sweat-stained racing gear she had on. "They won't let me dance in this, huh?"

"Unless the king likes his guests reeking of gasoline and motor oil," Rico said. "Come on. The car will keep. Time to raid the fun side of the closet."

Valerie tried the interior door on Damon's garage before she left, but it was still locked.

"Don't worry. He'll turn up," Rico said.

"Did you see him aboard the spectator train?"

"The mechanic car was packed like sardines. I wasn't about to go looking and lose my spot. I'm glad you didn't end up needing roadside repairs." He unlocked the outside gate and began tromping up the stairs to his apartment. "Once the train lost communications ability with you down in those moat tunnels, I thought we might never find you."

Valerie paused her walk up the stairs. "What are you talking about? I had coms in the tunnel. Damon was able to call me."

Rico stopped at the top of the stairs as he found his door key. "Then you were the only one. All the other teams were freaking out." He got the door unlocked and pushed through.

Valerie considered his words and tried to match them with the reality of what she had heard in the moat system. It didn't make sense. How would Damon have been able to call from the train with coms out? She finally followed Rico into his apartment and found him rummaging through his closet full of dresses. He held up an electric-blue dress with wild, multicolored ruffles. "What kind of image are you going for tonight? Center of attention? Look at me now?" He switched hands and displayed a sequined dress that flared at the bottom into a sparkly swirl of tulle.

"I need something that says, 'I'm here for justice, and if Jasper Sterling so much as touches me, I'll stab him in the face.'"

Rico considered the dresses in his arms, then scanned his closet. "Okay. A little more challenging, but yes, I can make that work. Go get cleaned up. When you get back, we'll get you dressed for revenge."

～

"Tell me you have everything ready for tomorrow," Jasper said. "Is it set?"

Blaise Cavendish was lounging on the chaise, examining the box of cigars on the lamp stand. "Our man is dropping off the package tonight after they do the final sweep of the island."

"And you're sure we can trust him?"

"He was willing to sell out his position on the security team for the miserable amount we offered. So, of course we can't trust him. What do you want me to say? But I did put the fear of God into him. I've researched all of his debts and made sure he knows I can call them in tomorrow if need be. Come morning, the package will be there."

Jasper checked his reflection in the mirror and nodded. "As long as he's discreet."

The door swung open. "Ah, here is an interesting sight," Lord Alister Sterling said, barging into the dressing room. His cold, blue eyes took in Jasper in his new suit. "The peacock in all his plumage."

Jasper fidgeted with his cufflinks and wished that, for once, his father's glare wouldn't instantly unnerve him.

"I plan to look good for my presentation to the king."

"Dressed to impress?" Lord Sterling replied. "I daresay the impressive tend to be so regardless of what they are wearing. Still, it's a good suit."

"I used your tailor," Jasper said. "I thought you would approve."

His father was wearing a similar cut of suit. This evening it was a pale gray that matched his silvery hair. Through the open doorway, the noise of guests already emanated from the ballroom downstairs.

Lord Sterling walked closer and grasped Jasper's tie, pulling the knot tighter. "You almost didn't get to dress for the occasion at all, it seems. It looked as though your would-be stepdaughter nearly took you out of the race."

"She didn't stand a chance," Jasper said.

"And yet she finished," Lord Sterling replied. "A loose end you have yet to manage." He gave Jasper's tie a last violent tug, making Jasper squirm.

When his father stepped back, Jasper ran his fingers along his collar. "Why didn't you tell me that King Logan had been friends with Il Orso Nero? That's information that would have been relevant to know *before* proposing to his widow."

"You didn't bother to ask," Lord Sterling replied. He crossed his wrists at his waist. "These are turbulent seas we are navigating. That's why it's imperative that the house of Sterling have more than one chance at the Round Table tomorrow." He turned to Blaise. "How many of the remaining contenders are still in your pocket?"

"Two," Blaise replied. "Not counting your champion."

"I assume you saw he barely finished the race," Jasper interjected.

"The Red Reaper? Yes. But he has many uses beyond driving." Lord Sterling reached into his pocket and produced a black-and-white photograph. It appeared to be taken the night of the tavern fire and showed a man carrying an ash-covered girl into a warehouse garage. Jasper recognized the girl as Valerie.

"That's your hired sword?" Jasper asked.

"He let me know he has been keeping tabs on your loose end, since it seems you have been less than effective at it."

Jasper snatched up the photo. "If he's that close to her, he's been compromised. He could be on her side of this for all you know. You should choose another champion to represent our house."

"And lose the best swordsman in the tournament? Not likely. He has proven himself most useful. And whatever his nocturnal activities with this girl have become, he remains the strongest contender for the win. If either of you win, we can still name you as the knight to represent us. He's your best chance to ever see the Round Table."

"I'm our best chance," Jasper argued. "We don't need him."

"We'll find out tomorrow, won't we? Just make sure that there are no more loose ends."

Lord Sterling walked out of the room, headed to the grand staircase. Jasper hurried along behind. He finally caught up to his father at the top of the stairs.

As they made their descent, side by side, one thought solidified itself in Jasper's mind. Whatever else came of the fight tomorrow, if Valerie Terravecchia was foolish enough to show her face in the arena, she was going to die.

Valerie stood before the mirror and marveled at the creature staring back.

"I don't even know what to say." She ran her hands over the form-fitting, blue-green dress that Rico had fashioned from multiple outfits. A layer of sheer black lace gave an undercurrent to the look, showing through cutouts in the silken dress. It hugged her curves until it fanned out in a fishtail at her calves. When she moved, the layers made a pleasing swishing sound like wind through grass.

The green and black continued across the textured bodice. It gave the impression of an ocean wave over black rock. One shoulder was bare, and the look revealed her prominent collarbones, but the single sleeve of the dress picked up the black lace that ran down to her wrist before cutting in a V at her fingers. This delicate sort of armor hid the bruises along her sword arm.

Rico had given her smoky eyes and pronounced cheekbones, finishing the look with a pale matte lip color. Her lips parted as she ran her fingers over the waist of the dress. Weeks of training had made a clear difference. Her waist was firm, and the fabric was tight but comfortable. She could breathe easily and relax without affecting the slender lines of the dress.

Rico had worked his magic on her hair as well, styling the places that had been scorched with accents of delicately twisted metal. Her hair swept up on one side but cascaded in curls down the other. A bracelet on her left wrist was also repurposed steel. It gave her a literal edge.

Beautiful and dangerous.

Valerie smiled as she took it all in. Until now, she had always thought of ball gowns as cumbersome things, bulky and inconvenient, but Rico had created something nearly as practical as it was beautiful. It was as though he had retrieved the design from somewhere inside of her mind.

"You're an absolute wizard," Valerie said.

"I'll come clean," Rico said. "I didn't just put this together tonight. I've been working on it ever since you said you might get to attend the masquerade and you told me about that pretty mask your boy, Damon, gave you."

"Oh no!" Valerie exclaimed. "The mask is still locked up inside Damon's garage."

Rico moved to the window and looked outside. "Actually, I don't think that'll be a problem."

Valerie stepped out the door onto the iron landing and looked down to find Damon standing in the driveway. He was waiting beside the Vulcan with her mask in his hands.

Valerie's breath caught.

"Thought you might need a ride," he said.

It had only been a day, but she was surprised at how much she had missed seeing his face.

She lifted the edge of her dress to descend the stairs, revealing the fact that she was still wearing boots. Footwear had been one thing Rico didn't have in her size.

"You look stunning," Damon said as she reached the bottom of the stairs.

"You don't look bad yourself." Damon was wearing a black suit and black shirt open at the collar. Calm. Confident. To top it off, she caught a whiff of the clean, earthy scent of him. Like a forest in a rainstorm.

She knew there were things she wanted to talk to him about, but for the moment she couldn't think of a single one. His eyes on hers made her lose focus, taking her into that blurry place where all that existed was the two of them.

"I'm proud of you," Damon said. "I've never seen anyone drive like that."

"The plan worked," Valerie said. "I'll finally get to see the king."

"Let's get you up there," Damon said. "As much as I'd like to keep this view all to myself, I suppose I ought to share." He opened the door for her.

Valerie turned back to Rico, who had descended the stairs, and gave him a hug. "Thank you. I wish you could be there with me."

"Don't worry. I'm gonna go bust my way into the hospital and visit Janet tonight. Now that I've been on a winning race team, we'll see if they still try to keep me out. We're gonna have our own party and celebrate your victory."

"Give her a hug from me?"

"You got it. Don't worry. She's a fighter. Like you."

Damon took Valerie's hand and helped her into the car. Rico waved as they pulled away.

"You've made a good friend there," Damon said.

"The best," she said. "I don't think I deserve him."

Damon studied her. "You have a power that I don't think you realize. People see it in you. The good. Why do you think I agreed to train you?"

"You said if I won, I'd give you the Guardian."

"Is that what you think I want?"

Valerie looked over and met his stare. It was there again, that hungry look. The wolf. She looked away, heat rising in her cheeks. She put her mask on to hide the flush of color that was no doubt appearing in her face.

Damon turned onto the Crown Bridge and headed through the Port Hyacinth city gates. Valerie flashed her invitation to the guards, and they bowed as they let the car through. They made the drive to Broadway and Main, then out to the peak of the city where the spires of Sterling Castle were all illuminated.

As they drove up the twisting road to the castle, her mind cleared enough to focus on the night ahead. She exhaled as she imagined meeting the king and tried to envision what to say. She wished she hadn't lost the proof of her case. The thought made her pause.

"I found something in your garage this morning," Valerie said. "Before I left for the race. A briefcase I took from Blaise Cavendish, Jasper's lawyer."

"It was in the street near the tavern the morning after the fire," Damon said, his eyes never leaving the road. "It was empty, so I figured you had what you needed. But I thought it was best to get it out of sight in case the City Watch ran across it."

"How did you know that I was the one who stole it?"

"You talk in your sleep."

Valerie's mind went into overdrive. Talked in her sleep? What other secrets might she have let slip during the night in his bed?

311

He turned to look at her. "Look, the king is a just man. If you tell him your story, he'll listen."

They pulled up to the round drive outside the entrance to the castle.

"I wish you were going in there with me," Valerie said.

"I'm just your chauffeur tonight," Damon said. "But you've got this. Jasper Sterling has it coming."

Valerie nodded, trying to regain the confidence she'd felt on the racetrack.

Damon climbed out of the car and walked around to open the door for her.

The broad steps of the entrance were jammed with attendees in elaborate masks and feathery hats. A court photographer was taking photographs along one edge of the walkway, and a long line of couples stood waiting for a chance to appear in the gossip pages.

Valerie looked up at the imposing towers of the castle.

Damon squeezed her hand. "Don't worry. There's nothing in there that you can't handle."

"Will I see you tonight? After?"

"I'll be here," he replied.

She nodded, then straightened up. An elegantly outfitted member of the royal guard approached to view her invitation.

"A finisher. It's an honor. I can escort you inside."

Valerie accepted the arm he offered. She turned to Damon, getting in one last glance.

He gave her a reassuring smile.

She exhaled and let her escort guide her across the drawbridge of the castle. The flags of the house of Pendragon flew alongside those of House Sterling. The cross and crown of the flag of Avalon flew above them all.

Her escort led her through the open doors of the castle and onward to the entrance of the main ballroom. Hundreds of masked faces crowded the room. Dancers whirled across the dance floor to the elegant music of a full, live orchestra in the corner. Somewhere among all of these faces was the king. Her escort bowed deeply and took his leave, returning the way they'd come.

Valerie turned and faced the waiting crowd, took a last deep breath, then stepped into the ball.

~

Damon pulled the car around to the garages, then rolled inside and cut the engine. He climbed out of the Vulcan and shrugged out of his jacket, leaving it in the driver's seat. He stared at the jacket for a long moment, then moved to the back of the adjacent vehicle—a charcoal-gray Easton Blackbird. He unlocked the trunk of the car, and the light illuminated the gear inside. A red hilted sword rested in the rack on the trunk lid. He reached into the interior space and slowly donned the metal-studded jacket. He then picked up the masquerade mask. It was a reflection of the dueling mask beside it, all black with a crimson streak across one eye.

He placed the mask over his face and let the world outside take on the tint of the lenses, then he slammed the trunk of the Blackbird and made his way to the castle.

31

MASQUERADE

Brilliant chandeliers cast prisms of color around the ballroom, a whirl of glittering bodies reflecting them back. Valerie had stepped into a foreign world of strange faces and mysterious laughter. The only comfort she had was that the mask she was wearing concealed her identity as well. She roamed the ballroom in search of someone resembling King Logan, but if he was masked, she would be unlikely to recognize him.

Eyes trailed her everywhere she moved. Gentlemen bowed and stepped aside. Women whispered and admired her dress and hair.

She approached a laughing couple near the bar and tapped the young woman on the shoulder. The girl was wearing a white-and-gold mask with golden feathers flowing from it.

"Excuse me, do you know if King Logan has been announced yet?"

The girl in the gold mask stared at her, leaning closer and squinting. "Valerie?"

Valerie immediately recognized the voice. "Thea? Is that you?"

"Oh my God!" Thea wrapped her in a hug. "I can't believe

you're here! I heard about you entering the tournament. We watched it all."

Valerie shrugged out of Thea's embrace.

The young man beside her pushed his mask up. "Hey. Looks like you do know how to drive after all."

"Remi Rothschild?" Valerie turned to Thea. "You came to the ball with Remi?"

"His dad got us invited," Thea replied.

"He's a sponsor of the tournament, so we have an all-access pass," Remi explained.

Valerie ignored him.

"I'm so sorry about when you called," Thea said. "I should have tried to get you that money, but you know how my dad is. He said we'd be shunned from high society. Can you imagine?"

"Yeah. I can." She didn't have time for this. "What about the king, Thea? Is he here yet?"

"He hasn't been announced," Thea said. "But the rumor is that he wanted to sneak in privately. That's why it's a masquerade. Everyone is trying to figure out who's who, like a game."

"Damn it," Valerie replied. "I really need to talk to him."

"I haven't seen him. But we did find the queen," Thea said. "She's over there." She pointed to a slender Asian woman in a sparkling dress. She was wearing a tall, intricate wig bedecked with jewels. Her mask was made of delicate, transparent glass. As far as disguises went, it wasn't exactly effective.

"If Queen Kimiko is here, then the king has to be around somewhere, doesn't he?" Valerie eyed the various masked men in the vicinity of the queen. She didn't see anyone that resembled the posters and photographs she had seen of King Logan, but she couldn't be sure. One face was clearly recognizable, however. Ice-blue eyes behind a shining silver mask. Jasper Sterling. Lady Charlotte was there too, having opted for a silver-and-blue mask that only obscured a quarter of her face.

Valerie slipped through the crowd, edging closer to the group and keeping her eyes on the queen. If King Logan was in the crowd, the queen was likely to give it away, wasn't she?

She picked up a drink from a passing serving platter and attempted to appear a casual bystander. Her dress worked against her in that regard as people kept coming up and complimenting her on it while making pointed attempts to ascertain her identity.

Valerie gave polite greetings and was in the middle of declining an offer to dance from a tall, spindly gentleman in a powdered wig when Jasper Sterling fixed his eyes on her and began to approach.

She grabbed the shoulder of the man in the wig. "Actually, I will take that dance after all." She took the man's arm and let him lead her to the dance floor. She affixed a smile to her face, and they whirled away into the crowd of dancers, leaving Jasper alone on the edge of the dance floor.

The dance was a complicated affair that involved a great deal of twirling and switching of partners. She found it difficult to keep her eye on the queen and kept craning her neck to manage it as she was swept from one end of the ballroom to the other.

To her dismay, Jasper Sterling entered the dance with a partner and was soon dancing nearby. She took the lead with her current partner and angled them both away. The group switched partners again, and due to her incorrect position, she was left standing on the sidelines momentarily. She turned to find the Red Reaper staring at her from behind his crimson-streaked mask. Valerie backed away, involuntarily bumping into a couple that was whirling by. The woman tripped and fell, sprawling onto her backside on the dance floor.

"So sorry," Valerie said, but then she seized the woman's partner and whirled him away. The young man looked back with an apologetic glance but then got a good look at Valerie and shrugged. They picked up the pace and were soon back in the thick of the dancing.

Valerie searched the crowd around the dance floor while

simultaneously attempting to keep her dancing partner at a distance. The young man seemed to have taken her intrusion as an invitation and kept angling in to try to kiss her. She spotted the queen moving toward one of the exits to the garden. Was she meeting the king?

The amorous young man attempted to push his face into Valerie's for the third time, and she caught it with her hand, pushing it back. She then gave him a swift knee to the groin. Her partner doubled over.

"Why don't you dance *that* off," Valerie said and swept past him, making for the door.

She moved to the outside balcony and caught sight of the queen slipping into the hedge maze. As Valerie rushed down the steps to the lawn, she noted that she wasn't the only one following. The Red Reaper emerged from the shadows near the far side of the lawn and entered the maze in pursuit of the queen.

"What the hell?" Valerie said and rushed across the manicured grass to the maze.

She paused at the entrance and peered inside, but there was no sign of her quarry. She entered the maze and worked her way down one avenue after another, attempting to keep her dress from catching on the hedges.

After a few turns, she felt entirely lost, but she continued on, finally making out the low murmur of voices ahead. She peeked around the corner of the next hedge and found the Red Reaper and the queen standing midway down the row. The queen was removing something from beneath her skirts. She handed a packet of folded papers to the Reaper. "Give these back to Sterling. It'll cement what we know."

"What about the girl?" the Reaper said, his voice a low growl behind the mask.

"There is still tomorrow. We need to see it through to the end."

Valerie leaned closer to the hedge, attempting to hear better, and a twig snapped under her foot. She held her breath.

"Someone is here," the queen whispered. "Find them."

Valerie fled.

She darted down the row and back the way she had come, attempting to navigate the way out. Somehow, it was even more confusing than the way in. Everything looked the same in the dark. The sound of footfalls the next row over hastened her flight. She rushed to a T in the maze and turned right, then right again, but hit a dead end. She froze as the footsteps grew closer.

She could hear the Reaper breathing on the far side of the hedge.

Not so much as a whimper escaped her own mouth as she waited, holding her breath.

The Reaper moved on.

She stayed hidden in place for half a minute, then moved again, carefully stepping in the softest grass and making no sound as she went. She came to a corner and peeked around the hedge and was startled to see the Reaper at the end of the row. But he was moving away with determined strides.

She followed.

He was least likely to search places he had already been, wasn't he?

But it seemed the Reaper was no longer searching at all. He led the way to the exit of the maze and strode across the lawn, never once looking back.

Valerie frowned at his retreating figure.

A clandestine rendezvous with the queen? Secret documents for the Sterlings? Something was going on here tonight. If she was going to convince the king of the Sterlings' dishonesty, she needed to know what it was.

She struck out across the lawn in pursuit of the Red Reaper.

The noise and lights of the ballroom washed back over her as she slipped inside the garden door. She traversed the hallways that skirted the ballroom and caught sight of the Reaper turning a corner ahead. She rushed to the corner and peered around it, but there was no sign of him in the next hallway.

Full suits of armor lined the walls, and between them, racks upon racks of swords. As she trod softly along the carpeted hallway, she recognized named blades from numerous houses. She walked to the end of the hall, but it was a dead end. The Reaper had to be in one of the rooms she had passed.

She carefully tried the door handles as she retraced her steps, peering into room after vacant room. She was just about to close a door midway down the hall when her eye caught on a sword hanging on the wall behind a broad desk. She froze.

The blade was out of its scabbard, mounted horizontally on the wall. It would have been recognizable anywhere, but they had even made a name plate for it. *Durendal.*

It was mounted like a trophy, no better than a gilded cup or a rack of antlers. Her family legacy was just a prize for them.

Valerie felt the anger rising in her as she strode across the room and crossed behind the desk. She was reaching for the sword when she heard the voices.

She froze again, listening.

The voices were coming from the bookcase.

And they were getting closer.

A click sounded from behind the bookshelf just to her left, then the shelf began to move.

Valerie backpedaled, pushing herself into the corner of the room. There was nowhere to go. It was too far to the door. She would have to cross directly in front of the opening.

She became a statue as two men exited the secret room. The first was the Red Reaper followed by Lord Alister Sterling.

" . . . and I cannot tell you how comforted I am knowing that these delicate items are safely in hand once again," the silver-haired lord was saying. "Jasper is rather impulsive in his methods and at times lacks the finesse of a wiser man. It becomes a father's duty to remedy his son's mistakes."

The two men had their backs to her.

"This Terravecchia girl has been an unexpected thorn. The documents she absconded with could easily have been misconstrued. It would be so unseemly to have to trouble King Logan with these matters during the royal visit, as you can imagine. You have saved us a great deal of inconvenience."

"I serve at your discretion, my lord," The Reaper replied.

Valerie studied the back of the man's helmet. Not looking at his face, his voice almost sounded . . .

"I have to admit, you had me worried," Lord Sterling said, crossing to the side of the room and pouring himself a glass of whiskey. "Some of the photographs my man took down at the dock district made it seem you were quite close to the girl. It's good to know where your loyalties lie."

"My loyalty has never wavered," the Red Reaper replied.

"Join me in a drink then," Lord Sterling said. He poured a second glass and held it out it to the Reaper. "To loyalty."

The Red Reaper removed the mask from his face and accepted the glass. He held it aloft. As he did so, he turned toward the light.

Valerie took a step back and hit the wall with a thud, knocking several books from the shelf.

No.

It couldn't be.

Both men turned at the sound, and she found herself staring at the man she thought she knew. Damon's glass fell from his hand and shattered on the floor.

Valerie ran.

32

SWORD

Valerie raced down the hallway, then shoved her way out the first door she could find. It led to a courtyard filled with partygoers. She angled through the crowd, walking quickly at first but then breaking into a run. She ignored the stares and whispered comments. She had to escape.

There was a wave coming, building on the horizon and swelling toward her. The pressure of it increased around her, a force that, at any moment, would crest and fall, crushing her beneath its weight. But there was nowhere she could run from this. It was as though the ground beneath her feet was betraying her, dragging her back toward this darkness. No matter how fast she ran, she couldn't outrun it.

She raced out of the courtyard and into the gardens.

Once outside, she tore the mask from her face, pausing for only a moment to stare at the beautiful blue-green colors. She tossed it to the ground.

She'd been a fool.

How could she have thought he cared?

This city belonged to the Sterlings, and they would never let up. They would simply crush her and everything she wanted.

They had proven that there was nothing she could desire that they couldn't take away.

Even Damon.

Her eyes filled with tears, and she rushed onward.

After a hundred yards, she took a glance back at the castle and saw Damon exiting the courtyard gate. His mask was off, and he was scanning the grounds, searching for her. He paused when he discovered the masquerade mask in the grass and stooped for it.

Valerie cut through a second garden gate and ran downhill, curving around to the circular drive where she had been dropped off. She located a pair of valets lounging against the wall. She wiped at her eyes and shouted, "You! One of you. I need a ride."

The young men both looked up in surprise. They clearly hadn't expected anyone to be exiting the ball so quickly.

"We aren't able to leave the grounds with vehicles," one of them said. "Lord Sterling's orders."

"Then find me a cab! There's a man chasing me, and I really need to leave." Her voice was on the edge of breaking. Tears kept welling up, and she continued to wipe at them, her fingers coming away stained with mascara.

The two young men stared at each other but did nothing.

"Fine. Never mind!" Valerie shouted. She lifted her dress again and ran down the drive, cursing the fact that she was in a dress. There was nothing elegant about this place anymore. It was a prison. A trap. A lie.

She had made it perhaps a quarter mile down the long, twisting drive when she heard the car. Headlights swept around the bend, accompanied by the roar of a powerful engine. It was a sound she recognized. The Blackbird. The Reaper.

Valerie plunged off the road into the woods.

The lace of her dress snagged on branches as she ran. She leapt over fallen logs and pushed through a patch of brambles before emerging on a lower section of the road.

It was too far. She could never run the entire way back. Not to Tidewater. Certainly not to her home in the valley. The headlights swept around a curve to her right this time, and she was about to flee back into the woods when she picked up the sound of the engine. It was a clunky, low-pitched rumble. Not the Blackbird. She stepped into the middle of the road and waved her arms. The car slowed. As she sidestepped the headlights and her eyes adjusted to the darkness, she got a look at the driver. He was a teenager. Fifteen maybe. In the passenger seat sat a girl, younger by several years but sharing an unmistakable resemblance to the boy. Just a couple of kids out for a joyride in their parents' convertible.

Valerie stepped up to the driver's side and addressed the boy who was staring at her with his mouth agape. "Please, will you help me? I need a ride."

The boy stammered the response. "We aren't supposed to stop for—"

"Please," Valerie interrupted. "In the name of chivalry. I'm being chased by a really bad man. I need your help."

"Help her, Curtis!" the little girl said. She smacked him on the shoulder.

At that moment another set of headlights appeared on the road a half mile back.

"That's him. Please!"

The boy glanced in the rear-view mirror but then nodded. "Okay, get in."

Valerie didn't wait for one of them to open a door, she simply flung a leg over the side and flopped herself into the back seat, staying low to keep herself out of sight of the car approaching from behind.

"Go! Go!" the little girl said. The boy shifted carefully back into gear and gave the car the gas. It lurched forward and began to move.

The little girl glanced in her mirror too, then reached for the automatic roof controls. The roof extended upward and over them, further protecting Valerie from view. The little girl latched the top, then slumped back in her seat.

The boy had picked up speed, but it was clear he was an inexperienced driver. There was no way he would outrun the Blackbird, even if the car stood a chance.

"Just drive normally," Valerie said. "Take it easy."

The boy's hands were fixed at ten and two on the steering wheel, his knuckles white, but he kept his eyes on the road as the headlights grew brighter behind them.

The little girl was now stiff as a board, her eyes fixed straight ahead.

The interior of the car brightened as the headlights filled the space with light. Valerie could clearly make out the distinctive growl of the Blackbird.

She slid as low as she could go in the back seat, lying horizontally on the cushion and attempting to disappear into the crevices.

The Blackbird swept into the passing lane and pulled alongside.

She held her breath.

Then the rumble of the engine increased again, and the war car pulled ahead.

The boy at the wheel eased off the gas and let the Blackbird gain ground. Finally the little girl twisted in her seat and popped her head into the back. "I think it's safe now."

Valerie rose slowly from her position and noted that the taillights of The Reaper's car were distant pin pricks. She exhaled.

The girl staring at her from the front seat was dressed up, attempting to look older, but she couldn't have been more than thirteen.

"I'm Chelle," the girl said. "This is my brother, Curtis. Why is that man chasing you?"

"He's just a very bad person," Valerie replied. "And a liar."

"Why do you know him?" Chelle asked.

"Because he was supposed to be my friend, but it turns out you can't count on anyone."

The boy shifted in his seat. "Where are we taking you?"

Valerie oriented herself to where they were. "Turn left up here. We need to cross the Crown Bridge."

Chelle glanced at her brother. "You've never crossed a bridge yet, have you?"

"It's fine," the boy replied. "I can do it." He flipped on his turn signal.

"You two are very brave for helping me," Valerie said. "I really appreciate it."

She couldn't help but notice the boy's determined posture, his set jaw. The two may as well have been Henry and her younger self out for a ride. They shared so many similarities.

But she couldn't think about that.

It was just a pair of good kids.

She stayed quiet for the rest of the ride, occasionally giving Curtis directions but otherwise letting Chelle fill the time with a rambling discourse on their friends, their school, and how much she looked forward to being able to drive herself in a few years.

When they reached the Crown Gate, she had them make the turnoff toward Tidewater, but the kids both looked concerned at the sight of the potholed road that led to the village.

"I'll get out here," Valerie said. "You can just drop me off."

Curtis pulled over and parked.

"Where are you going? Don't you need to get inside the city?" Chelle asked.

"It's okay. I have a car close by. I won't be staying long."

The mention of the car made them visibly relieved. "Mom says you should never drive through the rim districts because the people there will beat you up and take all of your stuff," Chelle said.

"It seems like that can happen in a lot of places now," Valerie replied. Curtis opened the door and moved the seat forward so she could climb out.

The sea breeze had picked up, and a cold mist was blowing across the bridge. She shivered. "Be careful getting back," Valerie said. "You two saved me tonight. Thank you."

Curtis was studying her bare shoulders and seemed to notice the burns and bruises. "Wait, are you a fighter? Were you in the tournament?"

"I was," Valerie replied. "But I've lost."

She left the two kids at the highway and made her way down the twisting road that led to Tidewater. The village was quietly subdued compared to the excitement prior to the race. A drizzling rain began to fall, and the fog settling in for the night muffled the village sounds as well as the light.

As she made her way to Lexington Avenue, she could no longer hold off the weight of the depression settling in on her. The closer she got to Damon's warehouse, the deeper she sank into the sadness and horror of his betrayal.

This entire time.

Her training. His advice. The way they'd touched. Kissed.

All lies.

She couldn't believe it.

He had been there when Henry died. Participated in the duel.

It was true that the Red Reaper wasn't the one who had dealt the mortal blow, but he had cleared Jasper's path to do so. If Henry had still held his sword, Jasper could never have hurt him. It was the Reaper's fault that Henry lost the duel.

It was Damon's fault that she no longer had a brother.

By the time she reached the warehouse, her dress was a soggy ruin. It was torn and stained, and the edges had been dragged through the mud. Her hair was no doubt equally a mess. The heavy fog clung to every bit of her, the drizzling rain condensing into droplets on her hot skin and running down her arms. It gave her chills.

The door to the warehouse was locked.

She rattled and shook the doorknob, but it wouldn't turn. The rolling garage door likewise refused to budge. The Guardian was trapped. Her only lifeline out of this infernal city and its continual labyrinth of nightmares stood beyond these doors. She picked up a rock and slammed it against the doorknob of the pedestrian door. It did nothing.

She needed something bigger.

She discovered half of a cinderblock in the alley beside the warehouse, but that proved useless as well. When she struck the doorknob, the cinderblock crumbled to pieces in her hands.

As the chalky bits of concrete rained from her fingertips, her tears began to fall as well. She punched the door, instantly regretting it. Her knuckles came away scuffed, and the door wasn't even dented.

Valerie stared up at the sky and screamed at the clouds. "Why won't you let me out of here!"

No response came from on high other than the steady dripping from the rain gutters.

The windows in Rico's apartment were dark. She pounded on the downstairs gate but got no response.

Finally Valerie shuffled into the street, making her way downhill.

It took her till almost mid-block of the next street before she remembered there wasn't even a phone to use anymore. The Twisted Tentacle was an ash heap.

The foundation of the tavern remained. There was little else of the facade. She walked up to where the front door used to be and stepped over the blackened lintel. The burned-out steel frame of the old car was still there, butted up against the structural support for what had once been the stage. It was hard to make out the shape of the rest of the room because the upstairs apartment had crashed down to the ground floor and subsequently burned.

Valerie's shoes left footprints in the sooty mud as she walked, surveying the ruins. There were no more bodies visible. Someone

327

had dragged away any remains they had found. That was a relief, but she had done nothing to help with the situation herself. She had focused only on her own goals. And what had it earned her?

As she stepped listlessly through the ruins of the bar, she reached the staircase that had run up to Janet's apartment. This one corner of the building had fared better than the rest, and a portion of the upper story still remained. There was a patch of dry foundation beneath the stairs.

Valerie turned back to make her way toward the door, and her foot struck something under the layer of ash at her feet. The something clunked.

She reached down and pushed the debris from the top of the item, discovering it was the ornate box she had seen upstairs with Ann. She crouched low and brushed away the cinders and ash from the rest of the lid, discovering one end had been blackened to a solid hunk of charcoal.

She lifted the box and carried it back to the dry area under the stairs and settled herself on the floor out of the rain. She set the box gently on the concrete.

The lock broke away in her hand when she pulled on it. Valerie lifted the lid, the hinges making a crunching noise as they strained the charred wood.

The sword was still inside.

The wooden handle that had once been an almost purplish brown was now a solid black. Valerie lifted the sword from its case. It was still perfectly balanced. The hardwood, despite being blackened, was still intact. The leather scabbard had blackened and charred, burning completely away in places, but even in the dim light from the streetlamp outside, the blade still shimmered. Valerie pulled it from the damaged scabbard. The metal had turned various colors in the heat, mostly shades of blue that seemed to change as she looked at them. The crossbar had also been marred by the heat. Its shiny finish had taken on a tarnished appearance. The tips of the crossbars and the end of the pommel were charred black.

Ten years of apprenticeship. Five years working on the sword.

A masterpiece and multiple lives all ruined in one night.

Her hand began to shake. It was as though the sword knew who held it and wouldn't tolerate it.

The rain started to fall in earnest. Big droplets splashed off the ruins of the tavern around her and made soft thuds into the ashes. She laid the sword back in its box and closed the lid, trying to quell the shaking in her limbs. Both of her hands were quivering badly as she lifted the box into her arms and hugged it to her body. She retreated from the rain, backing into the small corner of dry space under the stairs and curling herself into the smallest possible version of herself.

As much as this night had left her broken, she couldn't cry anymore. It was as though her soul was now as burnt out and hollow as the tavern. Her emotions had been exhausted like so much smoke from the blaze.

The sky continued to rain the tears that she couldn't.

She wondered if the ruined building might shift in the night and come crashing down on her. From her little corner of hell, she didn't think it sounded like the worst outcome. But as the sky continued to break open above, the building remained upright, and all Valerie could do was watch, wait, and mourn.

33

REBIRTH

"Valerie."

Valerie's eyes fluttered open.

She blinked and wiped at her face, and a figure came into focus above her, backlit by early morning light.

Ann.

The swordsmith was leaning over her wearing a hooded, weatherproof jacket and a flannel shirt.

"You're back," Valerie murmured.

Dawn had come to Tidewater. Fog still clung to the street, but daylight cast the world in a steadily brightening gray.

Ann's face was unreadable. As Valerie sat up, the folds of her dress she'd been clutching during the night shifted, revealing the box that was still laying across her lap.

Ann's eyes widened. "You found it."

"It . . . it was in the ashes." Valerie pushed herself to her knees and handed the box over. "I wasn't trying to—here, it's yours." She relinquished the box and rose to her feet.

Ann cautiously opened the lid. She bit her lip as she saw the sword and choked back a groan.

Valerie cringed. Was it worse for Ann seeing that it was ruined? Would it have been better if she had never found it? It was as though she just couldn't stop hurting the people she cared about.

But as Ann lifted the sword from the box, she exhaled audibly. "I didn't think it would survive."

"I'm sorry I didn't save it," Valerie said.

Ann shook her head. "No. You saved what mattered most."

Valerie studied Ann's face. "How is Janet?"

Ann's eyes stayed focused on the sword as if refusing to acknowledge Valerie's question. Finally she addressed the words to the sword itself. "She hasn't woken up yet. The doctors said she may not come back."

Valerie could find no words to reply. Nothing that could come out of her mouth would change any of this. Ann's and Janet's lives were both in ruins.

"She really likes you," Ann said, her eyes finally returning to Valerie. "She told me so."

"I can't imagine that's true now," Valerie said. "I've caused you both nothing but pain."

"She said that she knew you'd be trouble," Ann said. "Right from the start. But that doesn't mean she would do anything differently."

"This is unforgivable," Valerie said, gesturing to the burned-out shell of the tavern around them.

"You don't know her then." Ann shook her head. "That's the thing about Janet. She'll set you straight, no doubt about it. Always has. But her capacity to forgive is one of the only reasons I'm still here. We've all messed up."

"Why are you doing this?" Valerie said, unable to prevent the edge in her voice. "Why are you being kind to me? You ought to be angry."

Ann licked her lips and lowered the sword. "Oh, I am angry. I'm furious. This fire," she gestured to the charred remains around her. "This is nothing compared to what's going on in here." Her fist thumped against her chest. "But you have to be angry in the right direction." She raised her eyes toward the bridges overhead and the high walls of the city, and her mouth hardened into a line. "Come on. There's something I want to show you."

Without another word, she turned and walked out of the ruins. Valerie had no better option so she followed. As she passed the burnt-out car, her dress caught on a jagged edge of steel and ripped.

Valerie stared at the gigantic tear in the gown. She yanked on the fabric that was caught, but it only ripped worse. Finally she reached around her back and unzipped herself, stepping out of the destroyed dress and leaving it behind. She tried to summon the will to be upset at the loss of such a beautiful creation, but she felt as hollow and empty as the burnt-out shell of the car. The ornamentation in her hair went next. She pulled it out piece by piece, then tossed it into the rubble.

She walked out of the ruins of the tavern dressed in only her boots and undergarments.

Ann considered her briefly, then shrugged out of her jacket. She handed it to Valerie.

Valerie gratefully donned the jacket and hugged herself in it.

Ann led the way down the street and around the corner to the Otter and Oyster. The small tavern was already crowded despite the early hour.

"I invited a few more," Ann said. She pushed through the doors of the tavern.

Valerie felt horribly exposed; her bare legs chilled with goosebumps. The last place she wanted to be right now was in a crowd.

At least it was warmer inside.

She followed Ann through the doors.

The noisy chatter inside the tavern died. Valerie looked around the room to find dozens of eyes on her. Some faces she recognized from the race the day before. Connor Kane was there too, looking bruised. Most of the expressions of the other competitors were stony, men and women with furrowed brows and set jaws. A few members of the crowd had been regulars at the Twisted Tentacle, but the rest were strangers.

Ann walked to the center of the tavern and laid the charred sword box on a table. Then she addressed the room.

"Thank you for gathering this morning. I know it was unexpected. Most of you know me because you know Janet, and many of you have asked for news of her condition. All I can say is that the doctors have done all they can for now. The rest is between Janet and God. If you're the type to say prayers, she can use them."

A few members of the crowd murmured to one another and offered sympathy.

Ann brushed a hand along the charred box.

"As many of you know, the night of the explosion, Janet and I were judged by the Sword Masters Guild. I spent five years crafting a sword that I hoped would be a worthy masterwork. I believe it would have been had it not been for the fire."

More murmuring flowed around the tavern.

"But it wasn't to be," Ann continued. "As anyone who has lived in this village knows, once you've washed in here, it's not easy to get back out. The tide is always against us."

"They ain't ever gonna let us up," someone in the back said. "The fire proved it."

Several more people voiced agreement.

"We're cursed!"

"Damned to this hell we are," an old sailor muttered.

Ann lifted a hand and the room settled. "The fire might have seemed like it came from hell, Marco, but it has shown us a light." She took a few steps toward the old man. "The only way to escape Tidewater is through the system the nobles set out for us. That or death. Connor gave us hope that a champion of the people might one day beat their system." She nodded toward the big sailor. "He gave us hope that he could become the Knight Warden of the West, and finally we would have someone to speak for us. To speak for the people."

Several curses were audible from the crowd. "He ain't never had a real chance," someone shouted. "It's all rigged."

Noisy agreement erupted from nearly every table, and Ann had a difficult time regaining their attention. Finally the tavern's owner slammed a club on the bar several times, and the chatter died down.

Ann lifted a foot onto one of the open chairs and rested her elbow on her knee. "A few months ago, a stranger arrived to stay at the Twisted Tentacle. She was beat down and knocked around, and she wasn't one of us. When Janet told me that she had taken in yet another lost soul and given them a second chance, I wondered if this might be the time her reckless generosity finally caught up with us."

Several eyes fell on Valerie.

"Turns out I was right."

Valerie shifted uneasily, wondering where Ann was going with this.

"Since Janet made that decision . . ." Ann set her foot back down, "we've seen nothing but trouble. I've seen my dreams literally turn to ash." She flipped open the box on the table and lifted the sword.

The crowd murmured. More eyes found their way to Valerie.

"Yesterday Connor Kane lost at their twisted game, and our best hope for justice went with him. But not our only hope." Ann walked toward Valerie, the sword in her hand. "So the question is, what will you do with our last hope, Valerie Terravecchia? Will you stand up for us the way Janet did for you?"

Valerie's fists were clenched so tightly that her nails bit into her palms. She relaxed and let them fall to her sides. "I can't. I can't fight anymore. My car is locked up. My armor. My weapons. I've got nothing left."

"You don't have nothing," Ann said. "You have a sword." She turned the handle around and offered the grip to Valerie.

The eyes of everyone in the room were on her now.

"I don't deserve to be your champion," Valerie said. "Not after all the trouble I've brought down on you."

"Pay it back," Ann said. "Back to the ones who deserve it. Show them that trouble cuts both ways."

The room rippled with unspoken tension. Whispers. Glances. Valerie knew that her face must be flushed. Her skin was burning up. She slowly extended her hand and took the handle of the sword.

"For Janet," she said.

"For all of us," Ann replied. She released the sword.

Valerie raised the blade until it caught the light, shimmering with blues and purples.

A chair scraped the floor, and Connor Kane strode forward, stopping in front of her.

He pulled a wicked-looking falchion from his hip and stared her down. Valerie held his gaze. Finally Kane reached for his sword belt and unbuckled it. He stripped off the belt and dropped it on the table. "You'll need a way to carry that thing."

He turned around and walked back to his place.

A woman seated on a barstool next to them stood up. "No way I'm letting Connor get all the credit." She pulled a dagger from her hip and tossed it onto the table, then unbuckled the armor-reinforced leather corset she was wearing. She gave Valerie a nod and added that to the items on the table.

When the woman sat down, three more people were already making their way forward. The table began to fill with donated items. Gloves, gauntlets, hauberks, spaulders, and tassets. Before long there was far more in the pile than any one person could possibly wear.

"You won't get far with no pants on."

Valerie turned to find Rico standing at the door. He was holding the clothes she had left at his place before the ball. He held up a sandwich. "Carlyn says hello too. Egg and goat cheese. She said she burnt it how you like it." He strode forward, and Valerie went to him, wrapping her arms around his shoulders.

"Thank you," she said.

"Every fighter needs a second," Rico said. "I guess I'm yours."

"I don't think we're allowed seconds in this fight," Valerie replied. "It's every man or woman for themselves."

"Oh, thank God," Rico said, his eyes lifting skyward. "It was more of a gesture, you know? Like I love you, but I'm not so good with actual fighting."

Valerie smiled. "I'm happy to have you on my team, even from a distance."

"Not to interrupt," Kane said, "but if you plan to fight, you may already be late. Every fighter is supposed to be on the island by ten bells."

"I need to get changed then," Valerie said. She snatched the pants from Rico and began putting them on. "Does anyone here have a car?"

"I'll do you one better. I've got a boat." A man stepped forward from the crowd, and Valerie immediately recognized the old fisherman.

"Gaspar."

"A young feller on a bicycle told me someone up here might be needing a lift this morning. I'm happy to oblige."

Valerie turned to Ann. "Thank you for believing in me. I wish I could promise I won't let you down, but I don't know how this will end."

Ann rested her hand on Valerie's shoulder. "Just tell Jasper Sterling that Tidewater sent you. We'll be watching his face when you do."

Several people began scooping up the armor and weapons on the table to carry along. Gaspar gestured toward the door. Valerie buckled the donated sword belt to her waist and slid the blade into its place. She paused and looked at Ann.

"I never had a chance to ask you what name you chose for this sword. Did you ever come up with one before the judging?"

"I didn't. But it has one now," Ann replied. "I'm naming it *Fire Bird*."

"The phoenix from the ashes," Valerie said.

Ann rested a hand on her shoulder. "Now go show them what it can do."

34

DREADROCK

According to legend, Dreadrock Castle guarded the bay since the days of the first settlers. The rocky island was built into a fortress of black stone. It was rimmed with towers and battlements that stretched high enough to clear the oppressive sea fog and ensure that the lords and ladies who lived there always saw the sun.

Valerie imagined that the stories of the castle's glory might have been exaggerated, but no one was alive to remember it either way. The earthquake of '05 that damaged most of the buildings in the bay area did a particularly devastating job on the fortress. It was said that the towers sent fountains of water hundreds of feet into the air when they toppled. The castle that had once been an invincible bastion of strength at the heart of the bay was now a mostly submerged, cautionary tale that spoke only of the strength of nature.

Valerie thought it an ignominious place for an arena. The bridges that had once led to the heart of the castle had been reconnected to allow passage across the bay, but the fortress itself was abandoned. Its ruined walls were now a labyrinth of twisting passageways that most often ended in tide pools or the ever-hungry waves.

Today the bridges that crisscrossed the sky above the ruined castle flew a hundred colorful banners. Traffic on the bridges had been stopped, and stands had been erected in the lanes to give the audience a view of the action below. Additional bridges and walkways had been built to allow access to elements of the arena not visible from the bridges. The king's full orchestra was in attendance as well, providing a musical accompaniment to the action. The sound of the horns and drums carried for miles.

This aerial gallery would be the prime location for watching the final battle of the tournament.

From Valerie's perspective—motoring across the water in Gaspar's fishing trawler—the bridges seemed as far above her as the sun. Somewhere overhead, the king would be watching, but he couldn't help her now.

She concentrated on fastening the final few pieces of her armor and finishing the last mouthful of sandwich from Carlyn. When she was finished, she leaned over the bow and splashed several handfuls of seawater to her face, wiping away the remnants of last night's tear-stained makeup.

The cold water was invigorating.

She knew she wasn't a striking figure. The odd pairings of cast-off armor were bound to elicit more than a few sniggers from the crowd. But those who had been paying attention to the tournament would recognize the bits of armament as the best the defeated fighters from the rim villages had to offer. Despite the unusual combination, she now had far more of herself covered than in previous fights. Her dueling jacket was heavily reinforced, and the fighting corset beneath gave her an added layer of chest protection. While competitors in thick plate armor would be able to withstand heavier blows, she would have an advantage of speed, and the armor she did have would keep her safe from the worst cuts.

Her helmet and faceplate were that of a stranger, as was the knife she had selected as a secondary weapon, but carrying the pieces of dozens of separate fighters felt right. It was as though the varied colors and shapes of her armor only highlighted the body inside it. The muscles she had spent weeks honing made the ensemble cohesive. As she flexed her arms and freed her sword in its scabbard, she didn't even need to brandish it to feel as though she was armed. The sword was no longer the weapon. She was the weapon, and she was ready to cut someone.

Dozens of boats bobbed in the waves surrounding the island.

The rest of the contenders were already ashore. Several officials were convening in a circle near the remains of one of the old towers and turned to observe her arrival.

Gaspar motored his skiff past the nearest Watch patrol boat and shouted across the bow. "Got one more for you. Don't be starting without her!"

The officials ashore watched in consternation as Gaspar glided onto the rocky shore.

Valerie clasped his hand. "Thank you. I won't forget this."

"Can't stick around long. These waves are liable to sink me," he said. "But get up there and do us proud!"

Valerie leapt ashore and waited as Gaspar glided away. Once he was clear of the rocks, she marched up the beach.

One of the officials consulted a watch as she approached. "You've certainly taken your time in presenting yourself, but it seems you are still eligible to compete." He looked up to the announcers seated on the bridge overhead and keyed a handheld radio. "We have our final contender. Valerie of—" he glanced back for confirmation.

"Tidewater," Valerie said.

"Tidewater," the official echoed, this time into the radio.

As Gaspar's trawler motored out to the bay, Valerie took a deep breath.

The announcers up in the booth broadcasted her arrival over the loudspeaker.

"Valerie of Tidewater!"

The crowd gave a round of modest applause.

There was no turning back now.

"Follow me," the chief official said. He led her uphill to the heart of the old castle and the courtyard outside the great hall.

She had known what to expect, but the sight of the other warriors assembled in the center of the courtyard made her gut clench. Especially him.

Damon had his crimson-streaked mask on, but she could still feel his stare.

Betrayer.

For the first time in weeks, she had someone other than Jasper to focus her anger on. The fire inside her felt hot enough to scorch the very rocks they stood on. There would be enough rage for both of them to share.

Jasper was there, too, in shining, brand-new armor that looked like something from the pages of a magazine. It was made of thin, custom-fit plates without a single visible opening. His joints were augmented with piston actuators to relieve the weight of the armor and presumably aid in its motion. While the rest of them would fatigue at a natural pace, it appeared as though his armor would pick up the slack. She could only imagine what other secrets it might contain. To top off the ostentatious look, Jasper had added a ridiculous and inconvenient-looking silver cape that flapped in the morning breeze. Valerie wondered if she could strangle him with it.

She scanned the ring of other competitors. They all looked mean and ready for a fight. Several of them were sizing her up as well.

The music from the orchestra overhead died down, and the head referee stepped forward with a megaphone.

"The rules of the competition are as follows." The official was speaking to them but loudly enough that the entire arena could hear.

"Each competitor shall fight with longsword and one secondary weapon such as a dagger or hand axe. They shall fight in armor only. No shields, spears, or projectile weapons. Melee rules are in effect. Every woman or man for themselves.

341

Contenders shall fight until too injured to continue, at which time, should they be conscious, they may raise a white flag in the form of a handkerchief. They shall then be removed from the arena." The official held up a white handkerchief and waved it around to demonstrate.

"Once a contender has waved the white flag, they may not reenter the competition. The winner of the melee will be the last fighter standing, and they must be able to remain standing inside the grand hall in view of the king and queen to prove their victory." He pointed to the ruins of the building behind them. "We shall signal with trumpets when a contender is claiming victory. Should no other contenders remain to challenge them during that time, they shall be named the victor. If you all understand and agree to these rules, say 'aye'."

The assembled fighters responded with a collective and enthusiastic, "Aye."

"His Majesty King Logan Pendragon, first of his name, will now say a few words."

All eyes looked skyward to the central grandstand where the flag of the House of Pendragon was flying. Valerie squinted in the sunlight and placed a hand over her brow.

The king stepped to the edge of his box.

He was shorter than Valerie had expected. He wore a royal-blue cape over his shoulders today, and no mustache, but she recognized him as the man whose beer she had spilled at the car exhibition.

"Are you kidding me?" she blurted out.

A few of the other fighters gave her curious looks.

"Ladies and gentlemen, citizens of Port Hyacinth," the king began. "You do me great honor by committing yourselves to this tournament in my name. It is a tradition which goes back centuries. While many might say in this modern age that skill with the sword no longer holds the importance it once did in keeping the peace of this kingdom, I would argue that it is among the most noble of arts and steeped with meaning.

"A position at the Round Table is one that requires the most cunning mind and the truest heart. No one should undertake the position without consideration of the duties and responsibilities it requires. This tournament has already been a test of your will, your stamina, and your honor. Now is your finest hour. Do yourselves proud. I wish each house represented here good fortune, and may God be with you."

The crowd applauded enthusiastically, cheering and shouting their approval.

Valerie could only stare at the man she could have easily spoken to two nights ago. Now a dozen fighters stood between her and accomplishing that feat again.

The aggravation only fueled the anger she already felt. She flipped her visor down and drew her sword.

"You have heard the king," the official said. "You are now granted two minutes in which to remove yourselves to a position of your choosing on the island. At the sound of the trumpet blasts, the fight shall begin."

The drum section of the orchestra began an intense, rhythmic pounding, and a cheer went up from the stands.

Fighters rushed for positions, spurred on by the intensity of the music.

All except The Red Reaper.

He remained still, focused on Valerie. She had half a mind to stay as well, make him her first target, but she would only be doing every other fighter in the arena a favor.

Despite her anger, she needed Damon to face others first. This would be a game of attrition. It wouldn't be won in a single fight, though it could certainly be lost that way. She needed to be smarter than that.

Valerie turned on her heel and headed into the maze of ruins, searching for higher ground.

Castle Dreadrock had once been made of magnificent, black stone. Now lichen and barnacles decorated its lower surfaces, and a persistent smell of brine lingered in every crevice. Valerie climbed the ruins to what once was a watchtower, now reduced to rubble. It still offered an elevated view of the arena.

Three other fighters were in view. She recognized the young woman climbing the ruins of the old keep as Yuna Gozan. She was carrying the *Head Collector*, the legendary sword made by her ancestor Tomoe Gozan.

Yuna was one of three other women in the melee. Nikki Patel, also known as Night Frost, had made the cut and was carrying a legendary sword called *Chandrahas*. Valerie could count on her to be working with Jasper as her name had appeared on the document she had stolen from Blaise. The other two women, Freyja Eiríksdóttir, and Tara Sloane, were unknown to Valerie beyond their presence on tournament posters. Sloane, in true Celtic fashion, had entered the arena with the least amount of armor and the most war paint. The handle of her longsword, *Winter's Bite*, was said to be wrapped in the hair of warriors she had defeated.

Of the other men she was facing, Mervyn Doyle and Running Crow were worrisome. Doyle because he was allied with Jasper, and Running Crow because he was a formidable Native Avalonian warrior with a reputation for unstoppable endurance. Legend said that he once ran twenty miles in pursuit of a wounded deer, then carried the carcass home the same distance.

There were several other men in the arena she didn't know, a dozen competitors in all. How many she would face before the end remained to be seen.

Waves crashed against the rocks, and gulls circled the island lured by the presence of the food vendors in the stands. Valerie focused on her breathing, letting the salt air calm her nerves. The orchestra had begun building the intensity of the moment with the stringed instruments and drums.

Despite the danger, there was a thrill working through Valerie. She had made it to this final step. Her goal was in sight. Only eleven other souls stood between her and justice.

She called the image of her brother to mind. Not his last moments but the countless hours they had spent growing up. The teasing, the laughter, his bold smile. Today she would fight for him. She adjusted the grip on her sword and let the seconds tick by to the sound of the drums.

She scanned the arena.

The castle keep in the north marked the highest point of the original structure still standing, though several other towers had once stretched above it. Before the earthquake, the island had boasted over two miles of coastline. Now the island was broken into several smaller islands and inundated with tidal pools and rivers. Some of the islands were still linked by the original wall or connected by a series of patchwork, wooden bridges constructed by salvagers and treasure seekers who still dove the submerged rooms in hopes of discovering the castle's lost wealth.

Valerie studied the landscape in search of the best line of attack. She had a choice. Find a location and stand her ground, letting other warriors come to her, or go on the offensive and possibly catch her competitors in terrain that would work against them. She decided she'd rather be the hunter than the hunted.

The moment came for the trumpets, and they blasted from overhead, followed by the rest of the horn section. Another cheer erupted from the stands.

Valerie broke into a run.

A section of outer wall remained standing to her right. She scrambled to the top and moved east along the battlements, the direction in which she had seen several competitors disappear. She kept her sword in a front guard as she moved.

Fire Bird was every bit as long as the swords she had been practicing with at Damon's but noticeably lighter. The blue-gray steel glinted in the morning sun. She made a few cuts in the air to get the balance of it. It felt like a natural extension of her arms.

She reached the ruin of a guard tower at the end of the wall and paused, attempting to listen over the sound of the frenetic music overhead.

Somewhere to the west, metal rang against metal. The crowd shouted in approval as two warriors clashed. Spectators above used binoculars to make out the action. Valerie could see nothing of the fight from her current vantage point, so she pressed on, her senses vigilant for any sign of her quarry. She passed through the remains of the guard tower, stepping over fallen beams that had rotted and decayed. She had just reached the exit to the far wall when a pebble skittered across the flagstones. It was the only warning before a man in a skull-shaped mask rushed her. He swung a wicked-looking, double-edged sword that he used to cut at her from above.

Valerie met the blow with the forte of her own blade while dancing to the side as he charged through. Her heart raced as the man spun on her and slashed again, this blow shoulder high and aimed at her neck. Valerie ducked and dodged the blow, then instinctively moved to the attack, lunging forward and stabbing the man's shoulder. *Fire Bird* found its mark in the mail-covered arm joint.

Her attacker shouted in rage, then came at her again, hacking violently and using his superior height and weight to every advantage in an attempt to batter her to the ground.

Valerie took a breath and flowed into *Sighing Dove*, her movements smooth and natural. The man's rushed attacks and wide cuts left frequent openings in his defenses. Valerie slashed and jabbed at each opportunity, cutting first at the exposed rear of his knee, then following through with a thrust just above his left hip. The man lost his footing and crashed to the stones. He tried to rise, his metal-fingered glove scraping the stones, but he collapsed again.

The knight pushed up the visor of his helmet, revealing a prominent nose and bushy eyebrows. He winced and cursed. "I don't get it. You were supposed to be the easiest target in the arena."

"Is that what they told you?" Valerie asked.

The man swore as he probed the wound at his hip, and his

fingers came away bloody. He fumbled for his white flag, then waved it over his head.

The crowds on the nearest bridges cheered.

Valerie backed away, then descended the cracked steps that led to a lower courtyard.

High above, a team of safety personnel began lowering a stretcher. Valerie noted that another stretcher was already on its way upward at the far side of the arena.

Two down. Ten remaining.

Valerie scanned the courtyard on alert for more attacks. If the rumor had circulated that she was the least skilled fighter, she could expect more contenders would be hunting her as an easy target.

But not if she found them first.

She stayed moving, passing through an arched portico to another courtyard that looked like it once housed stables. A stone watering trough and several hitching posts with iron rings remained. The wall at one end of the courtyard had collapsed, and seawater was sloshing over the rubble.

"Rim rat!" a man shouted. "Don't you know you shouldn't have come here?"

Valerie turned to find Mervyn Doyle entering the courtyard from an angled hallway that had once had a roof but now was entirely open to the daylight. The old stones were overgrown with moss and lichen. Jasper's crony grinned a leering smile and raised his sword.

Valerie squared up to face him.

But then, as soon as he had entered the courtyard, a second man appeared in the angled hallway, striding deliberately toward Mervyn. It was the Red Reaper. Mervyn turned in surprise as the Reaper continued toward him.

"Hey, I've got her handled," Mervyn said. But the Red Reaper raised his sword and swung at him. Mervyn was barely able to get his own blade up in time to avoid being split in half. Mervyn backpedaled, anger visible on his face. "We're supposed to be on the same side," he hissed through gritted teeth. But the Reaper remained silent. Valerie watched with fascination as Mervyn was driven past her position with blow after blow of the Reaper's red-hilted sword until he was sent staggering into the foamy waves of the bay.

The thud in the middle of Valerie's back took her off her feet.

She landed on her hands and knees, her body still registering the pain from the blow. She rolled over in a panic, noting the thrown axe that had struck her lying on the ground near her feet and, more importantly, the figure of the female Celtic warrior rushing toward her with fire in her eyes.

Tara Sloane leapt into the air with a scream. The Celt landed overtop Valerie's prone form, and her sword came down like a hammer.

35

REAPER

J asper Sterling listened to the trumpet blast with a smile on his face.

He flexed his sword arm, the joint stabilizers in his armor making the weapon feel as light as air. The armor had been costly, and it hadn't been easy getting the custom-made, hardened alloy plates to pass the tournament judges' specifications. He was forced to dumb down their capabilities and the advantages they would bring him. The officials had worried the augmented power system would give unfair power to his sword blows. A few generous donations to their private accounts had eased their concerns.

The truth was that the armor itself was a weapon.

His fists were hammers. His feet were battering rams.

There were no chinks anywhere to be found. He was a walking fortress.

Still, one had to take precautions.

He circumvented the center of the island, careful to avoid the areas where he had seen Yuna Gozan and Gunnar Ragnarsson disappear. He would let The Reaper and Night Frost deal with them.

He would hunt easier prey.

Valerie Terravecchia was at the top of his list. He relished the idea of her blood on his sword, but he would need to get to her out of sight of the crowd if he wanted to make a true end of her. The king was watching. It wouldn't do to appear he had a vendetta. Her death would need to look unavoidable—if she even lived long enough to face him.

A figure darted across the path ahead, moving toward the ruins of the old church. Freyja Eiríksdóttir.

Jasper smiled and flexed the fingers of his armored glove before tightening them into a fist.

It was time to have some fun.

One of the many fallacies Valerie had faced in her years of training was that a sword fight should be elegant. As a child, she had mistakenly believed that armed combat between knights was a protracted, noble affair full of dexterous movements and skillful demonstrations of athleticism.

In reality, it proved to be a brutal experience: sudden, violent, and brief.

Tara Sloane's sword struck Valerie in the head, slamming her to the ground.

Her helmet protected her from the cutting edge of the blade but not the force of the blow itself.

Her ears rang.

Through the shock and ache of the impact, her mind raced to inform her of the next danger. It focused her attention on Tara's sword that was raising again, this time for a downward thrust.

Myriad tiny stars danced across her vision as she struggled to survive the next second of her life. Tara's sword came down fast, straight at her chest.

She rolled.

Awkwardly.

Gracelessly.

But fast.

Tara's sword plunged into the earth for only a fraction of a second, then was elevated again, swinging up over her head and back down again. Valerie scrambled to her knees and *Fire Bird* met the Celt's sword this time, the two blades crashing into one another and buying her another fraction of a second to live.

She was still dead if she couldn't get to her feet.

Sloane used Valerie's sword as a pivot point and angled her blade down to strike Valerie's shoulder. Her steel pauldron took the blow, and the movement left a brief opening. Valerie swung low and fast, trying to cut the Celt's legs out from under her.

Sloane was too fast, anticipating the blow and getting out of the way in time.

Valerie got what she wanted, however. In the second it took her opponent to clear away from the strike, Valerie was able to stand.

She brought her sword up to a front guard and flexed her back.

She'd gotten lucky. The axe that had struck her hadn't hit blade first. The blunt trauma of being hit with the axe head was bad enough, but it hadn't cut through her armored jacket.

"Ye should end your misery now," Sloane said. "Wave that flag while ye've still got arms to swing it with."

"You're fast. I'll give you that," Valerie said. "But if you're here for easy pickings, I'll disappoint you."

Sloane stooped and picked up her hand axe. "Looks like the boys be having their own fun."

Valerie risked a glance to the end of the courtyard. The Red Reaper had forced Mervyn Doyle out of the water and up a series of steps. Doyle was slashing wildly at the Reaper but seemed to be running out of ideas.

Valerie returned her focus to the fight in front of her and concentrated on her defense.

Tara Sloane was taller than she was but not by much. The real threat was her power. The Celt had muscles like iron and a no-holds-barred approach to fighting that meant anything was possible. Her red hair and blue war paint only enhanced the image of her wildness.

Valerie stepped into *Warriors Way*. Since she wasn't battling a height disadvantage, she could use the forms she had practiced for shorter fighters. Tara Sloane circled her, searching for an opening. *Winter's Bite* was a longer sword, close to being a greatsword, giving Sloan a slight advantage in range, but it also looked heavy to use one-handed. So far, the element of surprise had been her best weapon. With that gone, it was a fair fight.

Valerie concentrated on her footwork, each step precise, never letting Sloane catch her off-balance. They exchanged a few wary feints, their swords meeting in swift parries and counterattacks, but neither landing a blow. "Ye fight like a snail," Sloane taunted, still circling. "Ye sure ye don't want to go find a wee rock to hide beneath and let the real fighters have their day?" Sloane spun the hand axe in her palm, flipping and catching it by the handle again with a flourish.

Valerie read what was coming next and refused to be distracted.

Sloane hurled the axe.

Valerie dodged and didn't try to block the weapon. She instead kept her guard up to defend against the charging form of Sloane who followed up the axe throw with a screaming, two-handed sword attack.

This time Valerie was ready. She deflected *Winter's Bite* and rounded on Sloane with the same motion, the edge of her sword slicing cleanly across the Celt's leather breastplate. *Fire Bird*'s razor-sharp edge succeeded in cutting through the boiled leather, and when Sloane arrested her momentum, she registered the hit.

Her hand brushed across her abdomen and came away bloody. Instead of stopping, however, the wound only enraged her. She took another wild, two-handed swing at Valerie's head, but Valerie once again deflected and counterattacked, this time angling her sword around Sloane's blade and piercing her bicep.

Sloane shrieked and reeled away, her sword tip dragging on the ground. She stumbled a few feet and turned. It appeared as though she was rallying herself for another charge.

"Spare yourself," Valerie said. "It's over. Look at your arm."

Sloane snarled at her. "Nothing's over. It's a scratch." But as her arm continued to bleed, it went limp. Her sword fell to the dirt. Her other arm clenched at her gut, and she wavered. "Devil take ya." She fumbled for her white flag but collapsed to the ground, dropping it in the dirt. Valerie rushed to her side and scooped up the white flag, signaling the safety team overhead, then using the handkerchief to tourniquet Sloane's arm and slow the bleeding.

"Don't I look a right eejit," Sloane muttered, watching Valerie tighten the knot around her arm. "I lose to the girl everyone said was the gombeen of the bunch. What does that say about me?"

"You're not the first person to complain of that today," Valerie replied. "And you won't be the last."

"Right on, then," Sloane replied, gripping Valerie's hand with her good arm. "Go give these feckers a show." She laid back and rested her head on the ground. Valerie handed her *Winter's Bite*, and the Celt clutched it to her chest with a nod.

Valerie picked up *Fire Bird* and scanned the courtyard. There was no sign of the Reaper and Mervyn Doyle. Wherever they had disappeared, she would find them soon enough. The two victories she'd had so far gave her courage. She was warmed up and fueled with adrenaline. Wherever Damon and Jasper were, she was ready to settle the score.

∾

Jasper sneered down at the bloody girl crawling through the ruins of the old church. He pushed his flowing cape behind him and sheathed his sword.

Freyja Eiríksdóttir had, at least, put up a fight.

Her sword had struck him over a dozen times, but to no effect. His armor had performed perfectly. He hadn't even needed to block the blows with *Nocteflamme*. He had used the weapon but mostly to strike the girl in the face with the pommel. Freyja was now bleeding from her nose and a cut over her eye.

Jasper looked skyward, searching for the royal banners. He located the seat his father occupied near the king. Was he watching? He strode over to where his broken opponent was trying to reach her sword. He planted a boot on the blade, pinning it to the ground.

"You're a cheat and a coward," Eiríksdóttir muttered.

"I simply make my own rules," Jasper replied.

She spat on his armored leg, spattering it with blood.

Jasper kicked her in the face.

Eiríksdóttir was knocked onto her back, and her head lolled as she lost consciousness.

The crowd overhead grew eerily quiet. The orchestra music died down to a low, tremulous pulsing of strings and base drums. Someone booed.

Jasper frowned. Where were the victorious trumpets? Isn't this what they had come for? He was giving them a flawless performance so far. They ought to be cheering. He yanked Eiríksdóttir's white flag from her waist and dropped it over her face, then stepped over her as he left the ruined church. In the distance, a stretcher was at work, hoisting someone skyward to the medics.

The field was dwindling.

He made his way uphill and climbed a stone staircase that led to the top of one of the castle's interior walls. The battlements had fallen at one edge of the wall, leaving a pile of rubble down the other side. Jasper stood at the breach and observed the fighters in the area beyond. Nikki Patel, aka Night Frost, was putting the finishing touches on a duel with a knight in red-and-black armor. Night Frost wrestled the man's sword from his grasp, followed the move with a vicious elbow to the face, then used his own blade to stab him through the leg. The knight fell to the ground screaming.

Night Frost tossed the knight's sword to the dirt, then looked up and noted Jasper's presence. She walked over to the base of the wall he was standing on.

"How many have you defeated?" Jasper asked.

"Only this one," Night Frost replied. "I've seen other stretchers. Running Crow took out Gunnar Ragnarsson early. And the girl still lives. The scoreboard says she eliminated the Celt and the Spaniard."

"Dumb luck. It will run out," Jasper said. "Where's Doyle?"

"Out," Night Frost replied. "The Reaper cut him down."

"What?" Jasper snarled. "That wasn't the plan!"

"He's going off script, or it could be your father gave him different orders."

Jasper glanced up at the stands overhead. "My father has the same goal. He wouldn't sell me out."

"Then we have a Reaper problem," Night Frost replied.

Jasper tightened his grip on *Nocteflamme*'s handle. "See to it that you remember *your* orders. We have a contingency plan for this."

Night Frost nodded, then moved off toward the far end of the courtyard. The safety team rushed into view from the opposite side and began scooping up the fallen red-and-black knight, who was still moaning.

Jasper moved along the top of the wall and scanned the spectator bridges overhead, drawing his sword again. He angled toward the zone of the arena that was beyond the view of the closest stands. He descended the rubble outside the old wall and made his way down to the natural rock caves that the sea had formed in the cliffside.

With one last look around to see if he was being watched, he ducked inside one of the caves.

The package was where Blaise said it would be, tucked away on a shelf of rock and wrapped in a waterproof bag. He untied the cords and removed the weapon. The high-powered crossbow was small but deadly. It was camouflaged with gray and brown paint that matched the local stones and came with a built-in attachment for the carbide-tipped bolts. The final accessory was a reel in the shoulder stock that contained a spring-loaded tether.

Jasper quickly assessed the weapon, then reached around his back to pull his silver cape to the side. He brought the undersized crossbow around and clipped it to the ring at the back of his armor. With the tether attached, he could reach around his back, draw the crossbow out to fire, then stow it again in a matter of seconds. He tossed the cape around his back again to cover it. The pleats in the cape would do a fair job of disguising the bulge. It wouldn't fool a close encounter but would be sufficient to keep the spectators in the dark.

Jasper filled the empty bag with stones and tossed it into the bay on his way out of the cave. He then climbed cautiously back to the wall, even making a vague adjustment of his groin protection when he came in view of the stands. If anyone was suspicious of his absence, they might easily believe he had simply found a safe place to relieve himself.

He took a route that led him up and around the periphery of the castle. The sound of steel on steel could be heard over the beating of the drums and what sounded like electric guitar coming from the orchestra. If the music was to be believed, things were heating up.

~

One thing Valerie had no experience with was fighting multiple opponents at once. She circled the keep of the Dreadrock with her eyes flitting back and forth between her two targets. Running Crow and Yuna Gozan had been clashing with one another already when she stumbled upon the scene. Gozan had blood trickling down her arm from a wound under her shoulder armor. Running Crow was also spattered with blood, but Valerie wasn't sure if it was his own or a prior combatant's.

What she did know was that both warriors were eyeing her now, possibly as a way to draw the other into a compromising position. Valerie considered backing out of the confrontation, but it wouldn't do any good in the long run. There could only be one winner.

She trod carefully over the uneven terrain. One false step here could mean two swords in her gut in short order.

Yuna Gozan pulled a shorter blade from her belt and held it in the hand opposite the *Head Collector*. It was a bold choice as wielding the legendary sword one-handed would be more difficult, but it wasn't her first time in an arena, and Valerie couldn't count the move as a vulnerability.

Running Crow's secondary weapon was a club of bone and wood, decorated with feathers. His sword was all Avalonian steel. He maintained his two-handed grip and clenched his jaw beneath a horned helmet that was painted with the symbols of his tribe.

"Someone want to take the lead on this dance?" Gozan said.

"Ladies first," Running Crow muttered.

Valerie used a low guard, letting her arms hang loose. The anticipation was building with the sound of the drums overhead. The enthusiastic conductor was apparently determined to exhaust his percussion section.

Finally Gozan made a move, feinting right, then spinning and sprinting for Valerie. The warrior planted a foot on a piece of rubble and launched an aerial attack, flying through the air with sword extended to skewer her. Valerie somersaulted forward to avoid the surprise move and was back on her feet in an instant. She was now caught between the two opponents, however, and had to block the incoming blow from Running Crow. Metal clanged as their swords met. She shifted her feet evenly and refused to backpedal as she evaded his continued attacks. She wouldn't let him get her off balance.

The maneuver put Running Crow back in the center of the action, and he was forced to turn and parry an attack by Gozan. Valerie leapt into the fray, and the three traded blows in rapid-fire succession. The two women both landed hits on each other's armor, but nothing drew blood. Running Crow used his sheer power to knock their blades aside and attempted to hack through their defenses. But Valerie was too quick for him, and Gozan was able to use her secondary blade to deliver counterattacks. Running Crow retreated from the skirmish with a minor cut to his neck and several deep cuts in his boiled-leather armor.

The three were once again at an impasse, but the circumstances changed quickly as Night Frost rounded the corner of the keep and presented herself. Then Valerie's eyes were drawn to the opening of a nearby archway. The shadows took shape and The Red Reaper moved into the sunlight.

The crowd cheered and whooped as the orchestra took the opportunity to add bass to the horn section. The Reaper's arrival made this a five-way fight, and the spectators were eating it up.

Valerie locked eyes with the Reaper and grit her teeth.

Liar.

Two-faced, cheating bastard.

As the drumbeat once again ramped up in intensity, the tension grew in the circle. Running Crow let out a war scream and rushed Night Frost.

Then all hell broke loose.

Gozan and Valerie both sprinted toward the Reaper.

Overhead, cymbals crashed.

Valerie shifted into *Soaring Dragon*, and the Reaper met her blade as she expected. He had to shift his position immediately, however, spinning to evade Yuna Gozan's lunging, two-bladed attack. He moved with impressive speed, dodging Gozan and parrying and deflecting Valerie's continued cuts and thrusts.

Gozan shifted position and swung at Valerie, driving her back, before delivering a series of vicious cuts across The Reaper's chest and abdomen. His armor held but he was forced to retreat. Gozan whirled back to strike Valerie, cutting and stabbing with a flurry of motion that sent Valerie stumbling backward. She lost her footing and almost fell but recovered at the last moment as Gozan's blade passed just inches from her neck.

Valerie and Gozan exchanged a half dozen blows before they had to account for the Reaper again. He was back in the fight, and his *Sword with the Red Hilt* was a blur as he divided the two women and sent them scrambling for defensive positions.

The Reaper turned to deal with a renewed attack from Gozan, and Valerie saw her opening. He was using the *Coiled Viper* defense, which meant, in a moment, his side would be exposed. She ignored the doubts that tried to surface in her mind and focused on the movement that would reveal the vulnerable underside of Damon's arm. He raised his sword high and she struck. But before *Fire Bird* could penetrate his unprotected underarm, he turned, grasping her sword with his gloved left hand and spinning into her. It was a move she had only seen once before, and they were suddenly face to face as they had been the night they first kissed in the garage. Enraged that he would use that maneuver now, Valerie smashed his helmet from his head with her left fist and dropped to a leg sweep, sending him to his back. He caught the top of her helmet as he fell, dragging her off her feet. She landed partly atop him. Her helmet rolled away, and her hair fell about her face.

The fall had dislodged *Fire Bird* from her hand. As she sat up to her knees, she realized the sword was now in Damon's grasp.

She fumbled for the knife in her belt and drew it, holding it up to plunge it into him, but when their eyes met, she knew it was too late.

"I'm sorry," he said. He thrust the sword forward and stabbed her.

LOSER

V alerie stared at Damon's arm. The sting had only been momentary. A nick of the blade before his arm shoved all the way through her?

She stared down at her chest, but the blade wasn't there. The sword's edge had only grazed her side instead, piercing her jacket and cutting her slightly as it passed, but he had missed everything important, shoving the sword past her instead of through her.

Damon withdrew his wrist from beneath her armpit, and she heard the groan.

She turned to find Yuna Gozan directly behind her, the *Head Collector* still poised for a death stroke. But Yuna wavered, her arms dropping as she looked down to the wound in her chest.

"That sword . . . is so . . . sharp." The words dripped from her lips, and she collapsed where she stood.

Valerie scrambled to her feet, snatching up Damon's red-hilted sword and taking a guard position a few feet away.

Damon rose as well. He moved to Gozan to check if she was still breathing, then waved her white flag.

Valerie quickly scanned the area and found that Running Crow was slumped against the wall of the keep, his bloody sword resting across his lap. He was still alive but was bleeding from several wounds to his arms and chest. Night Frost was lying face down on the grass unconscious or possibly dead.

"Looks like we're almost to the end," Damon said. He glanced down at the sword in his hand, then offered her the handle. "Want to trade?"

Valerie considered the weapon she was holding. Its grip was too thick and long for her liking. She took a wary step forward and reached for the handle of *Fire Bird*.

Damon didn't let go. She offered the handle of the *Sword with the Red Hilt*, but as soon as he grasped it, she delivered a forceful kick to his stomach. Damon flew backward and crashed to the stones. She was on him in an instant, her sword flashing in a wicked cut that would cleave him in two.

"Liar!"

Damon barely got his sword raised in time to block the blow. He rolled away and staggered to his feet as he retreated before her fury. Valerie pressed the attack.

Roaring Inferno.

Sweeping Hurricane.

She delivered the blows with more energy than she had ever done in practice. Damon reeled away as her cuts found his armor and flew about his head. He counterattacked with *Whistling Grass*.

Too slow.

Valerie moved into *Fire of the Dragon* and instantly destroyed his attack. She put him on the defensive, driving him backward out of the yard of the keep and down a set of steps to a lower courtyard. Damon struggled to keep his footing on the uneven terrain as she advanced on him.

"I know you're upset," he said, desperately parrying a thrust at his face.

"Figured that out, did you?" Valerie said, swinging low and delivering a blow to his leg that sent him staggering. She pursued him out of the courtyard as he fled. He crashed into the stone wall of an alcove, then leapt behind a column as she swiped at him. She dashed around the other side of the ruined pillar and continued her attack. *Ripping Tide, Roaring River.*

Damon was fighting vigorously to keep her blows to his head from landing. She delivered several more cuts to his arms and legs, one of which found a gap in his leg armor and caused him to cry out in pain. He pressed his free hand to the wound, and it came away bloody.

They found themselves in a covered hallway out of view of the crowd. The porcelain tiles of the ceiling overhead were still intact and formed a mosaic that depicted a hunt.

Valerie paused to catch her breath. Damon did the same. The music from the orchestra died down, the conductor unable to score the action with them out of sight.

"I'm not what you think I am," Damon said.

"You're right," Valerie replied. "You're much worse than I could have imagined. You got my brother killed."

Damon panted his response. "I never knew Jasper would kill him after the duel. I only served as his stand-in."

"Only?" Valerie retorted. "That was enough!" She swung at him and began another dizzying flurry of cuts and thrusts. She backed Damon down the hallway into the darker recesses of the ruin. He descended another set of steps to what once was a dungeon. Barnacle-encrusted manacles and cages still adorned the walls. They splashed through several inches of water that had come in with the tide and flooded the room.

Damon sloshed his way around the dungeon, trying to dodge and deflect her vicious cuts.

"I know I deceived you," Damon said. "But I wasn't lying about all of it."

"You did say I shouldn't want to be with you. I guess you got that right." She punctuated the statement with a jab.

"There's more," Damon replied.

"More ways you betrayed me? I can hardly wait." She swung

at him again, cleaving a cluster of dried coral from one of the pillars.

Damon retreated, this time down a hallway filled with rusting jail cells.

Sunlight penetrated through a few chinks in the mortar overhead, and farther down the hallway, a wall had fallen in, allowing another access from outside. Seawater was cascading down the rocks like a waterfall. Bits of flotsam and seaweed bumped Valerie's legs as she renewed her attack on Damon. The clash of their blades echoed down the hallway, and they created waves as they continued their deadly dance. She met each defense of Damon's with a stronger attack. She battered his sword and made continued thrusts at his armor until finally a cut to his inner arm caused him to lose his grip on his sword. It disappeared into the rising water at their feet.

She pressed the tip of *Fire Bird* to his exposed throat.

"Tell me how it feels," Valerie hissed. "How Henry would have felt. Unarmed. Completely at your mercy."

Damon met her gaze. "You're right. He deserves justice."

"You betrayed me," Valerie said. "You said you wanted to help me. You were only helping yourself, selling me out to Lord Sterling this whole time."

The tip of her sword drew a drop of blood from his neck, and he flinched but didn't speak.

"Give me one good reason why I shouldn't run you through the same way your boss did to my brother."

Damon whispered his reply through gritted teeth. "Because you're better. Better than all of them."

Valerie narrowed her eyes. "You're just trying to save your own life."

"Do what you think is right then," Damon replied. He spread his arms, exposing his chest.

Valerie pulled her sword back to strike, but she wavered. His expression was stoic, but his dark eyes never broke contact with hers.

It wasn't a trick. He had to know she'd cut him down before he could defend himself.

She wanted to hate him.

She wanted the earth to open up and swallow him, or the ocean to suck him out to sea so that she wouldn't have to look at his irritatingly sincere face.

She couldn't help but recall the first night she had cut him. The way he had looked at her. His eyes still held that intensity now.

The tip of *Fire Bird* wavered.

She couldn't do it.

"Damn you!" She slashed through the air, her blade tip slicing through the water that was now up to her knees. She held up a fist as if to strike him instead, but she couldn't bring herself to do that either. "Why? Why did you do it?"

"Only with good reason," Damon replied. "When the tournament is over, I promise I'll—" His words were cut short, and he staggered forward a step, nearly colliding with her. She put a hand to his chest to steady him. That's when she noticed the arrowhead protruding from the upper corner of his chest plate. Damon looked down in shock, registering the blow. Then his eyes met hers and he fell, splashing into the water next to her. Valerie screamed and tried to keep his head from going under the water. Then she looked up to see the man standing in the section of knocked-down wall.

Jasper Sterling lowered the undersized crossbow. "I always knew that hired sword was soft." He snatched another bolt from the side of the weapon and began to reload it.

Damon groaned from next to her as he propped himself up on one arm. "Go! You have to take him out now!"

Valerie rose to her full height and gauged the distance to Jasper. There was twenty yards of knee-high water still separating them. She hoisted her sword and took a few steps toward him, but she was too slow. Jasper cocked the crossbow and seated the bolt, then leveled it at her chest.

Valerie froze. It was next to impossible to maneuver in the knee-high water.

"You've had this coming for a long time," Jasper said.

"I'm not letting you win," Valerie said. "Not while I'm still breathing." She tightened her grip on *Fire Bird* and started walking toward him.

"That's the idea, sweetheart," Jasper said. He sighted along the crossbow. "Say 'hi' to your brother for me."

He fired.

For Valerie, the moment broke into a hundred micro-seconds: the trigger on the crossbow clicking, and the snap of the bowstring, launching the bolt from the end of the weapon. The fletching on the arrow shaft caught the air and stabilized the projectile as it soared toward her.

Her muscles were already tight, her wrists twisting the hilt in her hand and bringing the blade of the sword in line with the incoming arrow.

"Aaaghhh!" she shouted as she swung, cutting down and right as she shifted her body to the left. The crossbow bolt ricocheted off the flat of the blade and danced across the surface of the water.

Jasper's eyes went wide.

Valerie didn't hesitate. She rushed him, her legs churning waves in the seawater as she ran. Jasper fumbled for another arrow, but his armored fingers lost their grip on it, and it fell, disappearing into the water. He was forced to toss aside the crossbow and draw his sword.

Valerie shouted as she reached him, swinging hard for his outstretched arms. Jasper blocked the blow and attempted a counterattack, but Valerie was all over him, slashing and cutting at his chest and legs. Despite her best combos, none of her strikes penetrated. Even his underarms were immune.

Jasper lowered his shoulder and charged her, not even bothering with a sword strike but tackling her into the dilapidated stone wall. Valerie struck the wall and dislodged a cascade of brick as she continued through it and landed in the water on the other side.

Jasper hacked at her with his sword, slicing the water and catching an exposed section of her leg just above her knee.

Valerie choked back a scream and scrambled back to her feet in a daze, retreating from Jasper's wild stabbing. She splashed her way into the daylight.

The room they had blundered into had long ago been eroded by the waves. The ceiling was gone, allowing in sun and salt air and putting them back in view of the spectators above.

A cheer went up from the grandstands as tournament fans spotted them. The percussion section picked up its fervent drumbeats, and the strings got back into motion as well.

Valerie scrambled up the ruined stone wall to higher ground, Jasper in pursuit.

She was hurt.

She had struck her head going through the wall, and it now throbbed at the back of her skull. When she pressed her fingers to the back of her hair, they came away bloody. Her armor was completely saturated, and the straps chafed and sagged as a result. She felt like she was carrying gallons of water in her gear.

The wound to her leg stung in the saltwater, but she didn't have time to check how deep the cut was.

Jasper climbed the ruins after her, his sword drawn.

Valerie stopped and picked up one of the stones at her feet, then hurled it at him. It struck Jasper in the shoulder and made him pause to maintain his balance on the shaky rocks but then he began climbing again.

As soon as he gained level ground, she steeled her nerves and moved into an attack position.

Flying Dagger.

She dodged his defense and rained jabs and cuts around his chest.

Whistling Grass. She stabbed at his hips and groin but to no effect. While the blows made him waver, it was like chopping at a tree with a spoon.

Jasper used his armor advantage to force himself ever closer, hacking at her with *Nocteflamme* and forcing her to continually flee ahead of him.

Valerie fought back the growing panic in her mind and scanned her surroundings. There had to be somewhere to gain an advantage.

They were outside the inner walls, caught in the zone that once would have housed craftsmen and stables. The outer wall had collapsed into the sea and was mostly submerged. Only a few sections of it remained above the waves and one old watchtower that rose from the sea like a lighthouse.

To the other side, the wall obstructed most of her escape routes except for a rotting gate that led back toward the heart of the arena.

Valerie headed for the water.

Jasper pursued her. His armor had to be heavy, but with the assistance of the joint actuators, he moved as though he wasn't even winded.

"There's nowhere to run now, little girl," Jasper said. "Nothing but a dead end out there." He moved to block the path back to the castle gate. He shifted his sword from one hand to the other and twirled it with a flourish.

Valerie splashed through the surf and leapt onto one of the hunks of wall that still protruded from the water. As Jasper waded into range, she struck at him, attempting to stab at the ultra-thin eye slits in his visor. Jasper swatted at her with *Nocteflamme* like he was waving away an insect. He climbed the rock and soon towered above her. She ducked as he took a powerful swipe that could have taken her head off.

Valerie retreated again, leaping to another rock and taking them even farther from shore.

"You can't outrun the end," Jasper said, leaping across the

gap and landing with a thud. A few bits of rock broke away beneath his feet and crumbled into the sea.

Valerie picked up another stone and hurled it at him. It glanced off his shoulder, and this time, he didn't even waver. He strode forward again. Anger boiled inside her. This wasn't how she imagined this moment.

She leapt across another gap and made her way toward the ruined watchtower. Waves were breaking across it and sending fans of spray thirty feet into the air.

There were only a half dozen sections of wall still above water out here, and the gaps between them were getting wider.

Her pant leg was covered in blood now, and she was forced to limp as she made a staggering run at the next section of wall and leapt. She cleared the distance but crashed into the stones and nearly slid into the water. She scrabbled at the rocky ledge and crawled on her hands and knees to gain the top.

Jasper took a slower route. He waded to an intermediary rock before leaping across to a lower section of the wall she was on.

Overhead, spectators jostled for position along the one bridge that had a view of their activity. The orchestra was still playing, but the music was drowned out by the waves breaking against the nearby tower.

Jasper was making slow but steady progress along the lower surface of the broken wall and would be at her position soon.

There was only one more section of wall accessible, and it was linked by a battered and dilapidated, wooden footbridge to the spot where Valerie was standing. It looked as though it had been constructed hastily by someone eager to loot the old tower, or perhaps the subsequent homeless who had used the tower for a place to shelter from the wind. The handrail had long since fallen into the sea.

Valerie crept out onto the shaky boards, testing each step. She reached a portion of the bridge where the wood slats were completely rotted away and had to balance herself along the sturdier sides. Placing one foot carefully in front of the other, she walked across the narrow support beam and reached the far side of the gap.

Jasper had nearly reached the ledge and would be at her position in moments.

If she could somehow get him off balance or get him to step on the rotting section of boards, she'd have a chance . . .

She retreated a few more feet to where the wooden footbridge met the last section of wall. It was little more than a ten-foot-by-ten-foot square of stone. The rest of the wall had been completely washed away. Beyond it, there was only thirty yards of choppy breakers to the old stone tower. She was trapped.

She turned to face Jasper.

Her foe had gained the top of the wall and was standing on the far side of the dilapidated footbridge. He took a few tentative steps, testing the boards.

"Come on, fall, you bastard," Valerie muttered. But despite her entreaty, the boards continued to hold his weight.

Jasper reached the portion of the bridge that had rotted away and stepped carefully onto the side supports. He maintained a front guard and looked up with each step to check Valerie's position.

"Why won't you die already!" Valerie shouted. She rushed him and made a sweeping cut at his legs, aiming to knock him off balance.

He was ready for her. *Nocteflamme* met her attack, then he countered with an upward slash that caught her across the chest. Her armor deflected most of it, but the tip of his sword nicked the corner of her jaw as it continued upward, slicing her almost to the bone.

Valerie screamed and backpedaled. Her hand went to her face and came away bloody.

Adrenaline was gushing through her veins in the form of

pure hate. It mixed with the rising panic from her continued failure to cut Jasper.

She made another attack, attempting to gouge beneath the facemask of his helmet, but the armored gorget around his neck deflected the point of her sword. Jasper swung at her with a vicious, downward cut that would have cleaved her head from her neck had she not raised her sword up in time. Even so, the force of the blow sent her stumbling backward, and she crashed to the pockmarked stone amid puddles of seawater. They were soon tinted red as her various wounds continued to bleed.

A few tears leaked from her eyes as well, spattering the already wet stone. But she brushed the rest away and refused to let herself cry. She pulled herself together and set her jaw.

Jasper approached slowly. His mask revealed no emotion.

"When I heard that useless magistrate had taken your name and sent you out with the beggars, I never imagined that you'd give me so much trouble. I thought for sure that you'd be found dead in a gutter somewhere. You've improved your ending considerably. But make no mistake, it's still the end for you."

Valerie climbed slowly to her feet not bothering to lift her sword arm.

"You may have won. You might have taken my land and my family, but you'll never be worthy of our house. You'll never be a bear."

Jasper took a step closer. He was in range of a strike now. "I have to say, I'm really going to enjoy killing you."

"No, you won't," Valerie said, "because I'm not giving you that satisfaction." She took a step back, then turned and leapt, plummeting into the waves.

37

JUSTICE

J asper stood at the edge of the rocky precipice and stared in bewilderment at the turbulent water. She'd just jumped.

He opened his visor and took a better look. She was gone.

Jumped.

In armor.

What an idiot.

He looked up to the bridges where the commotion was clearly evident as spectators jostled one another for a position to see what had happened. A contingent of loyal Sterling fans waved their silver dragon banners and cheered. Jasper put up a hand and waved back.

He'd done it.

He was the last man standing. The champion.

A smile parted his lips. Think of the acclaim. A seat at the Round Table. It was the greatest honor a member of House Sterling had ever achieved. His father would likely throw him a parade.

He sheathed his sword and waved with both hands to the crowds. His smile only broadened when he heard the distant trumpets, their jubilant tone carrying across the water. He turned to face the sound. He had only to make his way back to the center of the arena. The king and queen would be waiting to greet him. And, no doubt, his father would be with them.

A sense of elation rose from the soles of his feet, and it filled him with warmth. He hadn't felt so good in years. It was as though the entire world was suddenly new and waiting to be discovered. It was his for the taking. He felt so good that he pulled off his helmet and blew kisses to the crowd.

Kisses.

He grinned and strode back across the rocky section of wall, then began crossing the wooden footbridge, making his way carefully to the section that was missing. Another blast of trumpets made him look toward the castle. They were celebrating in earnest now. The conductor was playing "Hail the Hero."

That was for him.

"I'm coming, I'm coming," he said, still smiling.

He was about to step onto the support beam of the bridge when a stabbing pain lanced through his left foot.

He looked down at his shaking leg as the scream rose in his throat.

The armor covering his boot was pushed aside because the tip of a bloody sword had erupted through the top of his foot.

Jasper shrieked.

He stared in shock as the blade vanished again, back down through the crack in the boards. The next moment he registered the soggy hair and scowling face of the girl clinging to the bridge supports. The sword flashed again, this time lancing up between his legs and piercing the unprotected crevice behind his groin. He screamed again. This time doubling over.

Valerie swung upward and grasped the top of his knee guard. "This is for Henry." Then she pulled, buckling his knee and sending him crashing through the rotten boards of the bridge. His face struck one of the bridge supports, causing him to go numb, then he hit the water.

He fought to stay afloat; the air trapped inside his armor gave him a moment of hope. He caught the edge of the bridge structure with his fingertips, but the barnacles beneath them gave way, and the weight of his armor pulled him under, still screaming until seawater rushed to fill his mouth.

His silver cape waved in the current above him like a strange sea creature as he sank, obstructing his view of the light.

Then it was only escaping bubbles, darting fish, terror, and darkness.

⁓

Valerie Terravecchia crawled to the top of the wall and collapsed to her back. She stared up at the clear, blue sky, but in her mind, she was back home, lying on the dock next to the river. She saw Henry's face, finally smiling.

"You can rest now," she murmured. She wasn't sure if the permission was for Henry or for herself.

The memory faded.

She rolled over and sat up, then began shedding armor onto the rocks around her, piece after piece, relishing how light her body felt without it. When she had unbuckled the items from her legs and feet, she stood and stripped out of the rest, pulling the whole assembly over her head and dumping it onto the rocks. She was left in her undershirt, trousers and boots. It felt as though the entire weight of her anger went with it. Weeks of training. Long nights dreaming of vengeance. She'd done it.

She was free.

She reclaimed her sword belt from the pile of armor and strapped it back on.

After examining the wounds to her leg and side, she probed her face and limped over to the edge of the wall. She stared down at the waves where Jasper had disappeared.

She couldn't help but recall the feeling she had the first time Damon had sent her into the depths in her armor. There was no need to imagine the terror Jasper would be enduring at this moment. Was he still alive down there right now? He certainly wouldn't be for much longer.

Her eyes lifted to the distant grandstands. The king. The queen. Lord Sterling. They would all be waiting for her.

When she looked back to the water again, she noted the last few bubbles burbling up from the seafloor. She still couldn't walk away.

Damn it.

She took one step back from the edge, then ran forward and dove, slicing into the frigid water with her hands over her head.

She opened her eyes as she righted herself and looked around. She saw him a second later, a silver mass bobbing strangely in the undercurrent. His eyes were closed and his mouth was open. The current had shoved him closer to shore. Valerie grasped the front of his armor and pulled.

When Valerie emerged from the surf, she felt like a drowned rat, though the man next to her deserved the title. She had managed to dislodge a few pieces of Jasper's armor underwater, but the rest still clung to him and impeded her ability to maneuver him ashore. The fact that he was unconscious or dead wasn't helping.

Jasper's long, blonde locks floated about in the surf. She dragged him the rest of the way ashore and left him at the point where his head was high enough out of the water to not be submerged with every wave. Jasper's secondary weapon was a gaudy, jewel-encrusted dagger. Valerie plucked it from his belt and tossed it into the waves.

She then looked down at his limp body and tried to assess how she felt. He certainly deserved to be dead. But despite how much she had wanted him dead for the last few weeks, the sight of him lying there didn't bring the relief she had expected. She reached down and found the catches for his chest plate and removed it, pulling off the backplate as well. With that gone, he was finally light enough that she felt she could drag him out of the water properly. She seized his limp wrists and pulled, dragging him up the shell-covered slope of beach until only his feet were getting routinely submerged by the incoming waves.

"That's the best you get," Valerie said, staring down at his prone form. "And a hell of a lot more than you deserve."

She located his white flag amid the cast-off armor and dropped it on him. She then stepped on his chest as she walked over him, making her way up the beach. She had made it almost to the rotten gate in the old inner wall when she heard the retching coming from the beach behind her. Turning around, she noted that Jasper had rolled over, but was once again motionless.

She watched him for a few, long seconds, then made her way through the gate.

The quickest route to the center of the arena was via a long walking path overgrown with dandelions. She cut left instead and made her way back to the opening where she had crawled out of the old dungeon.

"Damon?" she called down the hole. The only response was the subtle lapping of waves as they sloshed into the detainment cells. She crouched low and peered into the darkness. There was no sign of him. It was possible the safety team had retrieved him and hauled him up to the medical tent. She considered descending into the cells to check, but her leg wound had begun to throb, and she was lightheaded. She straightened her stiff back and limped on, climbing the hillside toward the ruin of the great hall.

The orchestra began playing "Avalon the Beautiful," and she caught sight of the king's entourage descending from the heights of the grandstand. She picked up her pace.

By the time she limped into the center of the roofless great hall, the king was already in position. They had erected two thrones on a dais at the end of the hall, and a number of other nobles stood at attention around it. The royal guards observed from a respectful distance as Valerie limped up the center aisle that had been cleared of rubble.

King Logan was smiling. He rose from the throne and Queen Kimiko stood as well. They began to applaud. Even Lord Sterling put his hands together politely, though his expression was stone.

"In all my years, I have never seen a tournament to equal this one," King Logan said. "You have outdone my greatest expectations."

"Your Majesty," Valerie said, dropping to a knee.

"You have proven yourself a worthy contender."

"Excuse me, Your Majesty," Lord Sterling said. "I believe the rules of the tournament dictate that she must remain standing in the Great Hall for a period of time before she can claim victory."

King Logan clasped his hands together in front of himself and nodded. "You are correct, Lord Sterling." He gestured to one of his servants. "Tell the conductor to sound the ending chorus. If any fighters remain unaccounted for, they will know to present themselves."

The attendant nodded and spoke into his radio.

A moment later, the horn section of the orchestra in the stands blasted out several long tones.

The king nodded. "Now, if our young champion is as good a conversationalist as she is a swordswoman, I suspect we are in for an excellent time as we wait."

Valerie strained to stand, wincing as she did so, but she was able to stay upright.

Lord Sterling gave her a sour look.

"Your Majesty, I'm not here for the position at the Round Table. I'm here for justice for my family."

King Logan furrowed his brow. "Go on."

Valerie glanced from the queen to Lord Sterling and back. If she was wrong about where the king's loyalties lay, it was going to end badly.

"Lord Jasper Sterling and his family murdered my brother, Henry Terravecchia, in cold blood. They have conspired to cover up his murder, and they deserve to be punished."

"Your Majesty, this is absurd," Lord Sterling interjected. "Her case was already seen to in court and—"

The king held up his hand. Lord Sterling closed his mouth.

"I would like to hear it from Valerie first." He looked back to her. "Do you have evidence to support this claim?"

"I did have some paperwork. Documents that proved Jasper conspired to rig this tournament. I don't know exactly how he faked the terms of the dueling contract with my brother, but he is a liar and a cheat."

"Your Majesty, she said herself she has no proof of these documents. There is no evidence—"

"Lord Sterling, your king has asked for you to remain silent. He won't ask you again." Queen Kimiko's voice had an edge that brooked no argument.

Lord Sterling flushed slightly and took a step back. "Thank you, Your Grace."

Queen Kimiko turned to address Valerie. "You are the daughter of Sir Henry Terravecchia, are you not?"

"I am, Your Grace," Valerie replied.

"I knew your father well when he was younger. He was assigned to teach me swordsmanship when I was your age. He made me practice the most grueling forms. There was one in particular I recall. I believe it was called *Burning Sky*. Was he as fond of that with you?"

Despite the pain she was feeling, Valerie smiled. "We have that complaint in common."

Queen Kimiko smiled and turned to her husband. "Surely she has stood here long enough to satisfy protocol. The poor girl is bleeding. Let us end this so she can rest."

"I rather think you are right," the king replied. "It's clear she is the victor here." He held his hand out toward Valerie. "Please give me your sword."

Lord Sterling looked as though he was choking on his unspoken objections.

Valerie drew *Fire Bird* from its scabbard and presented it to the king, hilt first. He took it from her and lifted it, admiring the blade. "These colors are exquisite. And the workmanship. Where did you come by this sword?"

"A dear friend," Valerie said. "A smith in Tidewater."

"This village has quickly risen on my list of places I must visit," King Logan replied. "Very well. Let us get on with awarding you the—"

"No!"

The shout came from the back of the hall. All heads turned to see Jasper Sterling hobbling through the doorway. He had one bloody hand on his groin as he limped forward. "I haven't yielded!"

Valerie reached instinctively for her sword belt but found only the empty scabbard.

"She is not the champion. I am!"

Jasper continued to the front of the hall, his eyes boring into Valerie's as he walked. He strode up to the foot of the dais, and Valerie backed away a few steps to keep him in view.

"I never yielded," Jasper repeated. "I'm still here." He stumbled toward Lord Sterling. "Father, lend me your sword."

"You were recently the topic of our conversation, young Lord Sterling," Queen Kimiko said, taking a step down the dais to confront him. "We were discussing the accusations against you regarding the death of Henry Terravecchia. You were once in possession of a dueling contract that listed a duel to first blood. A contract you violated by killing Henry."

Jasper narrowed his eyes. "No. The duel was to satisfaction. The courts have the contract. It was witnessed."

"The courts have a *copy* of a contract," the queen replied. "But not the original." She slipped a hand into the pleats of her dress and removed two folded slips of paper from the hidden pocket. "This original."

Jasper's mouth opened, but no sound came out as he studied the queen.

She turned to Valerie and showed her the contract. "I received a tip from one of my covert agents and was able to acquire several items of interest pertaining to your case. Is this the document you and your brother signed?"

Valerie looked the form over and saw her brother's elegant signature on the line next to "Duel to First Blood."

The queen knew. She believed her.

A wave of relief washed over her, and she nodded.

Valerie recalled the documents passed to the Red Reaper in the Sterling Castle gardens.

A covert agent of the queen . . .

"This morning, while the city was engaged with this tournament, my Queen's Guard arrested a lawyer by the name of Blaise Cavendish," Queen Kimiko said. "When they raided his offices, they discovered a number of interesting items. One of which was a pad of contracts with mismatched form fields. A signer can indicate one selection on the front and different selections on the copies. An uninspired ruse, but one that was clearly used effectively within this court system." She handed the king two forms. "He also admitted to assisting Jasper Sterling in the rigging of this tournament."

King Logan studied the form fields and his brow furrowed. "An abhorrent misuse of the law." He turned to Lord Sterling. "And did you have knowledge of your son's misdeeds?"

Lord Sterling shook his head vehemently and raised his hands. "I swear I did not, Your Majesty. I had no knowledge of any of this." He glared at Jasper. "This miscreant has always been a grave disappointment. He has brought nothing but shame to this house."

Jasper turned to his father, his face stricken. "Father, tell them this is just a mistake! Tell them I'm the one they want for the Round Table!" His voice was nearing a shriek. "I'm your son!"

Lord Sterling's face settled into a stony glare. "I no longer have a son."

Valerie watched as Jasper's face fell. He seemed to wither into himself as the king began to expound on the severity of the situation. The queen and king were conversing about how best to proceed when Valerie noticed the shift in Jasper's expression. It was only a matter of seconds in total, but she recognized the fear morphing into hate, and she saw what was coming.

"Your Majesty!" she shouted, reaching for the king who still held her sword. But Jasper was already on the move. He lunged for his father's sword belt and pulled the blade from its scabbard. A shout went up from the royal guards, but they were too far away to assist. Valerie stepped in front of the king and queen, expecting that Jasper might turn on them, but Jasper's wild eyes focused solely on his father.

He screamed as he raised the sword. "Am I good enough for you now, father?"

Lord Sterling flung his arms up to block the blow, but it never fell.

Jasper suddenly staggered back, the sword tumbling from his hands and clattering to the stones. He looked down to see the crossbow bolt lodged in the center of his chest. He stared at the arrow, then fell, collapsing to the stone floor.

The king was holding the queen. Lord Sterling had his hands up to defend against any other sudden attacks. All eyes turned toward the shadowy figure that emerged from an alcove at the edge of the ruined hall. The royal guards sprang into defensive positions around the dais, raising their spears, but the man in black let the crossbow fall from his hand as he limped forward.

Damon.

His face was pale but determined. The tip of the crossbow bolt he had been struck with earlier was still protruding from the upper corner of his chest plate, just below his shoulder.

Valerie's heart leapt, and she pushed her way through the

guards, rushing to reach him as he stumbled forward. She caught him as he nearly fell.

"Hey there, Alley Cat," he murmured. "I knew I'd find you here."

Valerie slumped to the floor under his weight, and Damon collapsed into her arms.

38

INVITATION

The Port Hyacinth Hospital was a busy place. Post-tournament, nearly every bed was filled, so Valerie felt especially privileged that they had given her a private room for the night. She ran her fingers along her jaw until they met the adhesive bandage plastered over the stitches. It made her jaw stiff. The bandage crinkled when she opened her mouth, but otherwise, her face was okay.

She slid off the edge of the hospital bed and gathered up the crutch they had given her. She was wearing a sundress for the first time in what felt like forever, largely because the bandage around her thigh had made getting into pants an unpleasant experience. The cut there had required stitches as well, but all in all, she had survived the competition intact.

The tournament was still the talk of the hallway when she exited her room, though the staff had finally stopped applauding every time she showed her face. Now it was whispers and in most cases, friendly smiles.

She shuffled down the hall, making her way to the nurses station.

"Excuse me. Do you know which room they put Sir Damon Roark in?"

"That handsome knight? You bet I do," the nurse replied. "He's a catch. Is he with you?"

"I'm not really sure at the moment," Valerie said.

The nurse looked her over. "Well, if you decide to throw him back, you let me know, okay?"

Valerie continued down the hall, looking for the room number the nurse had given her. She was deciphering the arrows on a wall placard when a woman's voice came from one of the adjacent doors.

"I heard a rumor you were still too stubborn to leave town. Must be true."

Valerie spun around and searched for the source of the voice. The blonde woman in the bed was sitting up and grinning at her.

"Janet? Oh my God, I didn't know you were awake!" Valerie rushed into the room as fast as she could manage. She paused at the bedside. "Are you huggable? Will I hurt you?"

"I'll live," Janet laughed. She opened her arms, and Valerie leaned in to hug her, careful to avoid the few places Janet was still bandaged.

"I hear you have quite the story to tell," Janet said. "Tournament champion?"

"It's been an adventure."

"Did you get what you were looking for?"

Valerie brushed a hand down her forearm. "I don't know. I think maybe so."

"I'm sure your brother would be very proud of you."

"I couldn't have done it without you, and without Ann," Valerie said. "Where is she?"

Janet smiled. "Well, she's quite busy all of a sudden. She was contacted this morning by the director of the Royal Armory. Seems they've taken an interest in her work. Something about the king wanting her to design him a sword like the one you have."

"That's amazing! She's designing a sword for the king?"

"Maybe more than one. We'll see what happens."

"What about you?" Valerie said. "I'm so sorry for what happened to the Twisted Tentacle. It was my fault."

"I hear it's also your fault I wasn't left to roast in there," Janet said. "I'm counting it as a win. The tavern is a loss, but I've learned of late, you never know what new and better opportunity will rise from the ashes." She glanced at the door. "Speaking of the tavern, I heard one of your regulars was on this floor. A certain grumpy sword instructor. You see him yet?"

"Not yet," Valerie said.

"Tell him I said 'hi,'" Janet replied.

Valerie squeezed her hand. "I'll see you soon?"

"Don't worry. This place won't keep me long."

Valerie waved again at the door and made her way down to the other end of the hall. She found the room number she was looking for and peered through the small window in the door.

Damon was lying in bed, but his eyes were open and he was reading something. She knocked on the door lightly and turned the handle.

Damon turned to watch her as she entered.

"Hey," Valerie managed. "You still adding to your scar collection?"

Damon glanced at the bandage wrapped around his shoulder and chest. "I thought I needed something to remember this place by."

Valerie crossed to the bed and lingered next to him. "So. Covert agent of the Queen's Guard, huh?"

"A little less covert at the moment," he replied, shifting his leg and the blanket and giving her a place to sit. He leaned back against the pillow, and Valerie sank onto the mattress next to him. He folded the letter he had been reading and rested a hand atop it.

"So, you were under orders from the queen this whole time?"

"The Royal Guard gets all the big, flashy deployments,

guarding the king and queen in all their parades and galas. Everyone knows King Logan tends to look for the best in everyone. Queen Kimiko is less trusting. She likes to see what's going on behind the scenes. They make a good pair."

"She suspected someone would try to rig the tournament?" Valerie asked.

"We had a reason to investigate, but we didn't know what we'd find."

He handed her the letter he had been reading. Valerie unfolded it and found that it was a thank you letter from House Sutton. A photograph of a pretty, young woman in a racing suit was pinned to the letter.

"Lord Sutton secretly petitioned the queen to investigate the death of his daughter, Lady Magdalena Sutton. She died in a road race at the start of summer. He thought the circumstances suspicious. The queen said she'd like to see what the Sterlings were up to before the royal entourage made it to town. That's why she sent me ahead. She didn't know they were crooks, but she likes to verify before she puts her trust in a situation that might put the king in danger. In this case, we found a rat. At least, you did. When you sought justice for your brother, it turns out you were getting justice for Lady Magdalena as well."

Valerie studied the photo of the young woman, then set the letter aside. "I'm sorry I didn't trust you," Valerie said. "Turns out you were looking out for me the whole time."

"You were smart to be suspicious." Damon took her hand. "But the day I met you, I knew the king didn't need to have a tournament. If he was looking for a fighter with heart and honor, I knew right where to find one."

"Once you shot a few arrows at her and dumped her off a pier?"

Damon smirked. "Trust but verify."

"So, you think I should accept the position? The seat at the Round Table?"

"That's a decision no one can make for you. It's a big commitment."

A knock came at the door. They turned to find a nurse in the doorway. "Miss Terravecchia? There is a car waiting for you downstairs. Your ride?"

Valerie thanked her.

"You should go," Damon said.

"Will I see you again?"

"I'll catch up. You've still got my car, remember?"

Valerie narrowed her eyes at him. "After all this, you still want my car?"

"I guess you can borrow it for a while. I'll probably need a chauffeur."

Valerie punched him in the gut.

"Ow," Damon laughed. "I'm wounded over here, remember?"

"I'll give you some new ones," Valerie muttered.

Damon reached for her neck and pulled her to him. Their lips met, and her hands brushed up his arms until they rested on his biceps. His kiss was warm and firm, and his fingers twisted in her hair.

She missed this.

When their lips finally parted, his eyes found hers. "This is all I really want."

"You have a real way with words," Valerie whispered.

Damon smiled and pressed his forehead to hers. "Don't worry. We'll talk more soon."

When Valerie finally walked out the doors of the hospital, there was a convertible Easton coupe parked at the curb, and Lady Charlotte was hovering near the fender. She was modestly dressed today in jeans and a simple floral top. She uncrossed her wrists as Valerie approached and stepped forward to help with Valerie's bag.

"I've got it," Valerie said and tossed the bag into the back of the convertible.

Lady Charlotte stood awkwardly in front of the passenger door and shifted the car keys from one hand to the other.

"Are you . . . going to let me in?" Valerie asked.

"Actually I thought you might want to drive. Unless with your leg—"

"I can handle it," Valerie said. She snatched the keys and worked her way around the other side of the car. Lady Charlotte climbed in after her.

Valerie put the keys in the ignition and started the Easton.

"Val, before we go, I owe you an apology," Charlotte said. "For a lot of things." She stared out the windshield and seemed to be having trouble making eye contact.

Valerie leaned back in her seat and sighed. "Yeah. Look, I'm not saying you weren't awful. You were, but I know it wasn't all your fault. Jasper was—"

"Something I should have recognized."

"Well, probably."

"I was a fool," Charlotte said, putting her hand to her mouth. Her lip quivered. "You must think I'm just a pathetic, lonely, old woman. And you'd be right." She wiped at her eye to brush away a tear that was forming.

Valerie closed her eyes for a moment, then watched Charlotte fumble in her purse for a handkerchief. Valerie reached across to the glove box and opened it, then removed the extra handkerchief Charlotte always stored there.

Charlotte accepted it with a nod, then dabbed at her eyes and nose.

"I've been thinking," she continued, "that if you still want to go live at Villa Rosa, I can make the arrangements. The buyers backed out of the sale, and I thought that if you want it, then I could—"

"It's okay," Valerie said. "That was Henry's dream house. Not mine."

"Well, I know. But if there is something else that you wanted, I could try to make it up to you. I think it's time that you had something. You're an adult now, and if there's—"

"There *is* actually something I want," Valerie said, staring out the window at the horizon. "In Briarwood Village."

"The vineyard worker community?" Charlotte asked. "What could you possibly want there?"

Valerie shifted into gear and pulled out of the parking space. "You'll see."

~

A week later, Rico emerged from behind the new curtains of the Briarwood Theater stage and tapped his microphone. "Can anyone hear me? Is this thing on?" He fiddled with the cord. "Why must I always have these problems?"

"The new microphone is coming tomorrow. I'm already on it," Janet said from behind the bar. Cases of new wine and liquor bottles were stacked on the bar and around the floor.

"This voice is a finely tuned instrument," Rico said, stroking his neck. "I need to keep it warmed up."

"We can hear you fine," Ann said from the end of the bar. "Valerie and I can be your first audience."

"The first of many," Valerie said, filling her wine glass. "Later. Come have a drink with us."

Rico put his hand on his hip. "I know you are our new benefactor and all, but you need to know that this kind of talent can't just be bought with your fancy wine and your—" he waved his hand around, "—space with potential."

Valerie tried to keep her face serious, but the corners of her mouth kept creeping up.

"Oh, who am I kidding?" Rico said. "Yes, it can." He jumped

off the stage and strode over to join them at the bar. Janet began pouring him a glass.

"What should we toast to?" Ann asked.

"To your new contract with the Royal Armory," Valerie said.

"I'll certainly drink to the advance they sent for the work," Ann replied.

"To our new space to share with friends," Janet added.

"And to the friend who made it all happen," Rico said, lifting his glass and holding it out to Valerie.

She smiled as they all tapped their glasses and took a drink.

"What about drinking to new opportunities?" a voice said.

Valerie turned and located the man in the floppy hat who had slipped in near the front door. She nearly spit out her wine.

"Oh my God. King Logan!"

She slipped off her bar stool and sank to a knee. The others fumbled to find ways to do the same.

"No. Please," King Logan said, raising his hands. "I'm incognito again today. No need for formality. I just wanted to check in on you and find out if you've had time to consider my offer."

Valerie rose. "I'm still thinking about it."

"You mind if we take a walk?"

She set her wine glass on the bar and hastily joined him. "Of course, yes. That would be great."

King Logan nodded to the others, then held the front door open for Valerie. They stepped into the daylight and walked into the mostly empty parking lot.

The king put his hands in his pockets and turned to admire the partially repainted theater. Valerie noticed that they were standing in almost the same location she and her brother had been when they had daydreamed of fixing up the theater together.

Workers were endeavoring to hang a sign on a nearby garage. King Logan read the logo. "V8 Vines?"

Valerie glanced at the garage where her battered Rogue Fastback was still up on a lift, missing its engine.

"We're opening an automotive speed shop and wine bar next door," Valerie said. "Shop talk and charcuterie."

"A creative combination," King Logan replied. They walked toward the garage. The Guardian was sitting out front, its wounds only partially mended. A few spots of primer still dotted the paint job. The king leaned down and admired the interior. "L' Orsa Nera, isn't that what they're calling you now?"

"I think they just miss my dad," Valerie said. "We all do."

The king opened the door of the Guardian and gestured to the driver's seat. "May I?"

"Be my guest," Valerie said.

King Logan settled into the seat and placed both hands on the steering wheel. "He was a good man, your dad, and a great knight. His service to the kingdom was unparalleled. That's partly why I was so pleased to find you were his daughter. I know he would be incredibly proud of the woman you've become."

"I feel like I'm still figuring out what I'm supposed to become," Valerie said. "All of this is a lot more than I ever imagined for myself."

The king nodded. He brushed a finger along the hilt of her sword that was clipped onto the ceiling rack, then lifted himself back out of the car. "You know, one of the great traditions of the Knights of the Round Table was designed for just such a need." He rested an arm on the open car door. "Since the beginning of its formation, King Arthur would send his knights on various quests. Some thought the purpose of these journeys to be about fame or glory, or perhaps to acquire some notable artifact to increase the riches of the kingdom. But it was much simpler than that. These tests and quests gave each knight a gift. The gift of knowing who they truly were in the face of adversity and to test their character in times when there was no crowd or king to see them succeed or fail. It was a quest of self, and that, in turn, served the greater good."

"Are you saying that I still don't deserve the job?"

"No." King Logan reached into his pocket and removed an envelope and a badge carrying the seal of Avalon. He held the badge out. "I know we didn't have a chance to knight you properly with all the fanfare it deserves, but I thought we might do that at the palace. As you know, it's a bit of a drive."

Valerie accepted the badge.

"And if you do fancy yourself a road trip, there are a few things I thought you might look into along the way—as my representative." He handed her the envelope. "There's no requirement that you say yes. But if you do, I've left a map of the best routes with a certain agent of the Queen's Guard who is staying at an inn just up the road. He'll be happy to fill you in on more of the details."

"Thank you, Your Majesty," Valerie said. "It's an incredible honor."

King Logan rested a hand on her shoulder just as a black car flying the flags of House Pendragon pulled into the lot.

"Welcome to the Royal Knights of Avalon," he said. "I hope to see you again when you take your place at the Round Table." He squeezed her shoulder and smiled, then backed away and climbed into the waiting vehicle. Valerie caught a glimpse of Queen Kimiko in the back seat.

"Honey, what have I told you about wearing that hat in public?" the queen said. She shook her head and gave Valerie a wave.

Then the door closed. With flags waving from the fenders, the car pulled out of the lot and disappeared down the sun-dappled road out of the village.

Valerie climbed into the open door of the Guardian and slumped in the seat. She held up the shining badge emblazoned with the cross and crown of Avalon. It flashed in the sunlight.

She hooked it to the rear-view mirror where her father's watch was dangling, then tore into the envelope.

She only read the first few lines before pausing. A summer breeze was blowing through the lot and shaking the boughs of the trees. It sent leaves skittering down the road.

An invitation.

Valerie smiled and tossed the king's envelope to the passenger seat. She would have time to decide later.

She closed the car door and started the ignition, then shifted into gear and blasted out of the theater parking lot. The Guardian's tires left a cloud of smoke behind her.

The car shot onto the open road, scattering leaves in her wake. She let the engine noise try to compete with her shout of joy. Her heart raced along with the hum of the motor as she rounded the curve to take in the sight of the quaint, old inn and the Blackbird 900 parked in the lot.

She flew past with a smile on her face.

She'd see him tonight.

For now, all she wanted was the wind in her hair, the roar of the engine, and miles and miles of open road.

The End

The next adventure will be coming soon!

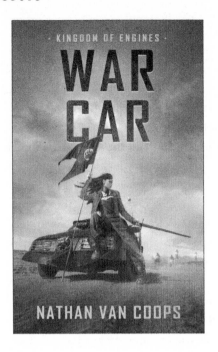

Preorder WAR CAR now and have it automatically downloaded to your device upon release.

Get it here! https://books2read.com/u/b5Q6ZA

ACKNOWLEDGMENTS

Thank you for reading! I hope you enjoyed this adventure.

Want more Valerie and Damon? Be sure to download the bonus epilogue from Damon's perspective at:

https://BookHip.com/VSJQSK

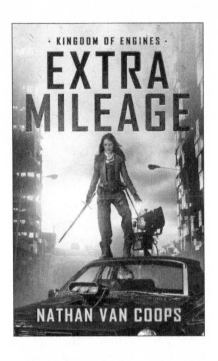

If you would like to leave a review on the platform you purchased from, it will be extremely appreciated. I will read and enjoy your comments!

No book conceived in an author's imagination ever saw the light of day without help.

This book had a lot of it.

I was toiling away on an entirely different novel when the idea for this story kept niggling me. If it weren't for the encouragement of Alan Janney, Lucy Score, and T. Ellery Hodges, I may never have given myself permission to switch projects and take the leap to this new world.

Several other author friends were vital to the marketing and launch process, especially Boo Walker, Jillian Dodd, and all of the St. Pete Author Lunch group. Thank you so much!

There is an extremely excellent podcast called The Story Grid Podcast that inspired me to dive deep into structure and plotting to make sure the bones of this novel would be in place before I ever started writing. I learned a tremendous amount from studying the methods of editor Shawn Coyne as laid out in his book, also called The Story Grid.

This story needed a test drive while I was still writing it, so I'd like to thank my alpha readers who gave me feedback to keep me on track and feeling inspired. Especially Maarja Kruusmets, Kay Clark, Marilyn Bourdeau, Bonnie De Moss, Ken Robbins, Josh Shaine, Felicia Rodriguez, June H. Van Riel, Marilyn Gast, Bill Hall, Linda Kerekes, Diann Marshall, Rob Stephen, Randi Milam, Lee Inks, Mark Hale, Matthew Taylor, Norma Grubb, Rick Bradley, Gary Smart, Claire Palmer, Dave De Camp, and Mike Hiltunen.

Author and editor H. Claire Taylor helped me align the story when I was still trying to wrangle it into some sort of shape. Her advice and willing ear were a godsend. She's also just a lot of fun.

I must thank my mom, Marilyn, for not only being a member of the beta team, but always going above and beyond to help make the stories I write the best they can be. The encouragement and positive support keeps me going during those inevitable writing days where I want to throw the whole manuscript in the garbage.

A special thanks to Kay Clark for doing a final proofread that went above and beyond and gives me the confidence of knowing that every sentence I write is getting her incredible eye for detail on it before ever seeing print.

Thanks to my friend and writer's group partner Emily Young who helps make every book I write better with her insightful comments on character and emotion. This writing gig is way more fun when we do it together.

For the beta team who volunteered to help sort out my prose issues and hunt down rogue typos. You are my rock. Every book I write has your fingerprints all over it and is so much better as a result.

Rob Stephen, Yvonne Mitchell, Andrew Freeman, Matthew Taylor, Lisa Mages-Haskins, Josh Shaine, Eric Lizotte, Bruce Green, Maurice Druck, Rick Bradley, Bethany Cousins, Kay Clark, Ray Clements, Marilyn J Bourdeau, Mark Hale, Joseph M Oakey, Diann Marshall, Marilyn Gast, Brett Parker, Gary Smart, Missy Burrows, Gerry Cohen, Logan DeVane, Gary C Smart, Nate, Walt Taylor, Geezer Roy, Tim Wright, Donnisha Jones, Melissa K Pritchard, Gary Lopiccolo, Elaine Davis, Laura Driskell, Andrea Sestak, James Morse, Seán, Philippe Jardin, Mitchell C Kelsey, Sylvia Walker, Abhinav, Rob Stephen, Marcus Baker, Tony Everett, Ben, Gordon Lee, Stephen Lafave, Thomas C. Altman, Lee Inks, Ginelle Blanch, Marijelle Moreno Bartholomewq, Stephen Bishop, Cindy Williams, Ken Robbins, Claire Manger, Amy Spicka, Ray Antonelli, Joseph Kane, Felicia Rodriguez , Paul Ness, Dave Bennett, Von Whitlock, Jason A Wolverton, Cle Montgomery, Mike Reed, Coleen Alexander, Rogelio Faco Franklin, Becky Alexander-Conrad, Dan McCrory, Fiona Holden, Karen Stansbury, George Beech, Alissa Nesson, and Larry Dietz.

The helpful staff and servers at my favorite restaurants kept me stocked with tacos and iced tea and are always incredibly kind to my dog, Atticus. I'd especially like to thank the staff at Grumpy Gringo, Poppo's Taqueria, Red Mesa Mercado, Chipotle, Banyan Cafe, and every other restaurant that let me occupy a seat for far longer than any customer has a right to while I toiled away over this manuscript.

And last but never least, my astounding wife Stephanie, who makes life better in every way. Your hard work and support for us as a family is what makes all of this possible. I love you to the moon. I hope you like this story.

ALSO BY NATHAN VAN COOPS

ABOUT THE AUTHOR

Nathan Van Coops lives in St. Petersburg, Florida on a diet comprised mainly of tacos. When not tinkering on old airplanes, he writes heroic adventure stories that explore imaginative new worlds. He is the author of the time travel adventure series, *In Times Like These*, and *The Skylighter Adventures*. Learn more at nathanvancoops.com.

Cover design by Damonza.com

Map by Nathan Van Coops

Author photo by Jennie Thunell Photography

Chapter header images designed by Julia Scheiber.

eBook ISBN: 978-1-950669-00-4

Print ISBN: 978-1-950669-01-1

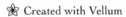 Created with Vellum

Made in the USA
Monee, IL
10 September 2020

42057381R00239